PRAISE FOR *A BEAUTIFUL CRIME*

"Deliciously diabolical. . . . What makes the crime in Bollen's stylish new novel so beautiful is that the perps' plan works out even better than they'd hoped—at least for a while. . . . A skilled purveyor of suspense . . . Bollen's wit sparkles on almost every page."

—*Washington Post*

"Bollen populates this utterly transporting novel with elegant, mysterious, and complicated characters worthy of Patricia Highsmith, and he delivers hard-boiled film-noir moments amidst the sensual decadence of a Visconti film. But somehow, masterfully, while his sexy, thrilling story pulls you ever forward, in the end it's Bollen's gorgeous writing that will leave you truly breathless. This is a first-class trip to Venice with an insider at your side taking you far beyond the tourist destinations. But be careful who you're with when you wander alongside that narrow canal and down that charming alleyway."

—Kevin Kwan, author of the
Crazy Rich Asians trilogy and *Sex and Vanity*

"Elegant."

"Entrancing. . . . Patricia Highsmith by way of Alan Hollinghurst: morally gray, utterly mesmerizing, and intensely erotic. Beginning with his 2011 debut, *Lightning People*, Bollen has displayed a fascination with how power works in America; his newest is an astute meditation on the ways financial inequality and racism affect one's sense of identity and interactions with others—including romantic partners."

—Alexander Chee, *O: The Oprah Magazine*

"Stylish. . . . A compelling take on the eternal question of how good people morph into criminals. Terrific."

—*People*, Book of the Week

"A brilliantly conceived international crime story with two complex, queer characters at its center. If you never thought the world of counterfeit antiques could keep you on the edge of your seat, think again. It's as complex and engrossing as *The Talented Mr. Ripley*, but don't be surprised when in the midst of the intrigue, the story breaks your heart. We wanted to follow these characters over and around the canals of Venice to see where they'd end up next."

—*Good Morning America*

"Extraordinary. A razor wrapped in silk, a cocktail spiked with poison—a novel both sophisticated and savage, inviting and dangerous. Death in Venice? You have no idea."

—A. J. Finn, author of *The Woman in the Window*

"With its delicate plotting, its fast-moving and elegantly transparent prose—not to mention a setting that for once is not rendered with a litany of platitudes—*A Beautiful Crime* is a novel designed to activate the pleasure principle, and, as with Bollen's own erotically charged characters, it does so."

—Lawrence Osborne, author of *The Glass Kingdom*

A Beautiful Crime

A Beautiful Crime

A NOVEL

Christopher Bollen

HARPER PERENNIAL

NEW YORK • LONDON • TORONTO • SYDNEY • NEW DELHI • AUCKLAND

HARPER ● PERENNIAL

HarperCollins books may be purchased for educational, business, or sales promotional use. For information, please email the Special Markets Department at SPsales@harpercollins.com.

FIRST HARPER PERENNIAL EDITION PUBLISHED 2021.

Designed by Leah Carlson-Stanisic

The Library of Congress has catalogued the hardcover edition of this book as follows:

Names: Bollen, Christopher, 1975–, author.

Title: A beautiful crime: a novel / Christopher Bollen.

Description: First Edition. | New York, NY: Harper, 2020.

Identifiers: LCCN 2019010893 (print) | LCCN 2019012934 (ebook) | ISBN 9780062853905 (E-book) | ISBN 9780062853882 (hardcover)

Subjects: | GSAFD: Suspense fiction.

Classification: LCC PS3602.O6545 (ebook) | LCC PS3602.O6545 S48 2020 (print) | DDC 813/.6—dc23

LC record available at https://lccn.loc.gov/2019010893

ISBN 978-0-06-285389-9 (pbk.)

21 22 23 24 25 LSC 10 9 8 7 6 5 4 3 2 1

FOR EDMUND WHITE

VENICE

Santa Lucia Train Station ⚲   ⚲ Scalzi Bridge

CANNAREGIO

SANTA CROCE

Rialto Fish Market ⚲

Rialto Bridge

Piazzale Roma ⚲

Scuola Grande di San Rocco ⚲

SAN POLO

Grand Canal

SAN MARCO

Campo Santa Margherita ⚲

Ca' Rezzonico ⚲

Campo San Barnaba ⚲

DORSODURO

Accademia Bridge ⚲

Gallerie dell'Accademia ⚲

Peggy Guggenheim Collection ⚲

GIUDECCA

0   500 yds.

0   500 m.

MURANO

SAN MICHELE

I Gesuiti

Basilica di San Giovanni e Paolo

CASTELLO

Piazza San Marco

Doge's Palace

LIDO

"You may either win your peace, or buy it."

—JOHN RUSKIN

"In loving him, I saw great houses being erected that would soon slide into the waiting and stirring seas."

—DAVID WOJNAROWICZ

A Beautiful Crime

Down below the cry of gulls, below floors of tourists undressing and dressing for dinner, below even the shrinking figure of his killer, a man lies crumpled and bleeding. He's been dead for only a few seconds. He's sprawled on his stomach, his body twisted at the hips, his left arm hooked in a U above his head. From a distance, from high above, he looks almost as if he is sleeping. It's the blood leaking through his pink shirt that gives the crime away.

Outside, the sun is setting on what is unarguably the most beautiful city on the planet. There are a lot of dead bodies in this town. Upstairs in the man's room, an English guidebook recommends taking a boat out to San Michele to visit an entire island of them. Among the legions buried there are the composer Igor Stravinsky, the ballet director Sergei Diaghilev, and the poet Ezra Pound.

This city is sinking and has been for centuries. Enjoy it while you can. The blood is pooling around the body. Screams are blaring from all directions. The killer is making a run for the exit.

But none of this has happened yet.

PART I

Setting the Trap

CHAPTER 1

The plane from New York landed just before dawn, its wheels tapping blindly along the edges of the runway. Nick Brink awoke to economy-class clapping and slumped forward with a quiet animal groan. His neck muscles were wrenched. Two bruises pulsed above his left ear. Somewhere in the cramped confusion below his waist, his legs were completely numb. It was not a good idea to be over six feet tall on a nine-hour flight in a discount seat. But as the plane decelerated across Marco Polo Airport, all he really felt was lucky. For Nicholas Brink, at age twenty-five, had never been to Venice.

No mythical city should be judged by its airport. Nick, born in a nonmythical city with a famous airport ("Dayton taught the world to fly"), knew not to expect too much from the view out his window. Still, through the dreary wash of tarmac grays, the few foreign words he spotted, USCITA and SICUREZZA and IMBARCO, read like promises of love and wild music. He had made it—or at least, he'd almost made it. The *real* Venice floated somewhere beyond this Gobi of concrete, and Nick had plenty of time to reach it. He wasn't meeting Clay on the Grand Canal for another three hours. If by some miracle he got through the airport in record time, he might even catch the sunrise while standing on one of the city's stone bridges.

Nick slipped his feet into his shoes just as the plane rolled to a defeated stop forty yards from the terminal. *Please, God, no*, he prayed. After nine hours morgued in the same position, he felt it might be beyond his endurance to sit still for another ten seconds.

"Folks, there's a delay at the gate," the pilot announced to the long tube of American sighs. "A very slight delay."

Nick watched helplessly as morning began to thaw on the tarmac. Eventually, a flicker of molten orange seeped around a distant tail wing. As the sunlight reached his window, he leaned his face into the glass. This is enough, he decided. It was midnight in New York.

When they finally taxied to the gate, a bell dinged and seat belts clattered. Passengers rushed from their rows only to find themselves stuck once again. They clung to their spots in the aisle like insects to a strip of flypaper.

"I'm here on a tour," a beefy young man in front of Nick announced to no one in particular. He wore a red NASCAR sweatshirt and nylon shorts hiked up to expose a talcum-white tan line across his thighs. He hugged a bed pillow to his stomach, and in his palm lay two earplugs, yellow and gnarled like extracted teeth. "I'm meeting my cousin. We're doing the whole bus package." He turned around to make eye contact with trapped Nick. "Milan, Perugia, Florence, Siena. I'm forgetting some places. What's that town with the famous wells? We've got two full days in Venice." He volunteered this information with a manic urgency, as if he were afraid this might be his last opportunity to speak to another American.

Nick listened to the guy ramble on about discount hotel rates and the tour's fifty-seat luxury coach with its state-of-the-art AC. It wasn't the ideal soundtrack for Nick's first morning in a foreign country; he would have liked to grab the earplugs out of the guy's hand and shove them in his own ears with a look of disdain. Instead, he nodded along dutifully and even improvised a few enthusiastic *Oh, cool*s. Although Nick had lived in New York City for seven years, he'd never developed the talent for rudeness. He believed in friendliness the same way he believed in his youth: he thought both would save him. His youth and friendliness were master keys to all future rooms.

"You're going to have a wonderful time," Nick assured him.

"Yeah," the young man conceded. "What about you? Is this a vacation?"

Nick smiled as the aisle cleared ahead of them.

"I hope not."

One delay bred others: first at passport control and then at baggage claim. There were no announcements this time, only the same group of passengers from his flight rearranged in a fidgety, classless clump by the conveyor belt. After forty minutes, the first-class bags began to rain down the ramp, each suitcase decorated with a neon-fuchsia PRIORITY tag. But Nick was in luck. Perhaps the Italian handlers had mistaken his neon-orange HEAVY, OVERWEIGHT tag as a special class all its own, because his silver-metal case tumbled down before the other economy flotsam. Nick anchored his shoe on the carousel's lip and hoisted the HEAVY, OVERWEIGHT suitcase onto still land. The suitcase contained every last possession he owned.

The spring air outside was moist from a recent rain and cut with fresh diesel exhaust. He wheeled his suitcase beyond the airport's automatic doors, pausing to help corral an elderly Canadian couple's runaway luggage. Near a huddle of smoking, bickering Italians, Nick veered off the walkway and rested his leather carry-on bag on his suitcase. He quickly dug through it for his passport and cell phone. Then he kept digging. He couldn't find the map of Venice that Clay had given him, with their meeting point circled in red. In his jetlagged state, all he could recall was that it was a dock on the Grand Canal. A dock with two words to its name—*or was it three?*

Nick patted his body for the folded square of paper, the panic building with each breath. He was in danger of botching up the plan on his very first morning in Venice. It didn't help his search that most of the clothes he had on were borrowed, the pockets still as unfamiliar to him as rooms in a stranger's house. Usually he'd wear jeans or sweats for such a long flight, but he'd wanted to enter Venice dressed like he belonged. He wore a pink button-down shirt underneath a billiard-green blazer that was already proving too hot for April in Italy. His twill pants were ocean blue and they felt heavy on his legs, as if he were indeed climbing out of an ocean in pants. The shoes were his, black alligator loafers that he'd saved up for months to buy and therefore rarely wore. Closet dust was still embedded between the scales.

The expensive borrowed clothes might have been a mistake. Yesterday, in New York, as he dressed for the airport, he tried to shove his wallet in the back pocket of his pants, only to discover that it was sewn shut. Nick couldn't decide whether he was supposed to rip the seam open or not. Ultimately he tore the stitch loose, but his ineptitude in operating a simple pair of pants hadn't been a boost to his international confidence. Now here he was, frantically frisking himself down outside the airport. He fought the urge to toss the ridiculous, too-heavy blazer in the garbage. Who was he fooling by wearing it anyway?

His hand struck a corner of folded paper: the map had fallen through a hole in the blazer's lining. He tweezed it out with relief. Clay had circled a dock called Ca' Rezzonico that sat halfway along the snaking Grand Canal. Nick couldn't resist taking the word for a joyride, singsonging it aloud—"Ca' Rezzonico. Ca' Rezzzooooniccooo. Ca' Reeeezzooooonicoooo"—each time exerting more gas on the vowels until they glided over the speed bumps of consonants. He had memorized only a handful of Italian expressions. Thankfully, Clay spoke Italian. Clay had once lived in Venice for eight months. His expertise would see them both through. "Ca' Rezzoooonicccooooo!"

"Ca' Rezzonico?" a woman's voice repeated, like a bird answering a call. Nick turned to find a thin middle-aged woman with gray-blond hair spilling out of a straw hat. The shadow of the brim fell over her eyes, leaving her teeth to do all the work of greeting. They were so square and bleach white that they might have been veneers. "Are you waiting for us?" she asked Nick.

An American family stood behind her—a slim, freckled husband with a cable-knit sweater tied around his waist; a teenage daughter, husky and pretty in a yellow dress with a plaster arm cast covered in signatures; a dark-haired boy of ten or eleven who, of the whole family, possessed the coldest and wisest stare. They were all sensible packers, each with only a wafer of a suitcase at their side. They exuded the unburdened ease of the wealthy who could simply buy whatever they needed at their next destination. Poor people like Nick had to act like donkeys with their own stuff.

"Did Giulio send you?" the older woman wanted to know.

Nick offered an apologetic smile. "I'm sorry. You have me confused for someone else." He glanced around as if it were his job to locate promising substitutes.

"Lynn!" the husband snapped at the same time the teenage girl whined, "Mom!" Lynn laughed. She clearly relished her role as the family clown. The husband lowered his voice. "I told you, Giulio isn't sending anyone."

"But this young man called out our dock!" she replied. "Ca' Rezzonico. And you said Giulio would send an American!" She reached for Nick's arm and tugged on his bicep. Perhaps the billiard-green jacket reminded her of parking attendants back home.

"And I told you, I canceled that palazzo. We're renting the one right across the canal, remember? San Samuele is our dock."

"Oh." Lynn released Nick's arm. She stared up at him and coughed out a laugh. "I'm sorry. I really did think you had come for us." Her eyes lingered on his face. Nick often attracted the curious attention of older women, as if he were forever being auditioned for some missing element in their lives: adopted son, sex partner, errand boy, devoted gay best friend.

"It's no problem," Nick replied. "I wish I could help."

"I wish you could too!" Lynn cried theatrically, as if to compensate for the mix-up. "You're so handsome!"

Nick was still unaccustomed to being called handsome. The lanky, awkward Ohio teenager had clung to him through his early twenties. Handsomeness had only crept up on him in recent years. (His mother had proved uncharacteristically perceptive when she'd told him as a child, "Wait, just wait, the best ones take the longest.") He balked at Lynn's flattery. Blushing, he glanced at the rest of her family—husband, daughter, son—as if expecting each to confirm the compliment. Instead they gathered their belongings, offered frail waves of goodbye, and followed the signs down a covered walkway for water taxis.

There were two ways into Venice: by bus or by boat. Even a first-timer like Nick knew that the princely mode of entry was by water. He watched the first-class passengers and their fuchsia-tagged luggage flutter down the same path the American family took. Clay had informed Nick that the bus was the cheap, reliable, and utterly romance-free option. "Take the bus and save money," he had advised. Nick steered his heavy suitcase toward the bus stop across the road. He gripped his wallet in his back pocket to ensure it was still securely buried in the twill. He couldn't afford to lose it; the wallet held the nine hundred dollars he'd converted into euros at JFK. It was the lion's share of his spending money. The wallet also contained one other essential ingredient for his plans in Venice: his old business card.

Nick reached the cement median in time to taste the burnt fuel of the bus he'd just missed. There was another bus slumped against the curb, its motor rumbling but with no driver at the wheel. Nick boarded the empty vehicle, stowed his carry-on and suitcase on the luggage rack, and took a seat by the window. The upholstery was a pattern of swirling confetti, and the air-conditioning vents produced a hot, whistling halitosis. Nick turned on his phone.

When the screen brightened, he learned that he only had forty-five minutes to make it to Ca' Rezzonico. He didn't have his boyfriend's new European cell number to warn him he might be late.

A text appeared, sent several hours ago. It was from his sister.

What?! You're moving to Venice?

That message was followed by variations on the theme.

You're kidding, right? What about NYC?

Nicky???? Only his sister and Clay ever called him Nicky.

I didn't think anyone actually lived in Venice. I thought it was all tourists.

Wait! Starting my shift, but do you mean Venice Beach, California?

At the departure gate of JFK, Nick had fallen into a last-minute tailspin about leaving New York. He realized the danger of texting any of his Manhattan friends: they might convince him to stay. His entire plan for Italy hinged on never going back. So instead he'd decided to reach out to his older sister in Dayton. Margaret Brink was a safe source of sentimental contact. Plus, he figured that at least one family member should be notified of his whereabouts.

The Brink siblings, all two of them, Margaret and Nicholas. Margaret was four years older. Through their vastly different childhoods, they had been close at some points, distant at others, like two radios scanning stations and occasionally landing on the same song. That happened with decreasing frequency as they both made their separate pilgrimages through their teens. Margaret, bleached blond and mahogany brown from weekly tanning-bed appointments, had the time of her life as a teenager—quite literally, she'd never top those flirtatious, attention-rich, alcohol-induced highs of her junior and senior years of high school. The world promised Margaret Brink far more than it could ever deliver, at least in their West Dayton suburb with its ranch houses decorated like country farms and its social jockeying modeled on the cosmopolitanism of nearby Cincinnati. All these years later, Nick could still picture his sister in her bikini, floating in their aboveground pool in the backyard, surrounded by the equally blond froth of her five best friends, Margaret's hawk eyes trained on the absolutely acquirable prize of the shirtless boy with the gold neck chain posing on the pool ladder. There is another Brink in this cheerful summer tableau, the thirteen-year-old Nick, hiding in the shadows of the second-floor window that overlooked the bright-blue circle of hose water and teenage lust. His eyes were also trained on the lithe chest and scraggly-muscled arms of the boy on the ladder. The world promised Nick nothing at that age but showed him glimpses of its finest possibilities.

Nick had the good fortune of a miserable childhood. At eighteen, there was nothing to miss and very little holding him in place. He went east for college. No Brink had ever visited Nick in New York. If they had, they might not have recognized the extroverted young man who lived there.

He could admit, in hindsight, that Margaret had been a decent sister. She'd watched over him, loved him at the right moments, and, perhaps most compassionately, left the secret grenades embedded inside him undisturbed. (All kids are afraid of the dark, but how many suspected while hiding under the covers that they might also be the monsters?) Nick and Margaret had never once spoken the obvious about his sexuality—she hadn't asked, and he never offered. As routinely happens with siblings, their relationship flourished in separate cities. Now in their twenties, they volleyed lighthearted jokes or heavyhearted animal news items to each other over text. Nick had gone back to Dayton for three Christmases and two Thanksgivings in his seven years since moving away—each time staying for no more than forty-eight hours. The world had changed drastically in seven years. Surely Dayton was part of the world. Surely it too must have changed and wouldn't care anymore whom he chose to have sex with. Yet Nick dreaded every return. For him, walking around as a gay man in his hometown was tantamount to being out on bail: he was free to go about his business, but everyone treated him with a heightened suspicion, as if unsure whether he had committed a crime.

As he sat alone on the bus, it would have been a comfort to hear his sister's astonished voice. "Venice, Italy? Nicky! You're crazy! You can't just move to Venice! Who does that?" It would have confirmed the audacity of the plan. Failing his family's approval, Nick delighted in their shock; in it, he sensed a hidden admiration for his gift of survival. Unfortunately, Nick knew that Margaret wouldn't answer her phone right now if he called her. Midway through her night shift as an emergency-room nurse at Dayton

Valley Presbyterian, Margaret was elbow deep in "manslaughter"—
that's what she called anything wheeled into the emergency room
between the hours of two and five in the morning; it was all men
and all slaughter. Margaret was only twenty-nine, but she was already married to her second husband and tortured by her first set
of stepkids. She'd been overlooked for a promotion at the hospital.
She drove the same car she'd been given by their parents at sixteen.
Life in Dayton had not been easy for the adult Margaret Brink.

He'd send her a photo of Piazza San Marco, he told himself.
He'd send her a plane ticket one day if he could.

Passengers began to fill the bus's confetti seating. Nick got up
to help a woman who was battling a fold-up stroller. When he
sat back down, he checked his phone: his forty-five minutes had
shrunk to thirty-five. What if he arrived at the dock an hour late
and he and Clay couldn't find each other and he had to spend all
his money on a night at a hotel? He searched out the window for
the bus driver and saw the beefy young man from the plane walking toward the bus. Worse, the guy was waving directly at Nick's
window. Fears of another package-tour monologue flooded Nick's
head. *Dude, save me a seat*, the guy mouthed.

Nick was already climbing out of the bus by the time the young
man reached it. "I forgot something," Nick said apologetically.
"Have a great trip! Enjoy the wells!"

Hauling his suitcase across the road, he followed the signs for
water. He hadn't gambled away the comforts of New York to
reach Venice on slow rubber wheels; he was going to enter the city
the right way. He hurried along the strip of white pavement. He
prayed he wasn't too late. He couldn't afford a ride on a *motoscafo*,
and he had no intention of paying for one.

The scheme that he and Clay had devised—a harmless con that
would settle their debts and set them up for years to come—involved

a single deceitful act on Nick's part. All that was required of him, really, was the gentlest of lies, a mere nod of the head and a few rehearsed sentences delivered with a reassuring smile. The problem with the plan was obvious to Nick: he was not a gifted liar. But he would use this boat ride into Venice as a trial run.

Ca' Rezzonico, he repeated in his head, *Ca' Rezzonico*. Then *San Samuele*.

The sky had darkened by the time he reached the airport's pier. Nick scanned the chaotic waterfront activity. Tourists lined up in front of wood docks that extended into the brackish lagoon. At the end of the docks, sleek brown motorboats the shape of fingernails idled while picking up passengers. Nick had imagined the waters of Venice as still as dusty glass, more a mirror than a motion. But the surface was surprisingly choppy, and seagulls skimmed it tensely before tumbling back over the waves. One *motoscafo* sped off toward a cloudburst of sunlight on the horizon, a couple standing at the bow, their arms intertwined. The image of the couple on the vanishing motorboat was so familiar to Nick that his mother might have shown it to him in his crib: "On our planet, this is what romance looks like."

Rain began to strike the water's surface with the ferocity of machine-gun fire, and those travelers not far along in line retreated to the shelter of the information kiosks. Nick took his carry-on bag in one hand, lifted his suitcase in the other, and ran through the crowd of trunks and toddlers and flowering umbrellas. On the farthest dock he spotted a teenage girl struggling to thread her broken arm through the sleeve of a raincoat. She stood at the front of the line with the rest of her family. Nick raced toward them as a *motoscafo* roared up and the father began shouting and gesticulating to the captain.

"Excuse me," Nick exclaimed, targeting the mother. "Lynn?"

She looked up without a hint of recognition. Her straw hat had vanished, and she was covering her head with a magazine. "Do you remember me? I'm the one Giulio didn't send."

Her eyebrows rose, and she flashed her white teeth. "Oh, yes, hello." She turned to her children and husband. "Look who's here! The one Giulio didn't send!" Lynn had stolen his joke and run off with it, which Nick took as a positive sign. The husband wiped his forehead, glanced warily at Nick, and then down at Nick's hands, as if he expected them to contain an item they'd forgotten.

"Did you say you were taking a boat to San Samuele?" Nick asked.

"That's right," the father answered coolly as he passed his family's suitcases over the dock's edge and into the captain's arms.

"Well, my dock is—"

"Ca' Rezzonico, we know!" the wife intoned. "Kids, get on before it pours." The boy was the first to take the captain's hand and jump down onto the deck. The daughter paused on the precipice, apprehensive about navigating the drop with her cast. Nick rushed over and guided her by her good arm as the captain intercepted her at the waist.

"Well," Nick stammered, left alone with the parents. Parents of any sort made Nick nervous, although these two didn't have much in common with his own. They looked exhausted by the strain of the past twelve hours, not by the past thirty years. "I wondered if you might consider sharing your water taxi," Nick said. "Our docks are right across from each other. We could split the fare."

"The driver wants two hundred and fifty euros to take us!" the father howled. "Because it's raining! Why would it cost more because it's raining? How does that modify the route from the airport? Do I look like a dupe?"

"John," his wife moaned as she shook out the magazine. "You're complaining to someone who's offering to cut the price in half." She eyed Nick sympathetically. "Of course we have room. Anyway, you'll get soaked if you stay here."

"But his suitcase is enormous. The captain will charge us—"

"John!"

"All right, fine," John groused. "Yes, let's split it."

Nick waved his arm like a maître d' to invite them to board first. Both Lynn and John descended and disappeared inside the boat's low cabin. Nick paused on the dock, double-buttoning his green blazer and ensuring that it concealed his back pocket. He hurled his overweight suitcase into the arms of the grumbling captain, then took the man's hand as he descended onto the deck. He ducked into the cabin and climbed onto one of the long chrome-accented benches upholstered in butterscotch leather. The inlaid wooden floor was pin-striped tan and chocolate. The Venetian "taxis" held little resemblance to their ripped-vinyl New York counterparts, and to Nick's initial appraisal, seemed worth every bit of the two hundred and fifty euros that John was going to shell out.

The kids sat on one side, the parents on the other. But as a unified family they stared down at Nick as if he were an intruder who'd just barged into their hotel room. He glanced at Lynn, relying on her camaraderie to ease the tension, but she didn't soften. The job was left to Nick.

"I'm so glad Giulio sent you guys to collect me," he proclaimed. The parents and daughter laughed, all but the boy slouched in the corner, studying Nick with a look of sullen boredom.

"I like him!" Lynn concluded as she nuzzled against John, as if liking a strange young man made her more susceptible to liking her husband. John wrapped his arm around her shoulders.

"Our docks are very close," Nick promised. "They're right across from each other on the Grand Canal, so it's really not out of your way." He had no idea if this was, in fact, the case. He was merely repeating John's earlier assertion. He should have studied Clay's map more carefully. Why had he even mentioned it? He'd already talked himself onto the boat; they couldn't kick him off now. Maybe he was alleviating his own guilt about sticking them with the fare. But really, what harm was he doing? They would have paid the full price for the *motoscafo* whether he was on board or not.

"Do you know Venice well?" John asked him.

The backward lurch of the boat saved Nick from answering. Through the swinging cabin doors, he saw the captain rotate the wheel and spin the craft in the direction of open water. The captain sucked on an electronic cigarette, which blinked with rainbow colors on intake.

"Is this your first time to Venice?" Nick asked.

Lynn gripped John's khakied knee. "Is it *that* obvious? I honestly don't know why it's taken us so long. Venice is the first place you're supposed to visit. We've been everywhere *but!*" She shot a look at her daughter. "August, stop it!"

August was inserting a ballpoint pen into the elbow-side opening of her cast. "It itches," she whined. According to the subway-grade graffiti covering her plaster cast, August was well liked, even occasionally loved, by her friends.

"I'm not saying you deserve a broken arm, dear. However, you should have realized . . ." Lynn trailed off.

August scowled at her mother and hid the cast in the folds of her dress.

Nick smiled at her sympathetically. "How did you break it?" he asked.

"Skiing," she replied with a determined tilt of her chin. "In Sun Valley two weeks ago. I was on spring break."

"Skiing!" Lynn wheezed incredulously, as if to refute the official story. Nick would spare asking August any particulars on the accident. He hoped she'd return the favor when a touchy subject came his way.

"It gets less itchy after a while," he promised her.

"Couldn't he pay for his own boat?" the boy yelled while kicking his wet sneakers on the cushions. Nick had harbored an irrational fear of little boys ever since he'd been one. Their fitful, unremarkable lives demanded so much—including victims.

"Magnus!" the father erupted. The man's freckled hands balled into pale fists. The abrupt pitch of John's anger frightened Nick more than it seemed to faze the little boy, who continued to glare at him from his corner. Nick wouldn't want John's anger turned on him.

"Sorry," Lynn said. "He's tired from the flights. We had to make extra connections because we booked so late. And you wouldn't believe the difficulty we had finding a palazzo last minute with a bedroom for each of the kids."

"I'm not sharing!" August griped, although it seemed to Nick that she had already won that argument.

"We pulled them out of school," Lynn whispered with a guilty wink. "We couldn't resist. And in light of what August did . . ." Lynn went mute over what was clearly an ugly incident in Sun Valley involving her daughter, or at least her daughter's arm. After a minute of uncomfortable silence, Lynn retreated to a description of the palazzo they were renting: its views of the canal, its oddly impractical and garish art-deco bathrooms, a private rose garden with a restored water fountain. Nick set his concentration on autopilot, wowing at the appropriate pauses. Meanwhile, his brain was scrambling over the next step in his plan. It was hard to concentrate amid the relentless, stomach-heaving slap of the boat against the waves.

Nick decided he'd better pull the trigger while he had the courage. He dramatically groped the front of his pant pockets, beating his palms against his upper thighs as if putting out small fires.

"I think I've—"

But August shouted over him: "Look!" She pressed her finger against the cabin's rain-streaked window. "Venice!"

Nick leaned forward with the rest of the family to gaze through the slender rectangle. There it was, like a tilted postcard in a frame. From a distance, it looked like a tiny raft adrift in the sea, piled with impossible treasures. The sun sparkled across the water, almost blinding Nick as he tried to make out the skyline. The beauty of it—or the expectation of its beauty—put a halt to his performance.

"The rain's stopped," John announced. He lifted his arms, unlatched a section of the cabin's roof, and slid it forward. The back of the boat was now open to the salt air. Nick and his newly adopted family climbed across the seats and stood together on the bow. The wind spilled over them, and droplets of seawater covered their faces and arms. Both Lynn and August were shivering. Nick was glad he hadn't tossed away his wool blazer. The borrowed outfit, which he'd deemed so ridiculous a half hour ago, was proving practical for weathering this chilly, glittering speedway across the lagoon—doubly so when he thought about it, as he doubted this family would have invited him on board if he'd been dressed in a T-shirt and jeans.

"I need my phone!" August ordered. Lynn hurried to retrieve it from her purse. The motorboat shot past overgrown islands littered with broken columns of brick and stone. A tiny Italian flag whipped around on the back of the boat, its tattered tricolor tail mopping up rainwater. The airport was long behind them. Ahead, the captain vaped, the light shimmered, the gulls swooped, and

Nick thought he could see the hazy pink peaks of San Marco. How could he have ever considered taking the bus?

August asked her mother to take her photo. Lynn demanded that Magnus be included, which set both Magnus and August off in separate directions of resentment. As the rest of his family argued, John nudged Nick's elbow. "I didn't catch your name."

"I'm Nicholas." Nick saw no reason to lie.

"Where are you from?"

Nick had two choices, and technically neither was a lie. He opted against New York. "Dayton, Ohio," he said. Did any city on the planet sound more trustworthy?

"Ahhh," John purred. "We're from San Diego, but my company does a bit of business over in Cincinnati. I've heard wonderful things."

"Cincinnati is very close to Dayton," Nick replied, also not a lie.

"Ohioans are good people," John said, "kind people." Nick had been told this fact his entire adult life by those who'd never stepped foot in Ohio. For some reason, the rest of the world felt the need to remind Ohioans of their inherent goodness. "What do you do for work, Nicholas?"

"I'm in antiques," Nick said, not a total lie, although the truth would require flexing the past tense. "Mostly silver."

"Ahhh," John purred again. "An antiquarian." Nick turned to face him. He thought it might be smart to study the man he was swindling. In direct daylight, John's freckles multiplied like cells in a petri dish. He was a blur even while standing still, the vast needlepoint of red-brown dots swirling around his fragile features. If anyone had to identify John in a lineup, they'd recognize him solely by his skin. Nick knew that the majority of white America must still see Clay the same way: as a blur of black skin. He wondered if Italy was different in that respect and if that was the reason it kept drawing his boyfriend back like a second home. Maybe there was less rage here all around. Nick hoped so.

"You know," John whispered confidentially, "we've inherited a set of silver candlesticks from Lynn's uncle. Eighteenth century. Boston maybe? That's what he told us. Nothing too valuable, but you never know."

"Not by Paul Revere?" Nick asked simply to gauge John's knowledge on the subject. The man shrugged. "Candlesticks are very rare in eighteenth-century American silver. But you're right, you never know." John grinned at this thrilling possibility. Nick understood one of the fundamental laws of antiques: nearly every American household was certain it owned at least one genuine relic. In a young country with an unreliable memory bank, anything passed down more than two generations was treated as a museum-grade artifact. But it didn't matter. Right now, Nick wasn't in the business of candlesticks. He was in the business of gaining John's trust. "If you send me some photos of them, I could take a look. I know a few collectors who might be interested. No promises, of course."

"Of course!" John dug into his shirt pocket and extracted a business card. "Email me directly." He pointed to the address printed below his name, JONATHAN ALBERT WARBLY-GARDENER. Nick slipped the card in his blazer pocket.

"Hey," Lynn yelled over to them. "While you two are conducting business, you're missing Venice!"

And they were. A tunnel of buildings had closed around them, mossy mosaics of brick and stone. The green-black waters of the canal lapped against rotted wood doors. The *motoscafo* passed through shotgun-thin alleys, under arched bridges so low Nick's head almost skimmed their underbellies, through a parade route of tourists loitering on all sides, half like neon angels in cheap plastic rain ponchos, the other half dressed for heat that hadn't yet arrived. Far above dangled balustrades and flowerpots and the exquisite embroidery of diamonds and crosses set in ancient, bloodshot marble. Every building was a new discovery. They stood together on the boat, struck silent in the religion of looking. Nick loved each detail that passed before his eyes: the seaweed shadows under the water's surface; the gondola prows bobbing at their mooring stations like rooster heads; the flash of olive skin and clothespinned laundry in the highest open windows. Nick loved *all of it*. A part of him had expected to be disappointed by Venice; surely the city had been overhyped his whole life. Now he faced the far more unusual prospect of agreeing with common opinion: Venice was a symphony playing inside a shipwreck.

"Isn't it something?" Lynn surmised.

The boat turned left onto the Grand Canal, affording the five passengers a view of an entire menagerie of palazzi across the water. The captain yelled over the cabin roof, "San Samuele?"

Before John could confirm the dock, Nick called to the captain, "Ca' Rezzonico, *primi!*" It was vital to his already regrettable plan that he be dropped off first. The driver's face creased in uncertainty. "*Due* stops," Nick faltered, holding up two fingers. "*Primi* Ca' Rezzonico. Then San Samuele. *D'accordo?*" The driver grunted and returned to the wheel.

John opened his mouth to counter Nick's orders but closed it again. There were too many amphibious sights and sounds and close calls with lumbering tourist-laden vaporetti to sweat the question of who should be dropped off first. August shook her phone at Nick. "Can you—?" she asked. Peace had been restored in the Warbly-Gardener tribe.

The family of four posed against the butterscotch bench with the scrawl of centuries drifting behind them. Nick clicked three shots. When Lynn exclaimed, "You should have been in the picture with us, Nicholas!" he felt like he might throw up.

Nick knew there was no more waiting. He groped his pant pockets. "Oh no," he gasped.

Lynn sat down on the bench. "Oh no, what?" she replied.

"I can't believe it."

"Are you all right?" John asked in a concerned, fatherly voice.

Nick must have turned green. He felt green, or whatever color matched the disgust crashing over him for taking advantage of these people—good people, kind people. His only consolation was the fact that they'd never know. He was stealing a ride; that was the extent of his crime.

"I don't have my wallet. Oh, Christ! I must have left it on the plane."

Lynn slapped her palm against her heart. "Are you absolutely sure?"

Nick performed a second perfunctory groping of his pants and wormed his hands up his sides, careful to avoid his back pocket. He stared at the family with a sincere expression of panic.

"All my cash and credit cards."

"Did you check your carry-on bag?" Lynn asked.

"Good thinking!" Nick replied. He opened his bag and made a show of rifling through it. Then he lifted his hands in defeat. "No, not there." He threw John an apologetic look. "Let's go directly to your stop, San Samuele. I can't give you my half of the fare. I'm sorry."

"No, no," John rasped. "Don't worry about that right now. The least we can do is drop you at Ca' Rezzonico. You should call the airline immediately—"

"I will." Nick patted the breast pocket of his blazer. "I have my phone and passport. I'll call as soon as I get off the boat."

"It had *all* of your money?" Lynn groaned. "You have no cash on you at all?" Hadn't they already established this fact? Nick was beginning to resent the gullibility of the Warbly-Gardeners. He would have to continue performing this inept charade as long as they refused to give up hope.

"Have you checked the cushions in the cabin?" August suggested. "Maybe it fell out there?"

"I'll look!" squealed Magnus, the only family member who didn't seem unduly bothered by Nick's loss. They heard the farting sounds of a child's hands squeezing into leather crevices. "Nope," came the report.

"Ca' Rezzonico," the captain shouted as the *motoscafo* tipped toward a rickety wood dock. A massive white palazzo loomed in front of him, set back from the water by a strip of pavement. Nick felt the weight of guilt lift just seeing the dock. He'd soon be free of them.

"Well, this is me," Nick announced, lifting the strap of his carry-on bag over his shoulder. "Again, I'm sorry about my half of the ride."

"Will you be okay?" Lynn worried. She climbed to her feet, only to be tossed off balance by the rocking waves. She stabilized herself against her husband's chest.

"I'll be fine. Thank you so much. It was really nice to meet you." He meant it. They'd been baptized into Venice together, and he was grateful for their half hour of kindness. Maybe he'd run into them again in twenty years and admit he'd been too poor to afford the ride. It would be funny in twenty years.

Lynn whispered urgently into John's ear. Nick couldn't hear

what she was saying and decided not to wait around to find out. The captain was already struggling to deposit his suitcase securely on the dock; the swaying of the boat was frustrating his efforts. Nick glanced beyond the sagging planks of Ca' Rezzonico, where a long brick walkway telescoped into the city's dark innards. He saw a figure advancing toward him, a mere pinprick expanding between two walls.

Nick crawled through the cabin and spun around to give one last wave to the family, only to find one of them missing. Instead, John was now ducking out from the cabin doors with a fan of orange euro notes in his hand.

"Nicholas," John said severely. "Take this." He waved the fifties, still crisp from the airport ATM.

"That's not necessary. I'll be okay."

"No," John persisted. "I insist. It's only three hundred euros, but it should see you through until you make arrangements with your bank."

"Honestly, I'll be fine." Nick's foot searched blindly for the dock step. "Really, you've already helped too much. I don't want to take any more."

Lynn climbed out of the cabin and clung to her husband's arm. "Don't be crazy. We're not going to leave you stranded in Venice without a cent. Take the money." John shook the cash in accompaniment to her pleas. "It makes us happy to help you. We'd feel terrible if we didn't!"

"I'd rather not," Nick whimpered. "I don't want it."

"You can pay us back," John reasoned. "You have my card."

"Please," Lynn begged. "You'll ruin our vacation if you don't accept it!"

These monsters, Nick thought, and at the same exact moment, *These wonderful people*. He lifted his eyes to escape them and gazed down the brick corridor beyond the dock. He recognized the beautiful orb of his boyfriend's head and his loose, darting stride that favored the right hip. Nick felt his throat catch with adrenaline and love. Nothing else mattered, least of all this stupid test to see if he could scam a free boat ride. He noticed that Clay had undergone a slight change in appearance since he last saw him: his hair was clipped short against his scalp and he wore a preppy blue-and-white-striped button-down. They were both new men in Venice.

"Email me when you get your funds settled," John instructed. "You can PayPal the money back to me. Don't forget, we have that bit of business to discuss anyway."

Accepting the money would be easier than arguing a case for refusing it. Nick opened his palm and slid the three hundred euros from the relentlessly generous Warbly-Gardeners into his jacket pocket.

"Did he take the money?" August asked as she too emerged from the cabin, banging her cast against the doorframe. Charity had become a family affair. Only Magnus remained in the back—Nick's new favorite family member—writhing across the butterscotch cushions like a child prince.

"Yes," Lynn exhaled. "But we had to threaten him."

"Um, if you're going to be in Venice for the next few days," August began, "we could—" But the invitation was interrupted by the captain's peevish grunt. It was time for Nick to disembark.

"Again, thank you. I really appreciate it," Nick said as he took the captain's hand and prepared for his leap onto the dock. He aimed for the shelf of wood next to his suitcase. But at the very moment he sprung, a wave struck the boat, pitching it downward. The impact muted Nick's trajectory, and he barely managed to anchor a knee and two palms on the splintered planks. His bloated leather bag slammed against his ribs. He'd nearly become a first-day casualty of the Grand Canal. But it was only when he got to his feet on the dock, with his right knee burning and perhaps bleeding, that he felt the lightness in his back pocket. His hand raced to recover what was no longer there.

His wallet was splayed on the pin-striped deck, his own abundant supply of euros spilling out of the billfold right at the tip of John's shoe. When the captain picked it up and reached out to return it to its rightful owner, Nick didn't dare make eye contact with the family. He grabbed the wallet with out-of-focus eyes.

The captain shifted the engine into reverse, and the boat swirled backward into the blue. Three faces stared at him from across the water. Silent, blank, only beginning to curdle with anger.

Nick's hands were shaking. He bent down, his heart pressed against his knee, breathing hard, with tremors moving up his windpipe that might erupt into tears or laughter. In the lottery of emotions, he wasn't sure which would win.

"Nicky!" Clay called as he rounded the corner. "See! I never doubted for a second you'd come!" Nick stood up, trying to straighten his jacket, trying to be the man he'd pictured yesterday when he'd put on these clothes. The act wasn't working. Clay slowed his advance. "What's wrong?"

Nick wanted to say something tough or witty. Failing that, he wanted to forget what had happened and bask in the lunatic beauty of Venice. He and Clay were still new as a couple, and first impressions mattered. But Nick had lost his courage, and out sputtered the truth. "Maybe this wasn't a good idea. I'm a really bad crook."

Clay grabbed the suitcase and took him by the shoulder. In the shadows of the alley, he kissed Nick on the mouth. "Don't worry, I'm not any better at it." He squeezed Nick's arm. "A bad crook is the best kind."

CHAPTER 2

The list of speakers for the dead wasn't long.

It was a freezing New York morning that past February. Inside the church vestibule, Nick scanned the program and found, to his relief, only five names printed under REMARKS. Today's memorial service wasn't the first that Nick had attended to honor a legendary New Yorker whom he'd never actually met in life. In their sixteen months together, Ari had brought Nick to half a dozen of them, and that total didn't count funerals or wakes. Nick would have preferred a funeral. The mourners tended to be too choked in grief to say much, and a sense of urgency hung over the proceedings, as if the coffin were a hot coal that had to be buried in the ground before it cooled and crumbled.

Memorial services were a very different beast. Because they occurred months and sometimes years after death, these "celebrations of life" gave everyone license to showboat. People spoke with anguished, saw-toothed voices; they used their moment at the microphone to rattle off decades of anecdotes, playing up their own parts and stealing all of the clever lines; some presented slide shows; a few took the opportunity to settle old scores; others had the audacity to sing. Funerals respected the sacrifice of an hour. But an 11:00 a.m. memorial service like this one for Freddy van der Haar could easily open a sinkhole in the center of the day.

Nick curled the program in his fist and drummed it against Ari's shoulder. Five speakers wasn't *too* egregious. He could handle five speeches.

"Hey," Nick murmured. "What did Freddy die of, anyway?" But a choir had erupted inside the chapel, and Ari was tugging him through the vestibule doors to locate seats.

"They're dying in droves," Ari had said in the taxi that morning as they threaded their way through Manhattan.

"Who are?" Nick asked.

"The old New York scene," he'd replied, drawing an intricate shape with his finger on the fogged back window. Nick tilted his head from side to side, trying to discern the image. All he caught were the blurry traffic colors of Second Avenue that the freshest lines let in. "So sad, all of that talent wiped out. It's been a terrible season for them."

Ari made "old New York" sound like a losing football team. But Nick understood what his boyfriend meant. While Nick was far too young to have any direct connection to the artists and bohemians who blew up Manhattan in the 1960s, '70s, and '80s, Ari had managed to breathe some of their final intoxicating vapors. Of course, Ari had the advantage of time and place. He'd been born and bred on the Upper West Side, an only child of posh, quasi-bohemian Sephardic Jews. At forty-three, Ari never tired of bragging about coming of age in a New York "right before the rabbit-toothed grim reaper Giuliani scythed the entire garden." He reminisced about wild nights in bars and clubs that existed in a far-off galaxy before the advent of camera phones. After two glasses of wine, Ari was prone to turn epitaphic: *It's gone. People talk like New York still exists, but it doesn't. It's not here anymore. Maybe it moved to your town in Ohio, while we're all stuck on this island searching for it.* Nick, annoyed at learning for the umpteenth time that his adopted city was actually a mirage, had to stifle the desire to scream, *Good, I'm glad it's gone! Now we can go on without the pressure of living up to it!*

Nick wanted to love New York in the present—right here, right now, in the brightest, energy-sapping neon of today. Well, maybe not right now, right today. In February, the worn-out animal of Manhattan took on the dull camouflage of its pigeons. February was the worst month for the city, a flat hangover stretch after too many holidays clumped together. Memorial services for strangers—that was a fitting ceremony for the season.

Nick had attempted to bail out of the one today. Wouldn't it be more respectful not to pay his respects to a dead man he didn't know? Waking under three blankets and a down comforter, he'd contemplated a sudden flu, even test-firing a few phlegmy coughs. But Ari, lying next to him in the tucked-up position of a cannonball diver, gripped his chest with a cold hand that had fallen free from the covers in the night. "No way, Nick," he grumbled. "You're coming. I promise it'll be interesting. Van der Haar was one of the last true eccentrics. Imagine the freaks and crazies that the service will draw." When that bait failed to lure Nick, Ari retracted his hand and sent it scouting across the nightstand for his phone. "Don't forget, Freddy was also a client."

Nick couldn't argue that point.

Inside the church he expected to find the usual misery of gray stone and stained glass. Instead, the compact, sunlit space looked more like a New England village meetinghouse. It had scruffy beige carpeting, opaque casement windows, and red velveteen cushions running the length of the pews. There wasn't a cross or a confession booth in sight. Still, Nick sensed a hostile welcome; a riptide of irritated glances made it clear that they'd arrived late, and on top of it Nick had failed to keep the door from slamming shut behind them. Six gospel singers—four older black women and two younger white men—clapped and swayed at the altar in a spill of shimmery purple. Their deep, harmonic voices were accompanied by the tuneless pings and bangs of an antique radiator. Ari grabbed Nick's hand to advertise that they were in the market for two seats together, and they scurried down the aisle with apologetic bent backs.

The last two pews seemed to be reserved for the homeless. Sleeping bodies, bundled in torn winter coats, were strewn across the cushions. That left the remaining ten rows crammed with upright guests who were here for Freddy. They whispered, giggled, dabbed tissues to moist eyes, waved flirtatiously to one another, shopped on their phones, and applied heavy doses of makeup. Nick spotted the odd dressed-down celebrity—musicians and artists who had been rediscovered so many times over the decades that their lives had been ransacked for any last item of cultural value. Some attendees looked conspicuously rich; the majority looked conspicuously poor; only one or two men conspicuously straight. But all were well above the age of sixty. By comparison, Ari, with his inky black curls and taut, stubbly cheeks, appeared like an ambassador from the kingdom of youth. Nick wasn't sure what that made him, nearly twenty years younger than his boyfriend. Youth's boy assistant? He was bound to hear a nasty comment or two. These cranky, seen-it-all New Yorkers could be so ruthless in their judgments. Even a simple compliment was usually delivered in the shrink-wrap of an insult: "Aren't you a cute little trick!" Nick wondered what his friends his own age were doing this morning. Sleeping in, just going to sleep, still in a rush to see it all.

Ari had located an air pocket in the third row. Begrudgingly, several sitters shifted over. One wailed "For fuck's sake!" to peals of laughter. Nick regretted not taking off his coat before he sat down; the radiator was as effective as it was loud. Technically, his gray-and-black houndstooth coat with leather buttons belonged to Ari. One of the boons of living with a man nearly your exact size was the doubling—or in Nick's case, quadrupling—of your wardrobe. Ari hadn't fared as well in that exchange. At first, Ari had bought Nick a few quality shirts and pants in an effort to safeguard his closets. Eventually he just shopped more frequently and tossed his boyfriend the overflow.

"What kind of church has wall-to-wall carpeting?" Nick whispered.

"It's Quaker," Ari answered. "It was probably the only denomination that would allow a service for such a hedonist. I'm also guessing it was cheap to rent."

"But weren't the van der Haars superrich? I mean, that last name . . ."

Ari widened his eyes at the obviousness of the claim. "Uh, *yeah*. Old rich. Like the oldest rich. They were one of the first Dutch families in New York. Nick, you should know about them from their silver collection. Are you forgetting everything you've learned at Wickston?" He softened his tone. "When I was a kid, the hospitals and museums had wings dedicated in their name. There was even a van der Haar fountain in Tribeca. That's all gone now. Newer money took their place."

"What did Freddy die of?" Nick asked again, but Ari leaned forward to tap the shoulder of a woman in the pew ahead. She had a gray wasp hive of hair; deep fissures scored her lips, in which foundation collected like shale.

"Ari, darling, glad you could come," she whispered. "I'm sorry it's so jammed. I know. We should have booked a bigger venue." She rotated farther around to grip the back of the bench. Tabs of canary-yellow nail polish grew from veiny, rake-bent fingers. "The church lets the homeless sleep in here at night. Usually they're swept out in the morning. But it was so cold today that some of them wouldn't budge." She grinned with mischief. "Who cares? Freddy would have loved that detail, don't you think?"

Nick wasn't convinced that anyone would want their memorial service doubling as a homeless shelter, but he gave a nod of earnest agreement. Ari introduced the woman as Gitsy Veros, Freddy's longtime gallerist. Ari asked her when Freddy's last show had been, and two of Gitsy's fingers strolled her chin as she tried to recall. "Ten years maybe? His paintings never sold. His photographs did. Well, less and less. Maybe they will again now." She slapped the back of the pew. "Were they ever the point? It was Freddy who was the real work of art!"

The choir ended on a soaring note. Gitsy glided from her seat and approached the altar. On either side of the podium stood two empty white pedestals; Nick wondered if bouquets or framed portraits had been forgotten in the flurry of morning preparations. Gitsy told a story about going up to East Harlem with Freddy in the mid-1980s to hear his favorite gospel choir—"He might've been cruising and using me as cover." She gestured to the front row and introduced the speakers. Nick studied the five elderly men who sat there, trying to assess their likelihood of rambling beyond a humane ten-minute window. The men were cadaverous, their skulls decorated with badly dyed chunks of hair, their bodies too thin for their clothes, two of them clinging to walkers. Nick tried to inflate their hollow chests with once-spectacular personalities. In this church, on a different occasion, they could have passed for veterans or survivors of a brutal war that had killed all of their friends and family. Being old was its own war, Nick supposed, reaching for Ari's hand. If these men kept their speeches short, they could be out within the hour and on the hunt for a Vietnamese restaurant in the East Village.

Ari hadn't taken Nick's hand. He was too busy twisting around in his seat, his eyes scanning the pews across the aisle.

"What are you looking for?" Nick asked.

"I wanted to see if the kid was here." Nick squinted his eyes to extract more information. "*The hustler,*" Ari whispered, "who swooped in and got his name added to the will right before Freddy died."

Nick grunted at his boyfriend's harsh description, and Ari responded with a roll of his eyes. "You can be so naive, Nick. It happens all the time to old gay men with money. Sadly, they tend to be easy targets. Lonely, no kids, hungry for company. A good-looking guy shows up, plays nurse with benefits for a few months, tends to them, swears love, and walks away with the whole inheritance."

"Is that what people think I'm doing with you?" Nick asked only half jokingly.

Ari prodded Nick's knee affectionately. "Don't blame me! I'm just telling you what I heard. I thought he'd be here, but I don't see him."

Nick joined in the search, perusing the rows for any other man under the age of sixty. He was curious what this hustler looked like. As a teenager, Nick feared he would eventually become something like his quietly miserable father, fixing radios in a Dayton basement. Then Nick feared he would turn into a version of his unhappy, Ohio-trapped sister. In New York, he worried he'd end up whispered about like this young man for his behavior around older men. Nick's entire biography could be summed up by the people he feared he'd become.

"I'm trying to remember his name," Ari muttered. "Cord? Cliff? Clay?"

"Did he get a lot of money?" Nick asked.

"Well, as you said, Freddy was a van der Haar. I'm sure he had a very nice egg tucked away. Plus, he owned a brownstone in Brooklyn that I know for a fact did go to the kid. That's got to be worth a couple million by itself."

"A couple million," Nick repeated in astonishment.

"The kid's getting too greedy, though. He called the shop about selling some of Freddy's remaining silver. I'll take a look at the pieces, but this whole business . . ." Ari shook his head.

"You don't think . . ." Nick felt he didn't need to finish that sentence, but Ari let his question hang there without acknowledging the implication. Gitsy was crying at the podium. She was recounting a story about visiting a hospital in the 1980s with Freddy, sneaking in marijuana and magazines to their sick friends to ease their suffering. Nick cleared his throat and whispered directly into his boyfriend's ear. "You don't think that this kid, this hustler, killed Freddy for his inheritance, do you?"

Ari grinned. Nick's childish imagination was a constant source of entertainment for him (would Nick ever be forgiven for suspecting that their building's super was dealing drugs out of the basement laundry room?). Ari shrugged at this particular allegation before waving to an acquaintance across the aisle.

Nick drove his thumb into Ari's thigh to recapture his attention. "Answer this question. What did Freddy die of?"

Another shrug. Ari reached into his jacket pocket and pulled out a tube of nicotine lozenges. He'd quit smoking a few years before Nick had met him, but he'd saved his lungs only to jeopardize his mouth.

"Well, let's see. Freddy was HIV-positive. He had hepatitis B. He was diagnosed with lung *and* liver cancer. And his kidneys were failing because he was also a raging alcoholic junkie in his seventies. I think all of those conditions were competing to see which one could finish him off first."

"And which of those illnesses won?"

"From what I heard, none of them."

The pews burst into applause. The oldest of the old men with the cheapest of walkers was struggling toward the podium. Grimy fluorescent-yellow tennis balls were staked on the walker's aluminum legs. The thick weft of the carpeting wasn't helping to smooth the old man's progress, and Nick instinctively rose to help him.

Ari grabbed Nick by the forearm and warned, "Don't. He wouldn't like that." Nick sat back down.

A spotlight was switched on from the rafters and shone its watery halo onto the podium. Several minutes later the old man filled it, clutching the microphone, his face a contusion of shut eyes and invisible lips. Then, as if lit by the sun, the old man changed. When he opened his eyes, he appeared years younger, agile and alert— and even, Nick thought, handsome—as if the only thing he'd ever needed was a stage. The pews roared bawdily in anticipation.

"Ladies and assholes," screeched the man's vinegar voice. "Pricks and punks, you glorious angels of muck and two-dollar virtue." Laughter scattered around the room. "Get comfortable because I've been waiting eighty years to roast this motherfucker, Frederica! When I met her, we were babies fresh out of the clink, only she had the golden last name and I had the golden mouth. We got along, as they say, like two toucans on fire. Who here didn't cop heroin with Freddy back in 'seventy-three?"

Oh no, Nick thought. There was no way they would be out of here within the hour. Instead, they would be sitting right here in the third row, hungrier and hotter. He desperately needed to shed his coat. Somehow, post-applause, the other sitters in his row had stolen ground while he had lost the precious extra inches he'd been secretly hoarding. He couldn't strip off the coat without standing, and that might make him a target of ridicule for the old man at the podium. Nick glanced at Ari, who was watching the one-man vaudeville routine with a giddy smile. Nick nudged him.

"Hey," he whispered twice before Ari broke from his spell. "You didn't say what really killed Freddy."

"Oh," Ari replied with a curt nod. "Some people agree with you. They figure the hustler did him in."

"I didn't say that he—"

Ari snapped his fingers. "Clay. That's his name. Clay something. Yeah, most people think that this Clay character killed him to get the money before Freddy could change his mind. That's just a rumor. I have no idea if it's true. Officially, Freddy's death was ruled an overdose."

"An overdose?" Nick repeated.

"Yeah," Ari said. "But in the end, whether it was drugs, murder, or disease, it comes down to the same thing. We all know what really killed Freddy. He died of New York."

Midway through the third speech—the leitmotif of which was Freddy in his gender-fluid Berlin years—Nick whispered to Ari that he needed some air. Crawling from the pew, he scurried down the aisle with his eyes combing the carpet to avoid the glares. He opened the thin door to the vestibule and the heavy red outer door that brought him out to the lower edges of Gramercy Park. His feet crunched the ice and salt on the steps.

The chill rinsed Nick's body, running around his neck and knifing up his pant legs. Soon this momentary relief from the stuffiness of the church would become its own form of torture, but for now he appreciated the icy slap on his skin. He swept his hair back so the cold could reach the sweat on his forehead. The radiator heat inside the church had merged with the endless, drowsy rotation of Freddy stories to the point that the past had started to feel like a temperature. Out here in the freezing noon, the cold felt to Nick very much like the future—healthy, invigorating, and a reason for his heart to pump fast.

The trees in front of the church—magnolias, Nick guessed, long stripped to their twiggy skeletons—were blooming with ice crystals. The church itself was buffered from the unending congestion of Second Avenue by a large rectangular park with a cast-iron gate. A hospital sat on the other side of the avenue, and most of the park's midday ramblers were nurses or interns, judging from the white or pale-blue legs that descended from their coats. Nick knew he should go back inside before the third speaker finished. A prolonged absence was bound to jeopardize the points he'd scored in sacrificing his Saturday to one of Ari's obligations.

Still, Nick allowed himself to rest for a moment on the cement wall by the door. It didn't seem right for him to be sitting up front in that crowded memorial service. He didn't get the references because he hadn't known the man, and thus every joke, robbed of any tenderness, made him feel like he was laughing at the dead. He bundled his coat collar against his neck and watched the hospital employees circle the dry fountain well. A young couple, an Asian woman and a white man, were passing through the park at a clipped pace, knit hats bobbing in unison, both of them slipping and catching themselves on a patch of ice. Nick pulled out his phone to text Leo—What did you do last night?—hoping to be amused by some raucous escapade that had his friend packed in an Uber in terrible shape at 7:00 a.m. But as Nick scrolled through their text history, he realized he'd been asking Leo this very same question once a week for the past six months. What did you do last night? What did you do last night? He was using Leo as his informant to keep tabs on nocturnal New York. Which bar were you at? Were lots of people there? Nick slid his phone into his pocket. He could scour Leo's Instagram account later.

A lone figure cut across the park, rounding the fountain, his breaths streaking white in the cold. When the man crossed the ice patch he didn't slip or even slow his gait. He was black, only a little shorter than Nick, and had a thin, athletic body with a slightly uneven stride, as if a sleeping pain existed in his right hip that he was trying not to awaken. His hair was short and frizzy, slightly longer on top than on the sides. Earphones dangled on a cord from his waist, reminding Nick of the tasseled tzitzit that Orthodox Jewish men wore under their suits.

When the young man exited the park, Nick was surprised to see him jogging directly toward the church. He slackened his pace only when he shuffled between two parked cars. Then he stopped and stared hesitantly up at the red door from the sidewalk. There was a movement at his mouth as if he were chewing on his lips. His fists punched the insides of his jacket pockets, and he walked up the stone path, his high-tops kicking up bits of ice. As he paused at the church door right in front of Nick, he took his hands out of his pockets but kept them balled. The skin at the knuckles was cracked.

Nick straightened up, and the guy glanced down and gave a

slight nod. But the crack of a smile, more upper gums than teeth, changed the entire forecast of his face. There was something inviting in that smile, and Nick could feel himself turning red. Luckily, the cold worked as cover. Nick took the opportunity to study the man closely. He was around Nick's age, probably just a year or two older. He had severe eyes, or rather soft brown eyes under a severe brow. His lips were badly chapped and lined with indents of his teeth. Nick found him sexy in a way that might not show up in a photograph.

The guy peered into one of the glass panes that bordered the church door. Nick didn't pin him as a late guest. The crowd inside was far too old, and it was entirely white. Maybe he was the son of one of the gospel singers, waiting for his mother to finish her gig to escort her home. In any case, Nick knew that the young man wouldn't be able to see into the church from the window. The vestibule doors blocked the view of the service.

The guy stepped back, and his eyes moved reluctantly down to Nick.

"Excuse me," he said in a deep voice, the kind of muscular baritone that teenage boys manufacture to sound like men when they answer the phone, tired of being mistaken for their sisters. "Do you know if the service for Freddy van der Haar is still going on?"

"Yes, it is," Nick responded, a touch too soprano. "It's probably about halfway through." He reached for the phone in his pocket to check the time but stopped himself. A phone shut down conversation, and Nick was hoping to encourage one, at the very least to delay returning to his seat. "It's packed in there. Lots of people."

"Ah, that's good," the guy answered. "I'm glad to hear that." He kicked his sneaker against the stoop but didn't reach for the door handle.

"What I mean is, you'll have a hard time finding a seat."

"Oh, I'm not going in," he replied. But now he gazed down at Nick with fresh interest. "Do you know if the flowers arrived?"

"Flowers?"

"Two huge bouquets. Peonies. Those were Freddy's favorites. They were supposed to go up by the podium."

Nick thought of the empty white pedestals at the altar.

"Uh-oh. Are you from the florist?"

The guy laughed at this idea, wrapping his arms around his stomach. For the first time, his hands lost the shape of fists.

"No, man," he said, recovering. "I'm not from the florist."

Nick was on the verge of stuttering out an apology, but there didn't seem to be any offense taken. "No," the young man said with a smile. "I'm a friend of Freddy's. I just wanted to make sure the flowers arrived and that enough people showed up. Those two bouquets cost a fortune."

"I have bad news," Nick said sheepishly. "I don't think they arrived."

The guy's expression stiffened. "Are you serious?" When he threw his hands up in frustration, Nick caught a flash of navy boxers and hairless, goose-bumped skin at his waist. "No wonder they didn't answer when I called. Dammit! Freddy would have wanted those flowers up there."

It was difficult for Nick to feel too bereaved about missing flowers, but it clearly meant something to the young man. "I'm sorry," he said in an attempt at consolation. "It's still a really nice service. I'm sure Freddy would be happy with it."

The guy nodded appreciatively as he coiled the cord of his earphones. Nick caught his gaze and felt a wave of heat and fright, the familiar vertigo of a brief flirtation. Ari always accused Nick of flirting with strangers, of trying to reel them in with shy glances.

Maybe Nick did tend to flirt. But when he was trapped with Ari's intellectual friends from Brown or his silver-haired colleagues in antiques or art, it was all he could fall back on. At twenty-five, Nick's eyes were wiser than his tongue.

"You should go in," Nick encouraged. "You might find a seat."

"Nah," he said with a shake of his head. "This is a service for Freddy's *old* friends. They put it together, and it's for the Freddy they knew. I don't want to interrupt."

"I don't think you'd be interrupting," Nick assured him, having no idea whether that would be the case. He was only trying to extend their conversation and get a second hit of vertigo. Yes, Ari was right. Nick did like harmless games of seduction. And once he decided to be seduced, nothing—not even the waning interest of the seducer—could throw him off the chase.

"You don't understand," the young man said. "I know I'd be interrupting. Some of those people aren't so fond of me." Nick offered up a look of disbelief. "It's okay, though. I'll have my own memorial for Freddy. He wanted to be buried in the Campo Verano in Rome or the Hollywood Forever Cemetery in LA. I couldn't make either of those happen, so I'll scatter his ashes in Venice by myself."

There was a colossal difference between bearing the responsibility of memorial bouquets and the final resting place of the deceased. Nick had wildly misjudged the relationship of this young man to Freddy van der Haar. He flailed his arms apologetically. He realized he'd just invited one of Freddy's closest friends inside the church as if Nick were the self-appointed memorial-service bouncer.

"I'm so stupid. I didn't mean—"

But the guy thrust his hand out, thumb to the sky, palm open. Nick took it and gripped down on the soft, warm flesh.

"I'm Clay Guillory," the guy said with a smile that exposed his purple gums.

The hustler, Nick thought, remembering Ari's words, the one who'd connived his way into the van der Haar inheritance. Nick had pictured a far sketchier figure, a scrawny white kid with bleached hair, a red Florida sunburn, and eye sockets like the heads of dirty spoons. Nick had taken "hustler" to be code for "escort" or "prostitute," whereas Ari might simply have meant "schemer," "con artist," "grifter," or basically "any young person without money or means who dared to survive in New York these days."

In any case, Nick reserved judgment. He himself had never accepted money for sex. But in his skimming-the-poverty-line college-dorm years, he'd engaged in a few dalliances with wealthy men that were unequivocally transactional in nature. Nick had been treated to expensive meals, to a designer coat, twice to a pair of sneakers, and to several weekends at mansions in Southampton. He was even once given a vintage Rolex for his birthday, which he'd stupidly lost a few weeks later. Nick had never received cash for those dates, but he was rewarded in the things that cash could buy. Was there a difference? To Nick, the answer was yes and no. He had never mentioned those starving years to Ari for fear of his reaction. But as he stared up at Clay Guillory, he wondered if he should be impressed or cautious. Clay was so young to have whee-dled a family fortune into his bank account—one of the oldest American fortunes at that.

Nick decided he was both impressed and cautious. "I'm Nick Brink. Nice to meet you."

Clay was the first to pull his hand away and, in the ensuing silence, seemed to be sizing Nick up with patient eyes. "You're not one of Freddy's old friends," he surmised.

"No. I never met him. I'm here with my boyfriend, Ari Halfon. He runs—"

"Wickston Antiques," Clay exclaimed, pulling his jacket's zipper up to his chin. His smile didn't change, but the spark behind it seemed to fade. "I've been talking to your boyfriend about Freddy's silver."

"Yeah, he mentioned that. I work at Wickston too. I'm an assistant for now, but . . ." Nick stumbled and let the pathetic sentence blow away in the wind.

"Freddy's family had one of the most extensive silver collections in America. A lot of it disappeared over the years, but he held on to a few last pieces. I thought you guys might want to take a look before I offer them to the auction houses."

"Absolutely!" Nick nodded before giving up the illusion that he'd be able to evaluate a collection's worth. "You should really talk to Ari. It's beyond my depth."

"That makes two of us!" Clay rasped. "Well, maybe I'll see you when I stop by the shop."

"I hope so," Nick replied too eagerly.

The choir started up in the church, muted by the two sets of doors that separated them from the rest of the mourners.

"I better go," Clay said. He spun around and hopped down the steps with his hands punched into his jacket pockets. Nick watched his leg muscles clench with each stride. "I was just checking on the flowers."

Nick held up his hand to the fleeing back. When Clay reached the street, he turned around and received the gesture with another smile. As he crossed into the park, a wave of loneliness overtook Nick, so sudden and bewildering he closed his eyes to wait for it to pass. Long after he lost sight of Clay to the yellow traffic of

Fourteenth Street, he remained sitting on the stone wall, nursing a flicker of heat in his chest.

For Nick, though, Clay had existed as a rumor before he'd become an actual person. When he stood up to go inside, it occurred to him that the same young man in charge of spreading Freddy van der Haar's ashes might also be his murderer.

CHAPTER 3

A ri predicted a bad year for silver.

In fact, there hadn't been an exceptional year for silver in decades. Once the bread and butter of auction houses that held silver antique sales on a daily basis, the Halfon family's decorative specialty had fallen mercilessly out of favor. Experts had several working theories for silver's popular decline: the loss of the dining room as a domestic institution; the preference for the cheap and the disposable rather than cumbersome utensils that you had to polish before they turned chimney-soot black; the soaring interest in contemporary art as the new status symbol of the global elite. Nick developed his own theory in the twelve months he'd been working as a poorly paid, highly perked underling at Wickston Antiques. He felt that semantics should shoulder some of the burden. There was a special medieval language for the glittering artifacts that filled the metal shelves in Wickston's climate-controlled basement storage room. What the hell was a salver, a porringer, a cann, a monteith? They were plates, bowls, and cups, for Christ's sake! Nick believed the problem was not that the world had fallen out of love with sparkling objects, but that the terminology had dated the whole enterprise out of relevance. Customers yawned before they ever touched sterling; they saw it as a tired history lesson. Nevertheless, Nick kept a small notebook in his shirt pocket to record the proper vocabulary (i.e., the difference between repoussé and chasing for ornamental effect). In lonely afternoons sitting at the front desk of Wickston's Park Avenue storefront, Nick's head felt heavy with metal, overloaded with fine-antique descriptions that had so far failed to transmute him from mere apprentice to passionate connoisseur.

When he'd begun dating Ari sixteen months ago, Nick had been working as a waiter at an upscale West Village steak house. He also shared a two-bedroom apartment in Greenpoint, Brooklyn, with three roommates—a mathematical problem of a living situation that encouraged staying out as late as possible and/or jumping into a long-term relationship. But when Ari entered Nick's life—he'd been seated one evening in Nick's section at the steak house and after two courses had gathered the nerve to ask for his phone number—he appeared as so much more than a temporary escape hatch. He was clever and handsome and hairy from head to toe, which for the twenty-three-year-old Nick registered as the apex of maturity. More to the point, Ari seemed as stable and secure as the Central Park West apartment building in which he'd been raised. Four months into their relationship, Wickston's longtime assistant moved to Scotland for grad school. Ari suggested that Nick fill the vacancy. "I'm tired of you smelling like cows and curly fries," he'd joked. Nick saw it as a chance to be delivered from the purgatory of mid-twenties aimlessness. Maybe silver could be his thing too. In early stages of love, all transformations seemed possible.

It didn't take Nick long to realize that no matter how many

arcane terms he memorized, he'd never acquire Ari's innate feel for precious metal. His boyfriend could close his eyes, select a vessel at random, run his fingers across its hammered surface, and by density and texture alone discern its date, style, and maker. Ari had an uncanny gift; in a heartbeat he could tell you a real from a fake, French American from American Huguenot, Boston from Philadelphia, 1770 from 1785. The flourish of an engraving on the side of a chafing dish could send Ari into an aesthetic-historical mystery spiral that ended two days later with the pronouncement that the chafing dish was produced in 1721 in New York by silversmith Peter Van Dyck as a gift for one Ethel Schuyler's wedding to Abraham Lodell. "Bad marriage, gorgeous result," Ari quipped, sucking on a nicotine lozenge while tilting the chafing dish so it caught the starry overhead lights. Nick did not confess his embarrassing historical blind spots: he couldn't begin to picture New York in 1721; he often got the Constitution and the Declaration of Independence mixed up; he could never remember the fuss that started the War of 1812. But Nick figured he had time to learn all of those collisions of American history. Ari was eighteen years his senior.

What Nick had learned most from Ari, though, was not sprawl but specificity. It was a thrill to tour a museum's silver collection with him. Most of the visitors ran straight to the lions and tigers of the gallery rooms, the enormous World's Fair punch bowls or British ceremonial swords. But Ari knew what all wise zoologists did, that the miracles of evolution were best observed in the smallest and oddest of creations. Ari taught Nick the beauty of details: the rolling curve of a handle, the scalloped bend in a plate rim, the minute scrolls on the serifs of engraved initials. It was magical to shrink the whole world down to a faint mark on a piece of metal.

Most mornings, after a half hour devoted to professional

jealousies—*which dealer sold a Neoclassical caster for how much?*—
Ari would sit at his mahogany desk in the back of the store, strap
on his magnifying goggles, and study every inch of an antique
brought in by some harried inheritor. Nick's workstation consisted
of the narrow glass-topped desk by the shop's front door. Patrons
had to ring the bell and be admitted by the press of a button under that desk. Nick was Wickston's official greeter, office-supply
stocker, phone answerer, package accepter, security guard, and appointment booker. Those disparate duties congealed into the la-
bel ASSISTANT printed across his Wickston business card. Most of
Nick's hands-on contact with silver comprised of polishing it with
a special patina-restoring foam at the basement sink.

Wickston might have aspired to an address in the blue-blood
blocks of upper Seventies Madison Avenue but had long ago settled
for East Sixty-Third and Park. Across the street loomed tinted-
glass corporate towers that shone in the sunlight like black ice and
glowed at night with the pearly fluorescence of an alien mother
ship. The shop's decor tried for old-world majesty. Swirls of plaster
molding garlanded the walls. The floors were oak herringbone,
and Nick couldn't resist the compulsion to fit his feet into the rectangular tiles every time he crossed the shop—pigeon-toed from
the front to the back, penguin-footed from back to front. The
sidewalk window read in silver gilt: WICKSTON FINE ANTIQUES,
EST. 1908.

What that sign didn't mention was that its current owners had
carried the Wickston name since 1969. Ari's grandparents had fled
Morocco in the late 1960s, holdouts but eventual escapees of the
mass Jewish exodus from Muslim North Africa. Once the couple arrived in Manhattan, the Halfons bought into a flailing Wall
Street antique store called Wickston Idyll. They cut "Idyll" but
kept Wickston. Like the shrewdest of immigrants trying to move

up in New York, they managed to get close but not quite into the red-hot center of the privileged city inside of the privileged city. That goal was left to Ari's parents, and they mostly succeeded by lasting. They focused the store's interest on early American silver and watched as the market constricted and the competition shuttered. Eventually, the remaining collectors descended into the East Sixties by cane and wheelchair to buy, sell, or authenticate. The cane and wheelchair reference wasn't hyperbole: the average age of the Wickston client was somewhere in the mid-eighties. Ari joked that they had one "sprightly young client" in his seventies who managed to walk into the shop unaided.

No question, antique silver was a dying trade—"The silver trickle," Ari called it. Occasionally while sitting alone at the front desk, Nick wondered if he were apprenticing in a field that would disappear before he ever mastered it. Worse, he imagined the opposite outcome: a future where he was forced to keep the shop running long after Ari died, a Brink ensuring the legacy of the Halfons under the name of Wickston.

Ari's parents, Haim and Deirdre, rarely set foot in the shop since retirement, but they were a constant presence everywhere else in Ari's New York. Nick had never understood the cult of a family before he met the Halfons. He assumed all families on the planet mimicked his own—a collection of loosely allied strangers forced to share a house until any member was legally allowed to escape it. The Halfons reveled in their time together. They spoke French and only grudgingly switched to English as if to accommodate Nick's special needs. As a rule, parents of boyfriends made Nick exceedingly nervous because he never felt sure how much they approved of his existence. That wasn't the case with the Halfons, that family of manic huggers. They swallowed Nick whole the moment they met him with their slim, cashmered arms. There was never a flinch from Haim and Deirdre about their son's gayness, no liberal resolve masking genetic disappointment, no plangent "Well, as long as you're *sure* it's what you want . . ." Ari told Nick that he came out back in the mid-1990s when he was a freshman at Brown. His mom had responded, "Duh! And we're so happy you've realized it!"—as if his parents had been waiting for the good news to reach them from Providence. Any open exchange of warmth between Nick and Ari—a kiss on the cheek, a quick pat on the ass—activated pleasure receptors in the Halfons. Their son was happy!

Nick liked Ari's parents, particularly Deirdre, with the pretty raised moles under her eyes. But the Halfons' absolute, unquestioning acceptance of their son had an unexpected side effect: it made Nick feel like a coward for never admitting the truth to his own family. Maybe if he had only spoken, the Brinks would have unleashed a hurricane of love too. Maybe the unhappiness that collected with the dust in their suburban Dayton house was due to his failure to come clean, and that unspoken truth had hung over all of them like a pressure front as they sat at dinner and steered the conversation away from anything near to the heart. Maybe that whole gray world back in Ohio had been of his own making. Nick knew he wasn't brave, at least not where it counted, not yet.

"You must marry my son!" Deirdre had blurted out to Nick in her kitchen that past Thanksgiving. It was after dinner, and she was tipsy on the cognac that Nick had misguidedly brought and no one else dared to touch. Deirdre was leaning against the stove with the yellow light of the oven's hood chiaroscuroing the shadows on her face. For a second, Nick felt he could have been in any kitchen in America, with its purring fridge and the efficient peace of its steel appliances—only this kitchen looked out onto a street of deflating cartoon balloons where some three million spectators had gathered that morning to watch the Thanksgiving Day Parade, and beyond that comic thoroughfare lay the frostbitten greens of Central Park. "You really should marry him," Deirdre continued. "You're perfect for each other. The whole family adores you. Who cares about the age difference? Ari is probably too shy to ask, so you should!" Ari had entered the kitchen right then, and Deirdre pretended to be scrubbing the stovetop with a community-theater actor's subtlety. Ari raised his eyebrows suspiciously, and they all snorted in laughter.

A month before Nick started at Wickston, he moved into Ari's apartment. The official excuse for their accelerated cohabitation had been mice. Nick's Greenpoint apartment was besieged with rodents, and it wasn't due to the inherent sloppiness of four gay twentysomethings bedding down together. The elderly Armenian woman across the hall spent practically her entire day cleaning her apartment, and she complained that every time she walked into her kitchen, there was a *whoosh* of fleeing mice. Nick had a healthy midwestern phobia of inner-city vermin; Ari pronounced his spacious two-bedroom apartment on Riverside Drive rodent-free, and that was all it took for Nick to agree to move in. But the real reason was that three months into dating, the world seemed less interesting apart than together.

Ari's apartment was not only rodent-free but rent-free. It had long cherry-wood planks that Nick walked across as if they were Olympic diving boards. To Nick's surprise, no silver antiques cluttered the shelves. Instead, Ari had pilfered some of his grandmother's Moroccan rugs and batiks and left the rest of the six rooms an echoey, minimalist white broken up by canvases gifted by painter friends; they weren't hung but left leaning against the walls, giving them the transient air of commuters on a subway platform. The apartment was on the sixth floor of a massive marble-stone pile on the corner of 104th Street, and the windows looked onto the trees of Riverside Park. As the year progressed, the leaves fell to reveal glimmers of the slate-blue Hudson River, and for the most brutal months of winter, they had an epic river panorama right outside their bedroom. Then killjoy spring came along and hid it again.

Their upstairs neighbor wore designer stilettos that echoed like thunderclaps from above, but their other neighbors had lived in the rent-controlled building for decades and were mostly orchestral musicians: violinists, cellists, concert pianists, a needling saxophone player down on the second floor. In the mornings, their individual practicing collected together to create an airshaft symphony. Ari's biggest regret was that he'd never mastered a musical instrument, but he played Schubert on the record player whenever he could. It was all Schubert all the time in the Halfon-Brink apartment. Schubert's Piano Sonata in B-flat Major; Schubert's Violin Trio in E-flat Major; Schubert's heavy strophic melancholy of Goethe's "An den Mond." Nick suspected the constant Schubert was part of his taste education, much like the books that Ari plied him with on New England redware pottery or the Basque cooking classes he'd signed him up for. To friends, Ari often described Nick as "very American," with its hidden implication that Nick should try harder to be a bit "somewhere else." Nick had already learned that gifts from older boyfriends were to be read as veiled demands—*I bought you this green sweater because I like you in green, understand?* But Ari was never a bully about it; he stammered if one of his presents appeared unappreciated: "Is it a misfire? Please don't feel any need . . ." But Nick *did* feel a need, mostly because he too loved the version of himself that Ari seemed to want. The Nick who could hum Schubert while stirring a spicy *piperade* in a redware vessel did feel like the right next Nick. That man would marry Ari.

Even if Ari occasionally called Nick out on his flirting, monogamy between them was a given. They'd gotten the awkwardness of sex out of the way on date two and the awkwardness of "I love you" on date ten. By the time Nick moved into the apartment there were few secrets between them, no former lovers texting dangerous memories in the night. Nick found sex with Ari to be set on medium heat; they rarely fucked, which didn't matter much to Nick because so far in his experience the act had only been clumsy or painful. Nick preferred kissing Ari and nuzzling his neck while jerking him off in bed. They were similar in size, Ari just a bit thicker, which excited Nick as he tugged and jerked and his elbow galloped against his own hip bone to bring Ari off. Nick enjoyed watching the storms grow and fade on his boyfriend's face.

Night set early in winter, especially when you were accustomed to gallons of daylight pouring through the apartment, six floors up. They didn't go out much at night anymore. Ari put on Schubert and stretched out on the sofa in the living room, reading the latest novel or biography. Ari read every night, chapters and chapters, while sucking on an after-dinner nicotine lozenge. Nick watched his brown eyes weave down the pages. He wondered how many miles Ari had read in his life when the lines were totaled up. How many times around the world? How far past the moon? Tonight Nick sat on the windowsill and watched the black disc of Schubert revolve. Nick hadn't seen friends his own age in months, nor had he danced or fallen down drunk. Before Ari, Nick had gone out almost every night, and each one of those nights had been a chance to set a world record for the most fun a human could have in New York. He'd once suffered almost daily hangovers, but he now couldn't remember how he'd fit those suicidal headaches into the corners of his days. Leo had long stopped asking him about his evening plans. The last time Nick met up with him at a bar in Chelsea, Leo had greeted him with the crack, "Nick, so great you're visiting! What brings you back to town?"

"Why are you opening the window?" Ari asked from the couch. "It's twenty degrees out." He crossed his feet and wiggled his hairy big toe that shot upward like an exclamation point.

"It's too stuffy in here." Nick yanked up the window. He thrust his hands out and felt the wind whipping off the water, hurtling southbound along with the car lights on the West Side Highway, everything outside in a hurry to get downtown.

On Sundays, in the Protestant tradition, Wickston was closed. On Mondays, Nick spent the morning running household errands. They were mostly Ari's errands, which Nick had initially enjoyed—there was something grown-up about picking up shoes from the cobbler or paper-wrapped halibut from the fishmonger on Amsterdam Avenue. It was exotic to Nick in the way that grocery shopping in a foreign country is exotic—the first dozen times at least. A year in, these chores had lost their sheen of romance. The Monday morning after Freddy van der Haar's memorial service, one of Ari's favorite suits had gone missing at the dry cleaner. It took an extra forty minutes of scrolling through the whirling wardrobe of the entire Upper West Side to locate the misplaced tartans. Nick took the crosstown bus and didn't reach his desk at Wickston until a few minutes after 2:00 p.m.

Ari was sitting in the back, typing on his laptop, his gold-framed reading glasses perched on his nose. He was sending out a flurry of invoices. A sizable chunk of Wickston's keep-the-lights-on revenue involved authenticity appraisals, certifying by expert opinion that an object matched a collector's claim. Nick turned on his computer, intent on devising a clever entry for Wickston's new

Instagram feed; it was Ari's idea to attract a younger audience to antiques. Under Nick's stewardship they had racked up 406 followers, which Ari deemed legion and Nick knew was a virtual ghost town. Nick and Ari often sat for hours at either end of the shop without once speaking. The showroom was the one place where Ari didn't play Schubert. It was often as silent as the moon, and the twenty feet of distance between them like twenty feet apart in outer space.

Ari pushed back in his chair, drumming a pen against his desk. "We had a visitor this morning," he announced. Ari waited eight pen taps to continue. "That hustler I was telling you about, the one who got his hands on van der Haar's inheritance."

Nick's fingers stiffened on the keyboard before he willed them into a pantomime of prolific typing. The news that Clay Guillory had come into the shop brought on conflicting waves of excitement and paranoia. Nick cursed himself for not getting in earlier so he could see the young man again.

He turned his head and searched Ari's expression for any sign that Clay had mentioned him. Nick hadn't told Ari about their meeting outside the church. Now he worried that Clay had mentioned it and that Ari might be reading too deeply into that lapse, might be taking it as an intentional concealment—which, to be fair, it was. Nick stopped fake typing and managed to say in the most disinterested tone he could muster, "The murderer?"

"What?" Ari asked while removing his reading glasses.

"You said at the service that he might have killed Freddy for his money. You mean that guy? The murderer?"

"I never actually said that," Ari replied. "You did. But yes, *that* guy." Ari opened a desk drawer and began rifling through it for some misplaced office supply. Gauging this reaction, Nick felt there was a good chance Clay hadn't said anything about their encounter, which both reassured and disappointed him. Maybe Nick had left zero impression on him. Maybe the guy had forgotten him the second he turned his back.

"Did he come about selling Freddy's silver?" Nick couldn't resist asking.

Ari nodded with a smirk. "I'd been waiting to hear from him. He phoned this morning saying he was in the neighborhood. He walked in fifteen minutes later with a cardboard box containing five van der Haar antiques. He just *happened* to be in the neighborhood." Ari rolled his eyes. "He's in a hurry to sell. My guess is that if we hadn't been open, he'd have taken the box straight to Christie's."

Nick squinted a silent question, and Ari answered, "Of course I said I'd take a look. Your murderer is coming back on Thursday to retrieve his box."

Thursday. Nick would sit at his desk all day on Thursday. What was wrong with a harmless crush? Nick's one-sided imaginary affair could still walk around on unicorn legs, now that he knew there would be a second meeting between them. He clicked on the computer's calendar with stony professionalism and scanned the entry for Thursday. Ari had a lunch appointment with a prominent collector down from Boston.

"Don't you want to know what I think?" Ari asked. He reached under his desk and lifted a cardboard box bearing the name of an adult-diaper brand across its sides. Clay Guillory either had a lot to learn about presentation, or was using a savvy strategy to prevent a possible mugging when carting around a fortune in silver.

"I'd love to take notes when you go through it," Nick said sincerely.

"Oh, I already examined them," Ari answered with a shrug. "I mean, we're talking about the van der Haars. I wasn't going to let them sit under my desk collecting dust." Ari opened the box to reveal five pieces wrapped in Wickston's signature light-blue tissue paper, which meant he'd already packed them back up for the owner's retrieval. Nick knew that wasn't a good sign. Ari could spend weeks poring over the illuminating features of just one significant vessel. Then Nick realized he'd been slow on the take all along: the potential sale of five authentic van der Haar artifacts would have sent Ari dancing around the shop in ecstasy. Such a trove would have been priced in the millions.

"No good?" Nick asked.

"Worse than I even feared," Ari confirmed. "I knew this kid was going to call, so I did my van der Haar homework. It's impossible to go by the family estate records. The 1758 van der Haar inventory has more than fifteen thousand pieces of plate. They had doubles and triples of everything, and that's just what's on the books." The antiquarian's first line of defense was always the reams of historical paperwork—the wills and codicils, the death inventories and domestic account logs—that traced silver back through the centuries to its original purchase. Unfortunately, Freddy wasn't the first van der Haar whose personal matters were ruled by the power of chaos. Ari explained that several van der Haar silver pieces now in venerable museums *could* be traced to their initial acquisition. But just as many could not. A multi-multi-multigenerational family like the van der Haars was a debris field of off-the-record gifts and snatchings, a silver teapot stealthily given to a nephew to avoid a death tax here, a silver snuffer stand sneaked from one sister to another there. Even a provenance geek like Ari gave up in clerical futility.

That's when it came down to the expert's eye. *Was the thing really the thing?* The first time Nick heard Ari compare colonial American silver to the Wild West, Nick had thought, Uh, I doubt it's quite that wild. But Ari had been right. Unlike England, which had long ordained a governing guild and *five* official hallmark stamps punched on every single piece of sterling, the United States never set a standard, never required a mark, and never assembled a regulating guild to keep track of its silversmiths. That's why colonial American pieces were so much easier to fake. The only helpful evidence punched on an American item was its maker's mark; occasionally even that identifier was absent.

The closest thing that the United States had today to those five telling British hallmarks was stacked in Nick's top-left desk drawer: Wickston's dove-white 32-bond letterhead, which Nick fed into the printer to be spitted out as an authenticity report. It only needed the blue-ink scribble of Ari's lasso-like signature. Ari was one of the few independent experts working on the East Coast who could bless an object as genuine or banish it to the halfway house of an uncertain past and future ("Hey, it's still worth its spot price as a precious metal," he often consoled a duped collector, "it's just not a precious antique"). Ari claimed he spotted fakes in the most revered museum silver collections in the country. But it came down to professional opinion: his versus the curator's. As Ari figured, better those forgeries existed in the eternal quarantine of a museum than floating around a sucker's market.

Ari unwrapped one of the van der Haar pieces from the tissue paper. "It's a shame," he muttered. "We all knew that Freddy had been selling family pieces privately for the past decade. He'd put one up for sale every few years, and a billionaire enthusiast would swoop in before it landed at the auction houses. They were authenticated over at Hawkes." Hawkes had been, until it shuttered two years before, the last major competitor of Wickston in Manhattan. It had been owned by Dulles Hawkes, a plump sixtysomething with a whinnying British accent who was also a notorious cokehead; instead of hiding his addiction, he incorporated it into his persona to the point that his sweating, fidgety, dry-gulping demeanor was considered part of his eccentric personality. Nick found him depressing, one of the people who scoured the shine off New York, and he didn't appreciate the way Dulles stared lust-fully at him but never asked him a single question when they were left in a room together. Ari vouched for his basic decency—"Oh, Dulles is all right, and he's always liked you, Nick." Ari occasion-ally still used him as a second opinion.

"Were those previous pieces that Freddy sold authentic?" Nick asked, walking over to Ari's desk.

"I always thought they were a bit wonky myself, but they were just on the right side of okay. These are on the wrong side. Way over."

A large tankard emerged from the tissue, which Ari placed on the desk. It had the right color, a dull, flat, copper-rich gray, the very opposite of aluminum foil. It also had the right patination, a scarring acne of dings and scratches running around its base. To Nick's untrained eyes, it looked authentic.

Ari opened the lid and pointed to the SS maker's mark punched on it. "That's a warning right there. It's only punched on the lid. Why not on the base of the tankard?" Ari lifted the vessel and held it out for Nick to intercept.

"It's lighter than I would have guessed," Nick said.

"Exactly! The lid and handle are heavier than the body. And if it's really a Simeon Soumaine, like the punch attests, where is the ornamentation around the baseline? Why are only the handle and lid decorated? No, it doesn't have Soumaine's flair. He was a Hu-guenot, but he was influenced by the New York Dutch style of the 1720s." Ari shook his head in flat rejection.

"So it's a fake?"

"Definitely. I think the lid and handle may, *just may*, be real. It's also been soldered on quite sloppily. Someone probably took an authentic lid and added it to an old, run-of-the-mill tankard base. It has the right marks, you could sell it in a photograph. But to hold it and to know Soumaine's instincts . . ."

Ari grabbed the tankard and swathed it in the tissue.

"It's the same story with the sauceboat, the porringer, the plate, and the punch bowl that your murderer brought in," he continued. "Each one is wrong for a different reason. One's trying to pass itself off as a Myer Myers, for fuck sake!" Myers was a Jewish eighteenth-century New York silversmith particularly close to Ari's heart.

"You don't think my murderer—" Nick winced. He wasn't *my murderer*, he was *the murderer, Freddy's murderer*, except he wasn't even a murderer, was he? Clay hadn't actually killed the old man. Or had he? Nick had no idea. He started over. "You don't think Clay is responsible for making these forgeries, do you?" How many crimes were they going to pin on this guy on a Monday afternoon?

Ari hummed skeptically. "It might have been him. It could very well have been Freddy. But it could also have happened a hundred years ago and entered the van der Haar household by error. The collections of all wealthy families are riddled with forgeries. The robber-baron clans of the nineteenth century were even worse, because they were such compulsive shoppers and would buy anything shiny."

Ari tapped the box on his desk. Nick knew he was expected to carry it down to the storage room for security. The quickest way for forgeries to become real was for them to be lost or stolen. The insurance would have to cover what it might have been instead of what it really was.

"But," Ari remarked, "the tankard was the most obvious phony of the five. The others are slightly more passable. I'm not sure your murderer could have pulled off that caliber of counterfeiting."

"He's not my murderer!" Nick snapped. "Stop calling him that!" He hated his voice when it flailed into high registers. It was the nine-year-old in him screeching around the playground fearing being pelted with a ball, the fifteen-year-old skittering away from school bullies in tears—they had written F-A-G in marker on his shirt and sent him back out into the world correctly labeled. That shriek brought all of those sad, earlier renditions of Nick into brief existence.

Nick quickly redirected the conversation. "So what will stop Clay from picking up this box and walking it over to the auction houses to try his luck there?"

Ari sat down in his chair and crossed his legs. He was beautifully dressed today, in a checkered black-and-white shirt with a gray knit tie fastened by a gold clip. There was an emerald chip embedded in the tie clip, and as Ari shifted in his seat, a tiny dot of raw green winked on his chest. The sobbing fifteen-year-old that Nick had been would have done backflips down the school hall knowing he'd one day have this gorgeous man to fondle and kiss any time he felt like it. Well, almost any time. Ari prohibited sexual activity during work hours, which was irritatingly when (and probably why) Nick wanted it most. He grabbed the cardboard box from the desk and pressed it against his stomach.

"I don't think *even* the auction houses will accept those pieces," Ari replied. Ari was convinced that auction houses set a considerably lower bar for authentication. "Now that Dulles is retired, what they'll probably do is call here to ask if I've ever encountered them."

"And you'll tell them the truth?"

Ari shot him an incredulous look. "Of course I will. Not only out of professional courtesy but because they're fakes!"

"So the guy won't be able to sell them anywhere?"

"No, not through the normal channels. Not in New York."

Nick felt sorry for Clay Guillory and the adult-diaper box of silver in his hands. He could imagine Clay thinking he'd gotten so close to a windfall—more than a million dollars in possible sales—only to be told that his inheritance was a mirage. At least Clay had gotten Freddy's brownstone. Houses couldn't be faked.

Ari glanced up at Nick and said pointedly, "Why don't you tell him I'm happy to look at any other pieces that Freddy owned. Each one is its own case."

Nick laughed. "Why don't *I* tell him? What do you mean?"

Ari picked up his pen and tapped it on the desk. "He's coming back at noon on Thursday. I won't be here. I have my lunch with old Ebershire from Boston."

Nick could feel his cheeks going red. He lifted his knee against the bottom of the box to secure his grip. "Ari, I can't! I can't tell him his inheritance isn't worth anything." His voice was threatening to crack again.

"Why not?" A corner of Ari's upper lip was rising slightly. "I'm writing a comprehensive report. All you have to do is hand it to him. If he persists, tell him we're not confident about their authenticity and we wouldn't be willing to procure a buyer. That's all you have to say. Honestly, how hard is that?"

"That *is* hard. Shouldn't you be the one to—"

"I think you can do it." Ari patted Nick's leg. "I have faith in your ability to hand him an envelope."

No one, not even a child, likes to be talked to like a child. Nick caught something new in Ari's face, something he wasn't sure he'd ever seen before. It was in the shape of his eyes and in the tight, uncooperative muscles of his jaw. Nick thought what he saw in Ari's face was jealousy. Perhaps Clay *had* mentioned their run-in on the church steps. Maybe he'd even complimented Ari on how overly friendly his boyfriend was. It occurred to Nick that Ari might have been waiting all of this time for him to admit that he'd already met Clay. It was too late now to confess without making the whole minor episode sound bigger than it was.

"If that's what you want, fine," Nick said lightly. "I'll give the murderer the news." He carried the box down to the basement.

CHAPTER 4

Everything in Venice was dripping. Water leaked from the battered white awnings of Campo San Barnaba and from the postcard racks standing sentinel by the corner *tabaccheria* and from the noses of statues peeking from the shadows of a church. The shower had lasted less than two minutes, and already the sun glazed the cobblestones a blinding white.

Clay had hoped for warmer weather. He wanted Nick to witness how Venice purred with possibilities in the Adriatic heat. But there were also merits to a chilly afternoon. It warded off an additional layer of tourists that made the narrowest alleys nearly impassable. In the stranglehold of dry, hot days, visitors clotted the streets like human glue, and cruise ships barged into San Marco's Basin with horns that blasted louder than any church bell. The invasion always intensified with the temperature. At least that had been Clay's experience ever since he'd first fallen in love with the city four years ago.

He hauled Nick's heavy suitcase over the uneven cobblestones, its rattling wheels mimicking the sound of suburban garbage cans dragged to the curb. Wheelie suitcases had become the unofficial soundtrack of Venice, a city that had triumphed for millennia on the very absence of wheels. Clay tried to lift the bag to quiet the noise, but he could only carry it ten feet before his muscles gave out.

"What exactly do you have in here, Nicky?"

"Everything," Nick admitted meekly.

"Right down to the pots and—" Clay cut himself off. He didn't want to mention pots or pans or any other metal vessel, fearing it might remind Nick of Ari and his life back in New York. Thankfully, Nick seemed oblivious. His eyes were too busy darting like uncaged birds over the wonders of the Dorsoduro neighborhood. As they passed a scaly wooden boat parked on the side of the canal selling vegetables, Nick stopped in his tracks. His mouth hung open. Nick's display of absolute wonder struck Clay as charmingly old-fashioned. Today, most people simply reached for their phone to take a picture. Three Americans stood behind Nick doing just that, letting their tiny machines digest the world for them. But Nick shook his head and stammered, "My god! Fresh tomatoes right off a boat! It's like, it's like . . ." No comparisons were forthcoming.

It was a secondhand high to watch a first-timer take in the city. "Come on, there's plenty more of that," Clay promised. He knew that encouraging Nick's love of Venice was a way of encouraging Nick's love of him too. It was like bringing a boyfriend back to your hometown—and since they'd met in Clay's hometown of New York, Venice was the only substitute he had. Nick's gaze drifted over every balcony and scurried down each alley, while Clay's eyes remained on Nick. He still couldn't believe he'd turned up. Nick had made good on his word, blown everything up with Ari, and now here he was with his dark-blond hair slicked with rain and dressed in a mismatched suit like the pickings of a color-blind poker champion. Clay had misjudged Nick from the very beginning. The day they'd met outside Freddy's memorial service, Clay took Nick to be another predictable cute white kid from the Midwest who dated adult replicas of the jocks and stoners they'd lusted after in high school. Clay was fairly certain that whatever Nick's freshman class looked like in Dayton, versions of Clay were in short supply. When Nick told him that he was dating Ari Halfon, Clay's bias cooled by only a few degrees. It always seemed to him that there was a failure of imagination at work when two attractive people became a couple. You couldn't blame someone for being beautiful, but you could glean a petty narcissism behind their need for a mate as pretty as themselves. It was as if they couldn't be bothered to delve into the deep, jarring jumble of the world. The deep, jarring jumble was where Clay proudly lived. But he'd been wrong. Nick had proved himself full of surprises, and here he was in Venice, just as he'd promised.

Clay still felt uneasy about implicating Nick in the con. Every time he tried to talk him out of it, Nick had replied almost braggingly, "It was my idea!" Nick's part in the scheme wouldn't extend beyond a ten-minute window, but his role, in its way, was the deeper betrayal. Folded up in Clay's shirt pocket was a photograph of their target. Clay had ripped it out of a Venetian society magazine to give to Nick so he could memorize the man's face—just in case he hadn't bothered to google him. Clay reached for the folded picture with his free hand but stopped himself. There was no reason to sour Nick's happiness right now. He'd let him remain the innocent sightseer for a little bit longer before broaching the ugly business of the scam.

They walked through a flock of pigeons that erupted around them, and Nick shot his hand toward the suitcase. "Let me take that," he said. "You don't need to carry my bag for me."

"It's okay," Clay replied. "You relax after your flight. I'll need your help carrying it over the bridge ahead." Clay was taking Nick on a slight detour to reach the apartment he'd secured for him. There was a shorter route up the *fondamenta* that didn't involve bridges, but that was far less scenic and Clay wanted Nick to appreciate the cloistered activity of Campo Santa Margherita. The square was a hive of university students who hung around the outdoor caffès. It might convince Nick that Venice wasn't solely occupied by tourists.

Clay stopped at the foot of a narrow bridge. He'd been having stomach pains for the past month. Right now, a little electroshock fired through his intestines, but he masked it with a few theatrical weight lifter breaths. Nick grabbed the other end of the suitcase, and they carried it like an ambulance stretcher over the stone arc. As they descended, Clay's nose picked up the sweet reek of the canal, a medieval waft of rot and brine. Unlike the rest of humanity, Clay loved that rancid Venetian perfume; it reminded him of his first days here, a middle-class black kid from the Bronx suddenly crowned a prince of Italy. Months and even years later, when he had been back in New York living with Freddy, there had been spots—certain subway platforms on humid summer days—where he'd catch a whiff of that familiar odor. The subway commute from Freddy's brownstone in Bed-Stuy all the way up to Clay's old neighborhood in the Bronx was a torturous hour-and-a-half ride, and its only reward was the dank smell of the platforms. The subway started out black in Brooklyn. By the time the train reached Manhattan, its skin had turned white, and it stayed that way until 116th Street, when the Columbia kids disembarked. Then the snake shed its white skin for black again and continued on in its original color, Clay's color, to its final stops in the Bronx. Sometimes he could find that smell on the Van Cortlandt Park stop, sometimes on 238th Street, and he'd wait there and breathe in the aroma of fetid water and rat death and it would bring back the tingling world of his first days in Venice.

"Stings your eyes a bit," Nick noted with a scrunched nose. "Do you ever get used to the smell?"

"Never," Clay replied. He commandeered the suitcase again, and they proceeded past a few gelato shops on the periphery of the square.

"Sorry about my bag," Nick said. "I'm sorry it's so heavy. I wish you'd let me take it." Gratuitous apologizing was one of Nick's midwestern tics. Nick was a one-man chorus of *I'm sorry* and *Pardon me*. Today, though, Clay didn't razz Nick for being so *sorry*. The poor guy was jetlagged and still shaken from his accidental theft of three hundred euros from the American family on the *motoscafo*. (Never in Clay's life had he been offered three hundred euros from concerned strangers; never had he been invited to share a motorboat from the airport.) Clay simply said, "It's fine. We're close now." They had reached the mouth of the *campo*.

The square spread out in a large rectangle that the strong one o'clock sun turned the color of elephant hide. A few lean chestnut trees were beginning to bud in the center. A fruit stand supplied painterly orbs of reds and yellows, while a nearby fish stand presented a science experiment of plastic tubs and rubber hoses. Around the perimeter, canvas umbrellas and metal chairs were herded in their separate pens, one caffè's allotment nearly indistinguishable from the next. It was a lovely springtime scene, although Clay never forgot the epic fistfight he'd once witnessed in this square late one night outside a bar. It was no mere one-two punch like the neighborhood fights of his youth. The unchecked violence went on for a good ten minutes, with two local men falling over tables and punching the teeth out of each other. It had been the only fight he'd seen in his eight months in Venice, but it served as a reminder that the city was a tougher place than its postcard appearance let on.

"Over there," Clay said, pointing to a yellow awning, "is a great pizza spot." He moved his finger a few storefronts to the right. "And that's the caffè I went to every day after work. I'd stay all night drinking red wine. It's close to Daniela's apartment, so you can hop over for a glass and watch the world stroll by."

"Uh-huh," Nick replied distantly, battling a yawn. Clay had the unpleasant sensation of a father giving his bored son a tour of his alma mater. Nick's fatigue was catching up to him, and he swayed zombielike while squinting his eyes. "We can't even sleep together," he abruptly exclaimed. "I wish we were staying in the same place."

"Me too," Clay said. "But that wouldn't really work for our plan, would it? We wouldn't get far on that arrangement."

"Still . . ." Nick's frail attempt at a fight trailed off.

"It's only a week. Two at most, and then we'll be together all the time. We can go south to Ravello or west to San Remo. We can even hide out in a hotel here in Venice on Giudecca."

"My feet hurt," Nick complained, so quietly it seemed more like a message he was relaying between remote parts of his brain. Clay glanced down at Nick's black alligator penny loafers, which were barely broken in and would definitely lead to blisters in this punishing walking town. Clay dug into his pocket, located a copper two-cent euro coin, and bent down to insert it in the empty leather slot on Nick's right shoe.

"You put one coin in backward for good luck," Clay explained. "Only on one shoe. Two is bad luck." For Clay, the coin made all the difference; the loafers looked owned now instead of borrowed. He stood up and smiled, presuming this gesture of affection would swing Nick into a sweeter mood. Instead, Nick grimaced down at his foot, as if he'd taken Clay's minor adjustment as a criticism of his outfit.

"Thanks," Nick said hollowly. "At least when I look down, I can think of you."

Clay gave a contrite laugh. "It will bring us both luck." He pushed Nick forward through the square. "*In bocca al lupo*. That's how you say good luck in Italian. 'Into the wolf's mouth.' And then you answer, '*Crepi!*' That means 'die.'"

"Huh? What are you talking about? A wolf dies?"

Clay decided to stick to essential facts. "You'll like Daniela," he promised. "Do me a favor and take her out to dinner now that you're flush with euros. By the way, don't call her trans. She doesn't appreciate that word. She's old-school. She's a woman. Not fluid, not trans. Got it?"

Clay waited for a reaction from Nick. Another person's idea of normalcy was always a foreign country, just as your own borders on that dominion were constantly expanding or shrinking, ejecting proud, long-standing residents while taking in exciting new émigrés that would have been denied entry the year before. Clay decided to make the judgment easy for Nick. "Daniela's the best person in Venice," he said. "The very best."

In truth, Daniela was Clay's one remaining friend in Venice. She'd also been the first friend of Freddy's he'd ever met. It had been back during that cold fall, or free fall really, after Clay had lost all employment prospects and was holding on to the city for dear life. In a sense, by introducing Daniela and Clay, Freddy had given them like gifts to each other. And Daniela had treated him like family—like a rightful member of Freddy's close-knit band of bohemian spirits. In the end, she would prove the only friend of Freddy's to see Clay in that light.

Daniela had been born a Henrik in Frankfurt, the son of banking parents, and she'd moved to Venice at age thirty to become a permanent expat under her new self-assigned name. The only reminder of that border crossing was a slit-like scar across her neck where her Adam's apple had once protruded. Daniela was now in her late sixties and stayed afloat exporting local Burano lace to Northern European capitals. When Clay phoned her last week to ask about the small guest room in her ground-floor flat off Calle Degolin, she'd been exceedingly generous. "Ah," she'd crowed. "Now your friend can say he is staying at the Daniela!"

Clay repeated the joke now. "You can tell everyone you're staying at the Daniela!" Nick's confused frown testified to his ignorance of the famous five-star Danieli hotel off San Marco. "Never mind."

They curled around the side of the square and headed toward a second bridge that took them over the same canal they had already crossed. Clay wondered whether Nick noticed the detour. Impossible. Venice really was all maze. After a right and another left, they entered a tunnel where strips of stucco were peeling off the brick like wet billboard paper. Nick had to duck so as not to hit his head. One more turn, and Clay opened a black gate to enter a tiny concrete garden with enough room for a clothes-drying rack and a circular wrought-iron table.

Daniela appeared as a red streak across the bank of dirty windows. She then emerged into the sunlight exactly as Clay had remembered her. She wore a red blouse with opal buttons and a pair of loose-legged magenta pants. Her hair was a two-tone confection of blond and wheat brown, cut into a practical suburban bob. Enormous red-framed glasses magnified her gray eyes.

"Oh, Clay," she cried with a hint of residual mourning. They had already grieved together twice by phone—first in a marathon two-hour tearjerker right after Freddy died, and again last week for a more celebratory fifteen minutes of memory volleying.

They kissed on both cheeks. Daniela turned to apply the same double kiss to Nick with bumbling, apologetic negotiations. It required a whisper of instruction on Daniela's part. "I am European. Let me kiss the other cheek, okay?" She stepped back and eyed Nick's enormous suitcase, nibbling on her thumbnail with concern. An "Effff" escaped her lips.

"I'm sorry I'm staying with you," Nick said clumsily.

She stared up at him with her thumbnail still wedged between her teeth. "Why?" She threw a sly glance at Clay, which spoke everything about her first impression of Nick—*Cute, but I'm not sure he's clever enough for you, doll.*

"I think he means—" Clay attempted a rescue.

"Whatever he means, welcome!" Daniela proclaimed in a warm tone. "It really is a pleasure to have you. How lucky! Your first time in Venice!" Clay worried she might make the Danieli joke. "Ah, but first, a glass of champagne!" She scrambled into the dark interior. Nick stood still, waiting to be formally invited into the apartment. Clay grabbed his hand to lead him through the doorway. He pinched Nick's pinkie affectionately and was relieved when Nick curled it around his thumb in a tiny embrace.

Daniela's low-ceilinged apartment was crowded with a lifetime of benign hoarding. Work papers, receipts, invoices, and swatches of lace were stacked across a thin kitchen table pushed up against the front windows. Dry flowers the shape of mop heads sprouted out of vases. A small refrigerator (which Daniela now opened to extract the promised bottle of champagne) stood next to a washing machine, and together the two units supported a wooden board for added counter space. A rowing machine leaned against the far wall. Clay pictured Daniela using it in her concrete garden every morning with her German sense of discipline, a stationary rower in a city of singing gondoliers.

She peeled off the gold foil and popped the cork with a toddler-like "*Wheee!*" It was the same exclamation that Freddy would make when he opened a champagne bottle. It became code for any point in the day when Freddy wished he could be drinking champagne, and he squealed it most insistently at the least appropriate moments ("*Wheee!*" as they inched along a hospital corridor leading to his chemotherapy session). Daniela gathered three crystal glasses from the shelf above the stove.

Nick stood quietly by the front door like a shy fan who'd managed to sneak backstage and now hoped to disappear into the scenery. Clay stared over at him, trying to induce a smile by example. His blond hair was curling around his ears as it dried, and his bottom teeth scraped distractedly against his upper lip. Clay experienced a flash of astonishment at how handsome his boyfriend was. A few feet away loomed the doorway to the guest bedroom. Daniela had made up the narrow bed with military precision. A square of cobalt blue from the room's shaded skylight shone across the white sheets. It excited Clay to think of sex with Nick on that bed, and the added exertion of having to keep quiet so Daniela wouldn't overhear them.

"You must have champagne the first hour you get to Venice," Daniela instructed as she poured. "Not prosecco. Champagne. It gives you your legs back after a long trip." She wiped her fingers, wet from overpour, on a dish towel. "You know who taught me that? Freddy."

"Of course he did!" Clay responded.

"He was so good with life knowledge, wasn't he?"

Freddy had done more than school Clay on the health benefits of champagne. Twice Freddy had saved him, taking him in when he'd been out of options. That ferocious, beautiful man had been the first or last of his kind—*first* or *last*, Clay could never decide which; maybe he was an *only*. But Clay didn't want to be lured into another grieving session, especially in front of Nick. That sort of grief didn't allow room for anyone else. He cleared his throat and muttered a dejected "Yeah." He considered switching to Italian so that Nick wouldn't detect the tremble in his voice. "Freddy taught me a lot of things."

Daniela smiled at him compassionately. "I miss him too. The other day, I found a picture of us from twenty years ago, snapped during *acqua alta*. We look like two gypsies. I left it out to show you . . ." She spun around, searching the countertops, but failed to locate the photo. She handed a glass of champagne to Clay and held one out for Nick, forcing him to join them. They clinked glasses and drank.

"Feel better?" Daniela asked her new roommate.

"Maybe you need a nap, Nicky," Clay suggested.

"I'm sorry I'm so out of it," Nick replied, wiping his face as if to manually clear his tired expression. "I'm really happy to be here. I'll try not to bother you."

"Oh, I live to be bothered," she assured him as she poured herself a second glass. "Make yourself at home. Your bedroom is right behind you. It's a bit cramped, but . . ."

After Nick steered his suitcase into the room to get settled, Daniela leaned over the counter with a whisper. "Do I call him Nick or Nicky?"

"He comes if you call him by either name."

She smirked. "You're so bad."

"Don't be fooled. I really like him."

"Oh, I sense that. Is he always so sorry for everything?"

"Yes! He is!"

"That suitcase!" She laughed as she tapped her nail on the counter. "He's a looker. I'll give you that."

It occurred to Clay that he was showing Nick off to Daniela, the silent brag of an attractive companion. She'd never known him to have a boyfriend or even a date in all the months he'd lived in Venice. "What about you?" Clay asked. "Are you seeing anyone?"

Daniela took a swallow of champagne. "Well," she said. "I've had my heart stomped on twice last year. But I'm seeing a prominent businessman from Shanghai, and I'll admit I'm unnerved by how smitten I am. You know, the Chinese have basically bought up all of San Marco. I mean, *all of it* in the past few years. So who knows? Maybe I'll become La Signora of Palazzo Barbaro yet!"

"Which is exactly where you deserve to be," he told her, although Clay felt sure that Daniela was destined to remain in this apartment until the day she died. She played up the part of the romantic, but she was too smart to let love save her from herself. Clay glanced around with admiring eyes. "The place looks great."

"This old bunker!" Daniela groaned. "For the last century two branches of a Venetian family were fighting over this pile of bricks. Last year, a Turkish ne'er-do-well strolled in with all the right forged documents, and now, according to the courts, he owns it. Venetian real estate!" She shook her head. "On the plus side, he didn't raise my rent." Daniela smiled and squeezed Clay's hand. "Are you staying at Il Dormitorio?" The Dormitory was the nickname for Freddy's toothpick of a palazzo. Clay nodded. "Freddy would want you there. Try to keep it for as long as you can."

Clay dropped his head at the mere thought of Freddy's muddled finances. He read the watch on Daniela's wrist. It was after one thirty.

"Crap, I've got to run." He spun around to find Nick just beyond the guest-room doorway. He'd taken off his green blazer and was squatting in front of his open suitcase. "Nicky, I'm leaving."

Nick's face paled at the news of abandonment. He jostled out of the room with the tripping momentum of someone ejected from a subway car. "Already? Can't you stay for a little longer? We could . . ."

The unfinished suggestion hung there in a void of silence. It was Daniela with her superior intuition who knew what must be done. She grabbed her keys off the kitchen table.

"I have to buy groceries. Clay, you stay a minute." She turned to Nick. Although she was speaking to both of them, she must have felt that Nick was more in need of this lesson. "You're so young. Be greedy with each other." Daniela took a canvas bag from the doorknob and disappeared across the concrete garden.

Clay pointed his thumb toward the blue square of light floating on the guest-room bed. He didn't have to ask what Nick felt like doing in their time alone.

CHAPTER 5

Sex with Nick was the best kind of greediness, because every hungry move on Clay's part was treated as an act of generosity. They'd tumbled around on the narrow bed for less than half an hour, and in that urgent blur of minutes there were no timid *sorry*s from Nick and no extra caution on Clay's part in handling this fragile, tired visitor. Afterward they lay on the mattress, the sheets having snapped loose from their corners and bunched around their legs. Nick tucked his arm behind his head, a blast of sand-blond hair filling his armpit. Clay turned on his side to study his boyfriend. It amazed him what a young person's body Nick still had at the age of twenty-five. There was only a two-year difference between them, and yet Clay's own frame was sharper and severer, more muscular and defined, his hips narrowing at the same point where Nick's seemed to widen. It was as if Nick were still swimming toward manhood while Clay was already waving from the shore.

On Nick's hairless chest, the cobalt skylight square turned the warm shade of a California swimming pool. Clay lifted himself on the whipcord of his spine, clenching his stomach muscles as he sat up. His fingers went purple when they entered the square of the light, and he softly pinched Nick's right nipple. Nick's arm shot up to block the squeeze, but he overrode the defensive instinct and smiled nervously, as if he were daring himself to withstand the pain. Clay let go and ran his fingers down Nick's torso, more rib cage than stomach muscle, all the way to the spill of brown pubic hair. He leaned in to kiss Nick on the lips.

"I have to get back to Il Dormitorio," he said. "Take a nap and then explore your new neighborhood."

He climbed out of bed, balancing his hand on a bookshelf crammed with cardboard boxes labeled by the year. A vertical mirror hung on the back of the guest-room door, and Clay examined himself in it, appreciating his own nudity in an unfamiliar room. He noticed lately that his body was looking more and more like his father's—not his father now, bloated at the stomach with pink stretch marks running across it like a marbleized bowling ball. His father had gone to pot, body and mind, when his mother died. No, he was thinking of his father's body long ago when Clay had been seven or eight and had been allowed to shower with him in their Bronx apartment bathroom with its avocado wallpaper and its halo of fluorescent light. Nightly, the two Guillory males could be found side by side, father and son, inside the textured-glass shower stall. Clay had stared up with worship and wonder as his father scrubbed his strong West Indian arsenal of a body, whitened at the stomach and armpits with suds, his muscles flexing, his broad feet stepping in semicircles, the runoff dripping from his chest onto his son. Clay didn't know if he'd ever gotten an erection during those showers. He only remembered being thrilled by the adventure of standing with his father while he bathed. It was later, in his teenage years, when every early memory is reinterrogated for sinister double meanings, that he realized how sexually confusing the experience might have been at that age. His father had put an end to their showers by the age of ten. *You're a big boy now, you take your own shower alone.* He'd whined and cried but did as he was told. It seemed right about that time that they had begun to drift apart. Clay had often wanted to ask his father outright, *Did I get an erection, is that the reason you put a stop to it?* But there were some family memories you couldn't ask a parent about.

Clay pulled on his boxers and stepped into his pants. He would soon be able to pay his father back—every cent of what he owed him, if their scheme went off without a hitch. He found his shirt balled in the sheets. He removed the photo of their mark from the pocket and tossed the folded-up clipping onto Nick's chest.

"That's him," Clay said, sliding his arms through the sleeves until his hands reappeared as punches out of the cuffs. "Richard Forsyth West." He watched as Nick unfolded the paper and stared at the white-haired American man grinning over a glass of yellow wine. Clay had purposely ripped Richard West free from the women flanking him at a party so Nick wouldn't view him in a humanizing context: older white men looked more like assholes when they were smiling alone. The paparazzi-style photo was taken close-up, and it captured Richard's wide Nebraska-shaped forehead with a mole dotting the left eyebrow, his falcon-like nose, his high cheekbones, and his unflappable smile. In the photo, he wore one of his trademark white suits, which Clay liked to think of as a flag of surrender. Unfortunately, Nick was studying the photo of Richard West under the skylight beam, which turned the entire image blue.

Clay circled the bed, picking up the coins that had exploded from his pockets when he'd removed his pants. It struck him as embarrassingly cheap to be gathering up every last glitter of spare change around a bed after sex. But the truth was, European coins were more valuable than their American cousins.

Nick spent exactly one minute looking at the photo before refolding it into a square.

"You should study it more carefully," Clay advised as he jammed his feet into his shoes.

"I saw him," Nick replied.

"There are a lot of rich old American men with white hair in Venice."

"Don't worry, I saw him," Nick repeated. "Or do you want me to tack his picture up over my bed? Would that make you happy?"

"Yes, that would make me very happy," Clay answered half seriously. "The last thing we need is for you to target the wrong man."

"I won't," Nick promised as he rolled over and nuzzled the side of his face into a pillow. "I'll get the right one."

"He's a terrible person," Clay said. "A devil. Remember that."

Nick tried for a two-fingered salute to his forehead but gave up and let his hand fall lethargically on the mattress. "You just text me when it's time," he murmured. His eyes closed tightly before softening into sleep.

As Clay closed the metal gate to Daniela's apartment, he was glad to be by himself again. It allowed him to contemplate every detail of Nick. It seemed to him that early on in a relationship the most intense feelings were experienced alone, the same way love songs always gutted the heart more deeply when the person you loved wasn't in the room. Clay walked along the *fondamenta* thinking of his boyfriend, marveling at the young man who had traveled across an ocean just for him. Clay felt sure he could trust Nick, and it scared and exhilarated him to put so much trust in someone else.

Freddy's palazzo was located in the northern neighborhood of Cannaregio. It would have been quicker to cross Campo Santa

Margherita and loop around the train station to reach it, but Clay couldn't resist taking the winding alleys east toward the Accademia Bridge. It was a sentimental walk for him, another reminder of his eight months living in Venice. Even the triangular white sandwiches—*i tramezzini*—in the caffè windows were sentimental to him, because they'd served as his primary food source for his first weeks in town. Egg and tuna, ham and artichoke, shrimp and olives—he'd sampled all their endless, mayonnaise-heavy combinations.

Those eight months in Venice had been the happiest and perhaps the loneliest of his life. Venice was the single global art capital that lacked any gay bars or reliable nightlife spots. Clay had tried his share of hookup apps, but they were mostly filled with closeted middle-aged tourists cruising for Italian boys and finding only the sad compromise of one another. Most assumed by the color of his skin that Clay was a refugee from Africa—*and who knew their real motivations once you let them into your hotel room?* The scraggly scrub-brush dunes at the far southern tip of the Lido, the one alleged "gay beach," proved more pudding-bodied nudist camp than testosterone-rich Fire Island pool party. Even after these early failures, lust drove him out into the night and hope kept him glued to a bar chair. Eventually he accrued two minor flings with locals, nothing with any real heat or noise. Clay drank a lot of wine that summer and fall.

He walked past the white-marble facade of the Accademia Museum with its trove of Veroneses and Tintorettos and began to climb the bridge. The Accademia Bridge rose over the Grand Canal like the peak of a wood Ferris wheel. As he reached the top, he shoved through couples taking selfies and peddlers selling items—model airplanes, squishy balls, cell-phone batteries—that probably shouldn't be sold at the top of a bridge. He managed to find a sliver of open railing to lean against and stared east beyond the Salute's gray hawk hood of a roof and the sharp fin of Punta della Dogana as the canal opened into the wider basin. The water was blue-green and sparkling like sequins, and the surrounding palazzi looked like canapés at a party far too elegant for the clothes that Clay and his fellow sightseers wore.

Clay concentrated on a low, white single-story house on the south side of the canal, the Palazzo Venier dei Leoni, otherwise known as the Peggy Guggenheim Collection. That museum devoted to modernist masterpieces compiled by the late American heiress had been Clay's life raft in the year that his family blew apart. Clay had studied history at Fordham University in the Bronx, but he'd taken a class on Renaissance art his sophomore year and became enthralled with the Italian paintings blown up on the lecture-hall screen. His professor, a southerner on loan from a Jesuit college in New Orleans, noticed Clay's interest and pushed him into other art-history electives. At the start of his senior year, the professor encouraged him to apply for a prestigious paid internship at the Peggy Guggenheim Collection. He'd already written Clay a glowing recommendation letter.

That Venetian seed was planted in Clay's mind right after his mother had been diagnosed with cancer but while she still appeared physically healthy. For a miraculous period, it seemed as if his mother's body could be condemned to harbor a terminal illness without ever suffering any of its symptoms. She had been the family's breadwinner, working in midtown Manhattan as the head of a dentistry journal's subscriptions department. She was small in stature, thin in the upper body, sturdy in the thighs, and while she wore her short hair tied strictly back, her eyes and lips were definitions of latitude and forgiveness. Clay loved her so fiercely it stung—his mother, who had only gulped once when he came out at age fifteen and then smothered him with love and acceptance after that single wayward gulp.

His mother had been especially delighted about the idea of her son, a graduate of a four-year liberal-arts college, living and working in Venice, Italy, for one of the most distinguished families in New York City—as if the Guggenheim heirs themselves were picking through the swamp of international applications and lifting up his envelope and saying, "Now who is this young Guillory?" Clay applied with zero expectations and, to his genuine surprise, was accepted. He hadn't meant to go into the arts and had already accrued a stomach-turning amount of student debt. But even Clay agreed that the offer was just too beautiful—*Who the hell gets the chance to be employed for a summer in Venice?*—to refuse. If the internship had been unpaid, it would have been accepted as foolish and impractical. But in the crucial hairline distinction of being a barely paid internship, the whole dreamlike prospect transformed into a possibility.

Clay was slated to fly to Venice in mid-May, two weeks after graduation. But during the last semester of his senior year, the dreaded abstract diagnosis finally presented itself in all of its horror. Even his resilient mother couldn't overcome the pain and exhaustion that followed. She checked into the hospital in March, promising the family apartment that she'd return to it soon. She never saw it again.

His mother insisted that he keep the internship. Clay balked. He wasn't flying off to Italy while she was lying in a hospital in New York. "You're going to Venice! End of discussion!" she griped right back. "I want you there, do you hear me?" These petty arguments actually seemed to stimulate and revive her during Clay's visits, and they would usually conclude in their laughing together at the absurdity of it all. (How did she end up at age forty-six in a hospital

ICU? How did her son end up being invited to work in a mansion full of art in a floating city on the other side of the planet?)

Soon enough, nothing was funny about the absurdity of his mother lying in the hospital. As an oxygen mask was taped to her mouth, as the needles and tubes and blinking machines began to swallow her whole in her bed, it became too excruciating for Clay. His father had taken a leave of absence from his security job to sit with her in her room every day. But Clay began to make excuses: exams were looming; final papers needed to be researched; if he didn't pass every single class, he'd have to take a summer semester, and that meant shelling out more borrowed bank money to the greedy Jesuits. He often rode the subway down to 110th Street and attempted to walk the single block to Mount Sinai, but his nerves would fail him and he'd swipe his MetroCard and wait for the uptown train. His father didn't *seem* to resent the increasing rarity of his visits; he *seemed* to understand—although Clay's absence would later be cited as the reason for their estrangement. On his last visit to the hospital, when his mother was still semi-lucid, she once again demanded he take his trip. Although now, his mother was mixing up Venice with Mexico, the place she'd always wanted to visit. Mexico had been her vision of escape. "You'll learn so much there, and you'll send me letters and pictures. It will be wonderful in Mexico. Promise you'll go." Dusk had begun to set outside the window, the soft purples of a late-spring sky in New York. Clay could just make out the faint outlines of their reflection in the glass, the two of them nestling creatures looking as if they were evaporating into the horrible beauty of a violet skyline.

She died the week of his graduation. In the course of a single week he was handed a diploma and punched in the heart. When all was said and done and the hymns were sung, he did get on the plane to Venice. It was as if Peggy Guggenheim herself had risen from her palazzo garden grave, where she'd long been interred alongside her fourteen Lhasa apsos, to rescue him from grief.

He loved the Peggy Guggenheim. Once he and Nick pulled off their con on Richard West, he would take Nick to the museum to show him his favorite paintings.

The sky darkened with the threat of another downpour, and Clay donated his spot at the railing to a honeymooning Korean couple wielding selfie sticks. He descended the bridge and threaded the crowds toward the wide expanse of Campo Santo Stefano. Along one side of the square, lone black men stood as tall as palm trees on islands of counterfeit purses: Gucci, Hermès, Prada, Louis Vuitton. These men were migrants from West African countries like Senegal or Mali, one eye hunting for the police, the other for potential customers. The young men haggled passersby in tones of menacing temptation, but they never said a word to Clay—not once in all the time he'd lived in Venice with his brotherly smile cast in their direction. They knew he was not like them, and yet he was enough like them to be deemed a waste of their time. They had desperate families back home to support. Unsurprisingly, all of Clay's friends in Venice had been white. Clay had been the only black intern at the museum that summer. Most of the interns initially treated him with a disconcerting overabundance of kindness—the sort of kindness that calls attention to the uneasiness it's trying to mask. Ultimately, though, the weirdness of living in Venice had leveled them all into allies. They worked together as gallery guards, as admission-ticket sellers, as tour guides, as coat-check clerks.

The rain began to beat down on Santo Stefano, and the purse archipelago was quickly dismantled. By the time Clay reached Cannaregio twenty minutes later, the sun had reappeared, burning gold across the syrupy canals. Clay crossed a small bridge and took three turns before he reached the alley that led to Il Dormitorio.

A green door stood at the end of the passage with iron-grated windows on each side. Perched in a tiny wall alcove above the doorframe was the sculpture of a turbaned man riding a lump of broken marble. According to Freddy, the lump had once been a camel; the palazzo's original fifteenth-century owners had been merchant traders.

Clay unlocked the green door that had originally served as the back entrance of the Gothic-style Palazzo Contarini. It was now the front and only door of the decidedly less spectacular van der Haar *palazzino*. Freddy's great-grandparents, two well-dressed hemorrhages of money, had bought Palazzo Contarini in the 1890s during America's obsession with the grand tour. Back then, the palazzo had a cavernous ground-floor *androne* and boat entrance nestled next to a lush rose garden, a spacious first-floor piano nobile replete with frescoes and stucco moldings, and arched Byzantine windows sculpted in Istrian stone. In the 1960s, Freddy's parents, in a frantic need for fast cash, had walled up one corner of the palazzo to keep for themselves and sold off the vast remainder of the house to a mining family from Bolzano. Most families would have divided a palazzo horizontally by floor—as was the local custom—but the van der Haars were true New York eccentrics in their love of verticality. So it was that this odd, cramped, towerlike house passed on to Freddy (who simply *adored* Venice) and his sister (who simply did *not*). Freddy's half now belonged to Clay. He was part owner of this slender slice of falling-down paradise. And, for the time being, he was able to keep his half of the home thanks to the Italian miracle of low inheritance tax.

The narrow, dingy entrance hadn't changed since the first time Clay had stepped over its threshold four years ago. Cables and wires snaked across the low, water-damaged ceiling, and the red-marble floor tiles were covered in cardboard squares to sop up shoe water.

In his final years, Freddy tried to make short pilgrimages to Venice every six months. And to pay for the year-round upkeep, he constructed a colony of upstairs bedrooms out of drywall and rented them out to the interns of the Peggy Guggenheim. They were ideal tenants—short-term, primarily from wealthy families, and too young and dizzy on Venice to complain about the lackluster accommodations. The supervisor at the museum, a shaggy-haired Italian woman who spoke English with a comical Irish accent, had alerted Clay to a cheap available room for rent in a palazzo in Cannaregio. "The house belongs to a very, *very* old American family," she proclaimed, clearly dazzled that there could be such a thing as an old family in a young country. "I can't name them, of course, but they only rent rooms to us." The single rule of the house was so bizarre that Clay really did feel as if he'd entered an upside-down universe. "One restriction," the supervisor warned. "You must be careful not to touch the ceiling!"

Clay trudged up the steps to the common area with its small, dumpy kitchenette. He'd met the latest band of intern renters when he'd arrived a few days ago, and the remains of their breakfasts cluttered the countertop: a spilled box of muesli, two banana peels, a disemboweled moka coffeepot. The place really did resemble a dormitory. Freddy had barricaded the walls in drywall to protect the frescoes and stuccos hidden behind it. But Freddy didn't have the heart to cover the extraordinary fresco on the ceiling—he loved looking at it too much.

Clay gazed up just as he had on the first day he'd moved in as a renting intern; only then had he understood the museum supervisor's warning. Across a dim blue rectangle in the center of the ceiling ran a frolic of pink and gold paint strokes portraying a floating Madonna surrounded by garlands and horny mating doves. According to Freddy, the fresco had been painted in 1698 by Sebastiano Ricci; the van der Haars had kept the main jewel of Palazzo Contarini for themselves. Clay never tired of looking at it, but now it came with the price of loneliness. Freddy was truly gone—even down to his ashes, which Clay had covertly poured into a nearby canal in a one-man ceremony the morning he'd arrived. He wished he'd brought Nick back to Il Dormitorio to stand with him underneath this forgotten masterpiece. The echoing sound of suitcases being wheeled along the pavement outside only made the loneliness inside the room more acute—surely the vibrations from that unholy, oblivious sound of newness was responsible for the cracks veining the ceiling.

Adjoining the common area, separated by more drywall and a locked door, was Freddy's (now Clay's) private chambers. It consisted of a bathroom and a bedroom flocked with the thick red velvets that Freddy favored, possibly for velvet's terrible propensity to trap the reek of cigarette smoke. Clay had already thrown out several of Freddy's old boxes—one contained a stash of needles and rubber tourniquet bands from the Great Venice Heroin Relapse of the early 1990s. Clay was sure to find more depressing artifacts in the closets.

Clay walked over to a wall of cabinet bookcases, the cheap linoleum-tiled floor whimpering at each step. The middle bookcase cabinet was a false front; it popped open on hinges to reveal a bolted Louis Seize walnut door. For reasons that Clay never understood, this solitary door remained the single connecting link between the van der Haar quarters and the rest of Palazzo Contarini. It had stayed like that over the decades and through its various owners. Clay knocked four times on the walnut door, the long-established signal between neighbors, and unlatched the lock as he waited for the approach of footsteps. Eventually, the bolt was yanked on the other side. The door flew open, letting in an explosion of afternoon light.

A tall white-haired man stood in the doorframe. He had a wide Nebraska-shaped forehead that was mildly sunburned; a black mole crested the wave of his left eyebrow, and white scruff covered his cheeks and neck. He was still handsome in his late middle age, and growing oddly more handsome as he receded into the soft years of retirement. This man looked at Clay with an expression of affection so blinding it was as if the light bouncing off the Rio della Sensa emanated directly from him.

"Clay!" he boomed. "We just got back from Capri." Clay nodded, and the man shifted his expression to one of puckered sorrow. "I'm sorry about Freddy. Jesus, I really thought he'd outlive us all. Did you get my flowers?"

"Yes," Clay said to Richard Forsyth West. "They were beautiful. Freddy loved lilies. I wish he could have seen them taking up half the brownstone."

"No need to thank me." West spread his arms. "Come here. I've been waiting to give this to you." And as if this small gift still confounded its recipient, Richard West named it. "A hug."

CHAPTER 6

In the middle of the night, Nick received the text he had been
waiting for.

He's back in town. Try him tomorrow at Mercato del Pesce/Rialto fish
market. He usually goes there @10 on Saturday mornings. Good luck. I
love you.

The "I" of the text was Clay, writing from his new Italian mobile; the "he" was their mark, Richard Forsyth West. But what
captivated Nick about the message—what left him tossing around
on Daniela's lumpy guest-room mattress—was the un-simple declaration of "I love you." Those words were a pure line of risk, and
Nick hadn't expected them from someone as guarded as Clay. Nick
drifted for minutes in the warmth of the phrase, sinking into each
word and battling his instinct to play it cool by not responding.
But he understood that a neck had been exposed and a vulnerable
vein held to the light, so he grabbed his phone and quickly typed,
I love you too and won't let you down. Then for the rest of the night
Nick did love him too.

Daniela had made ravioli for dinner, velveteen squares of noodle filled with dishrag-limp mushrooms. Over glasses of red wine, Nick said words like "ravioli" and Daniela corrected him by repeating the same words back to him; this tedious game of international tone deafness played out for the duration of the meal. After dinner, Daniela dug through a drawer to locate a spare set of house keys and encouraged Nick not to be afraid of the toilet brush—"Americans are so filthy with bathrooms, why is that? Tell me why you are so clean with your dogs but not with your toilet bowls?" While clearing the plates, she asked if she could take Nick out for a coffee the next morning. "I want to talk to you about Clay," she said with an unnerving tenseness. "I want to make certain things clear about him. Tomorrow, after you've had a decent night's sleep."

Nick was the first to wake in the morning. Headachy from the wine and still high from Clay's text, he carried a fresh pair of underwear into the bathroom to take a shower. Although he only urinated in the toilet, he whisked the plastic brush thoroughly around the bowl for fear of being blamed for any residual muck. By the time he had unlocked the bathroom door, Daniela was already dressed and waiting in the kitchen, peeling an orange at the counter with the long, unvarnished fingernails of an acoustic guitarist. Nick had a towel wrapped around his waist and his briefs on under the towel, but he crossed his arms over his chest in adolescent modesty.

"Good morning," Daniela sang with a slight ring of reprimand over the length of his shower. She was wearing the same magenta pants and red blouse that she'd had on the day before, switching only her jewelry. A meteorite of topaz hung from a long gold chain between her breasts, and several gold rings encircled her fingers. Nick was curious about Daniela's body—what she'd kept, what she'd improved upon. His close friend Seth in New York was transgender, and Seth had simply let all the hair grow everywhere while still debating about starting hormones. Seth wasn't even convinced "she" was better than "he" anymore and yet wasn't sold on the incertitude of "they" either. Daniela, however, whom Clay termed "old-school," had found her freedom in drawing far more certain conclusions.

"Well, get dressed," Daniela wailed impatiently, as if she'd been goading him all morning.

"*Che ora è?*" Nick asked. When he heard it was only eight fifteen, he figured he could have coffee with Daniela and still find the Rialto fish market by ten. He put on a clean white Oxford but decided to stick with the blue trousers and green wool jacket he'd worn the day before. Twice, he checked to make sure that his old Wickston business card was in his wallet.

When he opened the guest-room door, Daniela surveyed him through her enormous glasses. "Didn't you have that outfit on when you arrived?"

Nick was too polite to accuse her of the same crime. "Oh, yeah," he muttered.

"It will be too warm for that jacket today." Then she shot her finger up in inspiration and barged past him into the guest room to fish through a pile of bags. She emerged with a plaid blazer of thin blue, gray, and teal stripes—the pattern was called the Prince of Wales check, which Nick could identify only because it had been a favorite of Ari's father. "I bought this for my boyfriend, Benny, but it was too big on him."

Nick slipped it on and inspected himself in the mirror. The jacket was too short in the sleeves, but he scrunched up the cuffs and liked what he saw: a young man in a relaxed silk jacket who happened to be wandering a Venetian fish market.

"You don't mind if I borrow it?" he asked.

She patted his chest. "Keep it. Now, do you have your set of keys? I cannot be letting you in every time you forget them!"

They passed down the tunnel of Calle Degolin, and Daniela guided him around the curving gray backside of a Gothic cathedral. A slender canal glittered in the sun, and a warm breeze stroked their faces.

"In spring, the canal water is still fresh," Daniela said. "By summer, with all the tourists, it turns to sewage."

"But you like living here, don't you?"

"It takes a certain kind," she replied. "Eccentrics and individualists. Loners with good manners. The very opposite of the tourists." She sighed wistfully. "I'm afraid the tourists are finally winning. We've been conquered by a well-organized army of occupiers who have no interest in staying more than three nights."

Nick didn't bother to memorize the zig or zag of their path down side streets and across bridges. He was too absorbed by the discovery of every unordinary brick and stone. At the third canal, a gunshot blast of pigeons exploded over the water, and behind it lingered the tinny cries of seagulls. A teakettle screamed from an upper window, and in another window, green shutters were slapped open by saggy, matronly arms.

Daniela led Nick into a corner caffè on the white trapezoid of a *campo*. Older locals collected at the zinc bar counter. Daniela asked Nick what he wanted—anything approximating a large American coffee—and shooed him toward a table by the window. A minute later, she placed two coffees down and sat across from him. As Nick rested his elbow on the wood, twin splashes escaped from the coffee cups. He grabbed a matchbook from a nearby ashtray and ducked down to wedge it under the wobbly leg. It was an old waiter's trick that he performed almost by instinct.

When he resurfaced, Daniela gave a nod as if suitably impressed. She pressed her elbow on the wood to test his efforts.

"I don't know exactly how long you've known Clay—" she began.

"Two months," he told her firmly.

"Okay," she said in a dismissive tone. Nick knew that any answer he provided had already been deemed inferior. "I met him four years ago after he'd been an intern at the Guggenheim. Clay was in a bad place at the time, he'd taken a few punches in Venice. But, *oh*, when they met, Freddy fell for him hard. I could see it right away. Freddy was devoted to the teeth, probably in love, ready to throw everyone else aside to spend as much time with Clay as possible. He gave him little gifts, like a gold ring, a musty Emily Dickinson book—the kind of tokens that pass like secrets between two people. Clay was clearly being courted. You see, Freddy collected people."

"I got that impression," Nick said.

"I'll admit, I was initially skeptical. Understand, we're an old family of international psychotics and misanthropes. It isn't like today with this blind acceptance blasting on everyone in all directions. Now you could find someone like me on TV, couldn't you?" Daniela laughed. "Well, that wasn't the case back when. That's why we treated each other like brothers and sisters, a family that would always take care of our own, and we could be very suspicious of strangers who wormed their way into our group. Freddy was particularly susceptible because he had that gilded last name that spelled money. And let's face it, Freddy was incredibly lonely and had a weakness for youth. Clay wouldn't have been the first young man to try to charm his way through the door to take whatever he could."

Daniela rested her purse on the table and removed a folded piece of mint-green stationery. It looked to Nick like expensive paper, its texture almost the consistency of chalk.

"You've heard the rumors," Daniela said, nodding in affirmation for him. "They started circulating the day Freddy died. I was barraged with calls from close friends. Clay had murdered Freddy, just as they predicted he would. Clay had been alone at Freddy's bedside and delivered a fatal dose in order to get his hands on the van der Haar fortune." Daniela shook her head. "These friends meant well. Don't blame them. They were looking after their friend. And Freddy could have a wicked sense of humor, telling people that Clay was only sticking around to vacuum up the dollar bills once he croaked. But that wasn't the case. Not at all."

Daniela handed Nick the mint paper, which he unfolded to find a typed letter signed with a scribble of green ink.

"I received that letter from Freddy about a year ago when he was so far along on his death march that he could barely speak by phone."

My Dearest Dani,
Is the mail still slow in Venice? If it is, you may be reading this as haunted words from the dead. Boo! Peter had the nerve to call me yesterday from 29 Palms and ask Clay if I'm dying. Clay turned to me—I was bedridden on the sofa like King Sardanapalus in that Delacroix painting (did we see that in Paris? I'm forgetting everything)—and asked me, "Freddy, are you dying?" I belched out, "I'd say so!" Peter told Clay to tell me not to die until after his trip to Hawaii. Thus, I've acquiesced to a few more months of existence while Peter fails at surfing (or is he failing at the surfers?).
But now for the reason I write. Doll, I'm asking you for a favor. Tell our siblings to stop ganging up on Clay and spreading the rumors

about him gold-digging for my money. I've gotten separate visits/calls from Bruno, Laurie, Kiko, Jules, Gitsy, Nan, Marc, and, believe it or not, London Ted, each one expressly informing me that I'm being taken advantage of by a hustler from the Bronx. And out, out, out I must kick Clay to preserve my friendships and legacy. Dani, it just isn't true! You met Clay in the kinder twinkle of Venezia. You see him for the loving, good-hearted young man he is. Please share that impression with the family—convince them with your fascist willpower! They don't know what a godsend Clay is. He's the only one taking care of me—and how awful it must be to spend your vital days on a putrid old valetudinarian. Can you imagine either of us doing that in our gorgeous twenties? I honestly wouldn't be alive without him, and I'd happily give him what's left to repay his devotion. But [and here, in green ink, Freddy added a caret and wrote "*between us*"] *there is nothing left to take. Beyond nothing.* Niente.

Please intercede. I pray I will be strong enough to visit Il Dormitorio once again and we can dine like two hungry hookers at L'Incontro. I was just recalling the time we sneaked onto that private jet and landed in Le Bourget and were almost arrested on the tarmac. When was that? When were we last young?

Yours,
[And here an F was scratched in green]

Nick glanced over the top of the stationery where Daniela was staring at him with a look of vindication. Nick thought the vindication was misdirected. Daniela should have been sharing this letter with Bruno, Laurie, Kiko, Jules, Gitsy, Nan, Marc, or London Ted, not the lovestruck boyfriend of the slandered and blamed.

"Did you have any luck changing their minds?" he asked.

She took the letter from him, folded it, and returned it to her purse with tremendous care. "I tried my best, but they'd already made up their minds. Clay never had a chance." She tapped her nails on the table. "I thought you should know, in case you had doubts. Clay was loyal and dedicated to Freddy right to the end. He did more than any of us to help him."

"I don't have doubts about Clay," Nick assured her. "I know he didn't kill Freddy." Technically, he didn't know that for certain; he merely assumed it. *Did you murder your best friend?* wasn't exactly a question that flowed from the lips when falling in love. And love ruled out the possibility of that person being a murderer. Despite the New York rumors, Nick couldn't picture Clay maliciously ending a life, especially Freddy's, which he'd cared for more than his own. "Not a chance he murdered Freddy. No way."

Daniela gave a snort of satisfaction. "Good." She removed her glasses to pinch her eyes. The bridge pads had left red indentations the size of houseflies on her nose, and she blinked around with a scrunched face that seemed to mimic the world her eyes must be taking in. She slipped the glasses back on. "Now that I've been honest with you," Daniela said ominously, "I'd like for you to be honest with me."

Nick let out a gurgling laugh. "About what?"

"What are you and Clay plotting here in Venice?"

"Nothing!" he exclaimed, then lowered his voice. "Nothing at all. Clay was coming to Venice to check on Il Dormitorio, and I decided to tag along. He thought it was too crowded in the *palazzino* with all the stuff of Freddy's he has to settle. That's why he asked if I could stay with you." He hated lying to Daniela. But it was safer this way.

"Mmmm," Daniela hummed incredulously. "You should be aware of something. Venice is very small." Nick used to make that claim about New York—the mammoth global metropolis was really just a provincial village of nosy neighbors. New York did feel claustrophobic at times, but in reality that city could accommodate multiple selves and several double lives without much risk of ever being exposed. What Daniela said about Venice sounded like a threat.

"I'm glad to hear that," Nick replied coolly. "Because I need you to give me directions to the Rialto fish market."

Nick gave himself forty minutes to reach the fish market. Daniela promised it would take no more than fifteen and instructed him to follow the arrowed signs for the Rialto Bridge—the market was in the same vicinity, and at a certain point he could trust his nose to guide him. Nick entered the slow migration of sightseers, most of them seemingly as clueless to direction as he was. Cell phones had long replaced the messy paperwork of foldout maps, every screen blinking an electronic breadcrumb trail. What separated Nick from the other tourists was a purpose—he had somewhere to be, and, more anxiety-inducing, something specific to do once he arrived. From his years of living in New York, Nick understood that the distinction between visitor and resident often came down to a walking style. Nick tried for speed and sureness, hurrying confidently over bridges, awake to the stone-tap of his shoes, weaving eel-like through knots of window-shoppers and gelato-lickers. The coin that Clay had placed in his right loafer winked in the sunlight, a little amulet to remind him why he was about to con his way into Richard West's life.

Nick should have consulted his phone. He reached a dead-end alley, retraced his steps, and somehow managed to reach the same dead end ten minutes later. Finally, after a half hour of searching, he stumbled upon two lanes of T-shirt stalls at the foot of the Rialto Bridge. Near the bridge and just as a blister on his left heel was pronouncing the alligator loafers terrible footwear for Venice, a vast brick building introduced itself in gold letters as MERCATO DEL PESCE AL MINUTO. Nick fixed his jacket collar, smoothed his white Oxford, and told himself not to think of yesterday's fiasco with the Warbly-Gardeners. Still, he double-checked the wallet in his back pocket, for today it would need to be extracted. Nick entered the chilly, oceanic dark of the market. Puddles of water glimmered on the floor. In every direction, routine bartering and bagging was taking place over stalls of chipped ice.

Nick had memorized the photo of Richard Forsyth West, and he knew from Clay that the man favored white linen suits. He felt certain he could pick West out in a crowd, even one as chaotic and shadowy as the market. Locals crowded the stalls, barking out their fish orders. Tourists with bulky camera equipment and safari zoom lenses shot still lifes of sleek gray marine life with open eyes and white price cards pinned to its bellies. There was *scampi nostrani*, *branzini*, *di mari*, and metal buckets full of unnamed sea creatures. The safari zoom lens turned to shoot the locals ordering their provisions, attempting to capture a fleeting trace of normal everyday life that Venice so rarely provided.

Two middle-aged men, a couple, one in a denim shirt and the other in tangerine cotton, separately took notice of Nick with cruisy, admiring glances. Each hid their interest from the other in the guise of an overperformed scan of the market. "Maybe the scallops are fresher farther down, David," Denim Shirt suggested before sneaking a second thirsty glance. These ephemeral flirtations buoyed Nick's confidence; they had come to matter to him the way he imagined being recognized in the street mattered to a famous person—they worked as an empirical measure of his worth to the world. Nick never smiled back. Sometimes he rolled his eyes in irritation. But for the most part he was extremely grateful.

He sailed through the stalls, searching for an older man with white hair, a wide forehead, and a mole above the left eyebrow. Many of the rubber-aproned vendors had already sold out of their daily catches, leaving mere tissues of lettuce strewn across rectangles of ice. He hoped he wasn't too late. Clay had told him 10:00 a.m. It was now 10:17, and he was nearing the light-blue ribbon of the Grand Canal that signaled the end of the fish market. On the other side of the water, the peaches and yellows of palazzo facades glowed in the sharp daylight.

When Nick turned his head, he realized that the market continued outside the building in a tentlike jumble of metal roofs and tarps. This outdoor annex was reserved primarily for fresh produce, while also serving to collect the tourist overspill from the Rialto Bridge. The crowd thickened with the buzz and swell of souk activity. Sweat slicked Nick's forehead as he pushed through the aisles, fearing he'd underestimated the simplicity of his mission. Where was Richard West? Had he even bothered to come here today?

Nick tripped over a bucket of flowers and apologized to the vendor. He stopped to examine a crate of limes simply as an excuse to examine the crowd more thoroughly.

The back of a head gleamed salt white two aisles over. The head turned into profile, revealing a scruffy white five-o'clock shadow and a sturdy, handsome face. Nick let go of the limes and stepped cautiously in the man's direction. He was ninety percent sure this was Richard West. When some exotic delicacy caught the man's eye and he turned his head, the mole above the brow confirmed it.

Richard Forsyth West wore a cream cowl-neck sweater and white linen pants. Strapped to his shoulder was a large straw satchel that on a less commanding figure might have appeared twee. Clay had warned Nick that West was dashing, but Nick hadn't been prepared for how imposing he was. He had the leisurely, uncaring gait of a man who didn't calibrate his pace to anyone else's idea of the clock. The crowd barely jostled him. West turned a corner, and Nick followed in pursuit an aisle behind, noticing a pair of red-and-white-striped canvas espadrilles on his feet. It was a typical, inane accessory of the rich, a shoe designed for island rambles and easy removal on boat decks. As Nick kept stride several feet behind, another body cut between them. It belonged to a young man in his mid-twenties with his eyes glued to his phone, his thumbs tapping frantically on the screen. Even with his full attention on his device, he managed to keep on the heels of Richard West and avoid knocking into oncoming traffic thanks to the phantom third eye their generation had evolved to navigate two worlds simultaneously. Nick studied him. He was exceedingly pretty, even with the wisp of a hopeful mustache on his upper lip. He had curly black hair, dark and yet shallow-set eyes, and thin, very pink lips. His jeans were disturbingly tight, and he carried a large shopping bag on his shoulder. At first Nick took him to be Persian on account of his olive skin. But when Richard West attempted a phrase in broken Italian, the young man answered in the easy singsong of a native speaker.

Had Nick not already known that West was married to a woman—on his second marriage, in fact—he might have mistaken the young man for West's boyfriend. Judging from the way he sprang to West's side, it was more likely that he was an assistant. West pointed, and the young man gathered a carton of strawberries and a tin of almonds. West practiced his Italian on a vendor, and the young man interceded and handed over the exact amount of cash. Nick stopped to let the foot traffic sweep around him. West's assistant was proving to be a wrench in the plan. It was far easier to strike up a conversation with a stranger who was alone.

The awkwardness of the introduction would quickly be forgotten in the momentum of the ensuing conversation. Those chances dropped considerably when there was a witness to critique every detail later. *You didn't think it was strange that this random American came up and talked to you?*

To Nick's dismay, the situation was further complicated by the presence of a young woman who hurried up to West in the crowd. She held a bouquet of orange roses and a cheap wicker basket with a price tag dangling from its handle. The woman was thin, with long, lank, tea-brown hair and light-gray freckles that flecked her nose and encroached upon the edges of her pale mouth. She was not what Nick would describe as pretty. She was at once plainer and more sophisticated than that. She had darting eyes and the kind of uneven smile that suggested a propensity for sharp, biting jokes. She and Richard West were now laughing at the wicker basket, which she held in front of him and pretended to place on an invisible platform. The assistant wasn't paying attention, having returned to his phone. Nick couldn't guess the punch line of the basket routine, but he enjoyed watching the woman's performance. It caused him to like her, and he even found himself appreciating West for his genuine squall of laughter. Clay had warned Nick about the dangers of liking West.

Nick was on the verge of being stampeded by the throngs funneling around him, so he walked toward the trio with his face half turned toward the Grand Canal. West spun around to examine a display of sausages, and at the same time Nick felt the young Italian's eyes latch on to him. He aborted his plan to "accidentally" bump into West and quickly ducked into a side stall devoted to discount underwear. He pretended to scrutinize a three-pack of briefs as he watched West and his two companions drift toward the main fish market. Nick was losing his chance. His eyes froze on the wicker basket that jutted out from the young woman's arm. The basket was poorly made, with wicker spikes protruding from its weave. An idea came to him, one cribbed directly from the streets of Manhattan.

Nick had fallen for a particularly clever street scam twice when he was new to New York. A homeless man carried a Styrofoam container stuffed with noodles along a midtown sidewalk. When he found his target, someone naive and kind-looking and preferably from the Midwest—basically Nicholas Brink—who was distracted by the city lights, he would knock into him with force and send his Styrofoam container flying. The result of the run-in was a clump of noodles spilled on the sidewalk. Angry cries ensued— "Man, I spent all my money on that, twenty dollars, and now no food to eat tonight! Why don't you watch where you're going?" It was the responsibility of the naive, kind-looking midwesterner to hand over twenty dollars with a sincere apology. Once the dupe disappeared down the block, the con artist scooped the noodles back into the container and was ready for his next victim. It was New York street survival at its finest.

Nick silently apologized to Daniela for her generous gift to him that morning. He un-scrunched the left sleeve of the Prince of Wales blazer and followed its seam up the arm to a spot below the elbow. He hooked a pinch of the fabric onto the nail head that was holding the pack of briefs. With a quick jerk of his arm, he managed to make a tiny rip. Slipping two fingers into the hole, Nick ducked back into the market, rushing to find the group before they vanished or changed their configuration.

He found them just inside the semidarkness of the market, where the assistant was ordering a bag of sea snails. The young woman was standing next to West, distractedly talking, the basket still jutting from her arm. When Nick reached her side, he carefully gripped the sharpest, longest wicker spoke and slipped it into the hole in his jacket. He then sprang forward, walking briskly and bringing the entire basket along with him.

"Oh, no!" the young woman called behind him. "Whoa! Sir!"

Nick turned around with a look of shock. "I'm caught," he pronounced and instantly regretted the contrived fish joke. The young woman gave a confused expression as she reached for the wicker spoke that clung to Nick's arm. When she unhooked him, she saw the frayed threads by his elbow. "I'm so sorry! Shit, I've torn your coat!" She tucked the basket punitively against her side as if it were a nipping lapdog. Nick took a second to inspect the rip. It was important not to be too quick with his forgiveness.

"Ahh," he sputtered, rubbing the hole as if it were a bruise.

She stared up at him with gritted teeth in the limbo of remorse. "I'm so sorry," she said again. "It's such a nice coat."

He allowed a smile to break gradually across his face. "It's okay," he replied loudly to accentuate his American accent. "It's just bad luck, I guess."

"Eva, what have you done?" Richard West cried in mock outrage. He was grinning mischievously as he looked from the young woman to Nick, half in apology and half inviting Nick to see the incident for the minor matter it was. West had the playful, relaxed manner of someone who could afford to fix any problem. "Was it that damned basket? I told you that thing was going to get us in trouble. I thought it would be limited to Karine's wrath!" Nick knew that Karine was the name of West's current wife. "Now it's destroying the lives of innocent bystanders!" He cocked his head at Nick. "This is my niece. She's a terror. Make her pay for the tailoring."

"I *will* pay for it!" Eva snapped. "Of course I will! Except I'm out of cash." She laughed and knocked her forehead against her uncle's shoulder. "I spent all I had on this stupid basket just to annoy Karine."

"Don't worry, I'll take your roses as compensation," Nick joked. He pretended to reach for her flowers, which won him a round of laughter. The Italian assistant eyed Nick warily over West's shoulder. But it didn't matter now. He already had West's attention.

"Well, who told you walking around Venice was going to be painless?" West's voice was dense and steady, each unrushed syllable running on a reliable American motor. "If it hadn't been a rip, it would have been pigeon shit. And that stuff is impossible to get out. You should be pleased you got off easy."

"I'm still learning," Nick agreed. "This is my first time in Venice, so now I know to avoid women with baskets."

"We're a terrorist organization," Eva avowed. "Women with baskets. We've just expanded into Venice."

"First time here, huh?" West asked. He absorbed that fact with a heavy inhale through his nose. Nick understood why the mole above West's left eyebrow was such a trademark. It was the only feature that broke the perfect symmetry of his face. Nick had never seen a face so evenly proportioned. Even the white hairs of his jaw reached the same ridgeline on each cheek. West's wide head reminded Nick of the lion knockers on nearly every door around this city. "What a shame," West said, "that it took you so long to get here."

"I know!" Nick replied. "It's too easy to get trapped in New York and never find your way out."

He earned another thoughtful inhale from West. "Ahh, New York. The city?" When Nick nodded, he added perfunctorily, "I love New York City," almost as if it were required to say so out of cosmopolitan solidarity. "I was born upstate myself, up in Albany, although I've spent most of my life in Chicago. I don't get back to either place very much anymore."

Nick was trying to figure out a response that would keep West engaged—he could mention growing up in the Midwest, although Dayton shared few similarities with Chicago; he could return to the dilemma of his ripped jacket; he could ask West how long he'd been living in Venice. Nick's hesitation led to a lapse in the conversation, and in that expanding lake of silence, West turned to the young Italian, who triumphantly held up a bag of snails as if it were a severed head. Nick had lost West's interest.

"Will that be enough for everyone tonight?" West asked his assistant. "Don't you think we should err on the side of too much, Battista?"

"I doubt we need *that* much," Eva replied. "It's one of those specialties where you take two bites and feel you've done your adventure with hors d'oeuvres."

"Not true," West countered. "Karine loves them. It's like popcorn for her. I've seen her eat double that amount on her own."

They had turned their backs to Nick, and he hovered awkwardly on the sidelines like a man at a bar who couldn't accept that he was not going to be invited home. Any sane person would have walked away. But Nick had yet to accomplish the single objective in running into Richard West this morning. Thanks to Clay, though, he had one more card to play. This ploy wouldn't appeal to West's humor or to his ease with strangers, but, far more effectively, to his pride.

"Well, it was nice to meet you," Nick said, waving a hand to seize their attention. "I'm off to find this Titian painting of Saint Lawrence that was recently restored."

West slowly rotated his head. "Not the one at the Gesuiti church?"

"Yeah," Nick said simply. "I hear that now they've removed five hundred years of soot from the canvas, it's mind-blowing."

West snapped his fingers at his niece in delight. "Did you hear that, Eva?"

She nodded, cognizant of her role in West's self-admiration. She could attest to his altruism so that he didn't have to.

"You're talking to the man who paid for that restoration," Eva told Nick.

He looked at West as if he'd been talking to a celebrity in disguise. "You did? No way! That's amazing!"

"I can't believe you know about it!" West howled. "None of the experts thought it was worth the money. A minor work by a major figure. But I put my foot down. I knew it was an essential masterpiece. And now you've even heard about it in New York and were told it was restored correctly, and that people love it!" These weren't questions. They were declarations, and Nick nodded yes to every single one of them. He nodded wildly. Nick was wise enough to know that charm helped to secure a friendship, but often it was *being charmed* that cemented it. "I'm deeply proud of that project," West admitted. "And I'm only getting started with my work in Venice!"

"Isn't it considered one of the best night scenes in Renaissance painting?" Nick asked, repeating the information verbatim that Clay had fed him.

West dropped his straw bag so he could put his arm around Nick's shoulder.

"Eva," he ordered. "Hook your basket back onto this young man's coat. We're taking him with us!"

"Then he wouldn't be off to the Gesuiti to see your painting," she noted.

West removed his arm with the abruptness of someone who had broken his own protocol on personal space. He seemed slightly embarrassed. "Please let me know your thoughts after you visit the church," he said. "I want to hear your take on the pigments. See for yourself if they pop." West talked like he'd restored the painting with his own hands. But Nick couldn't have asked for a better opportunity to introduce his business card, which had been the explicit goal of this morning's expedition. He pulled out his wallet and removed it. He'd already jotted his cell phone across it.

"Here's my card. You can text me on my number here."

West stared down at the white rectangle. "Wickston," he muttered. "Silver, isn't it?"

"That's right," Nick said and launched into his prepared speech. "We pretty much rule the corner on colonial silver sales in New York. I'm actually in Italy because of a meeting with a client in Milan. He wants me to authenticate some recent acquisitions of German silver. That's my primary role at Wickston. Authentication. But I thought I'd give myself a week in Venice first. Why not, right? I couldn't miss Venice."

West flicked the card across his palm as if to test the quality of the paper stock. "You ever run into a guy named Dulles Hawkes?"

"Sure," Nick replied. "Hawkes was our only competitor in New York before he closed a few years ago. Between us, I always thought Dulles was a bit of a mess. Not exactly trustworthy when it came to sales either. But . . ." He discreetly trailed off.

West nodded in agreement. "Yeah, I tried to use Dulles for a purchase or two. He was a disaster." West flicked the card again before storing it in his pocket. "I have an idea. We're having a little dinner party tonight at my palazzo. It's nothing fancy, but why don't you join? We have plenty of room."

"Yes, please come!" Eva exclaimed as she wedged the bouquet into the shopping bag on Battista's shoulder. "It'll be our way of making it up to you for the damage to your jacket."

"I wouldn't want to intrude," Nick said cautiously. He hadn't expected an invitation to West's house. The plan had been to introduce himself and hand over his business card, nothing more. If he accepted the invitation, he would have to extend his act for an entire evening rather than a mere few minutes in a crowded market. Not to mention the fact that Clay would be right next door, separated from him like a secret buried behind the wall.

"Don't think too hard about it," Eva said, feigning offense. "You don't have to let us down gently. There are plenty of other strangers for us to lure home."

"No, no, of course I'll come!" Nick replied. Like so much in his life, he let the flow of the conversation decide his fate.

"Excellent," West said. "I'll text you the address. We're in Cannaregio." Nick already knew the palazzo's location. He'd considered walking over there last night just to see the setting of so many of Clay's stories. "Say seven o'clock?"

"Battista is a terrific dancer," Eva swore, grabbing the Italian's overloaded arm. "It's something to look forward to." She was clearly making an inside joke. A flame of embarrassment colored Battista's face, and Nick's stare fed its fire, reddening his cheeks even further. He must have humiliated himself by dancing one night in front of them.

Eva confirmed that Battista was West's assistant when she introduced him. They exchanged rote *Ciao*s at a range close enough for Nick to smell nicotine on his breath. West pointed Nick in the direction of the Gesuiti, which he now had the obligation of visiting. He was sure to be asked his impression of the Titian that night.

Nick skipped up the marble steps of the Rialto Bridge in a flush of success. At the top of the bridge, he briefly hallucinated a sighting of the Warbly-Gardeners in a *motoscafo* speeding right under him. But it was a different tourist family lounging on the back cushions, and Nick had already let go of yesterday's disasters. He was too busy arguing with Clay in his head that a closer friendship with West would only serve to help their scheme. It wasn't a betrayal to be welcomed into the man's house for an evening. Nick could still be one hundred percent faithful to the person he loved while standing on the other side.

CHAPTER 7

In the hush of early evening, Venice changed from past to present. Lights glowed in windows, pulling attention away from the ornate architecture to favor the haphazard clutter of modest rooms. The boat motors drowned out the murmur of sightseers. In the daytime, it was easy to forget that a sea lay just beyond the city and that the canals weren't mere cartoon strips of water. But in the evening, when the sun slanted to the west, a lonely, restless sea air rolled in with the Adriatic tides. Venice became a port town again, a struggling maritime capital trying to beat back the waves. The sea grew like an imagination in the dark.

Nick felt a sense of anticipation in the night ahead. He wore his green wool blazer, having dropped off the ripped Prince of Wales jacket at a tailor after his visit to I Gesuiti. Earlier that afternoon, paying the one-euro entrance fee, he'd entered the spacious, whipped-cream-walled cathedral constructed in the shape of a Latin cross. Nick found the restored, still-sooty Titian painting slightly underwhelming. He'd been far more impressed by the church's inlaid marble floor of green, white, and gold; the glitzy pattern spilled down the altar steps and spread across the nave like the kind of wall-to-wall carpeting preferred by Houston housewives. Nevertheless, Nick made an effort to study the Titian, right down to Saint Lawrence's chiseled torso and overly worked-out legs; while being barbecued alive, the saint raised a tentative arm toward a starry rupture in the night sky. It was with zero guilt that Nick assessed the sexiness of each armored torturer surrounding the saint. To the artist's credit, the painting did capture the pitch and sway of a crisis—Nick deposited those words, *pitch and sway*, into his memory bank to spend later on Richard West.

The only errand that Nick hadn't accomplished that afternoon was a text to Clay informing him of West's dinner party. By the time he returned to Daniela's, he'd convinced himself it would be smarter to see how he fared that evening before needlessly worrying his boyfriend. Nick might very well bomb tonight with the Wests and return to his minor background role in the scheme. Anyway, he and Clay were meeting up tomorrow in an out-of-the-way church. It would be easier to explain in person. Mission accomplished, he'd texted instead. See you tomorrow.

Approaching West's palazzo, Nick passed a long, lean alley that ended in a green door. He suspected it might be the entrance to Il Dormitorio. The tiny, derelict *palazzino* had crooked shutters, and bird's nests of weeds filled the crooks of the windows. There was no light visible, but Nick had to assume that Clay was home. He felt a pang of longing as he overshot the alley and continued toward the front door of Palazzo Contarini.

Nick briefed himself on his lies: *You work at Wickston. You're an expert in authentication. You're here by yourself before a business trip to Milan.* He checked the map on his phone and discovered that he was only four feet from the palazzo's entrance. The brick wall gave way to an iron gate with an enormous stone sculpture of a bird at its peak—it looked more like a pterodactyl, although Nick guessed the medieval artist was aiming for an eagle. The gate was ajar, and Nick drifted into a small garden where a square of mowed grass was pinned at each corner by a cypress tree. Blue vines wove through a rickety pergola. Against the far wall, the first flashes of white wisteria petals hung from flaccid branches. Two squat, leafless bushes were spring's last holdouts.

The inner iron door to the palazzo was locked. Nick rang a chrome bell and eventually heard approaching footsteps. When the door opened, it was Battista who stared out with an unwelcoming squint.

"Hi!" Nick chirped, putting so much of his heart into his smile he forgot to try out his Italian. Nick had developed a small crush on West's assistant and hoped they'd be drunkenly flirting over a plate of sea snails by night's end. Battista gave an unenthusiastic nod before stepping back into the darkness, which didn't bode well for Nick's chances. Battista wore tight camel-colored trousers that reminded Nick of horse-riding jodhpurs and a white button-down that still held the creases of its cardboard packaging. Stringy black chest hair erupted from the open shirt collar.

Battista led Nick into a murky cavern tiled in red-and-white limestone. Two wooden doors creaked against their chained lock. Nick noticed with a novice's fascination how moss-green water flowed under the doors and rippled over marble steps. There were water stains along the walls from previous floods, some as high as Nick's head. Battista leaned against a column by the staircase to light a cigarette and gestured curtly toward the staircase. His message was clear: Nick would have to find his own way into the party. Nick started up the steps, shouting back a belated "*Grazie, mio amico!*"

One flight up, after fumbling around in the pitch-black stairwell to locate the doorknob, Nick didn't so much enter the light as stumble into it. For a moment his eyes were blinded with brightness, the world gone as white as lit kerosene. Blinking, he focused his eyes on the floor and waited until they took in the polished tan-and-black terrazzo. Two pitch-black silhouettes stood nearby. As the colors slowly bled into the room, he saw two young women glancing over with amused smiles. One was Eva in a silk burgundy dress with straps tied like shoestrings at her shoulders. She came toward him with her arm extended.

"I know it's bright," she said. "We get this weird prolonged glare off the canal. We usually have to wear sunglasses in here." Eva wasn't kidding. She kicked a fabric box filled with sunglasses by the door. "Help yourself."

"I'm okay," Nick replied with a laugh. He didn't recognize the other young woman. She had large brown eyes, a smile containing very large teeth, and a pronounced cleft chin. Her hair was long and dark and fell around her face, and her skin held the ochre tan of a recent vacation. She wore a knit top and matching pants in a funhouse camouflage pattern of zigzagging peach and lime stripes, which Nick identified as the staple of a famous Italian fashion house. Eva looked so small and serious next to the striking Italian woman, her skin so pale that Nick could make out the circuitry of blue veins at her temples and wrists.

"This is Giovanna," Eva said. "She was just showing us her pictures of"—Eva grunted in search of the proper description—"basically skydiving into Piazza San Marco during Carnival."

Giovanna tapped the screen of her phone. Nick stepped forward to get a look. Sure enough, as Giovanna's scarlet fingernail swiped through an album, a giant human ball of tulle, lace, and wavy brown hair could be seen descending over thousands of revelers. Close-ups revealed not only Giovanna's supersized features expressing the supersized fear of falling but that she was harnessed to a black cable, which extended from the top of the piazza's bell tower to a wooden stage assembled on the cobblestone.

"I had to do it!" Giovanna squealed. "The Flight of the Angel is a tradition that opens Carnival!"

"Please don't scare us with those photos!" Richard West huffed as he swept into the room. He had on the same clothes he'd worn to the market that morning, right down to his striped espadrilles. The rope-soled slippers seemed a more practical accessory as he glided across the marble floor. He rattled a red glass filled with ice cubes. "I'm going to have a talk with your parents, Giovanna. How could they let you risk your life on that crazy wire? Why Nick, hello! You made it!" West smiled at him as he swerved toward a blue-clothed table where more red glasses sat beside liquor bottles and a bucket of ice. "Let's get you a drink. We're doing Aperol spritzes. Not very original, I know, but I hope you like them."

"I love them," Nick insisted. He'd never tried Aperol before and hoped it wasn't as horrific as grappa or absinthe or any of the other novelty European alcohols that Ari's friends routinely served at dinner parties.

"My parents were very proud that I was chosen," Giovanna swore. "It's considered an honor."

"This is why I don't have children," West said as he mixed prosecco with what looked like an economy-sized bottle of orange cough syrup. "Eva, promise me that you'll never trust Italian safety precautions when you agree to be swung hundreds of feet over cement. They could have at least suspended you over water. There happens to be a lot of that just now in Venice."

"I don't think I'm Descending Virgin material," Eva replied.

"I wasn't a virgin!" Giovanna stammered. She caught her own joke and laughed at it as she gathered her hair behind her shoulders.

West padded over and supplied Nick with his cocktail. The thick red glass had crisscross gilding around its rim. He took a sip of the bitter-citrus drink; the tart cringe of the lips was easily disguised by a smile.

"Are you having a good time?" West asked, as if Nick had been in the house for more than a few minutes. Nick glanced around the room again with clearer eyes. He took in the heavy yellow curtains lining each window, a tarnished mirror suspended over the fireplace, a showdown between chocolate velvet divans in the corner, and the cabinet bookshelf with chicken-wire glass that ran the length of the wall by the front door. A few muddy paintings hung here and there, glazed in a greasy green varnish as if seen through tinted sunglasses. A marble coffee table held a yellow vase from which the fish market's orange roses poked. Around the vase, glossy magazines had been left open. Nick presumed they might be deliberately turned to editorials featuring this very palazzo. It was, without question, a stunning room deserving of photo shoots. The only odd flourish was a luminous brass doorstop holding one of the balcony windows open; it appeared to be a replica of the human brain. At least, it would have struck Nick as out of place had he not already read up on West's wife.

"Your house is beautiful," Nick told his host. "Truly, it is," he added, as if West might have received a number of disingenuous compliments in the past. West nodded happily and patted him on the back. He turned to Giovanna.

"Karine and I couldn't deal with Venice during Carnival. Otherwise we would have been there to watch you drop. We went to Capri, where it's perfectly empty off-season, and we hibernated in the dead quiet of Hotel Quisisana for two months. God, it was wonderful. No offense, Giovanna, but Carnival's gotten too crowded and depressing." Giovanna grimaced at being forced to defend a tasteless holiday that had elected her as its symbol.

West glanced at Nick. "I took one look out the window right before Carnival started, and it was pouring. I don't mean rain, I mean people. People have become the weather in Venice. And for Carnival, it's all drunks from Padua with cheap plastic masks strapped to their faces, vomiting on every footbridge. It really has come to that! At two in the afternoon!"

Nick was about to make a comparison to the evil holiday of Santacon that pillaged downtown Manhattan for an entire day each December. But before he could speak, a male voice from deep in the room boomed, "Catastrophe!"

Nick didn't know how he'd failed to spot the skeletal old man sitting on one of the chocolate divans in the corner. If he *had* spotted him, he might have mistaken him for dead. He was pressed deeply into the sofa, his head slumped against the wall with his eyes tilted toward the window; his arms were splayed out on the cushions, and an expired cigarette was wedged between his fingers. An empty glass ashtray lay a short distance away, with a contrail of ashes drawn across the velvet. The liver-spotted Italian rotated his head to face his audience. He had a manicured gray beard and shiny gray hair, but his sideburns and eyebrows were jet-black.

"It is our mayor, bad, bad," he decreed in a garbled Italian accent. "He's from Mestre. Only cares about Mestre. Hates Venezia. Destroys our city with that hotel development he is building in Mestre right now."

"Giacomo's right," West told Nick. "The mayor's a mini Trump from the mainland. A self-righteous, self-made thief. He's filling his own pockets with *our* tourism dollars and doesn't care one shit about preserving our delicate ecosystem. It's disgusting. That new hotel site in Mestre is costing—"

"No more talk about the destruction of Venice!" a woman with silver shoulder-length hair announced as she entered the room. "You promised one evening's hiatus, Dick. No planning Venice's funeral tonight!"

West's wife was more remarkable-looking in person than Nick's Google searches had indicated. Karine had disturbingly prominent cheekbones—the image that came to mind was of vintage hubcaps. The sleeves of her blouse were folded at the elbows in origami-like precision, and its tails were tucked into a long pleated skirt. Her hair was parted so severely down the center, not a single strand had defected to the opposing side. She didn't introduce herself to Nick but simply took his hand and said warmly, "So glad we have someone new over for dinner." Nick found himself looking at Karine's teeth—there were tiny chips along the ridges of the top row. He complimented her on the house, although West must have done most of the decorating before she ever moved in. Perhaps Karine's lone contribution was the gaudy doorstop.

Karine West née Hirscher was born in Austria to American diplomats and had served as the CEO of a neuroscience research clinic in Leipzig, Germany, for thirty years. In a sense, Karine and West were still newlyweds, having only married two and a half years before. Nick sensed they had already fallen into a familiar marital pattern, West working himself into a frenzy on a topic and Karine sagely applying the brakes.

A pudgy Italian woman with magenta-dyed hair appeared in the doorway, carrying a tray of food. She aimed the tray at the man lying on the divan.

"Elisabetta." Karine held up a hand. "Stop helping! Sit down next to your husband. Let us be the hosts tonight!" Nick slipped from Karine's side, attracted mothlike to the piano nobile's Byzantine windows. The glare had finally receded from the room, leaving dusty halos around the interior lamps. As he walked across the marble floor, he realized that its surface was wavy, as if it had been molded over the centuries to mirror the shape of the water. Giovanna stood outside on a narrow stone balcony. Nick joined her, looking down at the skinny canal below. The water was pea green under the pink haze of the disappearing sun. They stared over the terra-cotta rooftops and into a distance of antenna-like spires and bluing night. A police boat screamed down the canal, and its wake slapped against the palazzo's mooring piles. Venice might be sunk in the past, but it wasn't Nick's past. To him it felt new and possible.

"*Che bello*," he said, and the gorgeous but not pretty Giovanna murmured in accord. The world from this view seemed magical with all of its strange beauty fading into night. Nick was too young to imagine himself ever owning anything substantial—not a house or an apartment or even a car—so he gauged his success on the rooms he managed to enter, on the forbidden gated enclaves to which he'd gained admission and was allowed, however briefly, to inhabit. By most odds, Nick Brink of Dayton, Ohio, shouldn't be here, and that's why it was so thrilling that he was. Already he'd come so far. In less than two days after touching down in Venice, he'd managed to stand on the balcony of a palazzo at sunset holding a drink next to a young woman who had been flung down a wire to open Carnival.

When Nick stepped inside, West was jabbering on about the death of an American friend who'd lived in Venice for decades. "Topper was a *huge* supporter of conservation. We couldn't afford to lose him. Of course, we all know *why* we lost him, even if no one could prove it." Nick went to the bar and poured more prosecco into his glass. "You agree with me, don't you?" West asked his oldest guests.

The elderly Italian couple on the divan made up a hung jury on the Topper scandal. Giacomo nodded with a verdict of guilt, while Elisabetta shook her head in uncertainty. Eva, sitting on the floor and tangling her fingers in the fringe of a rug, asked who this Topper character was.

"Didn't I tell you?" West rasped. He launched into the story of Topper Horn, a dapper gay septuagenarian heir to a grocery-chain fortune who owned a magnificent palazzo on the Grand Canal. Topper liked Italian boys, so it was no surprise to his friends when he mentioned meeting a young Venetian at the train station one morning. This Venetian worked as a low-level security officer, checking passports and escorting German shepherds around luggage trolleys. The guy already had a wife and an infant daughter on the mainland. "But, ohh . . . ," West cried. "Suddenly, we meet Luca, Topper's new motorboat driver. A month later, Luca has been promoted to Topper's private secretary. A month after that, none of us ever spoke directly to Top again. He only made contact *through* Luca. And that was it. The end."

But it wasn't the end. One day the Grand Canal palazzo was put up for sale, and a year later there ran an obituary for Mortimer "Topper" Horn, who died of natural causes at his home in Monte Carlo, age seventy-nine. The Venetian had quietly liquidated all of Topper's seizable assets and moved the cash (and Topper) to the tax-free safe haven of Monte Carlo. Luca inherited the whole bundle, and apparently he and his family were really enjoying Monte Carlo year-round these days, in case any of Topper's old friends had any doubts.

Giacomo laughed fiendishly, all open mouth and gold teeth. "Venetians are very smart! You underestimate us!"

"Smart, yes! And wicked!" West slapped his knees. "But how fucking unfair! Poor Topper never even got a kiss from the guy. He lost it all and didn't get one roll in the sheets! Give the man that much for his fortune!"

"Dick, you're going too far," Karine muttered as she picked at the hors d'oeuvres. But in Nick's prosecco-fueled estimation, it seemed a valid point. Poor Topper. He could have at least been allowed to see Luca naked.

"We have something of a similar situation . . . ," West said conspiratorially to Giacomo and pointed to the bookshelf that ran across the inner wall. He silently mouthed the rest of the sentence: *next door*. Nick's heart skipped, and he glanced nervously at the chicken-wire bookshelf. "I'm actually to blame," West said in a lowered voice. "I indirectly introduced Freddy to the guy."

"We miss Freddy!" Elisabetta pledged while selecting a fig from the plate. "I always picture him carrying off some ridiculous find from *il mercato delle pulci*."

"Well, this happened maybe four years ago. The kid was an African-American student visiting from"—West glanced over at Nick—"from New York, in fact." Nick widened his eyes in surprise, as if he couldn't believe someone from New York could be implicated in a Venetian scandal. But his cheeks were flushing, and he quickly took a drink from his glass to hide his face.

"He was an intern at the Peggy Guggenheim," West continued. "I was amazed he could speak Italian, because they can never learn the language." At first, Nick took "they" to mean African-Americans, and his eyes shot to Eva to acknowledge the overt racism of her uncle's comment. Eva was reaching for a fig, her expression concealed by her outstretched arm. Upon reconsideration, it was possible that West had meant young Americans can't learn Italian, or, even more likely, American interns at the Peggy

Guggenheim, which actually jibed with Clay's own account of his coworkers.

"I took him under my wing," West said. "I even offered him a full-time job working with me on my Venice projects." He lifted his palms as if being mugged. "I really dodged a bullet. Talk about catastrophe! Instead this kid went right for my neighbor. Of course, Freddy, poor guy, took to him *in-stant-ly*, like a fever. Eventually Freddy even brought him back to live with him in Brooklyn. You can imagine the rest." West blinked his blue eyes as he delivered his next revelation. "Guess who inherited the bulk of Freddy van der Haar's estate? Honestly, that kid should be thanking me. I won't go as far as to say he murdered Freddy . . ."

There it was again, for the second time today, a mention of that familiar suspicion. Nick winced, while Elisabetta stiffened in her seat. "You think that boy murdered Freddy?" she cried.

West gently shushed her. He stood up and, with a devious grin meant to keep his audience enthralled, sneaked over to the chicken-wire bookshelf. West popped a lever, and one of the cabinets jolted open. He pulled it back to reveal a walnut door.

"It connects!" he whispered, swinging his pointer finger back and forth as if testing the water temperature under a tap.

Nick stared at the door, imagining Clay on the other side. It was agonizing to think that he and the guy he loved were separated by a mere inch of solid wood; Nick should be on the other side of that door curled up with Clay, watching a movie on his laptop. Instead he was here on this side, drinking prosecco with strangers and snickering about stolen fortunes and not defending his boyfriend when his reputation was being bashed around like a piñata. Nick had expected a few stings from West on the subject of Clay Guillory—it was all part of the plan. But the prosecco was filling him with reckless fantasies of taking noble stands and ripping walnut doors from their hinges. The two drinks had given Nick the misimpression that the present mattered more than the future. He set his glass down and decided to wait until dinner for a refill.

"What is it like over there?" Elisabetta asked, as if she were inquiring about a foreign country.

West laughed. "Oh, god, it's like going from our side, which is Venice, right into Naples. Totally run-down, wires and broken sconces and rotting walls. Probably riddled with mice. It doesn't have a direct view of the canal, so it's as dark as night. And it's still basically a youth hostel for the Guggenheim, which I never complained about because I respected Freddy too much. But even I have my limits . . ."

West shut the bookcase cabinet. Just as he did so, the main door opened, and two more elderly Italians shuffled in behind Battista. Their dazed faces looked bewildered by the glimmering room, almost as if Battista had picked this couple at random off a highway and deposited them in a palace on the water. Karine ran over to administer double kisses. West clapped his hands.

"Eva, Nick," he said. "We are now outnumbered by Venetians! Which means it's officially an Italian dinner party!"

Battista relayed bad news: an important guest, the head of a renowned Venetian conservation nonprofit named Vittorio, had called to cancel. The royal family of Thailand was in town and demanded to be shown the sights.

Eva let out a grunt of disappointment. "So much for the setup," she said to her uncle.

West wrapped his arm around her. "I'm sorry, sweetheart. But if it's any consolation, Thailand is the wealthiest crown. Vittorio needs to rattle his tin cup for donations. It's a valid excuse. We'll corner him next time."

Karine picked up a bell from an end table and rang it to signal that dinner was ready.

Eva poked Nick's bicep. "I'm stuck sitting next to you," she said.

"Sorry," he replied. "Were you on a blind date with this Vittorio?"

"Sort of. I want a job at his organization. That's why I'm in Venice. I've been studying conservation in Toulouse for the past four years. But it's all tapestries and medieval castles up there. I want to work here in Venice, and this guy's the best there is. He restored the Frari, for Christ's sake!"

Nick didn't know what the Frari was but hummed with admiration anyway. "Couldn't you work for your uncle? It sounds like he's doing those sorts of projects."

Eva pulled Nick by the arm toward the dining room. "I don't have enough experience to tackle a public project. Venice wouldn't let me touch any of its treasures, even if Uncle Richard is paying the bill. This city is so insanely bureaucratic, it has to approve every single decision, and of course it only wants to hire Venetian craftsmen. But I *could* work on those masterpieces under Vittorio because he wears the golden ring. Oh well, he can't dodge us forever." She whispered menacingly in his ear. "I'm going to hunt that motherfucker down and make him hire me."

The dining room mimicked the living room right down to the wavy terrazzo floor. The only difference was that the yellow satin curtains were pulled closed; Nick suspected that those windows didn't overlook the canal. Perhaps they gazed out onto the entrance of Il Dormitorio. A large oval table was covered in a blue tablecloth; blue linen napkins folded into the shape of boats sailed on white china plates. The only clumsy touch was Eva's wicker basket decorating the center of the table. Karine had clearly one-upped her family on their practical joke by insisting on using it as the centerpiece. Nick thought he could still make out a few of his teal jacket threads snagged on one of the wicker spokes. Karine went around lighting candles with a trembling match.

As the guests collected in the doorway, West dealt silver coasters across the table for wine bottles. He flashed the last one in Nick's direction, the silver catching the candlelight and bouncing a beam into his eye. The coaster in West's hand scared Nick. He realized, a few steps too late, that he might have just walked into a trap. West might thrust the coaster into Nick's palm in front of his friends and ask him to identify its origin and maker, like a magician forced to perform a card trick in front of a skeptical audience. The truth was that Nick couldn't identify a French coaster from an Italian one, eighteenth from nineteenth century. At Wickston, Nick had cleaned and polished dozens of antique coasters, as they tended to be low-cost collectibles or affordable wedding presents. But Ari had been the one to authenticate them. As Karine announced that everyone should sit where they liked—"No order, no favorites"— West kept shining the coaster in Nick's direction, clearly enjoying how it threw the light on him. Nick froze with one eye blinded by the beam. *Please don't ask me about it*, he prayed. He'd been an idiot. He'd risked his and Clay's entire future on a free dinner in a fancy palazzo on his second night in town.

"Hey," West said to him in the playful tone of a challenge.

"Yeah?" Nick asked fearfully. He considered faking a stroke.

A timer rang in the kitchen. Karine, who was clearing Vittorio's setting from the table, warned her husband, "It's going to burn." Mercifully, West tossed the final coaster on the table and walked out of the room. The guests scattered to available chairs. Nick ended up with Eva on one side and Elisabetta on the other. The old woman dropped a digestion tablet into a glass of water and chugged the fizzy contents. "Devil stomach," she told him.

West carried in a steaming tray of baked pasta. "We were supposed to have this with sea snails," he announced, "but Karine already ate them. Please don't picture Karine with a pound of sea snail inside of her."

"Dick!" she wailed, tossing her napkin on her lap. "I had four! They were off! I'm saving you all from misery tomorrow."

The main course of pasta and chicken was followed by salad, followed by an enormous wedge of bone-dry Parmesan that was passed around with its own chisel. Five bottles of red wine were left open on the table, which allowed guests to refill their glasses with impunity. Elisabetta poured several rounds for herself and always topped Nick's glass off on the route back to the coaster. The table was warm with laughter. Even Battista, scrunched between West and Giovanna, appeared to lighten over the course of the meal. Most of the dinner was conducted in Italian, which allowed Nick to drift along unnoticed in the current of the conversation. Eva and Karine kept up impressively, while West blinked and wrinkled his nose with baffled effort. Only during the salad course did the discussion return to Nick's native tongue.

"Where are you staying?" Karine asked him from across the table.

Nick was prepared for this question. In fact, he had anticipated it ever since he arrived. He couldn't mention Daniela. "Venice is very small," Daniela herself had warned him. West might know her and might be able to trace her to Freddy, and from Freddy to Clay, and then there Nick and his boyfriend were, connected by a clothesline of intimacies. He had to be extremely careful about the facts he revealed tonight. It occurred to him that sitting at this table was not unlike family dinners back in Dayton when he visited over holidays in college. There, he'd learned how to dodge and evade dangerous questions, casting himself as an asexual, unthreatening lump of a person, a simple passer of potatoes.

"I found a place near Campo Santa Margherita on one of those apartment rental websites," he said buoyantly to Karine.

Karine glanced uneasily at her husband. West's face crumpled, and he put two fingers together in the shape of a crucifix or a riflescope.

"Not you too, Nick!" West groaned. "Don't say it! Those short-stay B&B rentals are exactly what's destroying Venice!" Giacomo, who was reaching for more wine, grumbled in solidarity. "That's why there are only fifty thousand Venetians left in Venice. Everyone else has rented out their homes to vacationers for a profit and split for the mainland! And they pay zero taxes on those earnings! Meanwhile, everyone who's remained here has a rotating circus of strangers as next-door neighbors."

"Dick, you promised," Karine warned. "No destruction of Venice tonight."

West couldn't help himself. "One of the few expectations in life is that your city is going to outlive you, but—" Karine shook her head, and he laughed out an "Okay, okay." He tapped his knuckles on the table. "Just promise me, Nick, next time you either stay at a proper hotel or here with us."

Nick was touched. Even if this were a onetime dinner, he'd made a good impression and was welcome back. He smiled appreciatively and asked Karine about Leipzig. Thankfully, she answered without catching his mistake. An innocent Nick wouldn't have known about her previous Leipzigian existence.

As the dinner wore on, Nick found it harder to dislike his host. West had been a nasty comedian in the living room, but he was far more considerate in the dining room. He was promiscuous with his humor, searching candlelit faces for signs of amusement to share. Over the cheese course, he talked about the various Venetian projects he was hoping to undertake—the restoration of a

Carpaccio painting in a Murano church; a wrecked doge's grave; an eighteenth-century carved bench that hadn't been refurbished after the La Fenice fire. In return for his money and efforts, all he asked for was a small accompanying copper plaque reading RE-SUSCITATION GENEROUSLY PROVIDED BY RICHARD FORSYTH WEST. "Because that's what we are doing! We aren't restoring, we're re-suscitating. We're bringing ghosts back to life." Like most zillion-aires, West didn't want to be remembered for how he'd earned his money but for how he spent it. Many lives might have been ruined in the amassing of his wealth, but now he was bent on uplifting lives by means of culture and taste.

As West recited a few more projects he was eyeing—should the local government get its act together and finally grant its approval—Nick noticed Eva's finger tracing ever-widening circles on the tablecloth. "Stop!" she finally erupted. "It's killing me that I can't work on those projects!"

"You'll get your turn," her uncle said confidently. "We'll make sure of it. But now," he crooned, "it's time to dance. It's our cus-tom. Nick, you aren't excused even if you're new."

Nick didn't realize until he stood up how much wine he'd drunk. The candle flames had burned into his retinas, and ghostly green diamonds pulsed around in the darkness. He somehow man-aged to find his way into the living room. Karine poured pro-secco into what she described as her "special glasses," which were wonderful embarrassments of bright glass squiggles with seahorse stems. The guests clinked rims as music exploded from hidden speakers. Scratchy 1970s Italian disco blasted through the room, all candy synthesizer flourishes, which caught everyone by their feet and rounded them up in the center of the room.

The dance floor had always been the one place where Nick could put his brain to rest and lose himself in the motions of his body. Before he knew it, he was dancing to the dumb fun of the disco rhythm, and so were the four elderly Italians, shaking their hips and flapping their elbows. Elisabetta was particularly impassioned, waving her hands around her magenta head. Nick had never danced with old people in New York. It was a shame. And he never once danced with his family in Dayton. All those radios that his father fixed lying around, and they never once turned them on to dance. In Dayton, they were also never allowed to drink out of the "special glasses," and they were forbidden to step foot in the living room except on holidays (for most of the year, the living room sat empty like a museum period room devoted to a twenty-first-century middle-class family in decline). Here, however, in the rich refuge of Richard West's palazzo, a normal night of existence was celebrated with the very best. *And why not? What was everyone so scared of breaking back there?*

Elisabetta was just getting started when the drum machine kicked in; she began climbing a steep hill in slow motion. Karine was giving it her all with one leg, endlessly squashing a cigarette underfoot. Eva was catching invisible balls in front of her to the beat. Giovanna appeared at Nick's side, and she lassoed her arms around his neck. Nick glanced down at her thick, fake eyelashes as he placed his hands on her hips. Giovanna was so warm to the touch, so beautiful really, with all her layers of long hair, that he felt the privilege of holding her. He put his nose near her neck to breathe in her smell.

Only Battista pouted on the sidelines. Nick remembered that Eva had ridiculed him at the market for his dancing—*Battista is a terrific dancer.* Eva snapped her fingers to call him onto the dance floor: it must be time for the clown's performance. Battista frowned in resistance for another second before springing into action and gliding across the terrazzo. He spun around on one heel and froze with his spine arched and his hands at his shoulders like he was about to lift an invisible barbell. His legs spaghettied and he shrank to the floor as cleanly as a cobra dropping into a basket. Then he jumped up with a smile on his face and lifted his arms in triumph.

Eva's remark at the fish market hadn't been sarcastic. *Battista is a terrific dancer.* Giovanna even let go of Nick to clap for him. Giacomo spotted this year's angel temporarily without a dance partner and made a move to take Nick's place. Then, as the music shifted to a slightly slower disco track, the unthinkable happened. Nick felt Battista's back press against his own. They were grinding shoulder blades to the supple synth beat and cries in broken English for "more, more love." Nick wasn't sure whether he was participating in a traditional back-to-back Italian folk dance or a secret flirtation. Battista was shorter than Nick; he could feel the Italian's sweaty hair against his neck and his round ass against his upper thighs. He imagined kissing Battista and reaching a hand inside his clothes to explore all the different parts of him. When the song ended, Battista abruptly ripped himself away. But when they turned to face each other, Nick saw West's assistant grinning with an unmistakable, inviting look on his face.

Nick's eyes fled to the bookshelf as if a portrait of Clay hung there. It wasn't a case of Nick being forbidden to mess around with other men, as it had been with Ari; he and Clay were open, free to be with whomever they desired, finally unleashing the pent-up, tree-sniffing body from the tired, tyrannical mind. No, Nick realized that his stupidity lay in choosing for a conquest someone who worked for West. He had forgotten himself for a moment, forgotten Clay and his entire mission in Venice. The coin in his loafer winked as he dragged himself off the dance floor.

West was standing at the makeshift bar. He gazed casually over at Nick as he approached and said, just as casually, as if it had only just occurred to him, "Why don't we talk in my study?"

"Of course," Nick exclaimed. Then he added, he wasn't sure quite why, "I'm sorry. I'd love to."

He followed West down a narrow hall lit by a series of recessed ceiling fixtures. One side of the hallway received most of the light's attention. It served as a portrait gallery of gold-framed photographs, all of them adhering to the template of West with a renowned figure, touching shoulders or shaking hands. The self-made mogul had risen up in the world just in time to meet a late-middle-aged Jacqueline Onassis and a young, prematurely gray Bill Gates. There were other figures Nick readily identified—two vice presidents, a bisexual Latin pop star, a famous children's puppet. Many others evaded recognition, but surely with a few more years of sophistication, Nick would find the entire constellation of faces impressive. West took a left at the end of the hall. Nick was turning to follow when a photo of his host with Freddy van der Haar caught his eye. In the snapshot, Freddy looked like a Rolling Stones groupie circa Altamont—a yellow bandanna tied around his forehead, a black leather jacket with eagle feathers pluming down both arms. It must have been taken on a fairly recent visit to Venice because Nick spotted Clay standing glumly at Freddy's side. Nick wanted to linger in front of this surprise appearance of his boyfriend—he liked being reminded of his eyes. But he was afraid West might catch him studying this particular photograph on an entire wall of somebodies. He passed on, sad to leave Clay trapped there in a gold frame alongside his dead best friend and his sworn enemy. He entered West's study.

"Welcome to my *wunderkammer*. Shut the door," West directed. But Nick found no door on the frame. "I mean the curtain. Pull it shut." Nick took a handful of thick tan velvet and tugged it across a gold rod. The fabric did a decent job of silencing the disco. Nick turned with a laugh, the wine and prosecco still tugging his brain in competing directions. The room was large, with piles of art books lining the walls. Many of them were still wrapped in cellophane. An oak desk stood in the center of the room; its top was decorated in tortoiseshell marquetry, and it was so wide that even Nick's extra-long arms couldn't have spanned it. One study wall was fitted with a mahogany cupboard that displayed a set of porcelain plates. The opposite wall boasted a fresco rendered in pellucid oranges and grays; voluptuous women were being dragged off on the shoulders of studly, armor-clad centurions. Nick thought the painting captured the pitch and sway of a crisis—and then remembered that he had saved that very description to compliment the Titian in the Gesuiti. Did all paintings in Venice pitch and sway with crisis? West hadn't yet asked Nick about the Titian. Maybe he had brought him into his study to discuss it now.

West leaned against the desk in the cool, relaxed pose of a high-school truant propping himself on the grille of a sports car. His white clothes took on the colors of the desk lamps, one shaded green and the other red. In the dim light, West looked younger and his body stronger, with an outline of pectoral muscles visible under his sweater. He crossed his arms, and his foot toyed with the espadrille that had come unhooked from his heel.

"What did you think of those German coasters at dinner?" he asked. Nick should have known this question was coming. And yet, unlike the inquiry into where he was staying, he hadn't prepared an answer for it. He'd been too busy dancing.

"I *thought* those were German!" he replied to buy time. "I couldn't really see them in the candlelight, but they looked exquisite." He knew the best method of evasion was to go on the offense with a question. "How much did they set you back, if you don't mind my asking?"

"I wouldn't know," West murmured. "They were a gift from Karine's brother." He smiled with the pride of a man who didn't keep tabs on the monetary worth of his possessions. "You're having a good time?" he asked abruptly, repeating the first question he'd posed to Nick that evening. West seemed to be building toward a sensitive topic and couldn't find the exact words to transport them there.

"Oh, yeah! A wonderful time."

"Good." West lifted his eyebrows like a dare and just as quickly dropped them. When his head fell toward the green lamp, his white hair and beard took on a toxic phosphorescence and his wrinkles deepened. Nick wished he'd remain in the green light so he could glimpse West as the monster that Clay saw. "We like it here in Venice so much, I want you to like it the way we do. It's too easy to get the wrong impression of the city, the brochure version, the ten-dollar tour-guide version with the operatic gondolier and a quick gawk at the Bridge of Sighs. That's all wrong."

"I can't thank you enough. I never want to see the Bridge of Sighs."

West clucked. "Did you get a chance to talk to Eva at dinner?" It was another swerve of a question, and Nick was still uncertain where West was trying to aim them.

"A little bit, when she wasn't speaking Italian. She seems eager to start on conservation projects in Venice. Like what you're trying to do here."

West nodded in agreement, but said, "No, Eva wants to get her hands dirty. I just put up the money to protect the stuff. Eva's the real artist. You know, she's pretty much the only family I've got left. She's very important to me." Nick wasn't sure if this confession was meant as a warning to stay clear of Eva or as an enticement to befriend her. He didn't get the chance to find out, because West dropped the subject as quickly as he'd introduced it. He lifted himself from his desk to stand in front of the fresco. He stared into it as if it were a window instead of swirls of dry plaster.

"It's stunning," Nick said. He had to be careful not to overflatter. One too many compliments endangered all of the ones that came before it.

"Yes, *The Rape of the Sabine Women*. It's really held its colors over the centuries. We didn't need to do too much to restore it. I also have two fantastic frescoes of Moors in my bedroom." West turned to Nick with a wan grin. "But all of my frescoes are painted by the disciples of Sebastiano Ricci. The van der Haars kept the real prize for themselves when they blocked up their corner of this house. They have a ceiling fresco of the Virgin Mary painted by Ricci himself." West boldly tapped *The Rape of the Sabine Women* with his finger. The Virgin Mary fresco must be on the other side of the wall. "Those fuckers," West added with a snort.

"Ha!" Nick blasted.

"Does that name mean anything to you?" West asked. "Van der Haar? They were the neighbors I was talking about earlier."

All this time, Nick had been waiting to deliver a few lines of poetry on Titian's painting at the Gesuiti. But right now Richard West was coming at him head-on with the main event, the whole crux of the scheme. Nick took an automatic step back, as if to weigh the moment from a safer distance. He regretted the last rounds of Elisabetta's heavy pour into his glass. He needed his wits.

"Van der Haar," Nick repeated pensively. "You mean, the New York van der Haars?" West nodded, but Nick wasn't awarded a smile for the correct answer. West's face had aged suddenly in a clench of seriousness. Nick quickly continued. "Of course I know *of* them. They were one of America's founding Dutch families. Their names were once chiseled into hospitals and fountains all over New York."

Ari's lines elicited the right response. "Yes, exactly, *them*," West said with a snap of his teeth. "So you must know about their silver." West grabbed a large monograph off the top of the nearest book pile and opened it to a page that was already marked with a yellow Post-it. The grainy, time-blurred black-and-white photograph showed a trove of silver artifacts—plates, trophies, tankards, cups, teapots, bowls—sitting on a large wood cupboard. Nick knew the photograph by heart. It had been blown up several sizes and hung in multiples around the attic of Freddy van der Haar's Brooklyn brownstone. The photo had served as the primary reference to the antiques that had once belonged to the van der Haars, and thus it had also served as a more recent reference on which pieces were still plausible for Freddy to own.

"I know that photo well," Nick admitted. "Everyone in my field does. The van der Haars had one of the great colonial American silver collections. It's been broken up quite a bit. Many of those pieces have found their way into museums." Nick pointed to a porringer with pierced handles that was on permanent display at the Met. "Most of the rest have gone into private collections. But a few of the best items are presumably still in the family's possession." Nick's tongue stiffened at the delivery of this lie, and he swept that wet, uncooperative muscle over his dry lips. He glanced up at West with cringing exasperation, as if he expected to find a skeptical glare. "I'm sorry," Nick said. "I'm probably boring you. But how funny that they're your neighbors! Or maybe that should be expected in a place like Venice."

West didn't grab him by the shirt collar and scream "Liar!" into his face. Instead he beamed. The serious, wrinkled man was now replaced with an impulsive, wide-eyed younger one. He held the book open in front of him and walked backward until he stood by his cupboard of decorative china.

"Do you see?" he asked, drawing his hand back and forth between the two cupboards. Nick already knew from Clay that Richard West was obsessed with the van der Haar family—and that their silver would be like candy to him—but even Nick hadn't expected West to build an exact replica of their Victorian cupboard.

"God," Nick sputtered. "It's so similar to the one in the photo. Almost perfect."

West shook his head. "Not almost. It *is* perfect. If you ignore all of Karine's Nymphenburg porcelain, you'll see it's the same exact one!"

Nick performed an ingratiating laugh while darting his eyes between image and reality.

"This photo was taken at the eighteenth-century van der Haar mansion on the south side of Albany," West explained. "The van der Haars once had a huge stone house near the river. By the time I was a kid, the family was long gone and the mansion was boarded up and abandoned. My friends and I used to break in and skate through the rooms. I'm sure I skated by this very cupboard! I'm sure of it!"

West tucked his hands behind his back and pretended to skate in front of the mahogany shelves. "You have to realize, I was the son of a mechanic. No money in sight, to put it mildly. But for me, playing in that mansion as a kid, the van der Haars represented impossible riches, our country's first kings." West snapped the book shut and returned it to the pile, his shoulders pulled back as if to reassert his manliness after his childish performance. West was one of the kings of America now; he was no longer a mechanic's son breaking into houses that didn't belong to him. "Anyway, after I'd made my own money and felt I could step away from the tech world, I fell in love with Venice. I saw all sorts of palazzos for sale, and many were far more spectacular than this one. I could have gotten one of the show ponies on the Grand Canal for the same price. But when I learned that Palazzo Contarini once belonged to the van der Haars . . ." West shook his head. "It felt like a sign. I swooped in a decade ago and bought it. I love it here. I love that the family whose mansion I played in as a boy once entertained in these rooms. Honestly, it felt like my duty to buy it and return it to its glory. It was in awful shape." West leaned wearily against his desk, as if winded by the sentimental trip back in time. "The cupboard arrived five years ago. I heard that the mansion in Albany was being renovated into a hotel, so I asked the owners if I could buy it. After all, it had served as the family's treasure chest. I thought the van der Haars would prefer it here rather than piled with brochures for river-rafting excursions or visits to Crossgates Mall." West smiled as he reached out and patted Nick on the shoulder. He touched him much more delicately than he'd tapped his wall fresco. "I hope you're listening closely. There's a point to my rambling. I want to know if Wickston has come across any van der Haar silver lately? I know you guys are the last game in New York."

Nick couldn't believe the conversation had arrived at this destination with such little effort on his part. It was frightening how much you could rely on the particular make of a person's greed. It was as if West had been doomed to take Nick into his home and rattle on about his impoverished childhood from the very moment he'd been handed the Wickston business card. Nick preferred to think of people as messy whirlpools of wants and desires, as unpredictable bundles of urges even when the appropriate bait was placed in front of them. But West was walking right into their con—in a sense, pulling a hesitating Nick along with him—just as Clay said he would. Nick felt a stab of guilt about their deceit, not so much for tricking a rich, retired dilettante as for betraying the dreaming little boy who imagined he'd one day own the spoils of his secret playground.

"Wickston never had any direct dealings with the van der Haars," Nick said steadily. "From time to time, a piece would pass through our hands that had belonged to the family. Very rarely, though. And they'd never stay long because they were in high demand. From my understanding, the last remaining heir—oh, what was his name? Freddy!—dealt mostly with Dulles Hawkes. I never met Freddy."

"There are two last van der Haar heirs," West corrected, putting his obsession with the family on display. "Freddy and his older sister, Cecilia. But you're right, Freddy seemed to have gotten all the silver."

Nick nodded with a weak smile. "Yes. Freddy sold a few pieces privately through Hawkes up until he retired. He never wanted the family artifacts to go to auction. That would be too public. These old families always try to be discreet when it comes to selling heirlooms." In general, this was true. But in Freddy's case, he had avoided the auction houses for fear of exposure—not so much out of a need for discretion as because a public auction would have allowed endless sets of expert eyes to scrutinize every relic for mistakes. "Now that Hawkes is closed," Nick said, "we would have been Freddy's likely choice for sales. But he never contacted us. We know he still owned a few extremely valuable pieces." Nick eyed West to ensure that he was buying every word. "Maybe Freddy wanted to hold on to those last treasures. They must have meant a great deal to him. They likely now belong to whoever inherited his estate."

Nick wanted to take a bow and flee the house. He'd managed to dispense his lies far more convincingly than he'd imagined he could, and he didn't want to botch the job by lingering at the scene of the crime. The wine had been a good conspirator, smoothing his nerves, and if West had possessed any doubts, Nick seemed to have survived them. He already pictured telling Clay tomorrow how he'd not only succeeded in giving West his business card but had already laid down the groundwork for the next step in their plan. Nick glanced at the velvet curtain over the door as if to suggest it was time to leave the study.

Unfortunately, West wasn't finished with him yet. "Freddy's inheritor is that kid I was talking about, the intern from the Guggenheim. He's in town right now, right next door." West paused a moment as if a mutinous idea had overtaken him. "Wickston never thought about reaching out to him after Freddy died in the interest of selling the silver?"

It was a smart question. But Nick saw in front of him a rather pretty dodge.

"We're not ambulance chasers, Richard." It was the first time Nick called his host by his first name, and he enjoyed the way it leveled them into equals for a moment. Nick thought he'd never sounded so grown-up in his life. "We're also not a pawnshop for heirs. We don't barge into homes and turn over saucers to see who made them while offering our condolences. If this kid wanted to sell Freddy's silver, he'd know to get in touch with us."

West nodded amiably. "You're a class act!" He dramatized another pause, as if a second rebellious thought had taken mutiny of his brain. Nick sensed that the pause was performed in order to appear offhand. "You wouldn't be willing to approach the guy next door—Clay Guillory is his name—and ask about his silver, would you? As a favor to me?"

Nick's jaw tightened. West's proposal was driving Nick and Clay together when their whole strategy had been to keep their distance so there could be no connection, no evidence of a plot.

West noticed Nick's hesitation and rushed to explain. "I hope that didn't sound too forward. I'm a greedy opportunist, what can I say? If you turn me down, I'll still consider you a friend. But, you see, I'm curious about acquiring the silver, whatever remains of the family collection. That's why I asked you about Dulles Hawkes at the market today. I tried dealing with him in the past when a van der Haar piece came up for sale. But Dulles was such an incompetent shithead that he could never get back to me in time, let alone negotiate a sale. So I thought maybe you could introduce yourself to Clay and ask about the silver. You know, you could check out what's left and tell me what it might be worth."

West looked so hungry for his chance to fill his ludicrous mahogany cupboard that Nick finally grasped the essential beauty of their scheme. West would be getting exactly what he wanted, and so would they. Many of the finest antiques in museums were actually fakes; what harm would a few van der Haar forgeries do sitting in the gloom of this far-flung palazzo, gathering West's admiration and fingerprints? They would satisfy West's ego, while supplying him and Clay with the cash they needed to live. It was possible to make everyone happy so long as no one pushed too hard on the mirage.

Nick faked a contrite frown.

"The problem is, Richard, I don't know Clay Guillory. So if I talked to him and leant my services, I would be doing so in an official capacity, under the Wickston name. Which means ethically I'd have to give him a fair assessment of the collection's worth and whether or not he'd be smarter to take those pieces to auction or show them to a number of interested buyers."

West puffed his cheeks at the annoyance of Nick's ethics—as if Nick's ethics had always been the problem between them, and a night of dinner and dancing hadn't softened them. But Nick already had a solution worked out. He would use his boyfriend's ugly reputation to his advantage—after all, West had been too happy to toss it around for his own enjoyment. "But," Nick countered with a raised finger, "if Clay is the kind of guy you say he is, a hustler who wormed his way into an inheritance, who all but murdered for money, he would probably take a decent offer of no-strings cash to get the pieces off his hands. It's not an unusual situation in my line of work, I'm afraid. *You* could go talk to him, Richard. You could ask him if he has any of the pieces here, or even photos from Freddy's estate. If you let me see them, I'll tell you what they're worth. That way, you could make a lowball offer and come out on top."

Even a rich businessman appreciated a bargain—especially a rich businessman. Nick felt certain he was winning West over. The man nodded in faster increments as the logic of the plan soaked into his brain. Nick, however, had to make sure he left no paper trail that could be used against him—just in case. "Of course, my appraisal would be purely off the record. I couldn't do a certified Wickston report, not without having to consult the office. So this arrangement would be more"—Nick rummaged his head for the term—"a favor. Just some informal advice between friends."

"Where the hell did you come from?" West demanded in the warmest tone. He offered a handshake but deemed his own outstretched hand insufficient and put his arms around Nick for a hug. Nick found himself laughing in the embrace, still dumbfounded by his success, with his arms at his sides and his chin buried in his adversary's neck.

"Let's have one last drink! A toast to you in Venice, my friend!"

As they swept open the velvet curtain and walked down the hall, the blasting disco music reached Nick with the same shock as cold wind after hours spent in a heated house. They entered the living room, where everyone was lying across the couches or sunk deep into armchairs, melting into the patterns of the house. They'd all worn themselves out, except for the lone holdout, Elisabetta, who was speed-walking around the terrazzo in circles as if she might find the right beat to set them all dancing again.

CHAPTER 8

Clay loved getting lost. It seemed like the whole point of Venice, built to trick and confuse. Taking a wrong turn and nearly plunging into a canal or skipping over a bridge that dead-ended in a brick wall was part of the town's fugitive magic. Only rarely, maybe once a year when climbing out of a midtown subway stop, did he ever lose his direction in New York.

He had already memorized a good portion of the city's terrain from his eight months living there. The northern neighborhood of Cannaregio, built on landfill instead of islands, took the shape of an elongated grid, with east-west streets stretching out like cello strings. The southern neighborhoods of San Polo and Dorsoduro were really a series of churches and squares, one feeding into the next like a trade route of interlocking kingdoms. The slow trudge of tourism around the area of San Marco turned every fast-food restaurant or brand-name boutique into an irritating landmark. Thankfully, there was still one neighborhood that Clay could count on for disorientation. In Castello he could still get hopelessly, irrevocably lost, the frantic brain tapping out the doomed distress signal, *Where the hell am I?* It was Castello where Clay arranged to meet his boyfriend at noon at the Basilica di San Giovanni e Paolo.

In theory, the massive tan-brick church should be impossible to miss. In reality, even Clay tended to stumble upon it by blind chance. He didn't even bother texting Nick more detailed directions than Follow the signs for the hospital, the church is right next door. That tip wasn't entirely helpful, as old signs for the hospital pointed one way and newer signs pointed another. In Venice, you couldn't worry about someone else's navigational chances. As with climbing Everest, you'd be lucky to make it yourself.

Sure enough, Clay found himself loping through the same minor *campo* for the third time that morning and shuffling down a promising side street only to realize he'd already gone past the shop with the delicate glass insects in the window. When he reached the Fondamenta Nuove for the second time, with its florist shops selling plastic bouquets to mourners awaiting boats to the cemetery island of San Michele, he laughed out loud. All these years, and the city could still throw his brain into slipknots. He dove back into Castello, took two turns, and for the third time that morning passed a woman in a red fedora walking an Irish setter. It was always like that in Venice: you encountered the same people over and over in the maze.

Light rain turned into a downpour. Locals collected under caffè awnings. Venetians were patient about weather. They waited with long-suffering grandparent smiles for the toddler sky to tire itself out. Clay accepted getting soaked and finally hit the basilica with one minute to spare. He entered the dark vestibule. A plastic screen had been erected just inside the nave to allow tourists a view of the interior without disturbing mass—or more likely to prevent them from entering without paying the four-euro admission fee. Clay could usually get around the fee by speaking Italian, but today he handed over two coins to the desk attendant. He felt buoyed by Nick's text message declaring his run-in with West a success.

The basilica was one of his favorite spots, not so much for its altar paintings as for its collection of interesting deaths. Twenty-seven doges had been buried in marble here—many were speed bumps randomly dispersed on the floor. But Clay's favorite was the side monument dedicated to Marco Antonio Bragadin. The sixteenth-century Venetian captain had been captured in Cyprus while fighting the Ottomans and had been treated to an unremitting barrage of tortures. His nose and ears were sliced from his face; he was dragged by a horse through the streets; tied to a ship's mast and whipped; and skinned alive from head to toe. The captain's skin had been sent to Constantinople as a war trophy. Eventually, it had been stolen back by a Venetian sailor and interred in this basilica, in an urn under the marble bust of a man gazing upward, his face saying mutely, *Wait, there's more?* It was a shrine devoted to how much pain could be inflicted on a person. But Clay knew there were other tortures, crueler ones, that the world could inflict. It could take away the people you loved. It could force you to watch them suffer without ever being able to help them. The world had endless, ingenious ways of smashing you to pieces. Clay skipped the visit to Bragadin's tomb today.

Down the basilica's center aisle ran a grove of marble columns the size of California redwoods. The air inside was cold, and the church's curved chancel reminded Clay of fingers cupped tightly around the flame of a cigarette lighter. There were few visitors this morning. Clay lingered near the front altar in the shadow of a column, checking the entrance for a sign of his boyfriend.

Nick didn't arrive at 12:05 or 12:08 or 12:13. But not long after, the door banged open and Nick slid in across the polished floor on his alligator shoes. Clay worried that Nick was going to run smack into the clear partition, but he managed to slow down in time to process it. Once Nick paid the entry fee, Clay stepped into the center aisle. They hadn't seen each other since they'd traded I-love-yous, and now Clay felt the pressure of having to test the real-time validity of those texts. Nick hurried down the aisle, his excited grin advertising good news about their plan. He stopped short a few feet away, in a puddle of white light shed from a high window. Nick's hands clenched and unclenched at his sides, as if he were hesitant to touch Clay in a Catholic church.

Nick finally lost his battle of restraint, grabbing Clay by the arm and pulling him behind the marble column. As soon as they were out of sight, he leaned in with his eyes closed. His lips initially missed Clay's mouth, catching his cheekbone with a streak of saliva, but made their way over with gentle precision. Nick was an excellent kisser. He had worked out a stealthy trick of modulation where his kisses went deep and lustful and then turned prudish and tentative as if he were battling second thoughts. After a minute, Nick pulled away. As he stepped back, he gave a slight wince.

"Blisters," he said. "My feet are killing me."

"You did too much walking in those shoes yesterday."

"Actually, it was too much dancing," he replied. When Clay looked up in confusion, he laughed. "You aren't going to believe it. Last night, I went over to West's house. He invited me to dinner at the market yesterday. Afterward, he put on disco music and we all—"

"What do you mean, you went over there?" Clay sneered. Last night, he had heard the music coming from West's side of the palazzo, just as he always heard it blasting through the walls during one of his neighbor's dinner parties. Clay had adopted Freddy's routine of sighing theatrically whenever the abominable disco tracks set the floors and bookcases vibrating. ("Of course he likes

disco!" Freddy used to hiss. "That stuff is ear poison! It's soulless-
ness set to a beat!") Clay had listened to the echoing music as he
sat in bed, his anger on a steady simmer as he went through Freddy's old diaries and drawing pads. But not once had it crossed his
mind that Nick could be on the other side of the wall, guzzling
prosecco and white-boy-bopping along with West and the other
assholes. His boyfriend had been dancing with the one man whom
he hated most. Whatever Nick's excuse was, it would still feel like
a betrayal. For a paranoid second, Clay imagined a scenario in
which he'd ripped Nick away from Ari Halfon only to deliver him
to Richard West.

"Wait!" Nick groused. "It's not the way it sounds. It's a *good*
thing!"

"Nick." Clay reached out to snap his fingers in front of his eyes.
"Can you hear me? That wasn't part of our plan. You were supposed to hand West your business card and wait for him to contact
you about the silver. You can't change the rules as you go along.
It's *our* plan, the one that *we* made *together*, and it only works if we
both follow it. It never involved you joining the Wests for dinner."

"Will you listen?" Nick pleaded. He stepped forward where a
blade of light struck his eyes—such a beautiful color, his eyes were,
a mix of autumn yellows and late-summer greens—and he immediately stepped to the side to escape it. "I knew what I was doing.
I went over there to gain his trust. A business card wasn't going to
cut it. Don't you see—he thinks of me as a *friend* now."

"Maybe you *are* his friend now," Clay said caustically. He regretted the cheap shot as soon as he uttered it. It exposed his inse-
curities too plainly.

Nick sputtered his lips. "You're being stupid. I couldn't turn
down a dinner invitation. Not after I gave him a whole story about
being alone in Venice for the first time and visiting the Titian he

restored. If I'd refused, he wouldn't bother to use my business card when the time comes."

"Does he still have that ridiculous van der Haar cupboard?" Clay asked, trying to reroute his anger onto the absent West instead of the fallible boyfriend in front of him.

Nick nodded. "Yeah, he showed it to me."

"Freddy hated him for collecting that. Despised him. West is a vulture who can't stop circling the van der Haar family carcass." Clay's own opinion of West clearly wasn't proving enough of a deterrent. He was hoping Freddy's might succeed where his failed.

"I know all about it," Nick replied. "He told me about growing up in the shadow of their mansion as a boy."

"Oh, god, that story!" Clay grunted incredulously. He wasn't entirely ready to forgive Nick yet. "Was that before or after you danced with him?"

Nick stepped forward, tolerating the stab of sunlight to the eye, and grabbed Clay's hand. "Don't be like that. I'm one hundred percent with you. And it *was* a good thing that I went over there. Don't you want to know why?"

Clay sighed in capitulation. "Okay, tell me why."

Nick began to describe the evening down to the dishware, his voice gaining texture and momentum as he set the scene for his expert handling of West. As Clay listened, he wondered whether Nick saw their plan as a game—not a life-and-death one either, but a little foreign-shore escapade that would later be glamorized into an anecdote of youthful misadventure. None of what they were doing was a game to Clay. He was depending on its success to keep his head above water. He had no backup plan if this one failed. And yet Nick was in a similar boat. He didn't have much to fall back on either. Their attitudes marked an essential difference between them, and maybe it went back to the color of their skin or how they were raised. Clay had grown up expecting every door to be nailed shut before he even reached to open it. At twenty-seven, his arms were numb from pulling on shut doors. Failure was expected. But that didn't seem to be the expectation for most of the young white transplants who flooded into New York City each year. Clay had watched them closely, as one does colonists on one's home turf. They treated the world as if they'd always be protected in it, as if they couldn't fail, as if even the dangers in the farthest corners of the night couldn't touch them. Clay wondered what it was like to feel that safe in the world.

Nick was describing entering West's office when he glanced down the aisle and his face went pale. Clay turned to find the source of his fright. Against the bright light of the open doors, a woman stood at the back of the church, her arm raised, waving a yellow handkerchief in their direction. She whipped her arm back and forth the way a cruise-ship passenger leaving a port dramatically waves goodbye. She wore a brown skirt and a white blouse and had a shadow for a face.

"Oh, shit!" Nick whispered as he ducked behind the column. "She saw us together! *Shit, shit!*"

Clay continued to study the woman, trying to figure out who she could be. When his eyes adjusted to the light, he realized Nick's mistake: it was the desk attendant, and she wasn't waving. She was wiping the plastic partition with a yellow rag. Clay laughed as he followed Nick behind the column.

"It's just the woman from the ticket booth."

Nick clutched his forehead. "I thought it was West's niece."

Clay felt relieved that Nick was at least taking matters seriously enough to be frightened of their discovery. "You still haven't explained why last night was a good idea."

Nick licked his lips to indicate he was nearing the best part. "I convinced West to go to you directly about the silver. Honestly, that was always my problem with our plan. It was too coincidental that I show up with my business card one day, and you knock on his door offering van der Haar antiques the next. But last night, West asked if I knew about Freddy's collection. I said I didn't. But I recommended that he talk to you about it and that I bet you'd take a decent offer in cash if there happened to be any lying around. Don't you see? It's so much smoother this way. And now you have the advantage because he's the one who's coming to you, and not the other way around. We're halfway there already!"

Clay had to admit, it was a much smarter arrangement. Nick had managed to propel them several steps ahead. "All right," he said nodding. "I give you credit."

"So you forgive me?" Nick asked with an anxious smile.

"Yes. But, Nick, listen. You've got to—" and here Clay stumbled because he couldn't find the right words to warn him about West. Nick seemed particularly susceptible to the approval and affection of older men. But Clay wouldn't risk saying that outright. In their two months together, they'd managed to stride boldly through a field of touchy subjects—money, sex, monogamy—where others would have inched on tiptoe. But there had been one ugly argument between them. It had been back in New York when Clay mentioned how crazy it was—this late in life, this early in a brand-new century—that Nick hadn't come out to his family. "Why don't you just talk to them?" Clay had asked flippantly. "Is it even a big deal anymore?" Clay had hoped a hard push would encourage Nick to take the necessary leap. But Nick's face went red and he took a choppy breath before replying with the counterpunch, "Why don't you talk to your father anymore?"

Clay measured his words carefully now. "I'm just saying, you have to be on your guard. West can fool you with his warmth and invitations, and you'll end up blowing the whole thing because you decide he's your friend. He's a manipulator. I was fooled by him once."

Nick nodded through the warning. He stepped closer, his warm breath spilling over Clay's face. "I'm not worried," he whispered. "Look, I won't lie to you. I don't hate him. I hope he never finds out he's being cheated. But he's not someone I care about. Can we go back to Daniela's for a little while?"

Clay snorted. "We can't use Daniela's apartment as a sex den all the time."

"Just for a half an hour. We'll be super quick."

Clay was about to risk another kiss when he heard an approaching squeak behind him. A tobacco-skinned old woman with a wedge of peroxide-yellow hair was pushing a similarly colored and peroxided man in a wheelchair. Both of their faces were sharp and pointed, but it was the wheelchair that struck Clay as fantastical. In Venice, it was nearly impossible to get around by wheelchair—there were pedestrian step bridges every ten feet. Clay knew there were other humans like him, so addicted to this city that they would go to miraculous lengths to stay as long as they could. The wheelchair stopped, and the intruding couple gazed apologetically. The woman struggled to turn her husband around.

Nick ran over to help; one of the wheels had gotten stuck in a doge's crypt. Clay was awed by Nick's endless reserve of kindness to strangers. It was one of the things he loved most about him. How had seven years in New York City not leached that quality out of him? Maybe kindness explained why Nick hadn't told his family the truth, and maybe it also explained why he was in Venice right now trying to save Clay from his quicksand of debt. Kindness was unrealistic and probably dangerous and certainly insane. And yet, as Clay watched his boyfriend free the chair and push the old man smoothly forward, he was certain it was the most beautiful trait in the world.

"I'm sorry I gave you a hard time," Clay said when he returned. Nick tried to respond, but Clay spoke over him. "You leave now. I follow in five minutes and meet you in the garden. But only if Daniela isn't home. And we have to be super quick."

Whenever Clay's keys clattered in the lock of Il Dormitorio, any interns who happened to be home scattered like cats. He could hear them scurrying to the sanctuary of their drywall bedrooms before he made it up the steps. From his perspective as landlord, the house seemed to be inhabited by a congregation of international, adolescent ghosts. Concert flyers, gutted care packages bearing postage-stamp quilts, and discarded pharmacy boxes littered the kitchen table. The dishes were never washed, juice bottles were tossed from well beyond the three-point line in the direction of the trash can, and foreign phrases punctuated with smiling or frowning faces crowded the refrigerator's dry-erase board. The interns were obedient only when it came to the single long-standing house rule: they managed to keep their mess off the ceiling. Everywhere else, it spread like a suburb.

Clay could have hated them for their clutter, just as he could have taken their avoidance of him as a personal slight. But he'd once been on the other side of this peculiar landlord-renter relationship, and he knew that the higher-ups at the Peggy Guggenheim had driven the fear of the very old, unnamed American family into each one of them. The interns were clearly wary of Clay, even after their initial surprise of finding that the heir of this very old, unnamed American family did not appear in the shape, color, or age that they'd imagined. In truth, Clay would have liked to take his tenants out for pizza. He would have willingly offered them advice on their museum tours or how to skip the line for vaporetto tickets. He was, after all, only a few years older than they were. But it was probably best to keep the relationship formal and remote. Only Clay had managed to cross the chasm between renter and owner, and he still wasn't sure it had been worth the price.

As he reached the door to Freddy's private quarters, he found a sealed red envelope wedged into the frame. One of the interns must have brought it in from outside. There was no indication of the sender, and only Clay's first name was hand-printed on the envelope's top corner. Nevertheless, Clay recognized the stationery. In fact, he knew from a brief stint working for its sender that the stationery came from a little shop on the Zattere, and that the sender stowed the sheets in a Florentine wood box in his desk drawer.

Clay unlocked the door, pulled off his jacket, and sat on the bed. He noticed that his shirt was misbuttoned. He'd dressed quickly after sex to leave Daniela's apartment before she returned. He didn't want to annoy her by adding to the intrusion upon her personal space. Nick had been predictably uncooperative, wrapping his arms around Clay's thighs as he was trying to climb into his pants. "Come on, stop," Clay told him. But eventually he'd relented and tumbled back onto the bed to collect as much of that inordinately long body as he could in his arms. Now, an hour later, Clay's body carried the achy reminder of those twenty extra minutes; his limbs felt as if they were moving underwater. Still, Clay could think of Nick naked right now and grow hungry for him all over again.

Clay slit the envelope open. West's gold initials crowned the top of the paper as they always had. The note was written in black ink, the scrawl a fluid, continuous forward tilt like a cresting ocean wave.

Clay,

Happy to be back in Venice? I again want to extend my condolences for the loss of our beloved Freddy. [*Our,* Clay reeled; there was no worse sin than inventing a close friendship with the dead.] *I'd love to invite you over for a drink <u>this week</u>. We haven't had a real talk in years, my friend.* [Friend!] *Also, there is a matter, a proposal, I'd like to discuss with you, one that might be mutually beneficial. It might even make life easier for you in dealing with Freddy's estate. I know we've had our differences. But as neighbors, it's time to put them behind us. Let me know if you're free <u>this week</u>—tomorrow, or even this afternoon?*

Sincerely,
Richard

Clay particularly appreciated the twin underlining of "this week." It might disguise itself as an eagerness to make peace, but Clay knew the real reason for the expedience: West's secret silver appraiser was only in town for a short time. He'd want to get those pieces in front of his new Wickston coconspirator before he left for Milan.

Could it really be this easy? Could West feel like he was pulling one over on him while all along Clay was doing him one better? Clay could forgive Nick for not wanting to hurt West with their scam. But for him, watching West fall victim to his own greed felt like justice. After his mother had died, he assumed he couldn't suffer any further. Nothing else could touch him, large or small, because he'd filled his quota on pain. But the loss of a parent doesn't immunize a person from betrayal any more than surviving a shark bite protects its victim from a car crash. West had cheated Clay when he was at his most vulnerable. Why should it bother him to settle that score?

Clay didn't wait another minute to answer West's letter. After all, it was essential that West get those pieces in front of his secret silver appraiser as soon as possible. Clay took out his phone and dialed. He couldn't hear the rings through the walls, but he liked imagining West rushing through his ornate rooms to reach them.

"Hello?" the familiar voice squawked.

"It's your neighbor."

"Clay!" West all but screamed. "You got my note. I handed it to an intern. But you never know whether . . . Well, it got to you."

"It got to me," he confirmed.

"I'm glad you called. How about a drink tonight at my place? Shall we say seven?"

Man, he was eager. But Clay wasn't going to make it too easy for him. He had promised himself never again to set foot on West's side of the palazzo. So, for once, they would meet on Clay's terms.

"I'm curious about your proposal," Clay said coolly. "But this evening's no good for me. How about you stop over here tomorrow around one p.m.?"

"Oh," exhaled a man unaccustomed to accommodating other people's schedules. "Okay. It's a bit early for a drink, but why not? Shall I knock four times on the connecting door?"

"There are too many boxes in Freddy's bedroom," Clay lied, simply to make the proceedings one degree more difficult for Richard West. "Come to the front door and ring the bell."

When they hung up, Clay unzipped one of his suitcases from New York, its handle still wrapped in the sticky tag marked JFK TO VCE. Freddy's ashes hadn't been the only contraband Clay sneaked through Italian customs. Digging through an outer layer of sweaters and an inner layer of Bubble Wrap, he excavated the five silver vessels that remained of Freddy's forgeries. As he set them around the room—on a bookshelf, tucked behind the lamp on the nightstand—he quietly recited his mantra for tomorrow. *I will not feel guilt or shame. I will not be sympathetic to him. I will take as much as I can get. He will lose. I will win.*

CHAPTER 9

Whatever one's particular opinion on the subject of horse statues, erect penises, or the Italian artist Marino Marini, very few visitors could argue that the bronze sculpture adorning the terrace of the Peggy Guggenheim Collection was not a thing of joy. The bulky body of a man, fully aroused, his dick pointing toward the basin of the Grand Canal, straddled a horse with arms outstretched and his head proudly lifted to the sky. The work is a hug to the sun, a giving over of individual life to the idea of life, the freedom of the flasher offering his imperfect body in the marketplace of human desires. Not a single day of Clay's internship went by without his drawing inspiration from Marini's *Angel of the City*. He wasn't alone in his appreciation. It had become a ritual among the museum's interns—whether straight or gay; female, transgender, or male; American, Portuguese, or Hong Konger—to give the erection a quick tug for luck when passing along the terrace. The Marini was, Clay felt sure, the most jerked-off artwork on the planet.

But there were other works inside the low-sitting, Istrian-stone palazzo that pulled with more ferocity on his soul. The lonely de Chiricos, the LSD-laced Max Ernsts, the chimpanzee trapped in a void of magenta in the nightmarish Francis Bacon painting. "I hope they give you long breaks," many visitors whispered to Clay when he was on guard duty in one of the museum galleries. "It must get so boring to stand in the same place all day!" They couldn't have been more wrong. Clay adored his days cycling through the rooms. He got to know every individual artwork as intimately as a heartbeat, every stroke of paint, every sharp ascending line of a polished Brancusi, every scrap of a Cubist collage. Clay was a freak even among the art freaks of the internship: Clay *loved* guarding duty. He also loved selling tickets at the front desk and checking bags and coats at the *guardaroba*. He could practice his Italian; he could give suggestions on special exhibits; he could dash off gossip about Peggy G. and her wayward, suicidal daughter, Pegeen, as well as Peggy's scandalous affairs with artists; he could promote his own twice-a-week tour of the grounds—all to spread the Good News of this nirvana-like institution that had saved him: saved him from America, saved him from what to do after he graduated from college, and, most of all, saved him from the gutting loss of his mother. Her death had taken on a geographical dimension. All that heartbreak existed across the ocean in New York. Here in Venice, and more specifically inside the marble walls of the museum, he was safe from it. Don't listen to therapists: it is entirely possible to run away from yourself.

His internship was supposed to last three months. His return ticket had him flying home on September 1. But Clay Guillory stuck out among the crop of summer interns, partly for his impressive grasp of the Italian language, and partly because his curious, unspoiled, ever-eager disposition made him the favorite of the senior staff. The shaggy-haired Italian supervisor reported back every time he received a visitor compliment. And the museum's venerated director, a quiet, erudite man with bushy, metallic-gray brows that hung like bunting over his eyes—a man who seemed to move phantomlike through the museum because he was rarely sighted by the interns—stopped Clay twice in the courtyard to praise him when he'd overheard a snippet of his tour speech. Clay had proved himself a dedicated member of the Peggy Guggenheim family, and he would have done anything—really almost anything short of murder—for the museum. When the supervisor asked if he'd like to extend his internship by three months—they'd pay for a new return ticket—he practically wept. Six months in his favorite museum in his favorite city! Six months in his tiny bedroom in Il Dormitorio and eating breakfast under the Blue Madonna fresco! Six months masturbating the Marini and pushing audio guides on culture-starved Nordic couples who had just been unpenned from their cruise ships! If asked, he might have agreed to sign on for life.

Clay deserved the praise as star intern. Most of his peers arrived in Venice with twenty cocktail outfits and not a lick of practical Italian. Clay had trained like a marathoner for six months before he landed. In Italy, his tongue caught fire. He was the intern to order for everyone at restaurants and to organize their weekend trips to Tuscany and to write down their exact hairstyle preferences so they had only to slip the stylist a piece of paper to make their instructions clear. Clay also became something of a guidance counselor for the new arrivals, many of whom, like himself, had never lived in a foreign country before. He discovered that his generation was particularly prone to homesickness. Clay, who wasn't homesick, who in fact associated home *with* sickness and who never wanted to go back, would take these misanthropes under his wing until they too discovered the Good News of Peggy.

Clay wasn't the only success story that summer. A twenty-two-year-old Swiss intern named Bridget Messmer had also been asked to stay on for three months. Bridget had white-blond hair that curled angelically across her tiny forehead. She had a very sweet smile and said very sweet things in Italian, French, German, and English. The other women on the internship hated Bridget for her prettiness, her Sorbonne education, and her indifference to fostering friendships with any of them. Bridget was the kind of person who didn't seem to want more friends; there were no reports of her ever displaying a sense of humor. Even the supervisor stopped bothering to invite her to the Friday-night intern pizza party in the downstairs break room. Bridget did not live at Il Dormitorio but in some unnamed piano nobile that her wealthy parents had secured. Clay really couldn't say a mean word against her, which, in his estimation, was a mean word against her. In retrospect, it seemed predestined that Bridget Messmer would prove the catalyst of his downfall.

Clay hadn't spoken to his father once since he left New York. He had not called nor emailed nor under any circumstance would he conjure his face in the watery portal of Skype. Clay felt bad about the distance, but every time he resolved to make contact, his stomach would spin on tumble-dry. He couldn't field questions about his mother just like he couldn't go back to that hospital room with its darkening view of Manhattan—not even for a few minutes over a telephone. Italy was his escape. Here, he was no one's son.

Instead, he wrote his father postcards, one each week, all sunrises and sunsets over the Grand Canal, with humdrum descriptions of his job at the museum. He included one lie. He told his father he'd found a boyfriend, a Venetian architect he was crazy about. Clay invented the architect so that his father wouldn't think of him as lonely; he might let go of his son more easily, knowing he had someone else. The truth wouldn't have paired well with the romantic postcard shots of gondolas slipping under the Rialto Bridge: Clay was lonely. Outside of the museum, he didn't have anyone at all. Then, in September, on a precarious rooftop ledge, he met Richard Forsyth West.

Looking back, West must have been haunting Clay's periphery in the Cannaregio neighborhood for months without his noticing. As dashing as West appeared to Clay once he knew him, as a stranger he would have been just another wealthy, well-dressed American retiree. They shared a wall, a canal, and a street that fed into their separate entrances. But they met at Clay's work.

Six days a week, the Peggy Guggenheim opened itself to all visitors who shelled out the twenty-euro ticket price. On certain nights, however, after the catering companies docked at the museum's slip with their coolers of food and racks of wineglasses, the museum's interiors and gardens were accessible only by invitation. Occasionally the roof of the palazzo was made available via a side staircase for drinks. There had been several such private parties over the summer, and Clay had been invited to none of them. But with his new status as favored intern, he had finally been asked to attend. "Smile, be respectful, talk to anyone who seems alone," his supervisor instructed. "And please, *please* let them know you've enjoyed your internship!" Clay was nervous, twenty-three years old, and unfamiliar with patron cocktail banter, but he was eager to exploit his privileges. Naturally, Bridget had also been invited. As he stood stock-still on the museum's rooftop, he watched pretty Bridget move like a veteran among the important guests. She wore a long cornflower dress and sipped prudently on club soda, and Clay suspected that this rooftop party hadn't been her first that summer. If Bridget exemplified the internship program's international sophistication, Clay supposed he embodied its diversity, a fact he loved and abhorred in equal measure. But he would do his internship proud tonight. He would smile. He would talk up the program. He would rescue the lonely from themselves.

The summer's humidity had clung to the Adriatic seaside that September. The evening light was a tarnished copper, coloring the palazzi along the Grand Canal a hazy, Middle Eastern umber. Late summer brought out the Byzantine. It also brought out sweat rings around the collar of Clay's one decent dress shirt. Dry cleaning in Venice was too expensive for his weekly stipend, so he wore the shirt buttoned to the Adam's apple.

Clay looked for people to save. He worried the supervisor would catch him doing nothing, talking to nobody, and it would be a strike on his record. The nearest bodies were blasted by the orange radiation of the sunset; behind them lay a shaded, impenetrable forest of partygoers. That's when Clay noticed a flash of white hair and the face it helmeted, a handsome older man who looked like he could be herding cattle in an old cigarette ad. Their eyes met, and Clay glanced shyly away. When he looked back, their eyes met again. It kept happening in this flirtatious manner, away and back, away and back. Clay appreciated the attention, particularly in light of his Venetian dry spell. In truth, he'd never found himself attracted to older white men. White guys in general had remained something of a mystery. His first boyfriend in high school had been Vietnamese, the second (his prom date) Bangladeshi, and he'd dated a Jamaican for two years of college, even introducing Mark to his parents (how his mother had swooned over hunky Mark). He figured his first memorable Caucasian would be a Venetian, but instead *nulla e niente*. Before he knew it, though, this handsome older man appeared at his elbow, wearing a crisp white suit and green velvet slippers. There was a tiny red slash on the lower corner of his shirt, right at his ribs; Clay initially confused it for blood, but upon closer inspection realized it was a monogram: R.F.W.

The man was chatting with a woman cocooned in navy lace, and he was using his wineglass like a magnifying glass to illustrate an anecdote. Suddenly a passing waiter knocked the woman in lace off balance. She fell against the white-haired man, who himself tripped backward, his feet drawing perilously close to the roof's low ledge. Clay thrust his arm out, grasped the man's shoulder, and tugged him away from the drop.

"Whoa," the man roared as he registered the jeopardy he'd been in. Thirty feet below the ledge was the erect Marini statue. "Thank you." Then he turned to the woman next to him. "Silvana, you nearly killed me!"

"Sorry," she muttered in the hostile tone of someone whose philosophy is never to apologize.

The man patted Clay on the back. "You're Clay Guillory, right?"

"Yes," he replied, taken aback. "I am."

"I've heard about you. Intern extraordinaire!"

Clay didn't realize he had a reputation. "Well," he answered demurely. "Let's not go too far."

The man laughed, raising an eyebrow dotted with a mole. "You're not making this easy for me!" He extended his hand, which Clay shook. "Richard Forsyth West," he said. West's fingernails were manicured, but his palm was calloused. "It's nice to meet you. I was told you might be interested in some extra work on your days off. For pay, of course."

An *Oh* escaped Clay's lips. It was a collective *Oh* encapsulating two distinct disappointments: *Oh, you aren't interested in me sexually.* And *Oh, the museum thinks I'm a charity case in need of extra money.* Clay's eyes sought out the traitorous shaggy-haired supervisor on the rooftop.

"I'm sorry. Did that come out badly?" West asked earnestly. "I get ahead of myself. You see, I'm starting my own preservation society in Venice." He laughed again. "Society of one, to be honest. You're looking at the one. I hope I'm looking at the second. It's an organization dedicated to the conservation of monuments that no one around here seems to be in a rush to protect, mostly because of the Italian bureaucracy and paperwork that ties every hand before it can so much as point." West nudged Clay's elbow. "What's Italy's biggest contribution to modern civilization besides pasta and paparazzi?" West had already stepped on his own joke, and Clay wouldn't indulge him by speaking the canned answer: *paperwork.* "Anyway, I asked Peggy Guggenheim who her best intern is. I want an American, someone smart, but I also want someone who speaks Italian. Peggy said 'Clay Guillory.' Only she promised I couldn't steal you from her. Apparently, you're too valuable. All I'm allowed to ask is if you're interested in helping out on my project on your days off."

West was a charming salesman for himself. His beseeching expression and self-deprecating humor softened the blow of dual disappointments. And Clay was certain that he sensed a playful flirtation in the wide eyes and the toying smile.

"Peggy told you all that, did she?"

West was studying his face carefully, his blue eyes flickering. "You can tell me to stop bothering you. Feel free to walk away."

Clay began spending his two days off each week from the Peggy Guggenheim at West's palazzo. Although they technically shared a roof and there was a rumor of a secret connecting door, Clay left Il Dormitorio on his free Sundays and Mondays, walked down the alley, turned left, commuted ten yards, passed through a garden, and used the key that West had given him to access Palazzo Contarini. Yes, the whopping three hundred euros per day was enough of an incentive—Clay was barely scraping by on the museum salary, and his college-loan payments loomed at the end of the year like muggers waiting outside the gates of Port Authority. But Clay actually enjoyed spending his days with Richard West. A majority of the work was relegated to menial assistant tasks—stocking office supplies, updating West's brand-new and ultimately short-lived website, making reservations at restaurants with local conservators, ordering his suits from tailors in Naples and Turin. But one afternoon each week was always devoted to "site visits," which consisted of the two men venturing out together to explore a small church on the island of Torcello or investigating a dilapidated Bellini painting in an abandoned barracks near the Giardini. They talked about their upbringings. West had grown up poor, "as poor as concrete because we didn't have a backyard with dirt, because dirt cost too much." He had earned his zillions in the 1990s investing in California technology from the comforts of his Chicago office. "People attack you if your money comes from the Internet," West said. "They think you've ruined the world. But don't blame the medium for what your fellow man used it for! My belief has always been, when you see an opportunity, take it. You can brood over the ethics later." West talked a tough game, but Clay sensed that the role of Evil Tech Lord had left its wounds. Perhaps that explained West's passion for safeguarding the relics of Venice. He wanted to do something that he could point to and say with absolute assurance, "There! It's better now."

Two days each week plotting strategies to save Venice, the remaining five keeping his true love, Peggy, guarded and coat-checked and buzzing with happy visitors. It was paradise with money in the bank. The arrival of Richard West hadn't entirely cured Clay's loneliness—his eyes still hunted for golden boys on his walks to work—but he'd found a companion, someone to confide in and to laugh with. West had been divorced for seven years and was "mildly maybe dating" a woman who ran a hospital in

Germany that specialized in research on the brain. And yet there was an intimacy to their walks and dinners and jokes that confused Clay; had West's vague flirtations ever advanced into an unmistakable expression of interest, he might have entertained the possibility of more between them. Once, after letting himself into the palazzo a few minutes early, Clay caught the reflection of West toweling off after a shower in the bathroom mirror. Clay allowed himself to examine the older man's thick, burly body, one foot anchored on the toilet seat, the purple sac of testicles hanging below his round ass, the circular scar from a childhood TB shot pressed like a time stamp into the upper arm, a slice of frost-white hair dangling over the prominent forehead.

For all of West's networking and social engagements, it was clear that he too was lonely in Venice. A month into their arrangement, the two began having dinners together on nights that weren't Sunday or Monday, at different Michelin stars around town. They often texted each other at night. Clay had never stepped foot in West's bedroom; the doors were always shut. But he liked to imagine West in bed on the other side of the wall, laughing at whatever joke Clay had just zapped over to him.

One night as Clay lay in his own bed, unable to sleep, slapping mosquitoes on his arms and counting the others perched patiently in the rafters—the mosquitoes in Venice were wilier hunters than the blood-drunk idiots that came right at you in New York—his phone beeped with an incoming text from his boss.

Please take a picture of it. I'm dying to see what it looks like.

I don't know, Clay texted back. Might get me in trouble. I wouldn't want anyone to know I'm sending it around. It's private.

I'm not going to tell anyone. Come on, just take a couple quick shots of it right now.

"It" was the Blue Madonna fresco by Sebastiano Ricci on Il

Dormitorio's kitchen ceiling. Clay knew all about West's un-
healthy obsession with the van der Haar family and the treasures
they'd once amassed—he uttered that last name, van der Haar,
with the kind of reverential awe that teenagers reserve for Italian
sports cars or French fashion designers. West had never managed
to secure an invitation inside Il Dormitorio from its current heirs,
and he occasionally drilled Clay on any hidden riches it still might
hold.

Clay sneaked into the kitchen, turned on the lights, and, in what
felt like a weird violation of her privacy, snapped a few photos of
the nude Madonna on his phone. He texted them over to West.
Ahh, wow, yes, beautiful, thank you . . . If only Freddy and his sister took
care of it like I would.

That busy, hopeful autumn passed too quickly. November
brought chilly Adriatic rains and a future in peril. The Venetians
had their tricks to mitigate the notorious *acqua alta* that flooded the
city during high tides. They boarded up the bottoms of their doors
with slats and assembled long wood beams as planks for piazza
crossings; they donned special plastic knee-high boots over shoes
to wade through *campo* lakes; they placed the legs of their furniture
in vases and cups to protect them from the surging water. Clay's
future, however, remained impervious to small acts of deterrence.
His internship would end along with the month, and without a job
or a visa, he was required to return to the United States. He didn't
want to go back. His very survival depended on staying.

Peggy once again offered salvation. One morning as Clay was
leaving the *guardaroba* station, the supervisor pulled him aside in
the garden. With an uncharacteristic grin, she notified him that
he was being considered for the Capo position. Clay was vaguely
aware that there had once been a job nestled somewhere in the
museum hierarchy between the interns and the supervisor, but he

had assumed it had long been scrapped due to budget cuts. No, the supervisor explained, there simply hadn't been any recent candidates in the intern pool to their liking. Now they had two candidates, and Clay was one of them—if he was interested. Was he?

The miraculous part was that Capo was a full-time post with a working visa and a living wage. No, he wouldn't get rich off the position, but it would allow him to stay in the city of his dreams and continue working in the museum he loved. "Yes, consider me! Please!" he begged the supervisor, who assured him that both candidates would be assessed fairly. It was only after she darted across the courtyard that Clay spied his obvious competition. Bridget Messmer was leading three rotund Saudi sheiks on a tour of the outdoor sculptures. The sheiks demanded to take a picture of pretty blond Bridget, and she reluctantly consented to pose in Peggy's iconic stone chair.

"I need this job," Clay confided to West over dinner that night at Da Arturo, a tiny, airless trattoria off San Marco. "I don't think I've ever wanted anything so much in my life. They *can't* give it to Bridget."

West nodded and pushed a plate of fried squid toward Clay. "You'll get it," he said confidently. "No one has worked harder than you or cares about the museum as much. This other candidate doesn't stand a chance."

"Bridget Messmer." Just saying Bridget's name caused Clay's mouth muscles to tighten. "She's supersmart, superambitious, super everything."

"No match for you," West replied and reached across the table to grip Clay's knuckles. "And if they're stupid enough not to pick you, something else will come along. Because you're young, this seems like the be-all, end-all. But, I swear to you—listen to an old man—there's more out there if this job doesn't work out."

Clay shook his head and pushed West's hand away. He refused the comfort of a soft crash landing. "You don't understand. There aren't other jobs. Not like this one. That museum is where I want to be. Plus, it offers a work visa so I can stay in Italy." He was on his fourth glass of wine, and the next declaration burst out without thought. "I can't go back to New York. Not after my mom died. My life is in Venice now."

West wiped his mouth with his napkin and poured more wine in their glasses. "You're going to get it, all right? Stop worrying." Clay noticed that West's eyes were glassy—not crying exactly, but more like the first symptoms of an allergy. West stared down at the table. "I suppose being Capo means you won't have time to work on our projects—*my* projects—anymore."

Clay laughed. It was a good feeling, this rarity of being in high demand. "Probably not," he said. "But you're going to need someone full time soon anyway. And, as Capo, I can send the best interns your way. Hey, I can still order your suits if that's what you're worried about."

West smiled and leaned back in his chair. "Even if we aren't working together, you can always depend on me. I want you to know that." West snapped his fingers and pointed across the table like a reprimanding father. "Under no circumstances are you going back, do you hear me?"

"Yes, sir!"

"*New York*," he grumbled. "Only in New York City and a few war-torn parts of East Africa is mere survival considered an accomplishment. New York's fine, but *Venice*—" he said that word like he said *van der Haar*—"is living."

It proved nearly impossible to outshine Bridget Messmer at the museum. Clay possessed American charm, the national anthem of a white smile and a friendly greeting, and the willingness to work morning to night on any task without complaint. But Bridget had her native country's formidable efficiency, her sober Swiss reason, the effortless, almost meteorological ability to forecast tourist congestion and direct visitor traffic flow. In the days before the final decision was made, Clay felt like he was dancing for his life, while Bridget was probably filing the museum's tax returns. Every morning before work he slipped into a different church, plunked a euro into the metal box as the signs charged per prayer, and lit a candle.

The supervisor led him downstairs into the break room, shut the door, and allowed him to sit down at the conference table before she delivered the bad news. The walls of the break room were painted the brightest yellow, a shade that Clay might later describe as happiness-at-gunpoint yellow. But as the supervisor spoke, all the yellow went gray. "We've decided to offer the job to the other candidate," she told him, her hands clenched in front of her in a defensive posture. Clay heard the verdict, although his heart must not have because it continued to beat. In fact, it was beating so loudly in his ears that for a few seconds its throbbing was all he could absorb, just his heart beating in the basement of a palazzo in a watery city four thousand miles from New York. "I'm very sorry, Clay. I know you wanted the job. And we've appreciated your dedication to the Peggy Guggenheim for these six months. I hope they've been beneficial to you. Of course, you can stay in the room you're renting for another two weeks. And, as promised, we *will* be providing your airfare home."

Clay's eyes were burning under the glare of track lights. The faux-wood conference table with its shiny veneer surface was equally painful to look at.

"So you chose the pretty white girl," he finally said.

The supervisor's eyes widened. She looked alarmed but also,

with her sucked-in cheeks, determined to withstand the fallout. "Please, Clay," she said sternly. "That's not fair to Bridget."

Richard West was the person he ran to for consolation that afternoon. Clay sat in West's living room on a leather footstool he'd dragged into a slant of bright winter sun, while West paced in circles behind him. Here, in this sanctuary, Clay could allow himself to cry. "I'm going back in two weeks." Two weeks; no visa; a one-way ticket to New York; his angry, miserable father.

"Complete idiots not to promote you!" West stormed around, bare feet slapping the terrazzo. "It's their loss. They'll never find anybody as talented and diligent. What idiots!" He circled and circled and stopped. Clay didn't dare to turn around. "You know, this doesn't mean you have to go."

"What?" Clay asked in a confused tone that wasn't entirely ingenuous. He had hoped that West might throw him a lifeline. "What do you mean?"

"Stay!" West cried. "You said yourself that I need someone full time once the projects finally get under way." He grinned down at Clay in a flush of excitement. "You can work for me! That way you don't have to go back! We'll figure out your visa. You're out of your mind if you think I'm letting you go!"

It was far from his dream job, but it would keep him in Venice. Clay's savior had spoken on cue.

One mild afternoon a few weeks later, Clay was hurrying through the neighborhood of San Polo, finishing up an errand for his boss. His mind was on his impending move from Il Dormitorio. He'd found a cheap garret studio by the Ghetto that was a six-minute walk from Palazzo Contarini. Distracted with thoughts of packing, he took a wrong turn and found himself in a small, unfamiliar *campo*. On one side stood a dusty porcelain shop and, on the other, a caffè with a pink-striped awning shading two outdoor tables. As Clay stumbled toward the square's iron cistern, he discerned an owlish face in the shadow of the striped awning. It was the director of the Peggy Guggenheim. He sat alone reading a newspaper, his tweed blazer caped around his shoulders. Clay's first instinct was to turn and flee before being spotted. But three steps into his escape, he stopped. Why should he run? He was allowed to walk through the city. He was even allowed to say hello to this man. Clay spun around and forced himself to walk calmly toward the caffè. Each advancing step offered Clay's brain time to propose new and persuasive reasons to flee. But it was too late.

"Hello, Mr. Guillory," the director said graciously, shading his eyes with his hand. The man remembered his name. Clay had expected aloofness, dismissiveness, or even downright rudeness; he was unprepared for kindness. "I'm afraid you've discovered where I hide myself after work to cheat on my wife with a crossword puzzle."

"I hope I'm not intruding," Clay said. The director shook his head and gestured to the empty chair across from him. "Oh, that's okay," Clay replied. "I really just wanted to stop to thank you." The director raised his bushy eyebrows in curiosity. "My internship at the Guggenheim—"

"—at the Peggy Guggenheim," the director corrected.

"Yes, the Peggy." Clay felt his face grow warm. "It meant the world to me. I loved every second of it. And even if I wasn't selected for the promotion, well, the internship saved me. I mean that literally. It turned my life around. So thank you."

The director gazed across the *campo* for a minute, as if pondering an answer for his crossword puzzle. His eyes drifted back to Clay. "You're welcome. And thank you too. Thank you not only for being one of the most dedicated interns we've had in recent memory but for marching up to me right now and saying what you did." The director picked up his ballpoint pen and tapped it against his newspaper. "Now that we have each other's confidence, I will say that I was taken aback when I heard what you thought of us. We've always prided ourselves on our inclusivity. I don't know what we could have done to treat you better, Clay, but if you were unhappy and felt disrespected from day one, I wish you had said something."

"What?" Clay's hands curled around the back of the empty chair. "What are you talking about? I never said I felt disrespected. I was never unhappy. I never had one bad thought about you or the museum! Not on day one or on day one hundred and eighty!"

The director's mouth shrunk to a lipless seam, as if he were smiling through a toothache. He managed not to blink first in the ensuing staring contest. "Let's not dredge it all up again," the director said. "I'm happy you enjoyed the internship. *Basta!* That's what matters. Whatever you said to Dick about the museum and whatever Dick told me when we were making our decision for Capo shall remain among the three of us. Does that sound fair?"

It would be an exaggeration to presume that Clay set the world record for the fastest sprint between that particular *campo* in San Polo and the doorstep of Palazzo Contarini in Cannaregio. Surely at some point in the past half millennium of their coexistence, somebody had not only run this exact route through the city but had also beaten Clay by a fraction of a second. Nevertheless, by the time Clay crossed the last stone bridge, his knees ached and he tasted blood in his mouth. He was running so he didn't have to think or hate or regret. He was running because he was in danger of exploding as soon as he stopped. In the palazzo's faded garden, he fished the spare key out of his pocket, opened the iron door, and took the steps two at a time up to the piano nobile of West's retirement home.

The lights were on. An orchestral piece, heavy on violas, warbled on the stereo. A pair of white trousers and a white sports coat lay in a sloppy pile on the floor. Clay's eyes landed on the set of oak doors that led into West's bedroom. For the very first time, those doors were open. Clay walked softly toward the bedroom. This must be how murderers or thieves walk through their victims' homes, he thought.

West had tricked him. He had robbed him of the one thing he'd wanted most in order to keep his loyal, grateful servant who could now be available full time at his beck and call. Clay stood at the threshold of the open doors, aware that he must be visible to anyone within the bedroom's darkness. He had no idea how large this room was or where it would lead.

"Come in," West called. "I need you."

Stepping into the dark, he picked up the scents of juniper and jasmine. He stopped in front of a bedframe. On the mattress he could just make out West's body: his muscly arms stretched out across a bank of white pillows, the chum of his hairy stomach protruding between a ribbed undershirt and a pair of boxer shorts. One leg was elevated on a stack of pillows, dangling a wiggling foot, which appeared in the darkness almost like an outstretched hand expecting to be kissed.

"Thank god you're here!" the voice boomed. "I twisted my ankle getting off the *traghetto* at Santa Sofia. I had to hop all the way home." There was a pause before the voice returned. "What's wrong? Oh, don't worry. An ice pack might be all it needs." A hand fumbled along the wall and found a light switch. The man he hated was directly in front of him, sprawled across his king-size bed.

West smiled cheerfully at Clay as if the twisted ankle was nothing more than fodder for a joke to be relayed over dinner that night. But his expression abruptly shifted. "Don't turn around," West ordered. "Or do. I've never realized how awful they are until this second. The past can be so offensive, can't it?"

Clay turned. On either side of the doors was the frescoed figure of a Moor. These two black men were shirtless. One carried the weight of a boulder on his shoulders; the other was posed in an effeminate contrapposto, holding up a bolt of diaphanous silk. Long-dead servants without names.

"Awful, isn't it?" West said when Clay glared back at him. "Unfortunately, we can't paint over them. But just because they're important artworks doesn't mean we can't cover them with a curtain."

Clay didn't care which horrible reality West was trying to amend. It was too late for any understanding between them. Clay's only thought was, You motherfucker. Tossing the spare key on the bed, he hissed, "I quit."

He bolted down the steps and across the garden. He ran for ten yards through the city he loved before he turned down the alley to Il Dormitorio. Once there, he slowed to a stagger with his hands braced behind his head. He got to the paint-chipped front door and crumpled against it, bawling into the doorframe. He cried for ten minutes or twenty, or maybe it was only two. He had no idea how long he stood there with his forehead pressed against the wood and his face muscles aching from the exertion. It was the sound of footsteps echoing down the alley that brought him back to the world.

"You there," a man behind him called. "Hey, you, by the door, crying." The voice was deep and gravelly, yet it possessed the warbling sprightliness of a 1940s movie heroine. Clay lifted his head from the door. A chalk-thin man stood a few feet away, holding a black portfolio. He wore a full-length mink coat that was suffering severe hair loss and, underneath it, a flannel shirt with mustard stains down the front. His left earlobe was pierced with a ruby. A peach silk scarf encircled his forehead, and from it emerged quills of greasy gray hair. Wonderful, Clay thought. Another old white dude pretending to care while trying to get something out of me. He assumed this one would try to find a way into his pants. Still, he felt slightly ashamed of his naked display of grief, crying out in the open.

"Hey, did you hear me?" the man asked as he put a cigarette to his lips. "I live in this house. Beat it. There are plenty of other places to sob your heart out. You're blocking my door."

Startled by the brazen rudeness, Clay stood up straight. And that's when he spoke his very first words to Freddy van der Haar. In five minutes, this encounter would spiral into tea upstairs under the Blue Madonna and, not long after, the closest friendship of his adult life—a bond so weird and sacred it could only be described as a family.

Clay's first words to Freddy were these: "You beat it, asshole. I live here too."

All these years later, West was still reliably punctual. As they'd agreed on the phone, at one p.m. the next day Il Dormitorio's buzzer droned. Clay bounded down the narrow steps in a pair of brown cords and a white wool sweater. A damp semicircle saturated the collar from when he'd stuffed it into his mouth. His stomach had been acting up that morning—deep chisels of pain, pain colored the worming orange of scrunched eyelids—leaving him moaning on the toilet with his collar shoved into his mouth until the pain subsided. The diagnosis was obvious—nerves, plain and simple, playing their usual gut-punch trick. He would need to drop by a pharmacy this afternoon. Freddy's medicine cabinet was packed with vials of painkillers, but they had mostly expired around the year Clay was born.

On the downstairs landing, Clay folded the collar over to hide the drool mark. Opening the door, he was greeted by a warmer day than he'd expected. Birds twittered promiscuously through the neighboring gardens. Baritone calls from gondoliers wafted from the Rio della Sensa. The air blowing through the alley advertised visions of headlong summers, sweaty afternoons shaded in the black crosshatch of a window screen, and long trips to chalky beaches. In Italy in particular, spring was summer's best PR machine. Richard West stood in the center of this bright season, gazing up at the four flights of the decrepit house. Clay hadn't bothered tidying up for his visit—he hadn't done much more than leave a note on the dry-erase board instructing the interns not to be home that afternoon. But, as the *palazzino*'s brand-new co-owner, he now regretted that decision. West wasn't disguising the fact that he was studying the house's condition. He was dressed in his usual white linen with a red-and-navy polka-dot handkerchief tucked into his blazer pocket. He dangled a bottle of limoncello at his side like a school bell.

"Clay!" West exclaimed, ringing the bottle at his thigh. "What a day! Thanks for making time for me! I've been looking forward to this!"

It took tremendous effort not to slam the door in Richard West's face. It took even more effort to mirror his smile. But Clay was not the same naive soul who'd worked for this man four years ago. In that interval, he'd learned to toughen himself. Still, he could hear the ghost of Freddy whispering in his ear: *Don't let this fucker in our house! Not for a second! Are you insane?*

"Come in," Clay said with a wave. The hallway floor was still littered with grimy cardboard squares. Clay pointed to the bottle of limoncello. "It's a little early for something so after-dinner, isn't it?"

West blinked down at the bottle and laughed as he stepped through the doorway. "Indeed! Karine brought back a whole case of it from Capri," he complained, a traitor to his own gift. "I'm trying to run through it as fast as possible. Don't narc on me if I accidentally leave the bottle here unopened." West gave a wink of collusion. Clay ignored it, jogging up the steps to the main floor and exclaiming, "Sorry for the mess. The new interns aren't exactly house-trained." But when Clay turned around, West wasn't behind him. He appeared a minute later, smiling innocently while feigning the slowness of age with a hand braced on his thigh. It was West's eyes, though, that gave him away. They were blurs of blue, inspecting every cobwebbed nook and rotted wire of Il Dormitorio. Those eyes now skipped over Clay entirely and feasted upon the dingy open room of the piano nobile. West thrust the limoncello against Clay's chest, as if diverting a child with a toy. Then he launched himself into the center of the room, his face lifted toward the ceiling in anticipation. His maroon loafers swirled over the linoleum in small, imprecise steps as he took in Sebastiano Ricci's Blue Madonna.

A tremor of anxiety flared in Clay's gut: Could West's real motivation for this visit not be the silver but simply to get his first real glimpse of this forgotten masterpiece? Maybe the ghost of Freddy had been right. Maybe Clay should never have opened the door to him. Clay knew he was betraying his dead friend by allowing West into Il Dormitorio. Freddy had shouted "Verboten!" at every attempt on his neighbor's part to gain entry over the years. All friendly overtures had been met with a brittle, nicotine-yellow middle finger. Freddy had hated West long before Clay and his story of betrayal blocked his front door. Freddy took his hatreds seriously—he was passionate about them in the manner that others are passionate about first loves. "He'll never take us alive!" Freddy had sworn, pretending to defend the bookcases from an imaginary raid with his skinny arms. He pressed his back against the shelves and glared at his sole audience member like a tragic starlet. "Do you know what men like West are really after, doll? They used to spit on me, which I could handle. Hell, I took it as a badge of honor. But then they figured out that we have something they don't. On top of everything else they've taken and stolen, they want to be *interesting* now too! But we're not going to let them take that from us."

There might have been some truth in that assessment. But Freddy was dead, and Clay was broke, and letting West into the house was only the first betrayal of the day. The second would come in selling him the silver. Those counterfeit van der Haar antiques had kept Freddy financially afloat in his last years, but he refused to allow even fake family heirlooms to enter his neighbor's collection. The single stipulation Freddy had put to his dealer, Dulles Hawkes, was that the pieces could be sold to anyone—really, anyone in the known universe—*except* to Richard Forsyth West. "I don't care if he keeps calling," Freddy had told Dulles over the phone. "His little cupboard will stay bare." For Freddy, it was a point of pride: in the last year of his life, he wet the bed, he vomited on himself, he couldn't remember the names of the men he'd loved, or even recognize his own face in a mirror. But he would die before West got his hands on another van der Haar trophy, even an ersatz one.

"Exquisite," West whispered in awe, his arm rising toward the fresco. His fingertips traced the nude Madonna in midair. "Absolutely stunning. I wish my niece could see this."

Clay cracked the seal on the bottle of limoncello.

"Do you want any?"

West lowered his arm and dropped his eyes, as if descending sharply from a dream. "Well, maybe a smidge. We'll need some ice, though."

Clay searched the freezer and found only empty ice trays. "We're out."

West sighed in resignation. "*Oof*, okay. We'll drink it like men."

Clay poured the pulpy, fluorescent-yellow liqueur into two shot glasses, unsure if it was humanly possible to drink such a substance "like men." Or "like women." It could only be drunk like fools. He didn't want to imagine his stomach's reaction to this goopy invasion. Clay slid one of the glasses across the counter. Before West took it, he motioned toward the ceiling.

"It desperately needs cleaning," he said. "Some water stains have gotten to it. Maybe even mold. You should have a professional take a look before it's too late."

"I've only been back a few days," Clay said.

West nodded and took a sip. He feigned a benevolent examination of the ugly drywall room. Two spinsterly chairs with missing arms seemed to plead for euthanasia. A cardboard mousetrap was shoved behind one of the chair legs, a pink tail snaking out of one side.

"So you own this place now?" West asked.

Technically, Clay co-owned it. Frederick and Cecilia van der Haar had conjointly held the deed as the two beneficiaries of the van der Haar family trust. Their names had been listed for decades in the *visura catastale*, which was the official record of Venetian property. But in place of Freddy, Clay's name now appeared alongside Freddy's sister. Clay had never met Cecilia, the long-lost "foul-weather" sibling. Judging by Cecilia's response to her brother's death—a note sent through a lawyer notifying him that "she's been informed and has asked, for the sake of the family, that

AIDS not be mentioned in any obituary"—he didn't care to meet her. Freddy refused to utter Cecilia's name. He canceled her out of childhood photos by drawing a black line down her body as if voiding a check. "They're wrong, doll. You *can* choose your family," Freddy would always tell him.

"Well?" West asked insistently. "Are you the owner?" His eyes probed his onetime assistant from across the counter. "Is it true that the place is yours?" Clay hadn't meant to lie on this point—he'd wanted to use up his allotment of lies on the silver forgeries. But in the crosshairs of West's condescending stare, he couldn't resist bending the truth. He doubted any other moment this afternoon would be as rewarding as notifying West that they were equals under Italian law. Long gone was the Clay Guillory that West knew, the young, Labrador-loyal assistant who had memorized West's suit measurements and favorite restaurant tables.

"Yep," Clay replied, savoring the nonchalance of his answer. "Il Dormitorio's all mine. Freddy knew how much Venice meant to me. We're full neighbors, you and I. Funny, isn't it?"

That funny fact registered like cold air on West's eyelids.

"What about the sister?"

"What about her?" Clay brought the glass to his lips and rinsed his gums with the citrus alcohol.

"She doesn't own a share?"

"No," Clay replied. "Freddy took over the house a long time ago in exchange for some other properties. His sister never liked it here. Who knows where she is now? Brazil, I think."

"Wow!" West marveled. "Lucky you! I'm impressed!" He winked, as if complimenting Clay on a clever chess move, as if Clay hadn't deserved his inheritance after four years of looking after his dying friend. "I can't help but think—" West cut his sentence off.

"Think *what*?" Clay asked sharply. He sensed an accusation

lurking at the end of that unfinished sentence: *What a clever hustler you turned out to be.* Clay steadied himself against the counter. The plan wouldn't work if he showed anger. Winning this minor fight wasn't going to help him. In fact, he'd only win today by accepting the role of the loser in need of some quick cash. Thus, Clay forced himself to take another sip of limoncello and repeated in a softer tone, "Think what?"

"I can't help but think how proud I am of you," West answered warmly. "Look, we had some ups and downs. But I'm a believer in not looking back with hard eyes. I'd prefer to be impressed by the man in front of me now." West lifted his hand off the counter, and it hung there briefly between them before he waved it around like a conductor. "Here you are, right where you want to be, as smart as you are, and still with so much time to enjoy it. I've always seen something special in you. I hope you don't mind my saying that."

"Thank you," Clay said coldly, avoiding West's eyes as he downed the rest of the yellow liquid. "Now what was this proposal you mentioned in your letter?"

West drifted from the counter, digging his hand into his pant pocket to fumble with some loose change. He seemed to want to gaze out of a window, but there wasn't one in the shabby kitchen. In its absence, there was only the Blue Madonna of 1698, and West's eyes shot upward as if for divine consultation.

"Dealing with Freddy's affairs must be difficult. We both know what a great big wonderful mess he was in life."

"Yeah," Clay agreed. "It's been challenging. I've really just started to sort through it all."

"I'm sure it's been tough." West made a slow-paced figure eight across the linoleum before standing still. "Let me tell you my idea. As you well know, I've always had an interest in certain artifacts that belonged to Freddy's family." He paused to ensure that Clay was following. "Particularly their antique silver collection." Another pause. "Word has it that Freddy still possessed a number of top-quality pieces. And I assume they've been passed on to you."

West paused again. Clay wasn't going to meet him halfway on this appeal. He wanted to watch West squirm as he tacked back and forth between his own greed and a veneer of civility. West finally let out an exasperated laugh. "Clay, you're so young. I can't imagine you want a bunch of eighteenth-century antiques clogging up your life. Those are decorations for us old guys." He stared down at his shoes. "So my thinking is, well, why not take them off your hands? We could avoid the whole drawn-out process of auction houses and private dealers, who always take a huge cut of the profit before you'd ever see a cent." West's focus remained on the floor, a rich man speaking shyly about money. "I'd pay cash up front and get some nice van der Haar pieces to display in one of their ancestral homes. You'd have money in your pocket to ease some of the difficulties in settling Freddy's estate."

West lifted his head to read the response. Clay performed a dramatic widening of his eyes. "I see," he stammered. "Huh! I wasn't expecting—" He quickly spun around, unable to contain the smile that shot across his face. He gave himself a full second to enjoy it before turning back around.

West leaned on the counter as he topped off his glass of limoncello. "I hope I'm not overstepping," he added. "If this sounds inappropriate, please say so. I'm happy to shut up about it. Maybe you want to keep those pieces for yourself. Maybe the rumors are nonsense and there's no van der Haar silver left. Maybe you'd prefer to risk your chances on the volatile, unpredictable open market, and if so, I wish you luck. All I'm suggesting is that you allow me to take a look at what's left and make a very handsome, discreet cash offer. You won't find a sweeter deal, I promise. All I ask is that you let me know right now. Next week I might feel differently. It's your decision."

West had waited most of his adult life for a chance at van der Haar spoils, but next week he might wake up a changed man. Clay had to hand it to him, his salesmanship was smooth. It helped Clay cut entire minutes out of the charade: a less convincing West would have required Clay to enact a series of uncertain heart-versus-bank-account mood swings.

"There isn't as much left as you think," Clay said flatly. "Freddy sold or donated most of the notable pieces. He only held on to four or five items, the ones that mattered to him the most."

Clay wasn't the only man in the kitchen battling a smile. West was beaming so hard it looked like his face might burst, his lips pierced like the knot of an overinflated balloon.

"And Freddy never bothered to have them appraised?"

"No," Clay replied with an idiotic shrug. "It didn't matter to Freddy what they were worth. He wasn't hoarding them for the money."

"Of course," West whispered respectfully. "And you haven't shown them to anyone? Like an antiquities expert?"

Clay again performed his idiot's shrug. "To be honest, I never thought about it. I haven't really had the time since Freddy's death to bother with those kinds of things. I lost my closest friend. I wasn't thinking about putting price stickers on his favorite possessions."

"I'm sorry," West said with a blush so genuine that Clay briefly felt bad about inducing it. "Excuse the questions. The market value doesn't matter to me either. Just so you know, that's not why I'm interested. My intention is to preserve them in a house that once belonged to the family. And I'd like to think that might also be what Freddy would have wanted. I'm not trying to flip them for a profit. It's about respecting the van der Haar legacy."

Freddy would have gone into cardiac arrest. All Clay had to do was resist rolling his eyes.

"You don't happen to have any pictures, do you?" West asked.

"Pictures?" Clay repeated as if trying to translate a foreign word. "Freddy took lots of pictures. He was an art photographer. Did you want those as well?"

"No, no," West sputtered. "I'm talking about pictures of the silver. Any documentation of the estate. I'd need to see what's there before I could make a reasonable bid. I'm sure they're legitimate, but even my untrained eye would have to take a look."

"Oh, that's easy," Clay said, allowing his smile its first moment in the open. "Most of the pieces are here."

"Here?" West repeated. "You mean, right here in this house?" Either West had caught on to the incredulity of the scam or he was basking in his endless streak of luck. He had a greedy young man right in front of him, a treasure in his reach, and a secret silver appraiser on call.

"Freddy brought them over from New York a few years ago," Clay lied. "He always intended to kick out the interns and retire here. But with how sick he got so fast, he never had the chance . . ." Clay didn't wait for another dose of sympathy from West. It hurt too much to lean on his friend's death to buffer his own advantages. He slipped from the kitchenette and opened the door into Freddy's quarters. He made sure to fling the door wide, so his movements could be tracked from the outer room. "Maybe that's why I never considered showing them to a dealer," Clay yelled. "They've been here collecting dust this whole time."

He glanced back to ensure that West was watching. He moved

swiftly around the velvet-flocked room, grabbing an ornamental punch bowl from the secretariat, a lopsided tankard from the bookshelf, and a large plate from the nightstand. After gathering a sauceboat and a porringer stashed behind the door, he strutted into the common area with a plunder of counterfeit silver in his arms.

In truth, Freddy had once possessed a venerable collection of authentic antiques, and his healthy drug habit from the 1970s to the mid-'90s had been kept flush by the sale of them. Freddy couldn't recall how many antiques there had initially been or when exactly they'd left his hands ("You might as well ask me who stole my color television in the personal blackout of 1990!"). Keeping up appearances by avoiding the hard truths of official documentation had long been a family practice. Even after his family money ran out, Freddy still had the golden ticket of his name. America didn't waste time with honorary titles; it had last names. The world trusted van der Haar out of habit, the way it trusted Rockefeller, Roosevelt, Astor, Schuyler, or Vanderbilt—and the way it didn't trust a Guillory or a Brink. Freddy's counterfeit operation predated Clay, but he'd talk about his forgeries as if they were something to be proud of, like illicit works of art. And he was careful never to let them stray too far from old family inventories that did exist. Ultimately, they'd yielded Freddy nearly two million dollars over the course of his last two decades. Unfortunately, with his spending compulsion, he owed far more than that.

Freddy's phonies weren't entirely fake. Like the best lies, each one contained a small nugget of truth. The tankard's lid and handle did derive from the family's illustrious collection, floating without a base for a few disembodied centuries before Freddy had his shady New Jersey silversmith hinge the lid and handle to a generic antique vessel bought off eBay for two thousand dollars. The punch bowl, meanwhile, had started its life as an inconsequential sugar dish. Freddy had preserved its decorative base, which was punched with a verifiable eighteenth-century maker's mark, before having it welded to a massive bowl of no distinction; thus, a minor antique collectible worth ten thousand became a rare treasure worth twenty times that amount. In Freddy's fantasy world, an ordinary spoon could dream itself into being a banquet dish. "Is there anything more American than that?" Freddy asked in joyous defense. The final step in his personal forgery factory had been a dip in liver of sulfur to speed up the aging process, then a few hundred shakes in a bag of nuts and bolts to deliver the necessary scratches and nicks.

Clay placed the pieces on the countertop. These were the last of the fakes, the ones that Freddy's dealer, Dulles Hawkes, said wouldn't pass the most gullible of professional assessments. They might fool an amateur, but they'd never withstand expert examination. Even a dying, destitute neurasthenic had given up the hope of selling them. But now, thanks to Nick, they had returned as deceivers from the dead. In the kitchenette's lamplit dimness, with the nude Madonna swimming overhead, they seemed to glow with self-importance. They looked particularly real under the excited blue eyes of Richard West.

"Oh, man!" West moaned. "And no one has seen these outside the family for centuries?" He dared to lift the tankard by its handle.

"I guess not," Clay muttered, uncertain whether to scare up some make-believe knowledge or keep to the idiot routine.

"Wow."

"There's an old photo where you can see a few of these pieces in the background of an old van der Haar sitting room. I'd have to look for it."

West nodded along to that information without interest. He had a better resource than a photograph. "Clay, can I ask a favor?

Would you mind if I brought these pieces over to my side of the palazzo for a night? I know that sounds silly. I just want to see them on the cupboard and think about what a fair price might be to offer you. I can't fall in love with them properly in a few minutes at your kitchen counter. You've got terrible light in here, my friend!" On the face of it, it was an absurd request, but Clay couldn't debate its flaws. West's borrowing the pieces was essential to their plan.

"I guess that wouldn't be a problem. I mean, I'd—"

"Thanks. I appreciate it." West gestured toward the trove. "Tell me. What do you think a fair price would be? What would you want for the lot?" Clay scrunched his shoulders in bafflement. His stomach was starting to protest the fermented lemon juice. "I have no idea," he managed through the pain.

West laughed as he drummed his fingers on his sternum. "Me neither!" he replied. "I'm no expert. I couldn't begin to assess their value. But since we've agreed to keep this deal out of the usual channels, I guess I'll just have to follow my gut. I have a very bad feeling that whatever I end up offering you will be horribly over-priced!"

He gazed fondly at Clay, so accustomed to winning he seemed to have forgotten he could lose. For once, Clay could reply with a genuine smile. He was thankful West had just lied to his face about having no way of evaluating their worth. The lie cured Clay of the guilt he'd promised himself he wouldn't feel but did anyway. West planned to acquire the pieces for a steal, and the whole time make it seem like he was doing Clay a favor.

The downstairs door squeaked open and feet pounded up the steps. Clay and West both turned to watch a young man with a long Teutonic nose and wavy, chlorine-copper hair slink into the room. He wore a Yale sweatshirt and a pair of wrinkled chinos. "I'm very sorry," he pleaded. "I'll be out of your way. I just forgot my laptop." The intern had been trained by the Peggy Guggenheim supervisor to be frightened of any adult who loomed within the aura of the Madonna fresco.

"It's okay," Clay told him.

The young man scurried down the hall with strides as gawky as Clay's must have been when he'd first arrived. He returned a second later with his laptop and made another round of apologies. Clay noticed West studying the kid as he disappeared down the steps. He felt protective over the renting interns.

"You aren't hunting for a new assistant, are you?" Clay asked defiantly, almost like a dare.

"Hardly!" West responded. "I have a great one right now, a full-blooded Venetian. It's a huge help for the projects we have in development. And he's a rare Venetian because he's trustworthy."

"Congratulations," Clay said bitterly.

West gave an unpleasant laugh of slowly fading snorts. In the quiet that followed, he tapped his wedding ring against the countertop. "You know," he said on the final tap of his ring, "I never really forgave Freddy for stealing you from me. Or you, for that matter, for running off with him and abandoning me just as everything was getting started."

That admission struck Clay with such force he had to will his throat into taking in air again. West had delivered those lines in a tone of absolute sincerity, as if he really did believe Freddy was the reason for their falling-out. Had he never realized that Clay had learned the truth? Or did he think sabotaging a low-level museum job was too trivial a matter to dignify with a spot in his memory? Clay opened his mouth to speak, but no words came out. All these years he'd carried around his anger, presuming West felt remorse whenever they crossed paths on his visits to Venice. But West hadn't felt an ounce of guilt. Worse, West had revised the entire incident so that he was the one who'd been wronged. Clay stared into his face, searching for any trace of sarcasm. West was glumly looking down at the counter, as if waiting for an apology. It was too unreal. But Clay wouldn't be provoked into anger. He wouldn't let West sabotage the plan to cheat him out of a small fortune.

"Freddy didn't steal me," Clay said instead. "I'm not something that can be stolen, Dick."

"It doesn't matter anymore."

"I wasn't Freddy's assistant. I was his friend."

"Let's forgive and forget. It's over. I don't judge what you've done."

Clay wondered whether the rumors infesting Manhattan had found their way over to Venice. Those rumors were inescapable now. *Why do you think that kid murdered our dear, delusional Freddy? For the van der Haar inheritance, of course.*

He gazed at the counterfeits on the Formica countertop. The tears straining his eyes gave their matte-gray finish a starry glimmer. He turned toward the sink and bent down to search a cabinet. He could feel his heart beating heavily, and he wiped his eyes on his knees.

"Take it all," he said to the man at the counter. "I'll find you a box."

He hoped Nick was enjoying the spring weather.

CHAPTER 10

Nick was promised a day of surprises. Richard West had woken him early that morning with a text: Hello, handsome! Eva and I miss you terribly and we've decided to wreck your afternoon with a few surprises. Are you free?

They picked him up at the foot of the Accademia Bridge. Nick wasn't sure whether they'd come by land or by sea, but finally he caught sight of West and his niece descending the bridge's steps. Battista drifted behind them with a black cardboard tube telescoping out of his backpack. As they neared the bottom of the bridge, Eva whisked a piece of fabric from a glossy shopping bag. The fabric was a grid of thin yellow and gray stripes, and it grew arms and a collar and lapels as she flapped it loose. Eva ran toward Nick and covered his chest with the sports coat, hooking it the wrong way over his shoulders like a barber's cape.

"What is this?" he asked as he pinched the expensive silk.

"We felt guilty for ripping your old one," Eva explained.

"Do you like it?" West asked with a grin that seemed sure of the answer. "There's only one decent men's shop in Venice, right above the Rialto. We guessed your size."

"I love it," Nick swore even before he slipped it on. It fit perfectly, right down to the extra-long sleeves. "You didn't have to. Seriously. It wasn't a big—"

"Oh, Jesus," Eva snorted as she shot a disappointed look at her uncle. "I knew we couldn't count on him to skip the American humility routine. Now we're going to have to spend the entire day convincing him to keep it."

"Okay, okay," Nick said in capitulation. "I won't even say thank you."

West let out an approving laugh. "None required between friends." Nick had trouble syncing this warm, generous man with the malicious double-crosser of Clay's stories. As he stood there wearing his new present, he started to wonder whether Clay's beef with Richard had all been a simple misunderstanding. Maybe West had even misguidedly thought he'd been helping Clay by squashing his chances at the museum. West saw more promise in his own endeavors, and anyway, wasn't the cutthroat poaching of assistants the norm in most industries? If it had happened to Nick, he might have taken West's scheming as a compliment—*he really wants me that much!* Nick would give his boyfriend the benefit of any doubt. But for all of Clay's street smarts, he seemed too easily thrown by the ordinary ugly dealings that spun the world. "More surprises this way," West promised. Nick followed Clay's nemesis across the cobblestones.

They walked east through the serpentine streets toward the tip of Dorsoduro. Nick flowed along happily in the human current, battered lightly by shoulders and shopping bags. Soon they were passing the entrance of the Peggy Guggenheim along an algae-green canal—"Great museum if you get a chance, Nick," West said casually, "the director's a friend." The second surprise took

them down a tight, winding corridor with an altar to Mary recessed into the wall. They emerged onto a dock in the tangerine
sunlight of the Grand Canal. Eva hurried onto a large, unadorned
canoe, while West dropped coins in the boat attendant's hand.
Nick stepped carefully onto the black, flat-bottomed vessel and
took a seat next to Eva on one of the wood benches.

"A gondola?" he asked, trying to mask his excitement. He knew
gondola rides were considered embarrassingly touristy, but that
hadn't stifled his hopes of taking one during his stay.

"*Traghetto*," Battista corrected as he took a seat on the opposite
bench.

"These little boats are the last deals in town," West said, joining
his assistant. "One euro per person. In ten years they'll either be
extinct or cost twenty euros for a ride. This one will get us to San
Marco in a jiffy."

The *traghetto* cast out. The rower stood at the bow, his oar stirring the stained-glass waves. All of Venice rocked and swayed as
they drifted into the iconic waterway. It was Nick's first Venetian
boat ride, if he didn't count the disaster of the shared *motoscafo* on
his arrival—and he didn't. He jostled around to absorb as much of
the scene as he could, ignoring the rap music escaping from the
rower's earphones. It was only Battista's gaze, taking note of the
too-excitable midwesterner, that goaded him into playing it cool.
Battista's backpack rested between his legs with the black cardboard tube leaning against his inner thigh. The backpack's front
pocket was decorated with a metal pin of the maroon-and-gold
Venetian flag. The words RESIDENTE RESISTENTE were inscribed
in a diagonal slash across it. Nick had to sound out each syllable in
his head in order to guess at the translation: "Resistant Resident."
He looked up at Battista, his resistant Venetian crush, and tried
smiling at him. After a few unrequited seconds, he gave up.

Eva must have clocked Nick's attempt at flirtation because she grinned deviously and asked, "Nick, do you have a boyfriend?"

"Yes," Nick replied automatically, before realizing the danger of the topic. "I mean, I did until recently, in New York. We broke up."

Eva turned to Battista to ask the same question. "What about—" But he glared back at her to shut down that line of inquiry. No doubt he didn't want to discuss his love life in front of his boss.

"The gondoliers have grown accustomed to making a fortune!" West said loudly as if over a nonexistent boat engine. "They've gotten too comfortable with the tourist money, and that means they won't be allies when it comes to implementing measures to protect Venice. Eva, did I tell you that Francisco took his entire family to the Seychelles last Christmas? How on earth are we going to convince gondoliers like Francisco to return to a sensible yearly income?"

Nick let the conversation drift on without him. The sloshy wake of a passing barge transformed their boat into a bucking bull. After the waves settled, Nick's eyes returned to the palazzi, one the color of a waterlogged tea bag, the next of peach sherbet. Nick didn't want the *traghetti* to go extinct in ten years. They seemed necessary to the world's fragile cultural ecosystem, and thus it was essential to save them, the way northern white rhinos in Kenya needed to be saved. Nick suddenly felt so grateful to have made it to Venice before the last of its magic died.

He tapped West's knee. "I'm glad you're working to save this city," he said. "I'm just now realizing how important your projects are."

"It's the same as your work with silver," West replied. "Making sure the gifts of history find the proper hands. We pass on the enchantments, one to the next, and hope that no one drops them."

The boat gently slipped into its dock, and they climbed out with

an overzealous round of *Grazie!!* to the oarsman. The third surprise of the day involved crossing Piazza San Marco, where crowds
rushed and shoved, marveled and threw tantrums and posed for
pictures, in that giant tourist playpen. Piano music tinkled from
outdoor caffès. Nick managed to keep with his group thanks to
Battista's poster tube, which served as a dependable mast over the
visitor fray. They reached the water's edge on the other side of
the square. Seagulls flew on scalpel wings, and signs advertised
express boat rides to Lido Beach. They headed toward the Palazzo
Ducale, its facade a brick pixilation of white and pink diamonds.
This next surprise required the retrieval of plastic VIP lanyards at
the admission desk.

Eva grew fidgety as they ascended the palace's courtyard staircase. She tucked wisps of hair behind her ears, straightened her
yellow cardigan, and adjusted the rolled silk scarf tied sailor-like
around her neck. Finally she blurted to Nick, "We're doing a tour
of the conservation room! And do you know who arranged it?
Vittorio!" When that name failed to induce a spark of recognition,
she whispered, "The head of the Venetian nonprofit I'm dying to
work for! Which means he might be here, which means I finally
get to meet him. Be honest." She stopped him on the stairs. "Do I
look employable?"

Nervous hives enflamed her chin, further reddened by persistent scratching. Nick assured her that he'd hire her on the spot
but was relieved that his words couldn't be put to the test. There
was no sign of the elusive Vittorio in the stuffy back rooms of the
conservation wing. Instead, the star figure was a solitary sixteenth-
century warrior, pitch-black from centuries of gypsum and soot,
which a blue-vested conservator was cleaning with a tiny laser pen.
They huddled around the statue and watched, while Battista filmed
the operation on his phone. The conservator removed a millimeter

of crusted black residue on the warrior's upper thigh as if erasing an unsightly college tattoo. Underneath lay the white scar tissue of Carrara marble. Eva machine-gunned dozens of questions at the conservator. Nick found himself envious of her interest. He had yet to find a calling of his own. Silver hadn't been the answer. He kept waiting for something to reach out and lift him by his armpits and announce, *I'm your passion.* In the meantime, he had Clay.

West did his best to console Eva on the way out. "Vittorio must have had a last-minute meeting," he said. "Don't be disappointed."

"Yeah," she replied somberly. "I just feel like I'll never get a chance here. It will be back to France to clean medieval tapestries." Eva excused herself to look for a restroom. She seemed to need a minute alone.

"It is time?" Battista asked as he touched his wrist.

"Yes," West said. "Go on. I don't want you late for the appointment." He nodded toward the cardboard tube. "And don't forget to bring the plans back with you."

Battista tightened his shoulder straps and, without a goodbye, disappeared down the marble hall. West shook his head in annoyance. "I could strangle Vittorio for not showing up today. Now he's avoiding Eva *and me*, because he knows I'm expecting him to find her a position."

"I'm sure once he meets her . . ."

West balked. "It's not so easy. Young conservators are a dime a dozen in Venice. Even with the strings *I* can pull!" Nick suspected that last detail was the most infuriating part for West. It must be galling to learn there were still people in the world who couldn't be bribed or cajoled. He had clearly promised his niece a job that he couldn't deliver. It hadn't been a good week for West's sense of entitlement. Over the phone last night, Clay had recounted his lie about owning all of Il Dormitorio and how wonderfully pissed off

West looked at the news that his former assistant had become his neighbor.

"Ridiculous! It's too difficult to get anything to work here," West muttered half to himself. "If I didn't love Venice so much, I might actually enjoy watching it sink."

Eva caught up with them at the entrance, her face dripping from the water she'd splashed on it. "Time for a drink?" she asked morosely. "I know I could use one."

"We can't," West said as he pointed at Nick. "I need this one's judgment sharp for our next surprise." He gave Nick a smile. "Are you ready for it?"

Nick furrowed his forehead in a show of bewilderment, although he already knew the surprise that was coming. He'd been anticipating it since his late-night phone call with Clay and had been rehearsing his part all morning. Still, as he accompanied West and Eva along Strada Nuova toward their house in Cannaregio, he grew increasingly anxious. As West kept busy trying to lift his niece's spirits—even resorting to the avuncular tactic of offering to buy her a gelato—Nick frantically recited antiquarian facts in his head.

Nick barely remembered crossing the last two bridges. Before he knew it, the three of them were standing in the garden of Palazzo Contarini. As West unlocked the iron door, he teased Nick with a warning: "Right this way, last surprise ahead." Then they were stomping up the dark staircase.

Karine was sitting in the far corner of the living room on one of the chocolate divans. She wore black sunglasses and was reading a science magazine. She must have taken to the corner to escape the sharp daylight knifing through the windows. Her foot stroked the brass brain doorstop that had also migrated into the corner. "Hello gang," she said to them. "Why, Nick, what a lovely jacket!"

Before Nick could thank her for what was essentially a compliment on her own husband's taste, West interrupted. "We're going into my office," he told her. "Why don't you join us? Full warning: the results of what we find in there might set us back a bit. Don't worry, your husband's been investing wisely. We'll make it back soon enough."

Nick was relieved when Karine shook her head. Eva was already one attentive witness too many, if her interrogation of the conservator at the Doge's Palace had been any indication.

"I'll leave the past to you," Karine said resolutely as she raised her magazine as if to squash a mosquito. "I'm investing in the future today."

"Suit yourself," West grumbled. He clomped down his hall of photographs and disappeared behind the velvet curtain. Eva and Nick followed. Near the end of the hall, Eva stopped so abruptly that Nick knocked into her. She was pointing at the picture of her uncle with Freddy and Clay.

"That's the one," Eva said, tapping her fingertip on Freddy's face. "The silver belonged to his family." Then she hovered her finger over Clay's glum face. "And this is the kid they belong to now." It was a struggle to resist telling Eva that this "kid" was a few years older than she was, spoke better Italian than she did, and had managed to land a first job in Venice without her uncle's help.

Eva leaned in to study the snapshot more carefully. Nick feigned curiosity and leaned in with her to examine the photo for a second time. Neither Freddy nor Clay looked especially thrilled to be stuck next to West. Freddy's ridiculous rock-musician getup made it impossible to determine the season (the wardrobe of rock stars knows no season), so Nick studied his boyfriend for a clue. Wrinkled pink shirt with no jacket. White jeans. But when his eyes reached Clay's shoes, he let out a slight gasp. His boyfriend wore a pair of black loafers, unexceptional but for the camera-flash-reflecting copper coin that had been wedged in the right shoe's slot. Should Eva drop her eyes right now toward the floor, she'd find a pair of loafers worn by an impartial silver appraiser with a copper coin wedged in the right shoe.

"Do you find him attractive?" Eva asked. "He's Uncle Richard's neighbor now. He inherited the van der Haar fortune. Can you imagine getting all of that at such a young age? I wonder if he did kill for it."

"Uncle Richard is waiting for us," Nick said brusquely. Eva squinted over at him with a look of confusion. Surely the coin was too small of a detail to notice. Surely it could be chalked up to co-incidence or a fashion trend or a secret, blinking indicator among young gay men the world over. Or could it? Nick's hairline was stinging with sweat.

"Do you see what he has on?" Eva exclaimed. "Are those eagle feathers on his sleeves?" She ran her finger down Freddy's arms. "What a fucking nutjob he must have been, right? And then to leave your whole fortune—"

Nick slipped past Eva and made a grab for the curtain. He blindly battled through the scrolls of tan velvet and resurfaced in West's office. The recessed ceiling lights were turned to full, invasive-surgery wattage. The light felt accusatory, although West must have cranked it up for Nick's benefit. Nick considered quickly plucking the coin from his shoe, but Eva was already right behind him.

"Well, what do you think?" West asked with self-congratulations as he gestured toward the mahogany cupboard. Five silver antiques stood on the shelf. Karine's evicted china was stacked clumsily on nearby book piles. Nick stepped forward and opened his mouth in a simulation of disbelief.

"You did it!" he thundered. "How did you manage to get them so quickly? These are the van der Haar pieces? From next door?"

West grinned as he crossed his arms. "Are you surprised? You wouldn't believe the rings I had to jump through to get them. Juggling, high-wire walking—the whole show just to convince that kid to let me borrow them for a night. But here they are! I couldn't let you leave Venice without taking a look."

Nick danced forward another few steps, as if so spiritually bonded with silver that he was irresistibly drawn to the element whenever it appeared in a room. At a distance of three feet, Ari would have been able to recognize the flaws that flagged them as phonies. Nick gave himself until the distance of two feet before he rendered his initial verdict. "Holy crap, they're amazing!" He spun around, his fingers balled as if holding himself back from touching rare treasures. "Do you mind if I inspect them?"

"Mind?" West hooted. "I'm not letting you out of this room until you do! That's why I brought you here. I need to know if they're legit. I don't trust that kid next door. I swear he'd cheat his own mother. But if they *truly* are authentic, I need you to tell me how much they're worth." West pinched his niece's forearm. "Thanks to Nick, we're going to get the deal of a lifetime. I'm going to lowball the hell out of my new neighbor with a cash offer. We're practically *stealing* them!"

Eva glanced skeptically at her uncle. Nick liked Eva. He thought of her as a friend. He wished she would suffer a debilitating headache and leave the room.

"Nick can determine all of that in one assessment?" she asked with her eyebrows drawn tight.

Nick stared at her as he picked up the tankard. It was the very piece that Ari had used to show Nick the unmistakable signs of a forgery. He smiled widely at Eva as she stood in front of a mural depicting a scene of rape and pillaging. "Of course I can," he said sweetly. "How do you think I make my living?"

It was all in the handling.

Ari Halfon had taught Nick the importance of a confident grip when examining antiques in front of clients. There was a bit of theater required in the role of expert. After all, an appraisal was, by definition, only an expert opinion; thus Ari knew the value in playing up that muscly adjective in order to protect its wimpy noun. "Don't look scared to pick up a vessel," he'd instructed. "It's not a rabid skunk."

To Nick's relief, for most of the appraisal, West and Eva watched from a respectful distance on the other side of the room, as if he were a country vet called in to deliver a breeching calf. They must have assumed that a considerable deal of silence and elbow room was required for concentration, and Nick took full advantage: tapping, sighing thoughtfully, flipping a vessel to check its base, running his fingers over chasings and engravings, examining a punch under direct light with an eyebrow cocked, followed by a subtle nod of reassurance. He poured his entire fourteen months' apprenticeship at Wickston into his performance, channeling the movements, expressions, and delicate eye-and-hand choreography of Ari Halfon.

The imitation came at a price. It wasn't guilt. Nick had already made his peace with using the Wickston name for their scheme. West had no intention of reselling these pieces on the market; Ari never visited Venice, so it was unlikely that they'd ever cross paths. More to the point, Nick wasn't providing any official Wickston documentation for this consultation. All he was doing was dispensing unfriendly advice. No, the hurt came in acting like Ari, in copying his small, precise gestures: the clearing of his throat when he picked up a new vessel, his gentle returning of it to its shelf, the hooking of a finger around his shirt collar while lost in thought. Those were the sure reminders of the man Nick loved and missed. Love couldn't have fixed them—if it had, Nick would still be in New York. The only thing that could have saved them was Nick's ability to shrink into the mold of the man Ari wanted.

After Nick finished his preliminary appraisal, he resurfaced in front of his audience with a protracted "Wow."

"Wow good?" West inquired. "They're legit?"

"I'll say!" Nick replied, rapping his knuckles on the desk. "They're definitely legitimate as far as I'm concerned. Beautiful specimens. They must have been with the van der Haars for centuries. It's amazing they weren't lost or divided up among twenty different branches of heirs."

"How can you tell they were in the family for centuries?" Eva asked.

West pinched her elbow to hush her. "Sweetheart, they weren't the kind of family to buy used. They were *van der Haars*."

Nick smiled and continued. "I'm not saying these pieces are the next Paul Revere 'Sons of Liberty' Bowl. They're not going to break box-office attendance records in a museum, although they *are* museum grade." Nick thought it best to underplay their historic significance. Nothing reeked of a con more than heralding a cataclysmic discovery. "But I can tell you they possess the hallmarks of some of the finest silversmiths of eighteenth-century New York. It's a shame I don't have my tools here, but I can walk you through some of the features appreciable to the naked eye."

None of what Nick was saying was improvised. The potency of his performance came from the weeks he'd spent researching and preparing it. If West possessed any lingering doubts about Nick's aptitude, his seemingly off-the-cuff encyclopedic knowledge would put those suspicions to rest. Nick picked up the tankard, which was, according to Ari, the least successful of the forgeries.

"Notice the *SS* hallmark of Simeon Soumaine punched on the inner lid. It was Soumaine's idiosyncrasy to punch his tankards only in this unorthodox location. His lids and handles were often bulkier than the central vessel, so it has an effect of both lightness and heft. He did a lot of work for the great Dutch families of the age. It's no surprise that the van der Haars used him. I'm guessing this piece dates to somewhere between 1720 and 1725, before Soumaine became a little too grandiose with ornamentation."

Nick found himself impressed by his own bullshit. It was undeniably top-quality bullshit. It sounded so erudite and convincing, even to the one who was spewing it. West ate it up, nodding with his arms clasped behind his back like a child on his best behavior. Only Eva, who stood behind her uncle, chewing on the insides of her cheeks, worried Nick.

"Do you mind if I ask you some questions?" she said.

"Of course not," Nick lied welcomingly.

Surprisingly, Eva's voice turned uncertain, all Southern California in its vertiginous ascents, and she threw marshmallowy softballs at him. Why did these pieces look so dull compared to the French and British silver she'd seen? Was American silver worth less than its European cousins? Did that curly engraving on the side of the vessel mean anything?

Nick fielded each question like a veteran. He began to wonder if his fourteen months at Wickston had, in fact, transformed him into a connoisseur. A part of him wished Ari could be here to eavesdrop; he might be proud of what he'd taught Nick.

"At school in Toulouse, I only did paintings, carpets, and frescoes," Eva admitted. "I dabbled a bit in marble and wood. But I never touched the metals." It sounded like she was listing the drugs she'd tried in college. Nick was thankful that Eva had never experimented with silver. She laughed as she stretched the sleeves of her cardigan over her hands. "I underestimated you, Nick. I fell for that baby face of yours. But, *fuck*, you know your stuff."

Nick next selected the punch bowl. The tankard might have been the most evident fake, but this piece had its own problems. A punch bowl would have been hammered out from a single sheet, but Nick could feel the faint globs of the soldering around its base. He held the bowl toward West and pointed out the engraved pattern running around its center ring.

"Do you see the gadrooning motif?"

"I see it!" West exclaimed religiously, as if seeing really was believing.

They went through each piece, with Nick gratuitously and inaccurately championing them for their beauty, artistry, and design. By the time they were finished, West was worn out from listening to antiquarian terms and Nick was equally tired from reciting them. He took a seat in West's desk chair, his neck stiff and his mind cramping. He was so drained he could have put his head on the desk and fallen asleep. But there was also a high that accompanied the deception. He'd made it through the performance and had succeeded in turning junk into sterling. Nick remembered as a kid spending hours at the kitchen table with his markers and pencils trying to duplicate a dollar bill so perfectly that it would be accepted as real cash. Every kid on the planet must try their hand at that cheating art. Kids dreamed of being counterfeiters just as they dreamed of being president.

West pulled out his phone and snapped photos of the van der Haar plunder, repositioning them in different arrangements as if they were visiting grandchildren.

"Congratulations," Eva said.

"Don't congratulate me yet," her uncle replied. "I still don't own them." He leaned against his desk and swiveled around to Nick. "So what do you think? Give it to me straight. How much are they worth?"

"Hard to say," Nick said with a sigh. But it wasn't hard to say. Nick and Clay had already agreed that they'd take seven hundred thousand dollars for the entire set. That would be enough for Clay to clear his loans, pay back his father, and leave them with more than three hundred thousand to live on for the immediate future. The lowest they would accept was six hundred thousand. Nick felt confident about their chances—so confident, in fact, that seven hundred thousand suddenly seemed pitifully low for a zillionaire to be united with objects he coveted. But Nick had to be careful. He couldn't get greedy at the last second. Naming an outrageous sum might encourage West to seek a second opinion. West had to feel he was getting a bargain.

"Those five antiques are worth well over a million dollars on today's market," he counseled. "They could go as high as a million three or a million four." West looked both delighted and horrified by these figures. "But that's only if there's a willing buyer. Right now, silver isn't particularly popular. It's cyclical. In five years, tastes will change and it'll be back with a vengeance. In the long run, we're talking about an extremely safe investment."

West didn't speak. He closed his eyes. He must be comparing his earthly desires against his monthly luxury allowance—or more likely, he was trying to determine the smallest cash offer that Clay was likely to accept.

"That's a lot of money," Eva muttered.

West opened his eyes and spat, "I know it is!"

"But the kid next door won't know they're worth that much,"

Nick continued. "Now, I'm sure he's not stupid. He could google recent auction prices and make an educated guess. But if you're offering cash on the spot"—Nick wanted more than three hundred thousand; he wanted five, seven, ten—"why not offer *eight hundred thousand*. Trust me, that's a deal of a lifetime! I worry if you go to him with anything lower than that, he'll be making a call to Christie's. Then you'll have lost them for good. They're worth more broken up. The auction houses know that. It would be impossible to reunite them all on your cupboard again. Even if you could, the taxes alone—"

"Of course, of course," West agreed. He slapped his knee. "Eight hundred thousand. That's a steal, right? I'd be making out like a thief?"

"You couldn't do better. I know collectors who would kill for just two of these vessels at that price."

"Eight hundred thousand," West repeated as if he were trying to acclimate himself to the number. "For these beauties, I think I can swing that."

Thank god, Nick wanted to cry. He imagined rushing over to Il Dormitorio to deliver the news. *Clay, you're finally free of debt!* Not only had Nick secured their future, he'd won them four hundred thousand dollars of extra spending money instead of three.

But the very moment Nick started celebrating, a seed of regret swam upstream. Sure it was a lot of money, but how long could even four hundred thousand last them in Europe? Maybe four or five years. Six if they really stretched it. Avoiding whole swaths of the Mediterranean where the rates were too high for their budget. How long before they had to skip meals or stay in less accommodating cities in order to stretch the remaining money? Every week there would be less and less of it. Clay could always come back to Il Dormitorio—that was his. But Nick would never be able to stay with him here as long as West was the neighbor. And after four or five years, when the money ran out, what then? Back to New York? Back to Dayton? Back to zero.

Nick knew his sudden swerve into pessimism could be chalked up to exhaustion and the high of his gamble wearing off. But tiny doubts began to nip at his mind as he sat under the astral lights of West's office: Should he have risked trying for a million dollars? Maybe a million two? Why couldn't he be greedy? Everyone else was. It dawned on him that the failure of their plan hadn't been its risk. Rather, it was that they had played it too safely. West had gobs of money at his fingertips. Why hadn't they tried for more?

He shook himself out of this spiral, blinking his eyes to bring himself back to the present. West and Eva were standing at *The Rape of the Sabine Women* mural, studying it under the bright wattage.

"You didn't let them use the solvent AB 57 on it, did you?" she was asking her uncle.

"I hired the best conservators available," West said in defense. "What they used, I can't recall. There was apparently a lot of animal glue on the fresco from an earlier attempt to brighten the colors."

Eva shook her head despondently. "AB 57 strips away a lot of the glaze and oils. I would have used something much more delicate. You know, we've come a long way in terms of cleaners and finishes in the past ten years."

West punched his hands on his hips and gave his fresco a vaguely incensed inspection. He seemed disinclined to weather a lecture on bad conservation practices from his beloved niece. "Well, you should see the one next door! It's a sin the way it's been allowed to decompose. Honestly, that kid is committing a crime against Venice as far as I'm concerned by not taking any measures to have an authentic Sebastiano Ricci restored!"

West described the rare Blue Madonna fresco he'd finally managed to glimpse while negotiating the silver with his neighbor. It was caked in centuries of soot, the Madonna's voluptuous, opalescent body as yellow and cracked as a ninety-year-old Sicilian's. "The doves that surround her are flaking off. Whole doves! They're falling to dust in the cereal bowls of the Guggenheim interns! And the blue background is basically the color of a black eye."

Eva inventoried each atrocity with expressions of outrage. West told her to try *not* to imagine what cigarette and oven smoke were presumably doing this very instant to the Blessed Virgin. "A travesty!" he cried. "But the van der Haars never had the Ricci listed in the government registers. So no one can really step in to save it. It's left to Clay Guillory. And I'm sure a restoration project is the first thing he's going to spend his inheritance money on."

"Is there any way I can see the fresco?" Eva begged. "Do you think he'd let me in to have a look?"

A peevish *pssst* leaked from West's lips. "Not a chance. *Not. A. Chance.*" West had saved face with his niece by turning his new neighbor into a devil. "I'm not saying he murdered Freddy. I won't go that far, although others—*believe me*—have. But there's no way he's going to let us in to inspect the place. He practically shot daggers from his eyes every time I looked up at that ceiling."

"What about when you return the silver? I could come with you."

"Oh, I'm not taking the silver back." West turned to consult his appraiser. "Nick, don't you think I should text him my bid? If he accepts, I'll wire him the money. I worry if I give the pieces back, he might change his mind or hold them hostage for more cash. And this way he can't send pictures of them to Christie's."

"Yes, that's best," Nick agreed. His mind had wandered again, or rather at some point while Eva and West were squawking over the badly damaged Madonna fresco, a bell had begun to ring in his head. It rang louder and more insistently, and it chased away his worries about money the same way the kitchen light in his crappy Brooklyn apartment had chased off rodents. Why couldn't he and Clay try for more money? They'd succeeded once. Why not a second time? Clay had inadvertently laid the groundwork with the lie he told West about owning all of Il Dormitorio. Why not make that lie true as well? It might be an insane idea—a risk bordering on a major felony—but Nick knew one thing: they'd never get this opportunity again.

"How about it, Nick?" West was asking him. "Let's go into the living room and have a drink. I owe you about a hundred drinks for your help today."

Nick rose. "Yes," he said excitedly. "I'm sorry. I'd love a drink."

CHAPTER 11

It had begun with the patter of tiny feet.

Except that wasn't how Nick first interpreted the ominous scampering across the ceiling of Ari's Riverside Drive apartment. Nick had followed the sound from the living room into the kitchen, where it magically evaporated. An hour later, as Nick stood at the coffeemaker, the faint phantom noise scurried across the ceiling again. This time, Nick followed it with fiercer commitment, tracking its movement back through the living room and on to the dining room, where Ari was leaning against the doorframe in his underwear. Ari was distractedly rubbing his palm over the curly black hairs that spilled from the waistline of his briefs—curlier only by a degree than the rest of the hair that shrouded his pale Manhattan body—while talking on the phone.

"No, that's too close to the city," he told a Pennsylvania realtor. "Yes, still a minimum of twenty acres. But now I'm also interested in a decent school district. I know I said I didn't care before, but I've changed my mind."

Nick glanced at his boyfriend to bait his eyes. He guided them up at the disturbing sound as it circled their lamp fixture.

"Tell me you heard that!" Nick cried when his boyfriend hung up.

"Heard what?" Ari replied, picking lint from his belly button.

"The scurrying! That's twice I heard it in the ceiling this morning." Nick shook his head with horror. "It's mice."

"It isn't mice."

"Yes, it is! I know what they sound like. They're in the walls."

"It isn't mice."

Nick snapped his fingers in revelation. "You know what? I haven't heard our upstairs neighbor's clip-clop stilettos lately. She must be out of town, and that's when mice take advantage. They love an empty apartment." There it went again, the scuttle across the ceiling. "You're telling me you don't hear that?"

"You moron," Ari said, laughing. "I ran into our upstairs neighbor yesterday. And you're right, she isn't wearing her evil stilettos anymore. Just listen to the sound for a second." Nick tried to listen *into* the disgusting rumble for a hint of what it could be if not mice. "You really can't tell what that is?" Ari asked. "Marcella adopted a toddler from El Salvador. That's the footsteps of a child."

In the weeks that followed, Nick would have preferred mice. He should have caught the clue in his boyfriend's conversation with the Pennsylvania realtor. Ari had asked for a decent school district. Ever since Nick had known Ari, he'd been mulling buying a weekend country house, spending free hours cruising real-estate apps without ever seriously considering driving out for an open house. Highly rated school districts had never previously been a concern. But one night, over the failed science experiment of Nick's home-cooked vegetarian lasagna, Ari asked, "If you had to choose, would you prefer adoption or fertilizing a baby from one of our sperms?"

"You're forgetting," Nick replied, "that the great thing about being an adult is I don't *have* to choose."

"Say you did."

"Wouldn't it be more fun to say I didn't?"

Ari shoved an orange forkful into his mouth.

"Anyway," Nick said, "doesn't that idea go against your cardinal belief in nihilistic bohemianism?"

"How so?"

"You know, our contributing to the endless arcade of kindergartens that most Manhattan cross-streets have become. Ari, you use every taxi ride as a personal tour of how old, mean-streets New York has been ruined by playgrounds."

Ari hunched over his plate. "People change," he said quietly. Then he tried a different tactic. "Obviously the Halfon gene is the superior life-form. I'm sure we'd agree to use my sperm." Here, Nick was supposed to defend the illustrious portfolio of attributes that came with a lifetime Brink membership. Instead he said nothing. What he really wanted to do was sink his face in the tray of lasagna and sob for Ari's forgiveness.

None of this baby talk was coming out of the blue. Nick was sure of it. Whether consciously or not, Ari must have realized that Nick had been cheating. And in Ari's beautiful, monogamous head, he figured the best way to keep hold of Nick was to move their relationship forward a step: its problem must be stasis, and thus its survival relied on a bolder, more irrevocable act of commitment. Children. Marriage. A decent school district in the tick-ridden hills of Pennsylvania. By this point, Nick had been sneaking over to a brownstone in Bed-Stuy three afternoons a week for the sole purpose of falling in love with Freddy's murderer.

It was all Ari's fault, Nick decided. If he hadn't insisted on Nick breaking the news to Clay Guillory in person about the counterfeit silver, they never would have gotten together. But it wasn't Ari's fault. It was Nick's fault. He thought of it more like a defect, a defective fidelity bone that caused him to wake up in the vicinity of Ari's slim, warm body and love him tenderly, all the while pining for equally warm Clay with his serious eyes and chewed lips locked in an eternal frown. Nothing made Nick happier than getting Clay to laugh against his will, unless it was leading him up the brownstone stairs to the small bedroom with its pilled gray sheets.

Nick wished it were only about sex, because sex had a reliable expiration date. But more often than not on these Bed-Stuy visits, Nick and Clay would just sit with legs and arms intertwined on the carcass of a downstairs sofa watching old black-and-white movies from Freddy's extensive DVD collection. Or Nick would help Clay craft elaborate descriptions of Freddy's bizarre curios to sell on eBay. A box of mannequin heads; lightly worn hand-crafted maharaja slippers; a collection of gay diaper-fetish porn ("Don't judge Freddy!" Clay growled protectively); a mother-of-pearl backgammon set with gazelle teeth for tokens; two hot-pink George Foreman mini grills; a vintage denim jacket purportedly stained with the puke of Candy Darling; twenty bootleg Greta Keller recordings. The month before Nick met Clay, an estate-auction company had sent a moving van to the Jefferson Avenue address to clear away Freddy's more valuable possessions. Those profits had covered nearly a year's worth of neglected electricity bills, and Clay was praying that the sale of Freddy's art-poster collection might keep the lights on until the brownstone found a buyer. "You can't sell a house at a fair price when the power has been shut off," Clay explained. "They see you're suffering, and they go in for the kill."

Nick had already learned the failure of first impressions. He'd completely misjudged Freddy van der Haar's finances by falling under the spell of his gilded last name. Far more crucially, he'd completely misjudged Clay's relationship with both Freddy and Freddy's finances. There was a growing stack of unopened mail in the foyer of the dilapidated brownstone, and there was a cassette tape on the antique answering machine filled with live and automated threats (finally the landline was disconnected and simply became another mailed bill). Sometimes when they were sitting on the couch Nick and Clay had to freeze until the persistent knocking at the front door stopped.

When you live and work with the same person, a secret affair isn't easy to coordinate. The excuse that Nick fed Ari for leaving Wickston at 4:30 p.m. instead of 6:15 three afternoons each week was a fictitious rock-climbing class in Brooklyn with his old pal Leo. Rock climbing seemed ludicrous enough to be believable, plus it offered a piggyback excuse for the reason Nick was refusing to have sex with his boyfriend ("Ouch! I'm too sore! Don't touch me! Everything hurts!"). Nick was dishonest and selfish and he hated himself to the core, but he found that he was emotionally incapable of having sex with Ari while doing so with Clay. That was the only point he accrued those months on his personal scorecard of dignity.

"From everything I know about Leo, I'm *shocked* he's going back for another week of classes," Ari exclaimed while brushing his teeth one morning. "Is there a go-go dancer at the top of the rock wall? An ecstasy dealer? Tell me, what makes Leo keep climbing?"

Nick laughed as he *chalantly* stuffed workout clothes into a gym bag. "Ari!" he sang in the faux aggrieved key of happy coupledom. "It's important that I see my old friends. Leo's the only one I've got from my early days in New York."

Ari peeked his head out of the bathroom. "You have my full support! And I'm looking forward to admiring your climbing muscles at the house we rent this summer in Pennsylvania." Everything about that reply from Ari said: *I love you, Nick.*

Nick began experiencing panic attacks. He locked himself in the Wickston bathroom to sit on the toilet and cry while punching the sides of his head. Then he unlocked the bathroom door and ran work errands with fresh gusto. He sweetened his voice when he answered the office phone. He assembled Ari's weekly calendar with the prowess of a teenager playing a brick-building video game. *Lunch Monday, 12:30 at Michael's with the curator of Winterthur; conference call 2:45 with Bonhams; 3:15 appraisal of 19th century shagreen-and-silver cigar cases.* For the months of February and March, Nick became a model employee and a model boyfriend. But three times a week when the silver hands of the wall clock by his front desk overlapped, he grabbed his gym bag and ran off to another world.

The reason he was falling so hard? Around Clay, Nick could stop feeling like an eternal apprentice. He felt, instead, like someone with his own interesting opinions. Clay did that—he made him matter; he made him feel rare. And he managed that feat without buying Nick a single present or telling him which color he looked best wearing. In the crumbling brownstone on Jefferson Avenue, Clay listened to him and asked questions, and when they disagreed, Clay didn't try to bully him over to his side. On those winter afternoons sprawled across Clay's bed, Nick was afflicted with an unbearable sense of his own youth—not youth as in amateurish or yet-to-be-trained, but bold, limitless, and thirsty for the world. More and more, Nick pictured a fantasy future where he and Clay were figuring that world out together, free to move around in it as they pleased.

In reality, though, Clay was even less free than Nick was. He was steeped in the kind of debt unimaginable even to members of a generation that had already leveraged their adulthoods to American banks. Clay's debt scared Nick. The depth and intensity of it was like being carried along in a shark's mouth, bleeding profusely but still alive, brought up to the surface to draw just enough air before being brought under again. "I don't regret it," Clay said. "It was to keep Freddy alive. You might think I was stupid, and maybe I was. But I couldn't abandon him. I'd do it again if I had to."

Clay planned to get jobs—two or three or four of them—once he finished settling Freddy's estate. Settling, in this case, meant selling. Everything would be sold in order to bring down the debt. But certainly, Nick posited, the Victorian brownstone was worth a small bundle. Bed-Stuy was no longer the geographical crime wave of decades ago. It was a gentrified, in-demand neighborhood where dog walkers and their mobile petting zoos had become the predominant sidewalk fixture. Unfortunately, the sale of the brownstone would barely cover the back property and income taxes that Freddy had been dodging for decades, along with hospital bills, pharmacy bills, credit-card bills, outstanding bank loans, long-term loans from Freddy's gallery—loans of all kinds jumping out from every direction. The worst of it was that Clay had taken out personal loans to help Freddy, and those collectors were knocking the loudest.

"Ironically, the only thing I can't sell is the most valuable," Clay told Nick. He'd inherited an equal share of a tiny palazzo in Venice, the other half belonging to Freddy's invisible sister who would never, under any circumstances, sell her stake. "Believe me, Freddy tried. He once asked her to sell when he was flush with money and wanted the palazzo all for himself, but she turned him down. And then he tried when he was destitute and badly needed the cash but she turned him down again. She hates Venice and hasn't been to that house in thirty years, but she keeps it, I guess, out of spite."

"At least you'll come out with something in the end," Nick bright-sided. "Half a palazzo isn't so bad."

"Oh, man," Clay moaned. "As much as I love Venice, right now I'd rather have a bill shredder."

In the end, it wouldn't have helped Clay had those last remaining van der Haar forgeries passed for authentic relics. If they had, Freddy would have sold them through Dulles Hawkes years ago to purchase more ridiculous trinkets and gewgaws that Clay would now be uploading to eBay. He planned to have the counterfeits melted down so he could sell the silver for scrap.

Nick and Clay were half-undressed, kissing in bed—Clay's silver belt buckle ice-cold against Nick's stomach—when an idea struck Nick with the force of a tidal wave. He pushed Clay off him and sat up.

"What if I appraised them?"

Clay stared at him funny. "Appraise what?"

"The counterfeit castoffs. What if, as a Wickston representative, I convinced someone they were legitimate? Privately. Away from the auction houses. Like how Dulles Hawkes sold them. Since he's retired now, it would make sense that you'd use a new dealer."

Clay shook his head.

"Just listen," Nick said. "We'd need to find someone rich who has no connection to Ari or the silver trade. Someone not in New York. This could work! I answer the phones at Wickston. I print out the appraisal reports. If we do it right, Ari would never find out and neither would the buyer. Everyone's happy." Clay was still shaking his head. "Hundreds of fakes are sold every year, they just have the right stamp of approval. Why should yours be any different?" Clay was now emphatically shaking his head. "It would have to be someone who believes in the van der Haar name. My god, a million people do. This could save you. This could get you out of debt. You could pay back your father!" Nick knew that last incentive would stop the head shaking. He just wasn't certain what other effects it might induce.

Clay leaped off the bed. He located his sweatshirt on the floor and dug his arms and head through its holes.

"No," he said, his glare fixed on a corner of the room. "I can handle my own situation. This has been fun, but I think it's time for you to go."

Nick scrambled off the bed. "Don't be like that," he begged. "I'm just trying—"

Clay yanked his arm away. "I'm not going to cheat someone, even if they're too stupid to realize it. Freddy did that, *fine*. He was an adult child. But I won't. Bringing them to Wickston was a mistake. And you shouldn't be lying to your boyfriend for my benefit. He's *your boyfriend*, Nicky. You seem to have forgotten that."

"I didn't forget." In truth, the world of Ari and the world of Clay were so separate in his mind that Nick couldn't even conjure an image of his boyfriend while standing in this Bed-Stuy bedroom. "Okay, it's a total fantasy. Maybe it's a dumb idea. But think about it, will you? Think about what it could get you out of. Think of the prison of the next decade paying off those debts. And Ari *will never find out* if we choose the right target. You can't be that good, Clay! Isn't there anybody you wouldn't mind screwing over? Isn't there anyone from Freddy's life that might want van der Haar antiques, no questions asked?"

"If I wanted to go that route, I wouldn't need you," Clay retorted. "Freddy had plenty of friends with criminal backgrounds. He had a crazy black marketer in Paris who could forge the right certificates if I wanted to sell those pieces. I don't need you to help me, Nicky. I'm good on my own. I'm—"

Nick risked grabbing his shoulder. "I want to help you, okay?"

He let the silence float between them. "Just think about it, all right?"

One afternoon in March, on the very day that Ari had driven out to Connecticut on a consultation job for a longtime collector, Deirdre Halfon stopped by the store. "How about lunch?" she asked Nick at the front desk. "My treat."

"I can't. I'm the only one here today."

"Just tape a note to the door. 'Out to lunch, back at two.'" Deirdre wore a patchwork sweater and a long pony-skin skirt that she would have been shocked and perhaps annoyed to learn was back in fashion. "Let me guess, Ari doesn't allow notes taped to the door. He's such a stickler." Deirdre's criticism also served as a brag about the son she'd raised. "Well, he can't blame you if his own mother does it!"

Nick reluctantly fetched his coat as Deirdre penned the note. Recently, he'd started to think of Deirdre less as a surrogate mother and more as an enemy spy.

They walked twenty blocks north through the Upper East Side, remarking on the recent urban blight of empty storefronts in the Seventies, and then, conversely, on all of the cloying new shops congesting the Eighties. Deirdre guided Nick into a brick-walled pub with tables covered in white butcher paper. She pointed toward a table in the corner. As Nick followed her through the restaurant, she said, "This place has been here forever. Jackie O. used to come for lunch!"

They both ordered Cobb salads, no bacon. For most of the meal they kept to safe topics like Haim's new obsession with birding and jogging ("No, I'm talking about birding *while* jogging," Deirdre elucidated), and the latest travesties protected under the Second Amendment. When their salads were reduced to lettuce scraps, Deirdre performed a theatrical survey of the restaurant, as if fearful of eavesdroppers, and leaned across the table. "Ari would kill me for telling you this. But I think he's going to pop the question by the end of summer." Nick's stomach dropped, and he stared into his salad bowl as if over a cliff's edge. "Maybe you like surprises, and I shouldn't have said anything." Her eyes were reddening at the corners. "Do you love him, Nick? Do you love my son?" She seemed to be overwhelmed at the thought of someone loving her son. Or perhaps she was overwhelmed at the thought of someone not loving him. Nick's lips quivered and his eyes began to leak. "Yes, I love him," he assured her. "I love him so *so* so much. Please know that!"

They were both crying now, and Deirdre steered her hand around the obstacle course of the salt and pepper shakers and the water glasses and the ramekin of pink sugar packets to squeeze Nick's fist. "We all want you in this family so badly!" She made the Halfons sound like a sorority into which his admittance would be decided by group vote. Nick excused himself. Hunched over the men's-room toilet, he vomited up his Cobb salad into the bowl.

How had this happened? Nick was making plans for the future in two very different worlds. Ari had narrowed down the summerhouse rental to one of three Pennsylvania cabins. "We get it May first to Labor Day. I can't believe I'm saying this—so *bouge* of me, what have I become?—but it really depends on the kind of pool we want. Salt, slate, or a plastic kidney bean with a diving board." The toddler in the apartment above them was growing at an astronomical rate, gaining an obscene amount of weight, judging from his constant heavy footfall across their ceiling. The clumsy pounding was worse than the stilettos and drowned out the airshaft symphony that Nick loved to listen to in the morning. "Also, Nick, in the fall, you should start coming with me to some of the appraisal appointments. We can hire a person to work the front desk, and you can sit in the back with me. It's time you took on more responsibility so you don't get bored."

On the other side of the river, Clay had selected the target for their scam, a despicable American zillionaire in Venice with a creepy fixation on the van der Haar name. He had a track record of trying to acquire Freddy's silver. "I can't stand this asshole. But you'll be able to sleep at night, Nicky, knowing the fakes will bring him a great deal of joy." The Venetian plan was mutating like a virus—Nick would no longer need to forge an appraisal report on Wickston stationery; he'd no longer have to cold-call Richard Forsyth West to peddle five miraculous eighteenth-century van der Haar antiques; Nick could be renting a room at Il Dormitorio and just happen to spot the treasures in the palazzo and . . . scratch that, too complicated and coincidental. Venice was a tiny town. Nick could bump into West on a vaporetto, give him his business card, and at the right moment lend him some pro bono advice. Nick got the sense that Clay was purposely minimizing his role in the silver scheme to protect him from any criminal culpability.

"And in the end, if you don't come to Venice," Clay said, "maybe you could talk to West on the phone. Or Skype. He'll want to see that angelic face of yours."

"I *am* coming!" Nick swore. "I told you, I can't stay with Ari. It's over. You're flying to Venice and I'm meeting you there a few days later. It's *our* plan, not yours. You'd better not look shocked when I step off the boat!"

They went up to the third-floor bedroom and undressed. Clay lay on his back and milked a condom over his erection. Clay always made sure to use protection: a condom when they fucked, a lean blue pill swallowed every morning that reduced the possibility of HIV to a near flat line. Nick wished he could take that lean blue pill too—hell, he wished he could walk around with a condom in his wallet. But those safeguards were prohibited for members of monogamous, lifelong relationships. In some insane, current-world logic, the people in monogamous relationships were now the ones most susceptible to STDs, while the most promiscuous went around unscathed. Nick straddled Clay's waist and flexed his biceps, because Clay said it turned him on to see the light-blue veins cobwebbing his muscles. Nick took a moment to appreciate how the bones of Clay's neck drifted into a concert of muscle, the hairless ridges of his stomach, and the pink, protruding knot of his belly button. Nick reached behind him, slipped his fingers down his own ass crack in preparation, and, with one eye anticipatorily squinted for the impending jolt, guided Clay inside him. Clay nestled his head into a pillow as if preparing for a long voyage. Staring down, Nick felt the kind of love that was too early to be named; naming it might destroy it. And beyond that feeling floated others that were just as elusive: Nick felt as young as his age, twenty-five, and the world itself felt real and round and unending.

"I prefer the slate pool," Nick told Ari that evening. "I hate kidney beans. And the slate pool is right above a barley field, which will be pretty in summer." Ari had brought Nick to his favorite bar in Morningside Heights, where brave opera amateurs climbed the stage to butcher arias. Right now, a middle-aged woman with a shaved head and shoulders wrapped in a shawl was failing to transport the room with her rendition from Così fan tutte.

"The house with the slate pool is my favorite too," Ari said with warm eyes. "That one's perfect for us. What's more, the owner is interested in selling. If we love the place, maybe we can talk him into counting the summer rental fee as part of the down payment. It's forty acres, and it's in a fantastic school district."

"Wait a minute! Stop! If he's selling the house, does that mean it isn't furnished? I don't want to spend half of May running around buying furniture." Nick was perfectly aware that in his other life he'd be far away from rural Pennsylvania in May—according to the plan he'd either be in Venice finishing up with their con or already traipsing through Europe with Clay and all the money in their pockets. But that other world was so disconnected from the one Nick shared right now with Ari in an opera bar on the Upper West Side that he didn't see it as a conflict.

Ari stroked Nick's back. Nick understood right then that what kept him attached was not the furious hunger of early love so much as the stable, unshouting promise of being loved—and maybe that feeling was infinitely more valuable. Nick stared at his boyfriend, who was sipping his beer as the singer aimed for a note as reachable to her as the moon. Generous, trusting Ari, who had given him a home and a job and an education. Nick knew he would never be able to put the bullet of abandonment into that forehead. He *couldn't*—it would be like killing himself.

"You look like you're about to cry," Ari said softly. "Why don't you? Come on, the poor gal is singing her heart out. It would make her night to see some tears."

Ultimately, time forced his hand, the silver wall clock ticking at the Wickston entrance. Clay told Nick that a lot of clocks in Venice had no hands: Napoleon's army had stripped as many precious metals as they could from the public monuments. While most had been returned—Clay pulled up an image of the four bronze horses in Piazza San Marco—the restoration of precise time hadn't been all that important to the Italians. But time mattered in New York. In fact, Nick had purchased a ticket with an exact end time stamped on it: a one-way economy ticket to Venice leaving on the evening of April 4. It was nonrefundable. He'd made his decision, and now he needed to come clean. But still Nick went to work every morning and existed as a man of umpteen smiles, and not a squawk of discord passed his lips. Instead, he pigeon-toed across the herringbone floor to discuss where his new desk would go. Meanwhile, Clay had finally found a buyer for Freddy's brownstone. It had been the last hurdle to their Venetian con. A part of Nick had prayed that the brownstone would remain on the market indefinitely.

By the last day of March, Nick had used up every spare mile and was reaching the point where the car must swerve or accept the cliff's edge. He and Ari worked later than usual in the shop that night, inventorying a collection of rare Guatemalan silver that Ari decided to sell and tissue-wrapping a collection of pre-Columbian gold that Ari didn't feel he had the expertise to represent. As they Ubered to a sushi restaurant around the corner from their apartment, Nick was aware that at that exact moment, Clay was hurtling through the air at 35,000 feet, halfway over the Atlantic Ocean en route to Venice, his suitcase stuffed with fake eighteenth-century colonial American silver. Somehow that bizarre fact was all Nick's doing.

The sky had been purpling when they entered the restaurant, and it was night by the time they exited. They walked in silence up Broadway, crossing the squares of pavement that sparkled with diamond dust. Ari stopped on the corner to give his spare change to a homeless man who was semi-visibly drunk and visibly bleeding from the sneaker. Ari made a habit of donating his day's pocket change to one of the local homeless. He might delight in witnessing authentic displays of New York cruelty, but he was never cruel himself.

They turned onto 104th Street and began walking toward the Hudson River. It was now or never. Nick had to say it right *now*. Or right *now*. Or right *now*. He would let the words cyclone from his tongue, just three or four of them and they'd build and accelerate and spin on their own. But every step along 104th Street held the promise of a next step and another after that one on which to wreck his world. Nick walked the entire block locked in fear. It was impossible to form the words in English. It would be easier to give up the next sixty years of his life to Ari than to devastate him for a single moment. Nick had been silent like this before, back in Ohio. He knew how to do it.

As they crossed West End Avenue, the real possibility of saying nothing occurred to him. He could just *not* get on his flight to Venice in four days. Clay would understand. He'd know that Nick couldn't risk sacrificing all he had with Ari. Hell, Clay probably already assumed that he wouldn't get on the plane. And he could still Skype Richard Forsyth West and vouch for the silver in a way that helped Clay's case but didn't tarnish the Wickston name. If he just stayed quiet, he would be free to spend the summer in rural Pennsylvania and raise a child that looked a bit like Ari and take up jogging while birding and still get wasted once a month with Leo at a club downtown. That life wasn't so bad. It was more than he ever thought he deserved. He was only twenty-five, still a kid really, and the fling with Clay could be chalked up to a kid's mistake. Ari would pop the question by the slate pool over a field of barley and he would say yes and ride that word all the way to old age.

They turned onto Riverside, and Ari dug into his pocket for the house keys. The park across the street rustled with shadowy movement. Another option came to Nick. Maybe a mugger would run out of the park, waving a gun and demanding their wallets. Nick could make a stupid move and the mugger would shoot him in the chest. That would be the cleanest way out. But New York was no longer that unsafe, and its citizens couldn't rely on a gun being pulled on them as they walked home at night.

"We should buy a car," Ari said as he slipped his key into the security door.

"Oh, god, where would we park it?" Nick replied as they passed through the lobby. The elevator took them up six flights, and Ari unlocked the dead bolt to their apartment. Nick didn't turn around to lock it after they went in.

Ari set the needle on the black circle of Schubert in the living room. A sad, slow melody poured from the speakers. It was Schubert's Piano Sonata in B-flat Major, D. 960. Nick had learned it by heart.

Ari popped a nicotine lozenge into his mouth and sat on the sofa, his arm stretched across its back cushions. Nick stood immobile in the hallway. All he had to do was shut up and be happy. All he had to do was sit down and listen to piano music. His entire future required nothing more than a few more footsteps. Within a year's time, he could be standing in this very passage as a husband and a father.

"What's the matter?" Ari stared at him. "Why are you standing there?"

Nick closed his eyes and uttered Ari's name. It came out as two warped syllables, with all of Nick's life caught in his throat. "Ari. I need to tell you something. Please just listen."

Now that Nick had performed his bogus appraisal, all that was left for him to do in Venice was wait. The next morning, West sent Clay an offer of $750K for the entire collection. That fucker! Nick wrote back when Clay texted the news. I told him to offer 800k! Ask for more. Maybe go as high as nine and see what he says? But Clay got cold feet about negotiating with a business shark. He figured $750K was already fifty thousand more than they'd initially hoped, and accepted on the spot.

It would take four days for the money to clear Clay's bank account. During those four anxious days, it still felt possible that West would come to his senses and call his dollars back home. Nick and Clay agreed it was best not to meet—not even to talk on the phone—until the money landed in the account. It felt like jinxing matters to celebrate early or even make out in a church.

Nick was far from idle. He spent those days making preparations, should he convince Clay to go along with his brilliant new scheme. He bought a bottle of silver polish and had it wrapped in foil like champagne as a present for West the next time he saw him. He sent Eva a spree of jokey text messages, to all of which she replied with witty rejoinders or obscene emoji chains. Nick might need Eva for his plan to work. On the third morning, he texted her, The client in Milan is delayed in Geneva, so I may be staying here a little longer. I'm sorry to put you at risk of seeing my face again. Eva replied with an emoji of praying hands.

Nick felt sure he had managed to win over Daniela during his stay. If he had become an expert on anything in his time in New York, it was being a conscientious roommate. He knew when his presence was wanted—when, for example, he could put his talent as a tall person to use by fetching high-shelved kitchenware—and when to make himself invisible. Nick's chore was the bathroom, which he mopped and scrubbed as if it were a crime scene. When he informed Daniela that he might be staying another week or so—"If that's okay with you, of course"—she merely nodded her consent and reminded him that she was promised a dinner on the town.

Nick wandered the city, gazing at listings in the windows of real-estate offices. He made an appointment with one high-end realtor, pretending to have inherited an apartment near San Marco that he was in a hurry to sell. Was it a complicated process? What was the fastest he could get it off his hands? "It can be complicated. But if we find an eager buyer, you wouldn't believe how fast!" the realtor swore with a wicked grin. "Many wealthy visitors fall under the spell of Venice. Our authorities have made it, shall we say, *expedient* to close the sale before they have a change of heart. That heart change usually transpires at the airport. We try not to let them get there before they sign."

One afternoon, Nick walked through Campo Santa Margherita and watched as university students hung a white bedsheet across a second-floor balcony. No Grandi Navi was printed across it, with a red slash through the image of a cruise ship. Another student with dyed fuchsia hair passed out flyers for an upcoming protest against the development in Mestre. Nick returned to the flat off Calle Degolin and found Daniela in the garden on her rowing machine. He debated whether home exercise was one of those moments where it was best to become invisible. Daniela wore a gray sweat suit with green piping. She had a strong, rhythmic stride, but her face was tilted off to the side, its far-off expression belonging to someone lost in thought at a library. Perhaps it was due to the fact that she wasn't wearing her glasses. The machine's whirling turbine created a light wind that ruffled a newspaper lying open on the garden table. Nick chanced sitting at the table. He teetered on the seat's edge, ready to evacuate it at the first indication of annoyance.

"Horrible!" Daniela said as she glided forward. Nick was about to apologize when, on her next forward glide, she added, "That story in the paper." Nick stared down at the article in Italian, meaningless to him, and at its accompanying photograph of a construction site on a coastline. The half-built cinder-block structures looked like mausoleums or sugar cubes. They were the same photographs that had appeared on the protest flyer.

"Thanks to our little mayor . . . ," Daniela began amid the natural ellipses of backward thrusts, "they're building an entire mini city of cheap hotel rooms in Mestre . . . tens of thousands of beds for tens of thousands *more* tourists . . . Guess who that helps? Besides our little mayor whose pockets have been stuffed for approving the development . . . It helps the town of Mestre . . . but those tens of thousands of *more* tourists aren't coming to see Mestre . . . They'll take the train in for the day to swarm Venice . . . All they do is walk around and use the plumbing." Nick decided that Daniela was obsessed with toilets. "That means more crowds and Carnival-mask shops, and out go amenities that Venetians need in order to live . . . No more dentists, dry cleaners, or butchers. How can you live in an unreal city? . . . We Venetians are going extinct! . . . And these anonymous foreign developers, who won't even name themselves for fear of repercussions, are getting rich off our deaths."

It was too bad that Nick couldn't introduce Daniela to Richard West. Their shared Doomsday-Venice prophecies would have rendered them instant allies.

Daniela stopped gliding and reached for a towel. Nick waited in silence, hoping thirty seconds might be a respectful mourning period for the city before he introduced a new topic. He'd interrupted Daniela's workout to glean some necessary information.

Daniela patted her cheeks. "Benny arrives from Shanghai in a few days. You'll love him. Wear that coat of his I gave you, yeah?" Nick nodded, avoiding any mention of the damage he'd inflicted on it. But, to Daniela's larger point, it had taken Nick more than an hour to locate a tailor to mend the sleeve. He'd passed a hundred mask shops in the process.

"I was curious to ask you about someone," he said.

"You *were* curious? What made you stop?"

"Ha! No. I'm still curious. It's about Freddy's sister, Cecilia van der—"

"*Older* sister," Daniela emphasized, like that lone detail was all Nick needed to know about the woman.

"Clay mentioned that they'd been estranged for a long time." He was baiting, but Daniela wasn't biting. "Clay said they didn't get along, and that no one even knows where Cecilia is."

Daniela folded the towel with precision, as if that activity might carry over into the delivery of an extremely precise answer. But when she was finished folding, she slapped the towel carelessly down on the cement.

"That woman is a beast!" she cried. "A true horror. Freddy hated her with a vengeance. He and his sister were mortal enemies. Clay told me that she only acknowledged Freddy's death through a solicitor. I'm surprised she did that much."

"Where is she—"

"Horses!" Daniela spat. She grabbed the handle of the rowing machine and held it out in front of her like an angry water-skier. "That's all she cared about. I'm a firm believer in obsessions, but Cecilia had only one thing on the brain since she was a little girl. Horses. She jumped and did . . . oh, you know"—she danced her feet along the ground—"dressage. Horse tricks. Cecilia was basically raised in a stable. Freddy always said that was the reason their parents spiraled into poverty. It was due to all the money Cecilia made them shell out as a stomping eleven-year-old to keep her in Andalusians and Dutch Warmbloods. But can you picture Freddy on a horse?" Nick could not. Even after months of handling some of Freddy's most private possessions, Nick still had trouble picturing Freddy at all. "He was a city creature from the start, born in a golden sewer grate. So, it was pretty much sibling warfare."

Nick tried his question again. "Where is she——"

"She didn't approve of Freddy's lifestyle. That's what they called it back then. A *lifestyle*. Like it's a hairstyle. Like loving boys and making art and living a radically free existence is akin to the upholstery you've chosen for your living-room sofa. *Oh, he's such an embarrassment. Oh, Freddy's ruining the family name. Oh, Freddy is a disgusting degenerate.* Well, he was a *great* disgusting degenerate, let me tell you. And yet little Cecilia van der Haar, with crinkly brown hair down to her ass, was decidedly not ruining the family name by plowing through the family money to feed and groom her own cavalry." Daniela dropped the handle. "I'm glad Clay never met her. I'm so glad that for once she didn't inflict more harm and decided to stay away. I know that if she'd found Clay sitting in Freddy's brownstone . . . Never in her racist, classist head would she have accepted him."

Nick decided against repeating his question, assuming that "Where is she?" worked as a password to set off a tangent. Instead he asked, "Did you ever meet her?"

"Once!" Daniela answered. "Once she came to Venice. She hates it here. We don't have horses. We also aren't impressed with dusty old names, which is really all she has in her favor. But little Cecilia van der Haar did come once. This was maybe the late eighties? She came with her new husband and naturally stayed at a hotel because Il Dormitorio, even back then, was far too run-down for her liking. But Freddy, for once, was eager to see his sister. He wanted to make amends. It was during one of his dry spells when he'd stopped using heroin. *Ahh!* Yes, that was one horse Freddy did ride back in the day. But when his sister arrived in Venice he wasn't on the nod." Daniela, with an open mouth, mimed falling asleep on her own shoulder. "He really tried to make peace with her. But Cecilia was having none of it! She attacked him the moment her shoe left the boat. She called him a faggot, a junkie, a humiliation. She blamed him for the attention he was getting for his photographs, demanding that he use a pseudonym so as not to blemish *her* name. She even threatened him—I swear to god, I was in the room—about the disgrace he'd cause if he contracted AIDS! How can you threaten your brother about a disease that was massacring his friends at that very moment? *How?* No empathy is how! Nothing human in her! Looking back, I'm afraid Freddy probably had already caught the virus by then. I'd hoped he'd be spared because he was a sissy top."

"A what?" Nick asked. "A *sss*—"

Daniela laughed. "A sissy top. That's what we used to call an effeminate gay man who prefers the top position." She waved her hand at the inevitable ephemerality of sex terms. "But, you see, Freddy shot up, and I'm sure it was the needles that got him." Daniela paused. "Where were we?"

"Cecilia was visiting Venice."

"That's right! And to Freddy's credit, he tried to stomach his sister's wrath, but it finally came to a head at a dinner she threw at the Gritti Palace. Her new husband was evidently loaded, and she wanted to show off in front of a bunch of Italian aristos. She organized a table right on the roof, and everything had to be just so, all that old-school social decorum that mattered to Cecilia. She drew up the seating chart, and it was *man, woman, man, woman* around the table. Do I need to tell you the rest?" Daniela thrust backward on the glider, as if to allow Nick a view of her body. "In the late eighties, I was already as I am now. A full woman. I have always been a full woman, for that matter. But little Cecilia van der Haar managed to jab a thorn into Freddy whenever she could, and she seated me between two women, where a man should sit."

Nick grimaced. "Evil," he said.

"I don't think anyone else even noticed," Daniela continued. "But I noticed, and Freddy certainly did. He stood up, called his sister a cunt first in English and then in Italian, and stormed out. Freddy and his sister never really spoke again."

Daniela pointed to a water bottle under the table, which Nick retrieved. As she drank, he dared to tackle his initial question. "Where is she now?"

Daniela shrugged. "No idea. She married two more times. Rich men who could pay for her equestrian whims. Last I heard she was in Brazil. Or was it Argentina? A horse farm somewhere in South America."

"But her name is still on the deed of Il Dormitorio alongside Clay's."

Daniela smiled. "I think that was Freddy's final act of revenge. Don't let Cecilia get her hands on his precious Venetian hideaway. Freddy must have loved the idea of his sister sharing a title with a young gay black man from the Bronx. But it hardly matters. She despises Venice."

Nick glanced up and noticed an elderly man smoking a cigarette on an upstairs terrace. His hairy arm straddled the railing, and he was peering down on the garden.

"Your neighbor is watching," Nick whispered.

Daniela looked up and shouted a greeting in Italian.

"Is that the Turkish guy who swooped in with the right paperwork to claim this building?" Nick asked. Even with her glasses off, Daniela managed to fix him with a suspicious glare. "I overheard you telling Clay about it the day I arrived."

Daniela smirked. "No, that's my neighbor Signore Breghetto. Until recently, he was under the impression that his family had owned this building for centuries."

"There's nothing he can do to fight the claim?"

She shook her head. "My new Turkish landlord is a very good con man. His only mistake has been choosing to settle now in Venice. No question he owns the building. But it's unlikely he will get to keep his life."

CHAPTER 12

On a calm day, a vaporetto can wind along its path with the unrushed pageantry of a parade float. Tourists help complete that impression, waving ceremonially from the deck at passing crowds. This afternoon, however, as the commuter boat launched itself across the lagoon, jostled by waves and rain squalls, the sensation inside the cabin was more like a stone skipping across the water right before it sinks.

Clay had already chewed three pink *mal di stomaco* tablets, and his intestines were still seizing up on him. The choppy lagoon water wasn't helping, nor was the teeth-rattling vibration from the vaporetto's overtaxed motor. Despite it all, Clay was happy. Happier than he'd been in a very long time, and he had Nick to thank. He glanced out the window as the boat lumbered by the island of San Michele. Spring leaves sprouted above the cemetery walls. Clay thought of wiring his father the hundred and twenty thousand that he owed him and finally putting their long-standing feud to rest. The $750K from West had landed in Clay's account that morning. For the first time in years, he could look into the future and find bright spots of optimism beyond the metal bars of debt.

Even today's bad weather was encouraging: The rain made it highly unlikely that anyone would stumble upon him and Nick together on the island of Murano. Even though the money was now in hand, they still had to maintain their secrecy until they left town. Thus, Clay sat on the 4.2 vaporetto line, being ferried across the bay to the distant meeting point. No Venetian would bother with a trip to Murano during a storm. Only dripping, die-hard tourists packed the waterbus.

He and Nick could leave for the south tomorrow. They could rent a room in Palermo and watch the fishermen reel in their nets of tuna on Favignana. Was it too early in the year to swim off Pantelleria? Yes, it was, but it wouldn't be soon. And there was the rest of Europe to consider. Portugal, Finland—and he'd always wanted to see Copenhagen. It was all waiting for them. Nick was his polestar now. That was all the future he needed.

Earlier that morning, Clay had gone alone to the Accademia Museum, as he'd done on a near weekly basis when he lived in Venice as an intern. For an hour he sat on the wood bench in front of his favorite painting, an enormous dinner-party scene by Paolo Veronese. It wasn't so much *what* he was visiting, but *whom*. There was a figure in the tableau, a young black man in a purple-and-white robe, ascending the steps in the canvas's lower left corner. Several black men inhabited Veronese's rowdy sixteenth-century Venetian banquet—servants, mainly, like the Moors in Richard West's bedroom, or turbaned emissaries blowing in from the exotic East. But Clay's favorite figure didn't fall into any of those stale roles. Something about the guy in the painting spoke to him, the way cameos of black men and women did when they'd flitted across the television screen in his youth, usually in the background behind the white leads who wouldn't get out of the camera's way.

Veronese's *Feast in the House of Levi* was one of the museum's masterpieces, although Clay doubted any visitor had spent as much time with it as he had. He couldn't pinpoint exactly what it was about the young man in the painting that fascinated him. He looked a little bit like his cousin Gad, who'd been "taken by the streets," as his aunt used to phrase it, when Clay was still a boy. (Clay often wondered if his being gay had saved him—saved him from walking down certain alleys and entering certain buildings. Being gay might have kept him alive.) No, it wasn't the similarity to his lost cousin. There was something in the young man's expression that kept Clay coming back—chin down, eyes darting to the side, head uncovered, eyebrows lifted as if to ask the viewer a defiant *What?*, carrying nothing more than his own attitude. He was out of place at this dinner party, as if he had somewhere more important to be. Clay spent an hour with this star figure, glad to visit him one last time before he skipped town. Who knew how long until he'd be back?

The vaporetto groaned against the concrete pier like a wounded elephant, heralding their arrival on Murano. The boat heaved and tilted as the attendant lassoed the ropes to the mooring piles. The tourists inside the cabin stumbled and swayed, knocked off balance with arms flailing. It was an odd way to reach an island known for its fragile glass. Clay hurried onto the dock and followed the masses up the lane lined in glass shops. The restaurant that he'd chosen was in a tiny *campo* that most tourists confused for a private courtyard.

Clay ran his hand over his hair before entering the trattoria, its windows of bull's-eye glass as thick as soda bottles. The restaurant was so old that Clay could smell the decades of wine that had seeped into the floorboards. He spotted Nick at a table at the far end of the room. He was wearing a navy sweater that was unraveling at the collar, and his skin was still wet from the rain. Sexy, adorable Nick with his *who-me?* smile. Nick had managed to wield that innocent midwestern charm like a weapon. Clay trusted his boyfriend too much to worry about that weapon being turned on him.

"Hi," Clay said happily as he sat down.

"I ordered us some wine."

"Good." He bent toward Nick and whispered, "I want to kiss you so badly right now."

Nick wrinkled his forehead. "Why don't you then?"

"Nah . . . ," Clay balked. But in an instant he leaned over the table and pressed his lips against Nick's. It felt bold to kiss him here, more public than in a shadowy church or in the safety of Daniela's apartment. He returned to his seat with a smile, readjusting himself under the table. "We did it! Thank you, Nicky. I feel brand-new today. All that crap in the past is no longer haunting me."

"I'm glad it worked."

"It's you who made it work." Clay opened his palm on the table and Nick took it. He was happy to finally be able to speak to Nick above a furtive whisper. "Honestly, I can't thank you enough. We can leave tomorrow if you want. You pick the first place, and I'll pick the second. That's how we'll do it, okay? How about—"

A waiter in a tuxedo vest inserted two glasses of red wine between them, each one poured to the rim. If the waiter had noticed them kissing, he didn't seem to mind. They both took siphoning sips before clinking their glasses.

"We're rich!" Clay toasted. Nick nodded meekly, tentatively. He didn't look like someone who had just come into hundreds of thousands of dollars. "What's wrong? It's your money too."

"Nothing's wrong," Nick replied. His eyes roamed Clay's face, and Clay instinctively wiped his mouth. "I'm sorry. Yes, we did it. And you've got what you need, that's the most important thing."

"What's the second most important?"

Nick laughed and took a sip of wine. "Well, I've been thinking." He exhaled deeply. "Three hundred and fifty thousand dollars after you pay off all your debts. I know it sounds like a lot, but is it?" The question worked like a dimmer switch on Clay's enthusiasm. His answer was yes, although Nick's tone made it clear it was supposed to be no. "It's not really a lot when you consider how expensive Europe is. Flights and hotels and meals every day. Clothes and toiletries and who knows what else. Medical bills if we get sick. I figure that amount could carry us for three or four years, max."

"Three or four years is a long time," Clay answered, his hand balling on the table.

"I know it is," Nick said with a meaningful nod. "And I'm happy to take that. I'm just wondering, what happens after three or four years? You've got Il Dormitorio, your very own house in Venice whenever you want it, but what do I have to fall back on?" Nick leaned into the table on his elbows, and for a second the rest of his body seemed to go limp between the twin tent poles of his shoulders. He let out a haggard breath. "Clay, listen. I don't want to go back to New York." Nick's eyes glistened as he said the name of that city. Clay suspected the ghost of Ari Halfon must flash through his head every time he thought of New York. Clay understood too well the fear of returning and how a hard loss could become the defining landmark of a place.

"I don't have anything back in New York anymore," Nick continued, his voice stronger now, more determined. "What if we could stay away longer, for as long as we wanted—with *more* money? What if we figured out a way to get our hands on a few *million dollars*?"

Nick again reached for Clay's hand on the table, and he felt Nick's fingers trying to worm into his locked fist.

Clay pulled his hand away. "A few million dollars sounds great," he said coolly. "But how exactly do you propose we get it?"

"I have an idea. Just hear me out, okay?" Nick straightened up, and a little frightened smile shot across his face like a test fire. "We sell Il Dormitorio to Richard West. Just like we did with the silver, we offer the house to him at an absurdly reduced price, which he'd be insane not to accept. We'd make it seem like he's taking advantage of you and landing the deal of a lifetime. We know he'd kill to have the run of the whole van der Haar palazzo. We get the payment in cash, and we go."

The present world briefly drifted away, and the past did exactly what it was good at doing: it engulfed Clay in guilt and sorrow. He pictured Freddy in Brooklyn, so sick he could barely suck down oxygen, begging for Clay to put a pillow over his face to stop the pain, but in his few lucid moments imploring him to hold on to the *palazzino*, at least until Cecilia croaked. He didn't want his sister to get her hands on his favorite earthly refuge.

Clay chose laughter as the safest response. "You're funny, Nicky. You forget that I don't own Il Dormitorio. I co-own it. Cecilia van der Haar is an equal owner, and she would never agree. She'd torture me over it, just as she tortured her brother. That is, if I could track her down."

"Exactly!" Nick cried. "She's so far out of the picture, she'd never know you sold it. She hates Venice. Who cares that an eighty-year-old woman on a horse farm in South America believes she still owns a sliver of property in Italy that she hasn't visited in thirty years? She's probably senile at this point anyway!"

Clay snorted. "Wow, you've really done your homework." This was not the conversation he expected to be having with Nick right now. Portugal. Finland. The Tyrrhenian Sea where it rubbed against golden Africa. "Then you'll know Cecilia's name is listed on the deed along with mine. There's no getting around that fact."

"You could make it seem like you're representing *her* and yourself." Nick's cheeks reddened. Perhaps he was embarrassed by how much thought he'd put into the intricacies of his plan. "Anyway, thanks to the lie you told West, he already believes you own the whole house. So what if Cecilia's name is still on some old Venetian ledger? The van der Haars were messy people who never got around to amending it. West has never met Freddy's sister. He doesn't know what she's like. She's too old to travel now, so you're representing the estate. Come on, if the deal of a lifetime is waved in his face, do you really think he's going to err on the side of caution? Not if we make it seem legit. Not if we make him think it's now or never. I haven't worked out all the details yet, but if we do it quickly—"

"No," Clay said firmly, his palms flat on the table. "No, Nicky. You're getting greedy. Getting greedy is what will get us into trouble. Let's be satisfied with three hundred and fifty. Look, even if we could figure out some way to cheat the records, eventually it would be discovered."

"In ten years!" Nick exclaimed. "Or twenty. Or never, like the Turkish guy who snapped up Daniela's building. You told me once you had contacts that could produce forgeries. And if, years down the line, it ever does come to light, we'd be so far away they'd never find us."

Nick was hallucinating. He was mistaking marble ballrooms and gilt facades and velvet-upholstered gondolas for real life. People went mad in Venice because it lacked the reality check of poverty and ugliness and ordinary struggles. Clay needed to remind Nick how hard the cement was in the rest of the world.

"And whose ass would be on the line if it was found out?" he hissed. "Mine! That's a prison sentence in Italy. I'd be the one to take the rap for fraud, not you." As Clay spoke those words, it hit him that the inverse had been true with the silver. Nick had willingly put himself under the blade, while Clay could have pleaded ignorance. He softened his tone. "Look, I can't sell the house, okay? It's a fantastic idea, and I don't blame you for dreaming it up. But I promised Freddy I wouldn't."

Nick tapped his finger on the table. "No, you promised him that you wouldn't let it fall into his sister's hands. If we sell it to West, she'd be cut out of the deal. Freddy couldn't have expected you to keep the place forever. It's not a mausoleum."

Clay shook his head. "I'm sorry, Nicky. I can't betray him. The answer is no."

Nick stared across the table in disbelief, as if Clay was the one suffering delusions. "*Betray him?* I get that you loved him. But Freddy's dead. You gave him everything when he was alive. Jesus, you borrowed money from your father just so he could keep living in that house. You broke your back for him. When is Freddy going to stop taking from you? He's dead and he's still taking from you." Nick threw his hands up to preempt any response. "Maybe I *am* being greedy," he said more calmly. "I did the silver deal to get you out of the debt that Freddy buried you in. But now, because of it, I can't come back to Venice. I guess you *are* planning on coming back. If you need that house to keep mourning Freddy, that's your decision. All I'm saying is that we have this opportunity right here, this rich guy ready to buy a piece of property that's in your name. When are we ever going to be in this position again?" Nick reached across the table and slid his palm over Clay's knuckles. "Look, even if we walk away now, I'm glad I gave up what I did. All I'm asking is that you consider it. Just think how long the future could go if we made this work."

Clay knew he was being asked to make a choice: Nick or Freddy, the living or the dead, Venice or everywhere else. Hours earlier, sitting on the wood bench in the Accademia, he had said goodbye to that lonely young man walking up the loggia steps, the one who spent the last five hundred years glaring out of the frame. Maybe it was Clay's last goodbye to him. Nick was right. He had been mourning for too many years, first for his mother and then for Freddy. He could go on mourning until it ate up the rest of his twenties and devoured his thirties and he ended up on some desolate shore where his father resided. He could do that, and hold on to the closet-sized palazzo to remind him of the loss of Freddy and his hatred of West. Or he could put it all in the ground. He and Nick could leave with a few million dollars, and they could slip together into the waiting world.

"How exactly would we pull it off?" Clay asked doubtfully. It was an insane idea. And yet so had been everything else up to now.

Nick retracted his hand, as if he hadn't actually expected Clay to go along with the proposition. It took him a second to find words. "We'd figure it out. We'd only do it if we were sure we wouldn't get caught."

"We'd have to be very smart," Clay said.

"We would be," Nick replied. "We will be." And, after a pause: "I love you."

It was a very dark day to let the future in. Flying high over the Venetian islands, a British Airways jet lowered its wheels for touchdown at Marco Polo Airport. On that plane, in the last aisle seat, sat a drunk, heavyset antiquarian dozing on his own shoulder. The elderly antiques dealer did not hear the pilot's warning about preparing for arrival, but it didn't matter.

Dulles Hawkes landed safely in Venice.

PART II

The Things That Get Caught in the Trap

CHAPTER 13

Clay murdered Freddy in the fall. He killed him on the first cold day in October, when the nighttime frost silvered the backyard porch and the morning sun was too weak to burn it clear. Clay always loved the first autumn days in New York—his spring, was how he thought of them, with their air of somber hope. This particular fall day, though, the heavy, puke-green curtains remained shut across the brownstone windows and Clay only stepped outside to let in the new hospice nurse. No murderer in human history had ever worked so hard to keep his victim alive. And no murderer proved more superfluous, for Freddy seemed to be dying just fine on his own. He hadn't eaten in weeks, and the nurse couldn't find a pulse on his wrist. "I think he's already dead," she whispered in her husky Haitian accent. Clay stared down at the withered, bright-yellow skeleton babbling about drugs from his bed. "Yeah, maybe," Clay agreed. "But he won't stop talking."

When Clay and Freddy met in Venice nearly four years earlier, they'd fallen for each other instantly. Their friendship was so fast and consuming, so tongue-and-groove, they seemed to have bypassed the polite get-to-know-you trial run and by day two were already rolling their eyes at each other's annoying habits. Clay realized he'd found much more than a temporary overseas companion or even a strategic ally in his hatred of Richard West. Clay sensed in Freddy a fellow orphan whose heart could only be opened by rare hands. He felt safe around him—safe to confide his secrets in him along with whatever uncensored thought happened to bounce through his head. Freddy gave the conflicting impression of a man who had experienced everything before ("I know what it's like to be broke and out on the streets without even a coat for a pillow") and one fascinated with the most mundane crisis ("Well, *go on!* What happened after the cashier told the woman they were out of stamps?"). He managed to warp the world until the big disasters seemed totally survivable and the smallest incidents transformed into acts of alien wonder. The rough spots in him were part of the charm, or at least he had the boldness not to hide his darkest shadows—the naps at all hours and the bad smoker's breath and the cackling laugh that vibrated Clay's fillings and the proclivity for filching ashtrays whenever he passed an outdoor caffè. Freddy was tough and unapologetic, a gay man from Clay's hometown with a fiendish humor, and he fit Venice like its finest piece of furniture. To Clay, their connection made perfect sense. It was as if, after six months guarding masterpieces in the aquatic galleries of the Peggy Guggenheim, he had graduated from artworks to artist.

Freddy too must have felt an immediate kinship. When the time came for Clay to move out of his rented room in Il Dormitorio, Freddy offered him a place to crash without ever presenting it as an act of charity. "Just drop your bags on my side, doll! Simple as daylight!" Clay understood, though, that Freddy was rescuing him. The other interns bunking at the *palazzino* watched in awe as Clay collected his belongings, crossed under the Blue Madonna, and carried them into the forbidden wing inhabited by the heir of the *very* old American family. The two stayed in Venice through December, celebrating New Year's with Daniela, and in the first fog banks of January, they headed to the train station. "Don't worry," Freddy said. "We'll come back." He spun an imaginary set of keys on his finger. "We can always come back. We own the place."

"You mean, *you* own it." Clay felt the need to make that heart-breaking distinction.

Freddy clasped his arm and stared at him with his veiny gray eyes. "No," he replied. "I mean the both of us."

They bought cheap train tickets to Paris, where they stayed gratis in a room at the Ritz permanently occupied by one of Freddy's "oldest and dearest" friends. Clay was soon to learn that an astonishing number included itself among Freddy's oldest-and-dearest, a global network of shady characters, and erstwhile artists, and drug addicts in decline, and gender-fluid freedom fighters who opened their spare bedrooms for him. At the Ritz, this oldest-and-dearest was of the warm and sketchy variety, an urn-shaped Frenchman named Antonin Marceau who told Clay flat-out that he was a key purveyor in the Parisian black market. "Just in case you need anything special," Antonin offered with a flirtatious wink. "And I do mean *anything*. Documents? A new passport? I take any request as a personal challenge when it is made by a friend." They were sitting around a gold-plated coffee table that held dishes of black caviar dolloped over baked potatoes. In the wake of Antonin's disclosure, the two muscly Lebanese men perched on the opposite couch seemed less like mute party filler and more like bodyguards or rent-by-the-hour offerings. Eventually, the portly Frenchman went to make work calls in the adjoining bedroom. "Midnight," Antonin explained cheerfully, "is when everyone wants something."

Freddy leaned over to whisper into Clay's ear. "Antonin doesn't own a cell phone *or* use email! But he can get semiautomatics delivered anywhere you want within five minutes! Isn't he extraordinary?"

"What do you need a semiautomatic for?"

Freddy sighed in disappointment. "Clay, you're missing the gift here. Tell me you aren't so brainwashed to believe that all you'll need in life can be found in a store."

From Paris, they went to Vienna and then on to Berlin, staying in the spare bedrooms of other oldest-and-dearests. Freddy was greeted as a beloved remnant of an otherwise extinct bohemian world; often their hosts would throw parties at which Freddy was paraded around like an old zoo tiger, a once ferocious animal that was now safe for kids to pet. Finally, Freddy grew tired of all the pawing and decided it was time to go home.

Clay was scared to return to the city he'd fled after his mother died. He couldn't imagine surrendering himself to that haunted Bronx apartment whose thin hallways were patrolled by his sullen father. He told Freddy he'd rather chain himself to a tree right there in the Tiergarten. "I understand," Freddy said, and for the second time offered him asylum. Clay could stay with him in his Brooklyn brownstone for as long as he wanted, and in return he could help organize Freddy's archive of art photographs. Bed-Stuy seemed a safe remove from the Bronx. Clay's plan was to return without going home.

"Are you sure I won't be in the way?" he asked to be certain.

"Don't you see?" Freddy replied, dusting cigarette ash from the front of his shirt. His gray hair had grown long and girlish, and his head jerked around with the movements of a long-beaked bird. "In the way is where I want you."

The Victorian brownstone on Jefferson Avenue had been Freddy's since the early 1990s, bought during one of the rare windfalls in his long and erratic art career. The exterior was best described as "the shade of twenty-eight Brooklyn winters," although Clay began to think of it as "rotted snail." Its interior made Il Dormitorio seem like a minimalist health spa. There weren't hallways so much as trails. Blankets could hide either a throng of whiskey glasses that had gone unwashed since 2003 or the sleeping body of an elderly friend who'd stopped by for a visit and never managed to leave. Freddy had a habit of collecting things, and not just on nights when he couldn't sleep and cruised online auction houses and eBay; a simple stroll to the corner for cigarettes could yield whatever random object he was able to drag onto the porch.

Clay should have realized Freddy van der Haar's dire financial straits the moment he entered the brownstone after their subway ride from the airport. None of the light switches worked. But like everyone else, Clay had fallen victim to the power of the van der Haar last name. Fancy white people who owned property in multiple cities couldn't possibly be destitute. Freddy was too proud to admit the truth, so instead, he lit candles and set them in baroque candelabras and in the spouts of empty soda cans. "It's more fun like this, anyway," Freddy concluded. And it was.

Clay knew he should be looking for a real job in the city, just as he knew he should call his father to tell him he was back. But the slogging, workaday world of New York didn't exist inside Freddy's brownstone. Clay felt that he had been admitted into a secret universe where the air crackled with art and wit and the clocks were always wrong and maybe it was still 1979 or 1983 or any time before the city streets resembled an oligarch's real-estate portfolio. If Clay decided to leave, he wasn't sure he'd ever find his way back, and he loved Freddy's universe too much to take that risk. It floored him that this grouchy, eccentric, mostly sofa-bound man, so acid-hearted around strangers, a glass shard in human form as soon as he stepped foot out of the house, treated him with such uncomplicated affection. Freddy had taken Clay in, and he kept letting him in, further and deeper into the back rooms of his life: "I want to show you the necklace of shells my first boyfriend made for me. It was an ice age ago, back in 1972, when he worked as a painter's assistant. He died later, of course, in the Great Plague, jumping off a fire escape before the disease got him. Go on, slip it over your head." It was Freddy's stories that enthralled Clay to the point of devotion; they were dispatches from a feral, war-torn city that seemed to share little ground with the one of his birth. Clay was determined to soak up the education Freddy offered while he could: a *queer* education—not just gay, but strange. Thus, as the months wore on, he and Freddy practiced their Italian; they killed cockroaches while making pasta dinners and reading aloud on the lives of Renaissance painters; they watched old movies; they cracked each other up. It was the closest Clay had felt to a family since his mother died. He told himself that in six months he'd find a real job. In six months, he'd call his father.

Meanwhile, Freddy really needed him. On Jefferson Avenue, Clay could flex his muscles as the responsible resident, the one who *did* make regular contact with Con Edison to keep the power on, who abracadabraed the blankets off mystery junk piles and secretly returned the broken birdcages and Hula-Hoops to their neighbor's trash. Clay dove headfirst into the job of organizing Freddy's photography archive, which was no small task. Freddy had captured tens of thousands of black-and-white portraits of himself and his friends over the decades—there was Freddy at age twenty as a pretty, long-haired twink in the middle of a Manhattan street wearing a halter top and jean shorts, eyebrows plucked, smoking a cigarette, camel-thin legs crossed coquettishly. Freddy had taken to the camera the way his friends took to drugs, compulsively, romantically, following a night's adventure through the early, beautiful highs and deep into the late, grievous lows of dawn. But his work wasn't all misbehavior and collateral damage; amid the stacks of photographs, like flowers pressed in a book, were softer, sweeter moments of love and companionship that nearly brought Clay to tears. He would often carry these photos over to Freddy and ask, so urgently it surprised him, as if he were asking for directions, *Who were these men? How did they live? How did they get so free?*

Over the years, Freddy's gallerist Gitsy Veros had milked most of the salable value from the shriveled teats of the photo archive. To be fair, Freddy had needed the money—he was always in "desperate danger, doll, for a tiny bit of cash." As a result, there were too many van der Haars clogging the art market for the archive to provide much of a nest egg. Even still, Gitsy and Freddy's other "back in the day" friends treated Clay like a last-minute party crasher who was trying to squeeze any last dollars out of their ailing friend. On their visits to the house, they stared Clay down with silent fury. They winced in displeasure when he and Freddy finished each other's sentences: "Doll, could you go get—" "the magnifying glass" "from the—" "sugar bowl in the kitchen" "so I can show Gitsy—" "the holes in the Persian rug" "in case she knows—" "what moth larvae look like." Freddy and Clay had crawled inside the madhouse of each other's head, and Gitsy, in particular, took it as a violation. (Gitsy would later say to Clay, "You didn't know the real Freddy. You only knew the sick Freddy, which hardly counts.") "Ignore her," Freddy said between drags on his menthol cigarette. "I'm sorry she's such a beast. I'll talk to her." Clay suspected that Freddy never did. No doubt he savored the idea of two people he cared about fighting over him.

Their friendship was never sexual. There wasn't even the usual one-sided pining of an old man for twentysomething flesh. Freddy wasn't always the easiest man to read. He could speak for days in quotations. He pulled quotes from everywhere, from Psalms to the QVC shopping network, from Edith Wharton to Barbara Stanwyck to Edith Piaf. Most of his references were plundered from old movie dialogue, always the cranky heroine or the spurned villain. It was an art form, a conversation collage, but Freddy could also go off script and speak with frankness. When Clay suggested he try online dating, Freddy rolled his eyes and said he'd given up the possibility of love and sex decades ago. He couldn't tap that tired vein anymore. "Sex was all I could think about when I was your age, like the loudest roar in my ears. Now I can't even remember what it sounded like." Many gay men in the city had found themselves highly desired late in life, more active in their seventies than they'd been in their youth. But Freddy had let that part of him go.

Clay presumed it was due to all the lovers who had died on him. If your heart broke nonstop for twenty years, maybe it finally shut off for good. Freddy often talked about French Paul or Canadian Eric or Trenton Mike, his great loves, all dead by thirty, first-wave casualties to a plague the size of an ocean. Clay had seen these boys in Freddy's photographs, living their last years as if they were their first, oblivious to their fast-approaching deaths. Try as he might, Clay couldn't imagine living through a cataclysm like that. Freddy had survived, but he had not been spared.

When Clay went out at night, he was careful not to mention his hope of finding a boy to go home with. But Freddy, dressed in his terry-cloth robe, could deduce his intentions simply by the round of pushups he did before he got dressed or the gel sparkling in his hair. "You're going out on the make tonight, aren't you?"

"I'm just meeting some friends," Clay replied as he threaded his belt through the loops. He knew it was ridiculous to feel guilty about leaving Freddy alone for the night, but he did.

"I wonder who the lucky fella will be," Freddy intoned. "You'll have your pick at the dance." He twirled the sash of his robe. "Now, don't wait for the perfect dream man, just grab a decent one. You know you can bring him back here if you'd like. I won't mind!"

"Yeah," Clay answered coolly, avoiding Freddy's eyes. "I know I can."

But Clay knew he couldn't. An intruder might have broken the spell between them. Freddy had ruled out sex, but he still had a weakness for beauty, and Clay didn't want to dangle a cute guy in front of him like a bauble that he wasn't allowed to keep. There was also a second, more selfish motive at play. Clay had grown possessive of his roommate. He couldn't risk bringing a new young man into the brownstone for fear he might discover Freddy's magic and try to claim him. It wasn't just neighborhoods that were gentrified; people with personalities the size of a borough could be co-opted too.

On those nights out, Clay took the subway almost as far as it ran. On the subway map, Lower Manhattan appeared as a massive octopus head, a bundle of nerves and glands, and its tentacles stretched out in every direction. Clay sometimes had to go all the way into the octopus head to follow a tentacle tip out as far as the airport. Climbing aboveground, Clay quickly dove underneath it again, into basement clubs where music and lights and friends spun around in the soupy, subterranean dark. He took his shirt off and danced for hours under metal pipes that heated strangers' apartments and flushed away their waste. And sometimes he would go home with strangers, black boys or Asian boys or white boys or some combination thereof, to their crowded, boxy apartments in Brooklyn or Queens. He would feel young and happy there, sleeping in snatches beside these smooth bodies whose first names he didn't quite catch. In these foreign beds, his sanity would briefly return and he'd decide that it was time to live full time in the New York of the present. He needed a real job. He needed to face his father, who thought he was still in Italy working at a museum. He needed a boyfriend, someone his own age and steady, rather than this occasional, semi-anonymous catch-and-release. Clay would slip out before the stranger awoke and take the train back to Bed-Stuy, often sharing a subway car with zombied morning rush-hour commuters. He'd shut the door of the brownstone, clean up a night's worth of crushed Newport Lights packets, and breathe a sigh of relief. The real world would always be there. He wasn't ready to pin his life to it yet.

There was such little money that Clay started to impose austerity measures, like cutting Freddy's hair himself in the kitchen and canceling the cable service. They already bundled themselves in coats and blankets at all hours to keep the thermostat as low as possible. Freddy cried elder abuse at his new haircuts and the television blackout, but even Clay knew these cost-cutting strategies were tantamount to cleaning up an avalanche with a snow shovel. Nevertheless, twice a year, they squeezed enough pennies to buy the cheapest economy tickets to Venice, and Clay and Freddy would race around their favorite city with their hearts hammering and their arms interlocked. Sometimes Freddy would make him study an altar painting for nearly an hour. Even as a onetime museum guard, Clay had never actually witnessed a person brought to tears by a work of art. But Freddy's shoulders would quake and his eyes leak at the normal Renaissance sight of a Virgin Mary swaddling her newborn ball of light. "Sometimes I'm scared that

I'm saying goodbye to them," Freddy confessed, "that I'll never see them again, that this is the last time." Clay squeezed his hand. "We'll be back. We own the place."

The end began as a shortness of breath. Back in New York, Freddy panted when he climbed three flights of stairs and a dry, high-pitched wheeze rattled in his chest like an alarm clock ringing under a blanket. "Are you okay?" Clay asked. Freddy waved him off. "Don't worry about me. I'm indestructible. I'm part cockroach." Eventually the wheezing grew constant. "I can't catch my breath," Freddy complained before grabbing the cigarette tucked behind his ear. "You've got to stop smoking," Clay shouted. "I'm buying you the patch!" "We can't afford it!" Freddy bit back, deploying the excuse of tight ends whenever it was convenient. Wheezing led to fainting in the tub. Fainting in the tub led to bloated ankles and vomiting one morning in the kitchen sink.

One doctor led to two, to five, to ten. The news was bad and getting worse by the hour. Freddy was x-rayed, mined for blood and urine, and forced to stand naked on an old-fashioned counterweight scale. Clay was with Freddy for each test and exam, during which the patient remained uncharacteristically quiet. It was almost possible, as he stood naked in the mint-green hospital room, to see his heart jittering in his thin chest. Freddy was afraid.

Clay broke into tears in the taxi on the way back to Jefferson Avenue. He knew what to expect from hospitals and treatments and tall tales from doctors on beating the odds. "Stop it!" Freddy barked. "I'm going to be fine. If you're going to cry, you have to move out." He rolled down the window and let the dirty Manhattan wind rinse his face. "Anyway, I can't die right now. I've got too much to live for."

"Really?" Clay asked in disbelief, wiping his eyes. "Like what?"

Freddy laughed. "Well, like you haven't finished archiving my work yet."

Clay knew that all of the photographs had been promised to Gitsy. In truth, he and Freddy had never spoken about the preservation of his archive beyond compiling it into a semi-coherent order. Did its survival matter to Freddy? Did he secretly hope it might secure him a spot in eternity? Clay stared out the window as the taxi lumbered over the Brooklyn Bridge. It occurred to him what a horrible weight it must be to have once been important. What a noxious task to worry over your legacy as your body crumbles like a leaf.

He turned to Freddy. The shadows of the suspension bridge were slicing the daylight all around them. "Do you mean you want to leave something of value behind?"

The question had come out crudely, but Freddy didn't flinch. His fingers, though, rooted around on the back seat until they found Clay's hand. He said quietly, "I am leaving something of value behind." They didn't speak for the rest of the ride home.

Freddy was convinced he was going to be fine. And to show just how fine he was, he spent the next month smoking and drinking more than usual, putting his lungs and liver to the test. These indulgences were minor in their destruction compared to the internal killers. An Axis of Evil was preying on Freddy's organs and had been for some time. The hepatitis had ransacked his liver and was running sorties on his kidneys. Cancer was squatting in the shells of his lungs and threatened to move into his bones. The HIV was the indolent superpower leader. It sat back and laughed as it strategically weakened Freddy's immune system while its rogue-state cronies did the real fighting.

"I have an idea," Freddy exclaimed. "Let's go to Venice!" Instead, he began chemotherapy. At first the chemo sessions seemed to help, and after a few coma-like days of lethargy, he appeared almost sprightly as he gamboled around the brownstone. Each time Clay rejoiced in the improvement, even though it was also the reason they were spiraling into a pit of financial ruin. For many months of Freddy's sickness, they didn't speak frankly about the danger. Clay was just trying to keep his friend going day by day. Freddy's insurance, however, was refusing to cover most of the specialist bills. Out of network. Exceeding lifetime coverage caps. Finally, Clay had no other choice but to ask Freddy outright if there was any secret, emergency van der Haar fund that he could access.

"Gitsy warned me that one day you'd come demanding money," Freddy joked as he lay on the ripped couch in the basement. Then he stopped joking. There was no money, no secret stash, no forgotten van der Haar trust. There was only a mountain chain of debt, peaks and summits adding up to millions of dollars in total. "I'm so sorry," Freddy said gravely. "You shouldn't waste your youth locked up here with me. I'm not your problem. Put a can of gasoline by the door when you leave and know that I love you." Clay knew that Freddy wasn't joking, not about the love or about the gasoline. But Clay wouldn't walk away. He'd done that once already when someone he loved was sick, and he'd barely survived the guilt of it. This time, through the searing worst of it, he'd be the good son and stay.

A week after the revelation about his finances, Freddy contracted pneumonia. His spleen was also infected, and he went into the hospital for three nights. Clay didn't bother imagining the costs accrued in that visit. He was starting to adopt his friend's *put-it-on-the-life-tab* mentality. When you're buried to your waist, does it matter if you sink to your chest? Freddy came out of the hospital with a new condition: edema. His legs were waterlogged, each calf bloated to the size of a neck. Special socks would be needed—as would a wheelchair and converting the downstairs parlor into Freddy's new master bedroom. The stay at the hospital had terrified Freddy. He swore he saw white ghosts walking around his bed at night ("You mean nurses?"), and he couldn't get the howls of the other patients out of his head. He would do anything, sign any paper, never to spend another night in that place again. Clay hated hospitals too, so it wasn't difficult when Freddy made him pledge not to leave him in one.

Not long after that, Freddy went on oxygen. It further confined his movements to the tether of the long tube screwed to the tank. Clay suggested throwing a fund-raiser for his medical expenses. "You're one of the last New York art pioneers. I'm sure your friends can scare up a few billionaire bankers to come to a cocktail party in your honor. We need the money. *Badly.*" Freddy refused. "I don't want people to see me," he said, motioning to his oxygen tube and swollen legs, "like this." But the real reason wasn't vanity. The only thing worse than death to Freddy was shame, and after seventy-three years of being a *New Yaak van der Haar*, he couldn't bear the public exposure of his condition as a beggar. He'd go with the gasoline option instead.

Clay had maxed out his own credit cards to pay some of the medical expenses. He accrued umpteen fines by defaulting on his college loans. Four banks had turned him down for a personal loan before the final, dodgiest branch extended him twenty thousand at an interest rate that would only appeal to suicide bombers. A chunk of that was eaten up merely by transportation to and from doctor visits. Freddy, with his wheelchair and oxygen tank, was too cumbersome to fit into a taxi; Uber drivers often threatened to go straight to an emergency room when they heard Freddy's hysterical gasping and moaning. The solution fell to renting a party van with a chauffeur. A party van cost a fortune, and its interiors were often decked out in blinking rainbow lights. But since the van's primary customer base was drunk teenagers, Freddy wasn't deemed that objectionable. In New York, all obstacles can be overcome with cash. The loan quickly evaporated, and Clay decided he had only one remaining option.

His father was managing the security for a new office complex in the Riverdale section of the Bronx. Riverdale was far more affluent than Clay's childhood neighborhood, but it still carried some of the borough's brash rhythms and street style. It didn't feel so bad to be back in the Bronx, even on a scorching summer day where people packed under store awnings as if they were rush-hour subway cars. The new office complex was constructed entirely of black glass and was built in the shape of three smooth onyx stones touching at their tips. The development must have cost hundreds of millions, but Clay bet that not a single person living around it—or even working for it—could tell you who owned it. There were no occupants yet inside the glossy buildings, but Clay's father was in charge of providing the impression of top-tier protection. The security uniforms, from ankle to neck, were a bark brown. From a distance, they faded into the color of the glass, causing an optical ripple effect when the guards circled the building.

Clay's father stepped out of an emergency side door. Although he was the manager of the security detail, his uniform was the same bark brown, nearly the shade of his skin, and he had walkie-talkies clipped at each hip the way a western sheriff might have pistols. In the nearly three years since Clay had laid eyes on his father, he had lost all of his hair and had gained a substantial amount of weight. All these years, Clay presumed he'd broken free of his upbringing by taking the internship at the Peggy Guggenheim. Standing in front of his father, taking in the crisp, brown uniform and the camouflaged sweat stains, he realized that his enviable museum job was simply another version of security guard.

"Look at you," his father said, offering his hand in the position of an arm wrestler. Clay clasped it, and his father bumped gently into his chest in an abbreviated hug. "You're looking older than I last saw you. Maybe a little thicker too from all that pasta!"

"I'm sorry it's been so long. I got back, oh maybe a month ago," Clay lied. "I didn't want to visit until I got settled so I could tell you where I was."

His father could have taken issue with that slight, but he simply nodded in resignation. His son was an adult now. They chatted for a while, standing directly under the sun in the sweltering heat, as if inviting Clay into the air-conditioned building would have been a breach of protocol. His father had never been a tyrant, but Clay couldn't help feeling that this chat in the pounding heat was a test of his endurance. His father spoke leisurely, filling him in on his cousins and aunts—who got married, who'd been laid off. After fifteen minutes, Clay introduced his reason for the visit.

"I was wondering . . . Mom's life insurance."

"Yeah?" his father asked with a squint. Beads of sweat rolled down his neck.

"I know she had a policy from the dental association. And I know the money went to you, but she said I should pay off my college loans with some of it. I was thinking, now that I'm back . . ."

His father adjusted his walkie-talkies. He kicked at his own shadow on the concrete. His mouth was moving under his sagging cheeks as if he were chewing gum, although Clay knew gum would be against the rules. The developers wouldn't want gum wads mucking up the smooth black pavement.

"There is some money," his father said. "And, yes, your mother would have wanted it to go to your education. How much do you owe Fordham University?" His father always recited the school's full name. It was never just Fordham.

"One hundred and thirteen thousand dollars." The truth was that he owed one hundred and twelve thousand two hundred and eighty-one dollars for his four years at the Jesuit liberal arts college. But Clay's portion of his mom's life insurance money wasn't going to touch his student debt. Clay was going to spend it on keeping Freddy alive.

His father needed a belt. At the mention of money, he pulled at his waistline. "Okay," he answered. "You give me your address, I'll mail you a check. How's that?" To Clay's relief, his father didn't look annoyed or doubtful.

Clay wrote down the address on Jefferson Avenue. His father took the piece of paper, studied it, and folded it up in his shirt pocket. "You go out to visit your mom at the cemetery?"

"Not yet," Clay said, staring down at his own tarry shadow on the concrete, jamming his heel into the back of his own skull. "But I plan to go. I promise."

Not long after the check arrived, Freddy's oncologist recommended a more vigorous and experimental form of chemo. Early studies indicated that it had a higher success rate with patients living with ("or dying with," as Freddy corrected) HIV. Freddy's GP was on the fence. "It can get risky to switch. Different chemicals, different reactions, different results. You may turn a different color. You may go into remission. You may turn inside out." But the oncologist wagged this delicious carrot: "You might also feel a whole lot better." It was nearly impossible to argue against feeling better—even if it was experimental, even if it was more expensive. "I'd love to feel better," Freddy agreed. "Even one day of feeling better. I just pray I don't lose my hair."

If the earlier chemo had rendered him a listing vessel, this new-and-improved variety flipped him over and sunk him deep. The pain was excruciating, and the cleanup was comparable. Freddy went screaming into unconsciousness, and woke up periodically to scream some more. He vomited so profusely that the parlor was littered with buckets. The diarrhea was worse than the vomiting because it couldn't be directed or contained. Adult diapers only helped so much.

Ironically, Freddy did not lose his hair. It grew a lustrous gray, perhaps conditioned by the night sweats and stomach bile. After two weeks, the pain ebbed enough that Freddy no longer screamed at all hours. A temporary calm returned to Jefferson Avenue. Clay called the oncologist. "Excellent," the doctor said. "We'll let him get his strength back and schedule the next chemo session for three weeks."

The second session yielded the same horrific results, only this time Clay finally hired outside help. Nurses came and went like thunderstorms. Most of them quit because the patient was "uncooperative." One nurse claimed Freddy had bitten him on the hand. Another marched out after proclaiming, "This man needs to be in a hospital!" Thankfully, nurses populated New York like aspiring actors: there could always be a fresh face from an agency waiting at the front door in the morning with only a scant idea of the horror movie underway inside.

One afternoon, as they were pulling up to Jefferson Avenue after an appointment with Freddy's GP, Clay saw the silhouette of a plump, older black man on the sidewalk, a few feet from the open gate to the brownstone. "Stay here a second," he told Freddy and the nurse, who were both crammed in the back of the party van. Clay climbed out and hurried toward his father.

His dad wasn't wearing his bark-brown uniform even though it was a Thursday. Clay feared he had taken the day off for this visit.

His dad held a piece of paper emblazoned with the logo of the bank where Clay had taken out his college loans. Clay had directed the bank to route all correspondence to his new Brooklyn address, but statements must have continued being sent to the Guillory household.

Clay knew what was coming, and yet in the eight white sidewalk tabs it took to reach his father he failed to formulate any justifiable defense.

"What is this?" his father shouted as he shook the paper in his grip. "Says here, you deferred on your loan. Says here you haven't repaid so much as a dime of it. Where's the money I gave you from Mom's life insurance?" His father was enraged, his voice louder and sharper than Clay had ever heard it. "Where is it? What did you spend it on?" Spit flew from his lips. He was visibly quaking. It frightened Clay to see his father yelling out on the sidewalk. Clay glanced around at the renovated homes, either in case a neighbor got the wrong idea and called the police or in case there might actually be need to call the police should his father rush toward Freddy in the van.

"Dad, please." He reached for the letter, but it was whisked away. "I needed the money. I will pay my loans back. What difference does it—"

"I gave you that money for your college tuition. Not for you to spend on anything you feel like." He glared over Clay's shoulder. "Who is that?"

Clay spun around. The nurse had not heeded his order to remain in the van. She'd opened the back door, exposing the frail old white man wrapped in a lavender throw and haloed by blinking colored lights. "What are you doing with that man? Did you pick him up from the hospital?" Clay's father smiled angrily. "You spending your mother's money on some rich white guy, *van der something?*" His father must have searched the brownstone's front-door mailbox. "What the fuck are you doing, Clay?"

"I'm helping him. He's sick," Clay managed. "I was taking him to the doctor."

"Oh, helping!" His father nodded vigorously. "What a good guy you are! Helping. Your mother could have used some help. I could've used some help." He raised his palm and spread his fingers wide. "Five! That's how many times you visited your mother in the hospital. I counted. Five! And she counted too. I was there every day for months. You managed to drop by five times to see your mother when she was dying. And now you're using her money on this old, screwed-up—" Clay wished his father would sputter a derogatory word, freeing Clay to hate him for uttering it—hating him for something would have helped him a great deal right now. But his father didn't use any of those derogatory words. Instead he simply clenched his hand. "I'm through with you," he yelled to his son. "Don't come back. Not even when you realize your mistake." He tossed the loan statement at Clay's feet and strode off, down the buckled sidewalk, until he was lost among the tattooed legs and toddler-weighted shoulders of Bedford-Stuyvesant.

When Clay walked back to the van, Freddy whispered through his cracked lips, "Who was that awful man?"

"That was my father." Clay reached into the back seat to slip his arm around Freddy's hanger-sharp shoulders. Long, soft fingers crested his scalp, Freddy's fingers. Their tips pressed against the indentation where Clay's skull met his spine. He froze, and Freddy's fingers remained there, exerting a tender pressure. They stayed like that for a minute in the darkness of the van, and it took all of Clay's strength to snap awake and pick up this frail body and carry it into the house.

Sometimes, late at night, Clay hallucinated that it wasn't a man he was trying to save but a piece of New York. If Freddy died, a vital chapter of the city would disappear with him, never to return, all of those righteous sins and transgressions, all of those young gay men in thousands of black-and-white photographs, all of his raw beauty, up in smoke. Freddy was the last bridge, and once he fell, that secret city inside him would be lost for good. Clay knew this much: there was no memory in New York; there was only the living. But in the end, it didn't matter who or what he thought he was saving. After four rounds of the new-and-improved treatment, Freddy couldn't take it anymore.

He would die soon. Every single hospice nurse claimed that Freddy would live only for a few more hours, a few more days. And yet summer ticked on, each month hotter than the last. The weeds wilted in the back garden. Flies died on the windowsills. And gasping, wheezing Freddy, whose every inhale sounded like the brawl of the century, continued to exist. It was very hard to kill a cockroach.

The new-and-improved chemo hadn't been the worst part of Freddy's illness. They had finally reached the worst part, the waiting for the abusively tardy angel of death to arrive. In his lucid moments, Freddy pleaded with the nurses: "More morphine, kill me with it, please." And the nurses would let out an exhausted groan as if to say, *Believe me, I'm trying.* One nurse told Clay in the kitchen, "I've given him the highest dosage I can. It's enough to kill a horse. Most hospice patients die from morphine, but I can only OD him within an acceptable margin of error!" The death that Freddy needed was apparently beyond that acceptable margin of error.

August and September crawled by, and all Clay could do was sit at his bedside and hold his hand. "Please put a pillow over, stop breathing . . ." Freddy's eyes would hound him from the pillow, his lips as dry as sand dunes. "Please. Clay. I don't. Want to." His fingertips pattered against the back of Clay's hand like light, insistent rain. Clay would squeeze his hand and bring a cold washcloth for his forehead.

On the first chilly day of fall, Clay let the new nurse in. They made small talk in the kitchen as he poured her a cup of coffee. Then she went to work, trying to find a pulse on Freddy, changing his IV, adding his morning dose of morphine to the drip. Freddy's muscles went slack like cut rubber bands. Clay sat in the chair by the bed while the nurse with the husky Haitian accent went upstairs to use the bathroom.

Clay rushed to the drawer and removed the needle. He'd pilfered it from the bag of a hospice nurse a week ago, the one who was too busy quitting to notice the theft. Clay had spent two years doing everything he could to keep Freddy alive. But now the only favor he could do for his best friend was to help him reach an end. Clay sat in the chair, leaned over the bed, and whispered in Freddy's ear.

"Make a fist for me," he said. "One last gesture, and that's it, I promise. Try to squeeze my thumb." Freddy managed to curl his palm around Clay's thumb. A single vein rose on the long, gray arm.

Clay pulled the cap off the needle. He hoped this amount of morphine, plus the horse dose already running through him, would be enough. He didn't dare google the question on his phone in case the police ever checked.

"Freddy," he gently whispered. "I love you." He kissed him softly on the forehead. He kissed him on each warm island of a closed eye. Freddy was squeezing Clay's thumb with all of his might, like a passenger in a downed plane gripping for mercy on an armrest. "Okay, sweetheart," Clay said. "It's time now." Clay was having trouble keeping his breaths steady. His fingers holding the syringe were shaking. "I love you so much. Thank you for everything. Thank you for letting me in." A nod. A little sad moan lost in the back of the throat. "Think of Venice, okay? Think of that fantastic city with all the lights on the Grand Canal. We're there on the water. I'm with you. I'm right next to you there. Okay. It's time." The needle prodded the vein, and Clay's thumb touched the plunger. "I love you. Here you go."

CHAPTER 14

FOR SALE BY OWNER, 15TH-CENTURY PALAZZINO, GOING FAST, MEDIOCRE CONDITION, LOWBALL OFFERS ACCEPTED AND PRICED TO MOVE. IDEAL FOR EXTENDING YOUR OWN QUARTERS, IF YOU HAPPEN TO LIVE NEXT DOOR. INQUIRE WITHIN.

It was a shame Clay couldn't plant a for-sale sign in the front yard and wait for Richard West to spot it. Clay and Nick agreed that the best way to entice West into buying the van der Haar *palazzino*—and thus restoring all of Palazzo Contarini to its original design—was to make it seem like it was his idea. That tactic had worked so flawlessly with the silver, thanks to Nick's guiding hand. But this time, Nick couldn't exert much influence without raising suspicion. The lion's share of the scheming rested on Clay. Of course, he could simply notify his neighbor that he was interested in selling, but that might give West the opportunity to do his homework. They wanted West hungry, scrambling, in danger of missing out, and trusting his instincts—confusing himself for the hunter instead of the prey. Ultimately, Clay devised a straightforward method for the news of the sale to reach his neighbor next door. Venice had the most baffling postal address system ever assigned to a city; the occasional mix-up among house numbers was inevitable.

"That's right, yes, I'm interested in selling my side of Palazzo Contarini," Clay said over the phone to a local realtor in Italian. "I'd like to schedule an appointment for you to come over and tour the place, the sooner the better." Palazzo Contarini's street number was 4228—shared conjointly by the van der Haars (4228A) and the Wests (4228B). Clay knew from his assistant days how much Richard resented being the Beta to the far paltrier Alpha. "Yes, noon tomorrow works perfectly. My name is Clay Guillory. The address is 4228B, that's B as in *bacio*. Ring the buzzer and make sure to tell whoever answers that you're here to do an appraisal to sell the house. *Grazie mille! A thousand thanks!*"

The next day, Clay positioned himself at the second-floor window overlooking the front entrance. At 12:12, a balding man in a loose-fitting maroon suit marched toward the door with an annoyed expression. Clay caught sight of West at the end of the alley, peeking around the corner. By the time Clay ran downstairs to greet the agent, West was gone.

"I'm sorry, did I say B? I swore I told you A as in *amore*. Anyway, come in." He gave the realtor a perfunctory house tour. Depending on the condition of the room they entered, the man's face publicized revulsion or delight.

"*Ha una sua bellezza particolare!*" It was indeed a peculiar property, very small, and a challenge to sell, the realtor admitted. It would have been far easier if the van der Haars had divided their wing by floor, instead of the awkward vertical cake slice down the side of the house. When Clay told the realtor that the Sebastiano Ricci fresco was not officially listed as *vincolato* with the Italian government's preservation board, he expected the response to be equally damning. "Oh, but that makes it so much easier!" the man exclaimed. "It would slow down the process by months if we needed to wait for permission! Don't tell them! The fresco will help the sale, and this way the new owners can do whatever they want with it!" The exposed wires and corroded sconces didn't seem to faze the realtor either; he'd simply target buyers looking for a restoration project. Still, Clay shouldn't get his hopes up. Venetian real estate was largely a western market. The cash-flush sheiks and Russians turned up their noses at palazzi: "Not *blingy* enough," the realtor said in American-accented English, as if to emphasize crass taste. "Too many restrictions. No pools or hot tubs. It is easier to park a yacht with all of those amenities in the lagoon." Clay's best bet was a rich European retiree—"We've had a lot of interest from the French recently." The realtor would have to crunch the numbers back at his office, but four million euros seemed a sensible listing price. At hearing that massive figure, Clay tried to look like his eyeballs hadn't been blasted into the back of his skull.

The best bet for the sale of Il Dormitorio was not a French retiree. The best bet was the American next door, and right on cue, ten minutes after the realtor departed, Clay heard four heavy knocks from behind the bookshelf in Freddy's bedroom. Clay opened the walnut door, temporarily blinded by the afternoon sunlight. West stood in the frame.

"How are you?" West asked with an urgency that didn't fit the question. Before Clay could respond, West yammered out an excuse for the interruption. "I wanted to check that the money for the silver made it into your account okay. Did it?"

"Yes," Clay replied. "Thanks for sending it. I hope you're enjoying the pieces."

"Indeed! You'll have to come over sometime and see them in

the cupboard." West gazed down at the floor and watched his espadrille draw an invisible line across the terrazzo. "Are you staying
in Venice awhile, or will you be off soon?"

Just ask, Clay thought. Just ask me outright if I'm selling the
house. Tell me you want it, and that you would make me a better
deal if I cut the realtor out of negotiations.

"I'm staying on a little longer," he answered casually. "I'm still
getting Freddy's belongings in order. There's been a lot to go
through."

"I can imagine," West said. And as if to buy time, he renewed
the half-hearted invitation. "When you do come over, you'll
have to stay for dinner. Karine would like that." Did Karine even
know that Clay existed? Was Karine aware that he had been her
husband's Venice companion before she'd moved here from Germany?

"A dinner would be . . ." Clay nodded vaguely instead of settling on a word.

"Perfect!" West said in a timbre of sincerity. "I'll check our
calendar."

Clay reached for the doorknob to indicate an end to the conversation.

"One last thing!" West blurted and blushed. "A man rang my
bell earlier. A realtor who said he was looking for you in order to
do an appraisal?"

"Ah, sorry about that. Our addresses . . ."

West laughed. "I still get gift baskets delivered from lonely parents in Wisconsin wondering how their daughter is surviving her
internship."

"I've told the interns to have their mail sent to the Guggenheim.
I'll call—"

"Oh, it's not *too much* of a bother." West drew another line with his shoe, and this time he was determined to step over it. "But about the realtor. I hope this doesn't mean you're putting the house on the market. I'm not losing you as a neighbor already, am I?" West glanced over Clay's shoulder, lifting up on tiptoe as if to signal how eager he was to get beyond the doorway. He made no effort to disguise his interest. West was a rare kind of person who had never been forced to hide his wants.

"I wish that realtor hadn't said anything."

"I don't mean to pry. But I am concerned. We do share a roof and a wall."

Clay paused for a moment, arranging his words carefully. Several million euros depended upon putting them in the right order. "The truth is I haven't made up my mind about what to do with the house. I love Venice. But I'm not sure how feasible it is to keep this place when I'm trying to build a life, post-Freddy, in New York."

"Post-Freddy," West repeated drolly. "Hurricane recovery."

"In a way, yeah." Clay took a deep breath and let it sputter out of him. "Anyway, you *might not* be losing me as a neighbor just yet. But if that does happen, I'm sure your new ones won't be the type to receive care packages from worried parents."

West pursed his lips. Clay knew that behind his seemingly innocuous joke about care packages, he'd delivered a pointed threat. A new resident inside Palazzo Contarini might be far more disquieting than a cast of rotating Ivy League interns on their best behavior. They could end up being even wealthier than the Wests, and thus more entitled, more demanding, and more outrageous in their plans for extensive renovations.

"I would hope that—" West broke off and tried again in a harsher, more businesslike tone. "When I bought my side of the building ten years ago, there was an implicit understanding—" He aborted this attempt too. It was too aggressive. "Selling is not something to take lightly," West finally rationalized in a calmer voice.

"I was only getting the realtor's opinion. That's why I wish he hadn't bothered you."

"What was his opinion, if you don't mind my asking?"

Clay demurred. "It was only a quick assessment. He didn't—"

"I understand. But what did he say?"

There was no point in being coy anymore. When Clay had been bargaining with Richard West over silver cups, there had still been a life to go back to in New York: an estranged father, boxes of his books and clothes, a degree from a local university. But Clay knew the stakes in selling the *palazzino*: there was a solid chance he'd never be able to return safely to that old life. One day, West would probably discover the fraud—a felony in Italy, punishable with prison time—and he'd come looking for him. Clay was going to build a future somewhere far away. In order to do that, he and Nick would need all the money they could get.

"He appraised it somewhere in the region of five million euros," Clay answered with a straight face. "Upper five." He was pushing his luck, but he had been pushing his luck for a while now. "The place needs work. But there's the Ricci fresco, which ups the value considerably."

West digested the "upper five" with a flare of his nostrils. "Really," he replied. "I wouldn't have thought it could fetch that much. No offense, but it's the size of some people's walk-in closets. He really said upper five?"

Clay shrugged. "It's a lot to take in," he granted.

"And you have all of your documents in order?" West asked. "I mean, everything's in your name. No contestation of the will from Freddy's sister? No delays with the Italian authorities or the *visura catastale*?"

"It's all in place," Clay lied and continued to lie. "As I told you, the sister's been out of the picture for a long time. And the realtor thinks any of the additional paperwork will be easy to process." Clay could tell that West's brain was absorbing these facts like nutrients. Could this actually be working? For the first time, the rickety plan that he and Nick had assembled in a Murano restaurant seemed genuinely plausible.

A woman's voice cried from deep in the sunlight. "Dick?" West turned his head and replied, "Yes, dear, one second."

West looked frustrated when he turned his attention back to Clay. "I'd like to talk to you about this further," he said. Clay nodded. "After all, it affects me considerably. It's been a mission of mine to preserve the integrity of this palazzo, which mattered to Freddy as well, no matter how he let his side go in the end." Clay stopped nodding. "I'd like you to give me some time to think before you put the house on the market. As you say, you're still mulling the decision over."

Clay had no intention of allowing his neighbor time to think. "I'm going to decide in the next few days," Clay replied bluntly. "I'm not sticking around for the summer tourist season."

West clucked. "Some of these properties sit on the market for years with their price slowly dropping. You should be prepared for that likelihood. You might be waiting awhile."

Clay smiled. "Yeah, the realtor said that does happen half the time. And for the other half, if they're priced to sell, they're snapped up in minutes."

Karine's voice called insistently again, and they exchanged abrupt goodbyes. Clay shut the door. Now that this crucial step in the scheme was completed, he set to work on the next one. He'd already scoured Freddy's papers to locate examples of Cecilia van der Haar's signature, and he knew from several nights of online research that a minimum of three official documents would be needed to convince an Italian notary. This next step was the most critical and least dependable. It required an act that could only be supplied by Freddy's orbit of lawless friends. There were benefits, after all, to a life built on the margins. No one had ever whispered a stock tip in Clay's ear, but thanks to Freddy, he did have connections that could deliver semiautomatic rifles anywhere within five minutes.

He googled the number for the Ritz in Paris off Place Vendôme.

"May I speak with Antonin Marceau?" he asked the receptionist in his twelfth-grade French.

"Monsieur Marceau doesn't accept outside phone calls," the receptionist informed him. "He only makes calls. He does not accept." It was a typical whimsical roadblock erected by one of Freddy's oldest-and-dearests.

"Can I leave a message?"

"Monsieur does not accept messages."

"Okay. But he *is* staying at the Ritz right now, yes?"

"*Mais oui*," she replied. "He is most certainly here."

"And he'll be staying at the hotel for the next week?"

"Monsieur Marceau is always with us," the receptionist said wearily, as if the portly black-market gangster were a French virtue or a troublesome ghost.

"Well, if you happen to see him, please tell him a friend is coming to town for a visit."

CHAPTER 15

The late-morning sun was strong on Nick's face as he crossed a wide, chair-rimmed *campo*. He carried the foil-wrapped bottle of silver polish that he'd bought for Richard West. Nick couldn't convince West to make a bid on Il Dormitorio directly, but there were other means of persuasion that might help to push the plan along. Earlier in the morning, he'd texted Eva to ask her to lunch. She sent the address of a seafood restaurant in Cannaregio off Sacca della Misericordia.

Passing down a narrow alley, its stones still slick from a night-time rain, Nick caught the dank Venetian odor that Clay loved. He tried to find some love for it too, although it reminded him too much of his childhood basement. The path ahead was blocked by tourists, leaving only a tiny ant-tunnel gap that pedestrians had to slip through one at a time. As Nick made his way through the gap, he spotted Battista approaching from the other end of the passage. He wore a black shirt with a blue silk tie. His backpack was tight around his shoulders with the familiar black tube sticking out of it. He appeared to be guiding an older Italian man shuffling right behind him. That man had rake tines of gray hair streaked over his bald head and an unlit brown cigarette clenched in his teeth. He held a bloated leather briefcase to his chest as if it were a pile of firewood. Midway down the alley, Battista stopped under a sign for a trattoria and gestured for the older man to enter. Nick shouted Battista's name before he followed the man into the restaurant.

Battista glanced up and for once offered a sincere smile. Nick picked up his pace as Battista pulled out a cigarette and lit it. Through the trattoria's window Nick watched the bald man reaching a table where a woman was already seated. She had a pile of folders on the plate in front of her as if paperwork were her meal, and her companion quickly added folders to his own plate. It had somehow escaped Nick that there could be tedious work lunches in Venice.

Nick didn't usually go for smokers, but Battista made the habit look seductive. The smoke drifted around the Italian's curly black hair, mimicking its waves and coils. Two mosquito bites rose along his upper neck, the lower one dusted in fine hairs he'd missed while shaving.

"I thought you had already left for Milano, Nick."

"Not yet," Nick replied with what he hoped was an attractive grin. He nodded toward the cardboard tube. "You're still lugging that around."

Battista reached behind him to pat the backpack. His RESI-DENTE RESISTENTE pin sparkled in the light. "These are very important plans for Mr. West's projects. We have been working night and day. I have been so busy lately." He winked as he added, "*Too busy.*" The Italian wink, Nick had learned, was a standard gesture of affection, rare in New York and virtually nonexistent in Ohio. Nick liked this friendlier version of West's assistant. Maybe he'd only been remote on their previous meetings because his boss had been looming in the background.

"You should ask for a vacation," Nick advised.

"No, I couldn't," Battista said vehemently, shaking his head as if such a request would be career suicide. Serving as the private secretary to a rich American must be a more prestigious position for a young Venetian than Nick had imagined.

"Do you like working for Richard?"

"Very much," Battista replied. He picked a piece of tobacco off his tongue, and as he gazed skyward, he seemed to be pondering the full depths of the question. "Do you know what it is like for young people in Venezia?"

"No," Nick admitted.

"It is impossible," he said as he lowered his eyes. "There are few opportunities for work that improves my city. I love the projects that Mr. West is planning, because they help Venezia, they bring it back to life. Most jobs for locals my age are about playing a fool, dressing up in costumes for tourists or driving them around on boats. Almost all of my friends"—he licked the sweat that was forming on his lip—"they had to move to the mainland after school to find work. All but two from my class are gone, and they won't be back. But because of Mr. West, I can stay and make a difference. I can work to keep my city alive. That is important, no?"

Nick tried to imagine caring about Dayton that much, about wanting to do anything for it besides flick it away with his finger. Maybe that was because Dayton wasn't sinking. Maybe that was because Dayton had made it very clear that it didn't need him. Nick found himself envious of Battista's love for his hometown.

"It's great you're getting that chance," Nick said. "Don't let Venice get murdered. It would be a very sad funeral."

"With how hard it is to get these restoration permissions approved by the local government, it seems like it is trying to kill itself."

Nick turned to the window, where the two bureaucrats inside were slowly picking through their paperwork. "What project are you working on with them?"

Battista reached over his shoulder and pulled out the cardboard tube like a samurai sword. "Important plans," he said vaguely. "Blueprints, certifications, architectural layouts. There are many signatures and inspections before we can get approval for our next restoration. Very complicated and top-secret." Nick was well acquainted with the self-important smoke screen of an underling—a snow of words to hide an ignorance of facts. He himself had used that technique at Wickston. He suspected Battista would deliver the cardboard tube to the table and wait outside until it was time to pay the bill with West's credit card. But Nick nodded along as if impressed. Wiser, kinder souls had doubtlessly done the same for him.

"I'm sure this one will get a green light," he said.

"It is only one project of many," Battista insisted. "Today I start research on a new assignment. Phone calls, tracking down names and dates. All a headache!" He flicked his cigarette and took his cell phone from his pocket. "Give me your number. I will WhatsApp you. Maybe we can have a drink before you leave for Milano."

Nick, trying not to picture making out with Battista after those drinks, recited his digits and then excused himself. "I have to meet Eva for lunch."

"I hope you can cheer her up," Battista said. "She will have to go back to France soon if she can't find a job. You see? This town is not easy for anyone young."

Nick shook his head in sympathy. For the sake of the plan, it was precisely the sad news about Eva that he'd been hoping to hear.

He had to sprint to reach the restaurant on time. Eva was already slouched at a corner table. She chewed on a drink stirrer as she read a local newspaper, turning the pages on the horrors of the apocalyptic new tourist development in Mestre and the threat of an upcoming transit strike. There was also a mass extinction of shorebirds under way in Tuscany, for those seeking misfortunes beyond the Veneto region. Bad news was perfect company for Nick. When he sat down across from Eva, she made the expression of a hissing cat.

"I'm in the worst mood," she warned him. "But I promise I'll pretend to shake out of it by the time we order."

"Why pretend when you can take me down with you?"

"Good idea!" She tossed the newspaper aside and banged her palm against her forehead. "This gesture is meant to summarize my last few days looking for employment. *Looking!* At this point, it's more like staring out of windows for employment. That counts, right?"

"Absolutely."

"You may have noticed that I've stopped Instagramming my days here. I'm tired of bragging about my life in a city that clearly doesn't want me."

"Oh, Eva. Post one more shot of a gondola nearing a bridge. *Please!*"

Nick was in his element with Eva—their humor matched, and their eyes held each other in the soft focus of mutual appreciation. He was also aided by the inherent loneliness of a fellow American adrift for too long on foreign soil. Nick needed her friendship in order to pressure her uncle. He felt sure that West would do almost anything for his niece. After they ordered, Eva continued to sulk.

"Don't be too down about your prospects," Nick said, tapping his fingers on the pink linen tablecloth. "What about that thing you and your uncle were talking about a few days ago? That was a brilliant idea."

"What thing?" she asked dubiously. She stopped chewing on the drink stirrer and began nibbling at the skin around her fingernails.

"Um." Nick feigned a pillage of his memory. "That fresco in Palazzo Contarini you said you wanted to restore."

"I love everything you're saying," she replied with a laugh, "which makes it extremely sad that I have no idea what the hell you're talking about."

He snapped his fingers over the breadbasket. "You and your uncle were talking about restoring—god, what was it? Why is it my job to remember your ambitions for you?—a ceiling fresco of Mary by—" He hesitated. "Tiepolo? Was it Tiepolo who painted the fresco in the house next door to your uncle?"

"Sebastiano Ricci!" Eva cried out. She grabbed a piece of bread as a reward for the correct answer. "Yes, you're talking about the Blue Madonna fresco. It's in terrible condition. Or so Uncle Richard tells me. I haven't seen it with my own eyes. The kid next door is not a friend. Evidently, he's a sworn enemy to the Wests and should be approached with utmost caution. But you're right. I do wish I could work on that fresco. What a fucking dream that would be."

"It seemed like Richard thought there was a way you could, right? Did I misunderstand?"

"Yes," she said. "Your English comprehension is deteriorating rapidly. I'm getting worried about you."

"I swear, your uncle said that. I can't remember if it was when we were all in his office, or afterward, when you had too many drinks in the living room."

"I did get blindingly drunk that afternoon."

"Yes, you did."

"I did not!"

"I was embarrassed for you. But seriously, your uncle did say how fantastic it would be if you could restore that masterpiece. And he's right when you think about it. That fresco isn't landmarked, is it? It's probably not even included in the city records. The local authorities wouldn't have any power to choose the restorer. It's on private property. My god, it's right there, rotting away on the other side of your uncle's wall, and no one is lifting a finger to save it. That's awful, especially when here you are with all of your training and all you can do to fill your days is have lunch with me."

"I know," she grumbled.

"It was a good idea for you to restore it."

"It still *is* a good idea!" she said defensively. Then she sat up straight. "You know, it really is a good idea. The Venetians couldn't stop me! I'd have total control and I'd do it right, unlike the chemicals they used to strip *The Rape of the Sabine Women*."

"I don't know why you don't listen to yourself when you're drunk."

"Because I don't remember. I honestly don't—"

"Well, I don't even know who Sebastiano Ricci is!" Nick raised his hands to underscore his total innocence.

"Wait a minute!" Eva started to gnaw around her thumbnail. "I *could* restore that fresco! Why not?" She eyed him harshly. "Did my uncle say how we'd get access to it? He hates the kid next door. He's spent entire dinners raving on about what an underhanded schemer he is. Do you remember exactly what he said?"

"I don't remember anything. You should ask Richard about it. I have no idea what you two were talking about. The whole idea sounds crazy."

"It isn't crazy!" Eva went quiet. "It really isn't that crazy at all."

"Especially when you think how long it's taking for your uncle to get any other restoration projects approved."

She wasn't listening, her eyes roving across the pink tablecloth. Nick didn't need to push any further. He reached over and gently batted Eva's hand away from her mouth. "Don't fill up on cuticles. We have swordfish to share."

As they ate, Nick steered the topic away from the Blue Madonna, hoping to put distance between himself and the idea. But Eva's wax-and-wane attention was an encouraging sign that she was already plotting a way into the neighbor's house.

When the bill arrived, she snatched it up. "My treat," she said. "You might have just saved my life."

He slid the foil-wrapped bottle of silver polish across the table. "Can you give this to your uncle for me?"

"Give it to him yourself. We're only a few blocks from the house, and I know he'd love to see you."

They walked together through the spring heat. A group of young gondoliers passed, each in a straw hat with red ribbon. In their bright, new uniforms, they had the excitable air of fresh recruits being sent to the front lines to replace the tired and wounded.

"If Karine's home," Eva said, "don't mention the Ricci fresco."

"Why? Would she be against it?"

"Well, she and Uncle Richard have an agreement. He gets to invest in his projects if she gets to invest in hers. I think they've been arguing about how much he's been spending. So I don't want the idea brought up while she's in the room."

"What are her projects?" Nick asked. They were nearing Palazzo Contarini, and Nick had to keep himself from glancing down the alley that led to Clay's door.

"She's all science, all brain-mapping research or whatever she was working on in Leipzig. It's a terrible marriage in theory, two people with money and opposite interests on where it should be spent." They entered the garden, and Eva unlocked the iron door. Before they took the stairs, she turned and offered him the wide, Teflon smile of a career criminal. "Don't worry. I'm going to get to that fresco if I have to take a sledgehammer to the wall in the middle of the night!"

"You scare me, Eva," he replied happily.

When they opened the door to the living room, it was not Karine's voice that echoed from deep in the house. Nick heard West's monotone reverberating from his office, followed by a man's cloying laugh punctuating each sentence. When the stranger spoke, Nick couldn't make out the words, and yet the warbling British accent seemed disturbingly familiar. It made the hairs of his neck stand on end. The velvet curtain parted, and West strode down the hall. Nick held up his gift and prepared to launch into a lecture on proper polishing techniques.

"Nick!" West reeled as he entered the sunlight of the living room. "What a surprise. I was planning on calling you today."

Before Nick could respond, the stranger shouted from the office, "Make mine with no ice, okay?"

Nick flinched at the sound of the voice. West stepped toward him, speaking in a whisper. "Don't take it personally. It wasn't for a second opinion, I swear. I have absolute faith in your judgment."

"What second opinion?" Nick asked, either aloud or to himself. He wasn't sure. His pulse roared in his ears, and the blaring light on the silver foil in his hands was making him feel nauseated.

"I only reached out to brag," West said with a guilty grin. "I know it's childish. But after years of that drunk fool not being able to get his hands on a single piece of van der Haar silver for me, I couldn't resist sending one snide email. I won't lie—it felt great! Don't worry, I told him I had *you* to thank." West squeezed Nick's shoulder. "I've got my own Wickston man."

"What?" Nick said faintly. He didn't have the strength to speak any louder. "I don't know . . ."

One second of silence elapsed before the office curtain screeched farther across the rod and Nick's nightmare took specific shape. Dulles Hawkes had widened in the months since Nick had last seen him, but his skin was still washcloth damp, his loose shirt still bleeding sweat rings at the armpits. Dulles blinked at the sunlight and put his palm above his eyes in order to see. West stepped back, as if he were inviting two dogs of the same breed to sniff each other.

"Dulles!" Nick cried in the tone of an insult.

"Nick, Nick, Nick," the older man sang in a fey vibrato. "What luck to come across you here in Venice!" Above Dulles's seal neck, a smile hung. Nick couldn't determine whether that smile was one of animosity or charity, of cruelty or humor. Certainly, even if Dulles's twin hobbies of alcohol and cocaine had amped up in retirement, he'd still be able to deduce that the van der Haar antiques on West's cupboard were forgeries. In fact, he already knew they were fakes because he'd advised Freddy not to bother selling them. Dulles probably also knew that Nick was no longer a Wickston employee. Nick considered escaping to the bathroom. He imagined wiggling through a window, falling into a canal, swimming toward the airport, and phoning Clay while waiting for a plane to take off. But he kept the smile on his face, the only escape route available to him.

Dulles extended his hand. Nick took it and felt a mean, knowing squeeze on his fingers. There was a struggle over Nick's fingertips as he ripped his hand away.

"Richard was just telling me how you advised him on those last remaining van der Haar antiques!" Dulles nodded jovially. "You can always trust a Wickston appraisal! The best in the business, now that I've retired."

Nick laughed and turned toward the sunlight in the room, the only direction that seemed safe.

"I was at my flat in London when I received Richard's email. As I happened to be flying to Rome, I thought, Oh, why not stop in Venice for a few days and see these paragons of colonial American silver."

"They're beautiful, aren't they?" Eva said, sitting on the sofa in the shadowed corner.

"Oh my goodness!" Dulles rasped. He pulled a red silk handkerchief from his pant pocket, dabbed his sweaty cheeks, and bundled the fabric in his fist. The red silk bloomed between his chubby fingers. To Nick, it looked as if he were kneading raw meat. "They're exquisite! Freddy was a close friend as well as a longtime client. I'm livid he didn't share them with me while he was alive. Bad, *bad* Freddy!"

Nick could feel Dulles's eyes crawling all over him, and he purposely kept his attention on West, standing at the bar. Dulles's platitudes about the silver had put a bounce in their host's step, literally dancing as he poured a jigger of vodka into a tumbler.

"A little more, please," Dulles encouraged. "Hell, just keep pouring. I'm retired! I'm finally allowed to drink!"

West glanced over his shoulder. "Do you want one, Nick?"

"No, no, thank you," Nick stammered. "I actually have to go. I have a meeting—" His brain couldn't generate the simple fiction of a name or a place. His only conviction was to leave without looking Dulles in the face. "I just wanted to drop this gift off to you."

West carried a full, iceless glass of vodka over to Dulles and then grabbed the present from Nick. He ripped off the foil and chortled at the once-clever present. Now it seemed like a taunting reminder of Nick's deceit. "Silver polish!"

"Oh, that's the best brand," Dulles confirmed, although it wasn't. "Nick must clean *thousands* of pieces at Wickston. He knows the good stuff. I was just telling Richard, it's my theory that dishwashers destroyed our industry. No, no, listen . . . ," he ordered, raising a steadying hand to hush the nonexistent dissent. He took a gulp of vodka before proceeding. "No one wants to waste time polishing dining service anymore. Silver takes work to keep up. It requires respect and elbow grease. Beautiful things, meaningful things, *sacred things*, take effort. The automatic dishwasher is the domestic god of ceramic and plastic. But it's a devil to us. For god's sake, most people don't even have dining rooms anymore." Dulles began to giggle as he glanced at his audience. It was then that he must have grasped Nick's ploy to avoid eye contact, because his next sentence was sharpened for maximum effect. "Nick, speaking of the business, how's Ari? I owe him a call."

"He's great," Nick said as he gave Dulles what he wanted, his eyes. The mention of Ari's name pushed him toward tears. "I really need to be going."

Dulles smiled. "That's too bad. But why don't we meet up this afternoon? I'd hate to miss the opportunity for a reunion before you skip off to your Wickston client in Milan."

"Oh . . ." Nick shook his head.

"Yes, come on," Dulles thundered. "I get to New York so seldom these days. It might be the last time we see each other." Dulles gulped his vodka, and his fingers groped blindly through the sunlight for West's arm. "Richard, suggest a quiet museum for us. Somewhere Nick and I can meet in, say two hours, with wonderful art and no tourists stampeding from every direction."

"The Scuola Grande di San Rocco!" Eva interjected from her

corner seat. Her foot kicked at the brass brain doorstop. "It's got the best ceilings in Venice." Eva grinned mischievously at Nick. "I love ceiling paintings. Don't you, Uncle Richard? Ceiling frescoes were my specialty in Toulouse."

"San Rocco has divine Tintorettos," West affirmed. "You both really should see them."

"Yes, Nick, we *must*," Dulles drawled. "Does San Rocco in two hours sound good to you? I'm really looking forward to catching up."

It did not sound good. Neither did the two hours before San Rocco or all the hours after. He and Clay should have left town when they had their chance. But they had gotten greedy. They had stayed in Venice a day too long.

The sturdy, geometric white-marble facade of La Scuola Grande di San Rocco could have been the prototype for a corporate bank. It was located in a *campo* across from the Frari, not far from Daniela's apartment, and, unfortunately for Nick, a shorter walk than he'd anticipated from West's palazzo. It left him too much time to worry and regret and hatch elaborate, quickly abandoned plans while pacing frantically outside a gelato shop. Nick tried to replay the encounter with Dulles over again in his mind, but he'd been so spooked, it was as if his brain had failed to record all the relevant details. That failure now allowed Nick to reinvent the interaction. He almost convinced himself that Dulles *did* believe the silver pieces were real, and he *was* genuinely hurt that Freddy had never offered them up for sale, and now all that the old, sweat-drenched alcoholic wanted was to catch up under a quick heaven of Tintoretto paintings before they went their separate ways. Nick decided not to alert Clay on this problem. Why upset him prematurely? It was his job to handle it. Maybe Dulles would laugh about the ruse: *God, I can't stand Richard West either! I'm delighted you pulled one over on him! I'm proud of you! I tried for years but Freddy wouldn't let me!* Nick was trying to lead a circus of optimism through a hopeless wasteland. But optimism was far better than the reality of what Dulles might threaten to do—or, for all Nick knew, had already done in the past two hours over several more glasses of vodka. He could have already ruined them.

At 3:00 p.m., Nick accepted his fate and paid the eight-euro admission fee at the Scuola's entrance. His feet echoed through the ground-floor hall, and he climbed a stone staircase without noticing the enormous Antonio Zanchi paintings of Mary soaring over a plague-ridden city. The second floor opened onto a sprawling gilt ballroom. Nick searched the murky chamber for Dulles. Instead, he saw visitors wandering around the room as they peered down into the glowing iPads in their hands. As Nick drew closer, though, he realized the screens weren't iPads but mirrors. The visitors were examining the ceiling through its reflection, looking down in order to gaze up.

Nick grabbed a mirror from a side table. The room's walls were covered with carved wooden figures. Some of the bodies were tranquil and angelic; others seemed to thrash and writhe. It was a dark forest of serpents and chains and screaming mouths. Nick preferred the Tintoretto canvases above him, all toppling saints and white-lit skies. It took him a moment to adjust to the mirror, but his brain reorientated, and soon he was lost to his own steps as he followed the biblical scenes around the coffered ceiling. He stopped when a monstrous gray-green face eclipsed his view.

Dulles stood before him, holding a glossy booklet. One of the wall figures was featured on the cover: a long-haired blindfolded man shoving out his tongue.

"'The Beauty of Virtue and the Ugliness of Vice,'" Dulles quoted the cover's subtitle. "It's usually the other way around, don't you think? The ugliness of virtue, the beauty of vice." His voice was frail, less whinnying, almost teetering on compassionate, which might be an attempt at intimacy, or due to the mandatory hush of a museum, or because the walk across the city after too many vodkas had sapped his strength. Dulles thrust the book into Nick's hand before bundling his red handkerchief against his dripping nostrils. "Take it," he said. "I bought it for you in the gift shop."

"Thanks," Nick replied hesitantly. He wasn't sure how to react. Back in New York, when Dulles dropped by at Wickston, Nick reacted by avoiding contact. Desks, doors, and staircases were the preferred barriers. Nick now pretended to skim the booklet with interest.

Dulles pressed his wet palm over Nick's hand to shut the book.

"Nick," he purred. "What kind of scam have you gotten yourself into?"

"What do you mean?" Nick asked coolly as he took a step back.

Dulles stepped forward with a grunt. "Don't," he warned. "We both know those van der Haar silver pieces are about as real as your business card. What shocks me is that Richard actually believed such a sweet, dimple-faced twink"—Dulles swept his knuckles toward Nick's cheek, but Nick pulled away—"could actually be a reputable antiques appraiser. You must have really floored him with your tap dance." Dulles let out a laugh and seemed to appreciate the way it reverberated around the room. A man sitting in a folding chair, drawing in a sketchpad, stomped his foot to demand quiet. Dulles didn't lower his voice; he simply moved closer to his victim. "My real question is, how are you and the Guillory kid splitting the seven hundred and fifty thousand? Is it even-steven right down the middle? Because you deserve at least seventy-five percent for the performance you must have put on."

"Clay doesn't know anything about it," Nick fired back. "He doesn't know that the silver isn't real. He inherited it from Freddy and thinks it's authentic." It seemed smarter to take all the blame. Not only would it protect Clay, but he had a better chance of convincing Dulles to spare him if he thought he was acting alone.

Dulles whistled incredulously. "Give me a break. That little New York hustler knows. I don't buy it. Freddy was dead broke at the end, and the trick wants his money for his time and effort. Why the fuck else would he clean up van der Haar vomit for months on end?" Dulles took the opportunity to study Nick's face, and his eyes lingered over its features. "You look very handsome, Nick. I like you with a little sun on your skin. I always told Ari what a beauty you are. I take it he doesn't have a clue what you're up to?"

When Nick didn't respond, Dulles patted Nick's chest. Then his hand descended in light, caressing swirls down his abdomen. "Ari doesn't have a clue at all," Dulles answered for him. "Can you imagine Ari doing anything dishonest? But don't worry, I understand. I've been through a lot of lean years in this business. You do what you have to do to survive. Ari can afford his scruples because he has his wealthy family. We aren't so lucky, you and I." Dulles's fingertips stopped at Nick's belly button. "But some advice for next time. Try to flog pieces that are a bit more passable. It was smart to choose a novice like West who has big eyes and no interest in educating himself on what he wants. But eventually, in a few years, someone's going to come for a visit to his palazzo and set him straight."

"Thanks for the advice," Nick said. He stepped back, leaving Dulles's hand to float in midair. "So what do you want?"

"What do I want?" Dulles mused as if he were surveying a menu. He wiped the sweat from his face. The question seemed self-evident. What he wanted was what he was doing, to torment Nick.

"You weren't on your way to Rome when you got West's email, were you?"

"Actually, I will go to Rome in two days. But no, a trip to Italy wasn't initially on my calendar. Rest assured, though, I've traveled farther for a lot less. As I said, I've always had my eye on you."

The realization of what Dulles was intimating rose like bile up Nick's throat. It wasn't money he was after, which would have been so much easier. They could slip him fifty thousand dollars to keep his mouth shut.

"Come on, Dulles," Nick whined.

"You aren't with Ari anymore. It won't be a betrayal. I'm sure you'll recover your dignity in no time."

"I don't want to," he said flatly.

Dulles grunted. "Of course you don't." He grabbed the booklet out of Nick's hand and reached into his jacket pocket for a pen. He scribbled in red ink across the back page. "I'm sorry it can't be tonight," he muttered. "I have dinner plans with an old friend, a princess. If you must know, she's a Thurn und Taxis." Dulles's commitment to name-dropping at the very moment he was using blackmail for sex made Nick despise him even more. He noticed that Dulles's back teeth were black at the root and faded to a lemonade yellow, while his front incisors were porcelain white. But it was not the time to find more physical flaws in Dulles Hawkes. Dulles shoved the booklet against Nick's chest, and he opened it to see what he'd written. The lettering was nearly illegible.

"What does this say?" Nick asked. "Hotel—"

"Hotel Grazia Salvifica," Dulles translated. "Room five-oh-three. Five p.m. tomorrow? The hotel is by the train station. Don't get your hopes up. I'm afraid it isn't even three stars." Nick closed both the book and his eyes. Dulles took the opportunity to pat him lightly on the ass. "A few hours of fun," Dulles whispered. "That's all I'm asking. I promise I won't be too hard on you. Deal?"

A group of schoolchildren ran like warring invaders up the stone steps.

CHAPTER 16

Nick's brain was doing it again, separating worlds. It didn't occur to him until deep in the night that the meeting at Dulles's hotel conflicted with his plan to see Clay off at the train station. Clay was due to roll out of Venice just after seven, and Nick wanted to see him off at the platform. The Santa Lucia *ferrovia* station was a cement slab shaped like a sandwich press, with tourists and their luggage oozing from every side. It was the safest place in the city for a furtive encounter; no one wandered the station unless they had good reason. It was a short walk from Hotel Grazia Salvifica, but Nick didn't know how long that meeting would last or what kind of man he'd be when he left it.

He lay in bed all night with his eyes shut and his mind awake. The guest-room door was closed, but Daniela and her boyfriend were two lovebirds thrashing around in the kitchen—laughing, kissing, racing for a fresh bottle, inventing minor gripes that required tender explanations. Benny was a dashing man in his early fifties. Like most couples over the age of thirty, Daniela and Benny made no sense together until they were actually in the same room, where they made perfect sense together. Benny had black hair gelled and parted with surgical precision and a chin that tilted upward, even when he wasn't talking to Daniela's tall houseguest. Nick had assumed Benny would be older, more guarded, and less delighted to find another man in his girlfriend's apartment. But as soon as Nick met him, he too was smitten. Daniela had spent days preparing for his visit from Shanghai. Nick had helped her scrub the floors and hang a green sheet over the cement garden like a caravan awning. They'd invited Nick to join their dinner, but he declined. He knew he'd be awful company. Imprisoned in his room, exiled from the oblivion of sleep, head submerged under two pillows, he clocked eight of the next ten hours in his own awful company. Nick left his bed the next morning more broken than when he'd crawled into it.

He lingered through the morning in the darkness of Daniela's apartment. The lovebirds had flown out by ten to leave him in peace. When Clay phoned, Nick was collecting bottles and dirty plates in the kitchen. "You aren't going to believe it!" Clay shouted through the receiver. "I think we got him."

A corner of the green sheet had come untied in the garden, and through the window Nick was watching the fabric rippling in the breeze.

"Aren't you going to ask what happened?" Clay prompted.

"Yes," Nick said with a jolt. He poured some warmth into his words. "Yes, sorry. I'm here. That's great!"

Clay laughed testily. "What I mean is, this morning I get a message from West. He wants to talk. He asked if he could bring his wife and niece over to tour Il Dormitorio. Oh, man, he even asked if I'd consider a *scrittura privata*, which is like an unofficial agreement with a deposit down to hold his claim. But I just want to get it all done so we can get out of here. Nicky, this is really happening! I'll be honest. I didn't think it would work. I thought we were insane!"

Nick knew it was his turn to speak, but his tongue wasn't co-operating. Worse, his throat kept making a strange clicking sound when he tried to summon his voice.

"Nicky? Are you there?"

"Yeah, I'm here. That's great news!" Nick grabbed for a more logical reply. "What did you tell him? Did you name a price?"

"Not yet. I said I was going out of town for two days, but he could bring the family over when I'm back. It's good to keep him waiting. Nicky!" Clay shouted his name as if calling out for some-one lost. "We could be millionaires! Us! Can you believe it? We'll be set."

"We'll be set," Nick repeated. He could swim for hours in the warm flow of Clay's voice.

"It comes down to Paris. It's the last piece we need. I pray I can convince Antonin to help us. He did say any time . . ."

"You'll make it work," Nick replied. "It'll happen and we'll be out of here. Let's not wait much longer, okay? Let's do it and go."

Nick felt he'd injected a convincing dose of enthusiasm into that last exchange. He only realized he'd failed when Clay asked, point-blank, "What's wrong? You're not sounding like yourself."

"I'm fine," he insisted. "Everything's fine. I just can't, uh . . . I can't meet you at the station tonight. I'm sorry. Something's come up."

"Something's come up?" Clay didn't have to state the obvious: What could possibly come up in a foreign town where Nick barely knew anyone? Nick exhaled into the mouthpiece. "There's a little glitch." Before Clay could ask the nature of it, Nick dove forward. "It's nothing to worry about. I've got it under control. It's about the silver. Well, it's more about my job at Wickston than anything to do with the van der Haar deal. I'm making it sound way bigger than it is. I'm sorry." He needed to stop tying his sentences in knots. "It's nothing. Really. You just concentrate on Paris, okay? Everything's fine. I'm handling it."

"Nicky." Clay released a heavy sigh. "Should we stop before we get in any deeper? Tell me the truth. Maybe we let things settle down and don't jump into trying to sell—"

"No!" Nick cut him off. "It's fine. I shouldn't have brought it up. It's a very minor snag that I can take care of. Will you trust me? I can handle things too, you know. I'm not completely inefficient."

"I know you're not."

"Go to Paris. We're so close now. We'll get the money and be out of here."

"Do you want me to stop by Daniela's before I go?"

On any other day Nick would have said yes. But today he didn't want that. He couldn't take an afternoon naked with Clay before "a few hours of fun" in a two-star hotel with a man he could barely stand looking at. The contrast would be too unbearable.

"Benny's visiting," Nick said. "We should let them have the apartment today."

"*Ooohh.* Is Benny a good guy?"

"Yeah. He's pretty irresistible. Daniela's so far over the moon she's currently orbiting Proxima B."

Clay laughed, and Nick felt calmer hearing his boyfriend's tone lighten.

"I love you so much," he said and waited, with eyes stinging, for those same words to echo back to him in a different voice.

Five p.m. was a spiteful hour in Venice. The excitement of the day had faded, and nighttime diversions hadn't yet ridden in on darker skies. Even the vendors along the loud tourist gauntlet of Strada Nuova soured on their cheap, overpriced souvenirs; at this hour, the salesclerks would shrug and feign no comprehension of English rather than check in the back for additional sizes and colors. There was still enough foot traffic flowing between the train station and the Rialto Bridge to camouflage Nick as he followed his phone map to the Hotel Grazia Salvifica. This was not the first time in his life that Nick had gone to a seedy hotel for a sex date. It wasn't even the first time he'd gone to a seedy hotel for a sex date while in love with somebody else. But this was the first time Nick knew exactly who the man waiting for him was, and it was the first time he couldn't simply walk away without a second thought.

Grazia Salvifica looked like many of its competitors along the crowded span of Rio Terà San Leonardo. It had a scarlet awning stamped in fat gold letters. Automatic doors swooshed open by motion sensor, and the smoked-glass windows boasted printouts of TripAdvisor reviews and the decals of credit cards it accepted. The five-floor pink stucco building had never been an equal to one of the imposing Grand Canal palazzi, but it had no doubt once served as a regal abode for a Renaissance family. Seventy years ago, a hotel chain had taken up residence inside its grand shell, chopping up the interior into guest rooms and installing a long faux-marble reception desk, a glass elevator shaft up the core of the staircase, and a room off the lobby that offered single-serving cereal boxes and unwieldy pitchers of orange juice as a "continental breakfast."

The lobby was luxurious only in its air-conditioning, turned to full blast in late April. A scarlet runner striped with the tread marks of luggage racks bisected the narrow lobby and stopped at a chrome elevator bank. There, a man was on his hands and knees on a white drop cloth, bowing before closed elevator doors. Nick sailed by the front desk of the Grazia Salvifica, noticing that it had been left unattended. As he approached the elevator, he saw tools laid out on the drop cloth. The kneeling man was using a screwdriver to pry open a panel. A pimply Chinese manager in gray pinstripes stood at his side, yelling down at him. Behind him, an old, arthritic Italian woman with a firework of gray hair was yelling at the manager. Nick could see the stuck elevator car through the glass shaft. It dangled a few feet above the ground. Trapped inside was a woman holding the hand of a young girl, both wearing visors with the word VENEDIG written across their brims, both with money belts clipped at their waists, both sporting futuristic walking shoes. Their expressions communicated the early minutes of an emergency where panic was only beginning to set in. They hung suspended over the lobby like a perfect specimen of tourists preserved in amber.

The manager clapped his hands, disappeared into a back room, and returned with an orange traffic cone, which he placed in front of the drop cloth. The prehistoric Italian woman screamed at a middle-aged couple crossing into the lobby from the breakfast room: "Out of order. No order. *Finito!* You take steps, *steps!*"

Nick knew Dulles's room number. He circled wide of the traffic cone and followed the couple up the carpeted steps. The staircase curled like a pencil shaving around the elevator shaft, and the carpet got dirtier and more hole-ridden the higher Nick ascended. The couple exited onto the third floor. Nick could still hear the banging of tools far below.

He was sick to his stomach by the time he reached the fifth floor. Televisions hummed from distant rooms. A housekeeping cart was parked halfway down the corridor, stripped of towels and cluttered with dirty cups as if it had been left abandoned for days. The numbers counted downward along the hall: 507, 506, 505 . . .

Bleach stains were spattered across the red carpet. He located the brass doorplate for 503.

Nick took a few choppy breaths before knocking. No emotions, he told himself. Remember what you're doing this for. He was doing it for himself and for Clay, for their future, for the seven hundred and fifty thousand already in the bank, for the possibility of millions of euros more. That was worth a few hours submitting to someone else's idea of fun. He knocked.

Dulles took thirty seconds to answer, but when he did, pulling the door wide with more force than was required, Nick was relieved by the provisional fact that he was fully clothed. He wore a wrinkled, pink Oxford over a pair of stained, baggy chinos. His stubby toes gripped the carpet fibers and his fly was unzipped, with the edge of a pink shirttail hanging out of it.

"Nick," he groaned almost apologetically. "Come in. Please." There was no coy smile as Nick had expected, no I-got-you tone. Nick was the one to smile first, followed by a rumple of his lips to indicate an attempt at a détente. They could both still walk away. Run, really.

Dulles closed the door behind him. The drapes were drawn across the windows. The combined smell of aftershave, uncorked alcohol, and a chemical carpet sanitizer took up a larger presence in the room than an odor should. A lamp on the bureau provided enough light for Nick to make out a collection of red-crusted wineglasses, a half-drunk bottle of whiskey, a square wallet-sized mirror smeared with white residue, two cell phones, and a torn map of the Doge's Palace. A small silk-covered box sat open on the nightstand. Where a more introspective man might have stowed a set of meditation balls, Dulles had compiled a stack of condoms. Dulles made his way across the room, knocking his hip against the bureau and leaving Nick alone by the door with a pounding heart. Maybe Dulles was already too drunk to try anything. Maybe he was on the verge of passing out. Nick couldn't decide whether that prospect would save him or merely prolong the misery.

"Do you want a drink?" Dulles asked. He steadied himself on the arm of a sofa chair before sitting.

"No, thank you. My stomach's a little off." Nick gave what he hoped was a pitiable smile. "Are you all packed for your trip to Rome tomorrow?" It was clear by the state of the room that he wasn't.

"It's such a nightmare when it comes time to shove everything back in the suitcase. It's like your possessions have gained weight on a holiday, isn't it?" Dulles smiled stiffly. "Have a seat," he implored, extending his hand toward the side of the bed. The cheap, machine-quilted nylon bedspread suppressed a faint whimper of hinges when Nick followed the instructions. Dulles reached under his chair to locate a glass filled with a large pour of tawny liquid. He then brought the glass to rest on his lap with the exhausted sigh of a grandparent lifting a toddler. Dulles swilled his drink and sipped. "I'm sorry I've asked you over like this," he said, his watery eyes glinting with the scant daylight that seeped into the room. His jaw was trembling. "I've been very lonely, especially since I've closed the shop." He took a bigger sip, and the glass muffled another exclamation of "very lonely." Nick sat on the bed with his fists jammed into the mattress at his sides, like a gymnast on a pommel horse. "I should never have retired. Don't ever retire, Nick. It's death," Dulles advised. "It can't be pleasant for you to be with a man my age."

Actually, a couple of times, Nick had been with a man Dulles's age. He remembered appreciating the way those men had gone out of their way to ensure his pleasure as well as their own. But Nick wasn't about to correct Dulles on this point. He still harbored a distant hope that he might be let off the hook.

"Oh, Christ!" Dulles cried. He downed the rest of the whiskey and rose with effort to his feet. "What a mess I've made." He stepped sideways to wipe the white powder off the mirror. Two fingers acted as a toothbrush with which to rub the residue into his gums. Then he lowered those fingers to his shirt collar. He started to unbutton his Oxford from the top down.

"This can still be fun," Dulles promised hollowly. He walked over and pressed his palm against Nick's inert leg. The palm seemed to be the canary sent to test the safety of exploration. The hand lunged for Nick's chest. It gouged his left pectoral with several nipple-missing pinches before flailing higher to cup his chin. "You're a very beautiful young man," he whispered. "Take your clothes off."

Nick stood up. His fists wanted to be useful and punch Dulles in the stomach. He had a clear shot of it now that he'd removed his pink Oxford. The skin of Dulles's body was white and smooth, like the skin of an inmate who hadn't been allowed into the prison yard for decades. The flabby wilt of his chest and elbows reminded Nick of melted candle wax. He purposely didn't inspect Dulles's body any further. *Get this over with.* Nick took off his shirt and unbuttoned his pants.

"Slower," Dulles ordered, falling back into the chair as he tried to step out of the puddle of his own pants. "Go slower, dammit!" Nick went faster. Shoes kicked off. Pants and socks removed. Nick grabbed for the waistline of his white briefs. "Wait!" Dulles shouted. "Not yet! Stop!" But Nick didn't listen. He slid them off and sat down naked on the bed, his eyes on the torn map of the Doge's Palace.

"Are you sure you don't want a drink?" Dulles asked. "Or something more?"

Nick saw from the corner of his eye that Dulles had removed his boxers. A gray cloud of pubic hair haunted a fleshy hip bone. "Let's just get this over with."

Dulles inhaled with hurt satisfaction. Nick's insult seemed to be exactly what he was hoping for. It erased any lingering sympathy he held for him. Now Dulles could use him without remorse.

"Get on your hands and knees. In the center of the bed."

Nick did what he was told. He thought of the handyman on his hands and knees in the lobby five flights down. He thought of the screaming Italian woman in her scratchy blue housedress and of the polished Chinese manager dragging out the orange traffic cone. He thought of all of them and of the mother and daughter holding hands in the elevator, but Nick did not allow his mind to travel beyond the hotel's automatic doors. He kept his thoughts outside room 503 but within the confines of the Grazia Salvifica. He wouldn't let them contaminate the rest of Venice.

"Spread your knees farther apart!" Dulles demanded from somewhere behind him. Nick, on all fours, moved his knees eight inches apart on the nylon bedspread. "More!" Nick moved them ten inches apart. "A little more!" Another inch. "There! Perfect! Yes! I can see it all now." There was a long pause. "How tight is that little ass of yours?"

Nick didn't have an answer to that question. He didn't want his participation to extend into words.

Dulles growled, "Dad wants to know how tight it is, boy?"

So that was the make of this old man's fantasy: father/son. "Tight," Nick murmured, simply to end the debate.

Nick felt a hand grip his testicles, exploring the sac with ungentle squeezes, followed by a painful, milking tug on each ball. Nick was not the slightest bit erect, and when he allowed himself a peek behind him, he discovered with a mixture of vindication and despair that Dulles wasn't either. Below the swollen stomach and the wisp of gray hair hung a shriveled newt-like penis. The tugging hand let go.

Nick heard the recognizable acoustics of sex preparations in the darkness, as familiar to him as the clattering sounds of a table being set for dinner: the pop of a prescription bottle, the gulp of a pill, the deep, single-nostril snort of poppers, the plastic snap of a lube bottle, the flimsy metallic rustle of a condom wrapper.

"Relax," Dulles commanded. Slick palms steadied themselves against Nick's hips. "You're going to be like this for a while."

"I don't want to do this," Nick muttered, feeling the need to lodge a final objection—to whom, he wasn't even sure.

"Good. Squirm for me like you don't want it. Beg a bit. I like to hear you whimper, and the more you cry the longer it will take."

All Nick could do was study the bedspread, its weft infinitely complex in the dim evening light, its color the chapped tan of a blighted desert that many before him had crossed but where no one would choose to live.

According to the antique silver traveler's clock on the nightstand, the act took one hour and twenty-three minutes. Dulles peeled himself off the bed, more sober and steady-footed now, and turned on the shower in the bathroom. Nick lay on the mattress, his eyes on the glowing pink column between the drapes, thinking that if he hurried he could still catch Clay at the station. He imagined Clay walking there right now, perhaps not even a hundred yards from this hotel. If Nick ran, he could see him off, maybe even buy a last-minute ticket and take the train up with him to Paris, where they could walk around in the open without any worry of being seen together. They had never been able to do that, not in New

York and not here in Venice. Nick let that vision of Paris play on in his mind until the shower shut off. That was Nick's alarm to jump from the bed and get dressed.

He desperately wanted a shower, but he wasn't willing to spend an extra minute in this room. He slid on his underwear and pants and was fumbling to button his shirt when Dulles drifted out in a cloud of steam with a towel knotted around his sucked-in stomach. Nick jammed his feet into his laced-up shoes. He picked the condom off the bed, stepped into the bathroom, and flung it in the toilet. He flushed it down, washed his hands in the sink, and splashed water on his cheeks. Mercifully, the mirror was fogged so he didn't have to catch sight of himself.

When Nick returned to the bedroom, Dulles had already finished dressing and was gathering up a stack of euro coins from the bureau.

"How about a drink over on the canal?" Dulles asked. The old man poured out a tiny shot of whiskey from a bottle on the bureau and tossed it back, as if the very mention of a drink proved too much of a temptation. "My treat. Or there's a great *cicchetti* spot around the corner with the most delicious sardines."

"No, thank you," Nick said dryly as he started toward the door.

"Wait!" Dulles ordered. He crossed the room and stood in front of Nick. Then he lifted up on his tiptoes and leaned in for a kiss, his eyes shut romantically. It was as if the entire hideous sex act had merely been a preamble for what Dulles was really after: one evening of reliable company in Venice.

Nick pushed Dulles back with a hand to his chest, lightly but firmly.

"No, Dulles. I already did what you wanted. We're finished."

The man sniveled as his heels dropped to the floor. "We're both leaving the hotel at the same time. The least I can do is buy you a Campari. Come on, it's twenty more minutes of your night."

"No," Nick said more defiantly. "We had an agreement. We made a deal. I fulfilled my part. This is the end."

"End," Dulles repeated. "What end?" He clapped Nick's arm as Nick reached for the doorknob. "Okay," he said quickly. "It's fine if you aren't free tonight. I'll see you back here tomorrow. Does five p.m. work for you again?" Nick's fingers froze on the knob. Dulles was smiling, a blush blooming on his cheeks. Perhaps he was ashamed of his nastiness, but the shame hadn't stopped him from inflicting it.

"I'm not coming back," Nick replied. "You won't be here to-morrow anyway. You said you were leaving for Rome."

"I've changed my mind. I don't see the point in rushing off." Dulles tried to rub Nick's back, but Nick flattened himself against the door. "Besides," Dulles said, "we got a good start today, but there's still more I'd like to try with you."

The words were out of Nick's mouth before he registered them. "Are you fucking insane? I'm never doing that again!" There was no chance Nick was going to enter this hotel room a second time. The thought of it broke him. It slumped him watery-kneed against the wall.

Dulles took a step backward, just beyond reach. "We also still haven't discussed the money part."

"What money part?"

"Well." Dulles glanced down at his fingers as they fidgeted with his room key. "You and your partner made—what? seven hun-dred and fifty thousand?—off Richard. Certainly my silence as an accredited silver expert is worth half of that. Let's say three hun-dred and seventy and I walk away. I'll even confirm they're real and what a brilliant job you did. That's fair, isn't it? And with my stamp of approval, you can probably sell more pieces to him in the future."

"What?" Nick's saliva had transformed into glue. His tongue was stiff, and his lips weren't moving correctly. The amount of hush money that Dulles was demanding wouldn't leave them with enough to pay off Clay's debts, let alone see them through the next few years in Europe.

Dulles sprang for the door and managed to open it wide enough to slip out into the hallway. Nick grabbed the doorknob and chased after him down the red-carpeted corridor. "Dulles," he whispered in a voice far calmer than he imagined himself capable; his ears were ringing, and his breath didn't seem to be reaching his lungs. "Dulles, please. Wait a second."

Dulles ignored him. He continued to move swiftly down the hall, either to indicate he meant business or to avoid a physical altercation. Nick shouldn't have let him escape his hotel room. He should have grabbed Dulles by the collar, shoved him against the wall, and threatened to kill him if he didn't leave for Rome tonight. Nick could have walked him to the station and watched him board a train. But Nick had no experience as a thug. He had survived on earth for twenty-five years without once punching another human being. He used to be proud of that fact, but now he realized its crucial disadvantages.

"All right!" Nick cried. Dulles stopped at the housekeeping trolley and allowed Nick to catch up to him. "All right," Nick said with his head bent, his neck yoked in shame. "I'll come back tomorrow. Five p.m. One more time. And then we're even, okay?" Nick was on the edge of tears. "You can do whatever you want. Okay?"

Dulles looked up at him almost sympathetically. "I should have been clearer from the start. I'm afraid it's not an either-or prop-osition." He glanced down the empty hall to ensure that no one would overhear his confession. "The thing is, Nick, I'm broke. Too many debts of my own since retirement. I've gotten myself into a jam." He bunched his lips, as if sorry for leading Nick on. He hadn't come to Venice for disgusting sex—that was just a bo-nus. He'd come to refresh his bank account.

"You can't have the money," Nick spat with a shake of his head.

Dulles closed his eyes, spun around, and launched himself down the hall. Nick followed a few steps behind. Dulles stopped at the elevator doors by the stairwell and pressed the call button. The button glowed with IN ARRIVO printed in black across it.

Nick was about to inform him that the elevator was out of order, when Dulles turned around to face him with a smirk. "I'd hate to call Ari and tell him what you've been up to these past few weeks. That would really break his heart, wouldn't it, to know you be-trayed him like you have?"

The elevator bell dinged. The doors parted to reveal a gaping hole from which the hellish sounds of hammering and a child's screams arose. Nick gazed at the enticing void over Dulles's shoul-der, and for a second he gave himself over to its power as a solution. This five-floor drop was really no different from the one a few feet away at the staircase. It wouldn't be difficult for Nick to push Dulles over that low iron railing when they took the stairs down to the lobby; Nick could point to something on a lower floor and wait for Dulles to lean over to see it. But Dulles wasn't standing in front of a railing. He had his back to an open drop while taunting the young man he'd just abused in his hotel room for an hour and twenty-three minutes. The empty shaft in front of Nick was mon-strously tempting, the perfect human disposal system.

"Dulles, you should be careful—"

"I should be?" He fluttered his outraged eyes. "Do you *want* me to call Ari? Because I will. I'll put him on the phone with Richard West myself."

That last threat had done the trick. Nick smiled warmly and extended his hand. "The elevator's here."

Dulles spun around and brought his right leg forward into the nothingness. Some instinct must have fought through the drugs and alcohol and greed in his brain to warn him of his imminent danger. For as Dulles dropped his right foot toward a floor that didn't exist, he managed for a trembling second to recalibrate the physics of his body and teeter on his left leg, his arms flailing by his sides. Nick watched Dulles in that second, mesmerized: it seemed as if the force of a mere breath would decide his fate. Nick didn't wait for the breath. His hand shot out, his palm spread wide as it rammed into Dulles's shoulder blade. Nick's eyes shut, and he heard a blunt *thwack* followed not five seconds later by a deeper, more conclusive thud at the bottom of the shaft.

He stood there, eyes closed, lost in the outer space of his head. When he opened them, he saw a smear of blood on a metal beam inside the shaft that Dulles's head must have struck on his way down. Now there were real screams, a chorus of sopranos surging from below. The screams seemed to echo up the stairwell rather than the shaft, as if they were taking the safer route.

His legs shaking, Nick took long, panicky steps backward. Gravity seemed to be pulling him toward the open shaft, as if to devour him too. He tried the knobs of several doors—508, 507, 506— before ducking behind the housekeeping trolley. As he squatted on the floor with his palms clamped over his mouth, more shouts wafted from the lobby. Doors on lower floors slammed. Nick realized he'd soon hear sirens and feet marching up the stairwell, and if he remained where he was, crouched in a child's hiding spot halfway between the open elevator and Dulles's room, he'd be IDed as a suspect. His only option was to beat the sirens to the hotel's front door.

He stood up, straightened his clothes, and steered toward the mouth of the staircase. He forced himself to slow his pace into the rhythm of a confused, curious onlooker as he took the flights in rushing descent, on each floor joined by more guests who had heard the commotion below. "What happened?" he asked a woman in a bathrobe on the second-floor landing.

"Is there a fire?" she asked in reply, before they were separated by a family of Spaniards. As he took the final turns of the staircase, Nick kept his eyes from the body on top of the elevator car. The mother and daughter were still stuck inside the cube, lying on its floor now, the daughter sobbing and shrieking while the mother hugged her to her chest.

The Chinese manager stood frozen by his traffic cone. The handyman was frantically trying to pry open the elevator doors with his bare hands. The Italian grandmother was directing the guests outside with wild gesticulations. Nick did not look back. He exited the Grazia Salvifica and turned left onto the crowded footpath. He made it two blocks walking slowly, fighting the urge to break into a full-throttle run. He crossed a stone bridge and kept going with the tide of meandering restaurant seekers. French children were counting up all the lions they could spot on door knockers, flags, and cornices. They were up to eighty-nine.

Two bridges farther on, tourists licked gelato, their expressions blissfully ignorant of the death that had just befallen one of their own not a quarter of a mile away. How far did Nick have to walk until he was free to run? How much distance did he have to put between himself and his crime before the security footage of a young American sprinting down a side street would not be linked to the death of a drunk British retiree in a two-star hotel? Nick still had traces of Dulles's spit and semen all over him. But to his relief he also had his own wallet, phone, and all of his clothing. He'd left no macroscopic evidence behind in room 503.

He checked the time: 7:06 p.m. Clay's train must be hurtling across the lagoon right now, making its own distance, rushing toward the border. Nick would give anything to be with him, half-asleep with his temple against Clay's shoulder, soon to cross into another country that spoke a different language. When Nick spotted the Rialto Bridge, its twin arcades shining with spotlights, couples leaning like kissing gargoyles over its balustrades, he finally gave in to his impulse. He ran across the Grand Canal as fast as he could, and he didn't stop until the sun set.

CHAPTER 17

Nick took the night boat into the lagoon. He'd waited thirty minutes in various states of consciousness for the off-hour vaporetto to snail up to Piazza San Marco. He couldn't remember how he'd managed to make his way to the dock at four in the morning and extract a ticket from the machine. He could have simply crawled under the turnstile, but Nick had always been a good boy. Such a fucking good boy, his entire life. Forget finding Piazza San Marco, how the hell had he managed to hold on to his wallet all night?

He stumbled through the vacant waterbus cabin, unsure whether the boat's fierce pitching was disguising or dramatizing his drunkenness. He struggled with the back-door latch and banged his head on the frame as he stepped onto the stern's outer deck. He fell onto a plastic seat. From here he could watch the twinkle of Venice recede against the tarry waters. The city was now nothing but a strand of white Christmas lights. White Christmas lights were reserved for the wealthy sections of Dayton. His family, like the other suckers in their middle-everything neighborhood, went for the tacky glory of reds and blues and greens. The motor grumbled as the vaporetto accelerated into open water. Soon they'd touch the sea.

After he'd sprinted over the Rialto Bridge earlier that evening, he'd kept running until he wandered down a narrow alley that dead-ended on a shoelace canal. On one side, there was a thin stone ledge, and Nick balled himself up there. He covered his eyes with his knees and tried to delete all memories of the Grazia Salvifica, but they kept flaring up—the bedspread, the elevator shaft—more so when his eyes were shut than open. Eventually he returned to the alley, his footsteps thunderously loud on the stone, and made his way to Campo Santa Margherita. It seemed safer to be around people, especially ones who didn't speak his language. He picked the noisiest jam-packed spot on the far side of the square. "Vodka con club soda," he told the bartender. He was served a vodka con tonic water, which he promptly chugged, and downed the next one that he ordered and the one after that. Nick was trying to flood the elevator shaft from his head. A sweaty Italian with a goatee bumped into him while trying to get the bartender's attention. He clapped Nick's shoulder and called his friends over to marvel at the lone, morose American drinking in their student dive. They were university kids studying in Venice. Four girls, three guys. Nick couldn't have said whether they were attractive. He was only judging people on whether they seemed like threats or not. They acted friendly as they joined him at his drinking pace. The goateed Italian even bought him a vodka.

"Andiamo! Come with us, American!"

Nick went along with the group, heedless of the direction, happy to submit to someone else's plan. All they seemed to want from Nick was his Americanness, and he felt shielded by these Italians on their home turf. He followed their footsteps and singing through the streets. "Our only discotheque in town. *Piccolo*. We bring you, but in trade, you promise to take us clubbing when we visit you in Manhattan."

"Uh, yeah," Nick replied. "Sure."

They knocked on a gleaming brass door and trudged down a narrow staircase to a bleak basement retrofitted in bedazzled mirrors and black-lacquer benches. Drinks were skinnier and double the price. But Nick felt safe underground, and the vodka untightened his body enough for his hips to crank back and forth as the others jumped around him on the dance floor. *Clubbing*, what a stupid, embarrassing word, and yet right now it seemed perversely accurate for the fist movements the crowd was making around him. Lasers flashed on the ceiling. In the flickering pyrotechnics, he spotted a husky young woman in a yellow dress standing not five feet away, her fleshy American face staring at him in recognition. She was the daughter of the Warbly-Gardeners, the girl on the *motoscafo* from the airport that first day. She knew that Nick was a thief. She might call the police on him. Nick tried to disappear into the dance floor, but he was immediately pushed backward by a muscly Italian. He fell drunkenly against August Warbly-Gardener, her arms catching him before he could take her down with him. Scrambling, he grabbed at her shoulders for stability. This young woman had two working arms, no cast. She was not the young American. As he looked at her, her face sharpened into Eastern European features, and a man behind her glared menacingly with his fist raised.

Nick fought his way to the other side of the basement, and the world went black for a while. He didn't know how long he stayed in the subterranean club, filling his credit card with drink purchases. He wasn't entirely sure that the youths he left with were the same ones who had brought him. But it was still night when he reached the surface, and there was still too much fear in his head to brave it alone. He followed his new friends down a web of alleys to an iron-spiked door. Inside, the abandoned palazzo's walls were crumbling, its garland-molded plaster worn through to scabs of brick. Red swirls of spray-paint made a Persian carpet across the marble floor. The staircase had caved in, and American hip-hop blasted from a set of speakers. The only furniture in the room was a ring of mattresses surrounding a pond of melted candles. In the corner, painted signs and protest banners lay drying. Someone handed Nick a half-filled bottle of wine. He sat down on the closest mattress, right next to a couple who were making out, and he drank down the rest of the bottle. His Americanness seemed to have lost its novelty. No one noticed him. "Hey," he whispered to the two Venetians next to him. "Hey." They stopped kissing and stared at him. "Do you know if there's any more alcohol?" They didn't respond; Nick wasn't sure he was even speaking clear English. "Or drugs? Do you have drugs? I'll take anything really." He laughed. "You wouldn't believe how much I need them." He somehow managed to crawl to his feet and find the front door.

He couldn't go back to Daniela's in his current state. She and Benny might still be up, sitting in the kitchen, their eyes reading his guilt. Worse, he couldn't handle being locked up alone in the tiny guest room. The leash-tight walkways of Dorsoduro were already starting to close in on him like a straitjacket. He was glad that Clay was off in Paris. Otherwise, he would have lost his self-control and shown up banging on Il Dormitorio's door, crying loudly for his help.

An idea came to him: the Lido, so close that boats went there from Piazza San Marco. The Lido was open beach. He could breathe out there unseen, away from the city.

Almost an hour later, slumped on the back deck of a vaporetto,

Nick realized his mistake. The straitjacket had been keeping him from harming himself. He'd been safer around strangers; now he was alone with the memory of what had happened. He stood up and gripped the railing. It was too low to prevent him from falling over if the boat lurched; nothing in this world had been designed with him in mind. He rested his head against the railing's cold metal to quiet the growling of his brain.

Finally the vaporetto rubbed against the landing platform of the Lido. Nick scuttled off with a weary *grazie* to the boatman. He crossed a wide, paved road that cars must drive down—the world of automobiles seemed momentarily exotic to him. Streetlights illuminated a row of tidy hotels and houses. The facades here looked quaint and village-like, as if they belonged to the rose-dotted waterfronts of Southern France. Nick cut down a side street with arrows pointing toward SPIAGGIA LIBERA. He passed shuttered boutiques and swimsuit shops before reaching a series of enormous dark monoliths looming against the blue-black cloud cover. These were the Belle Epoque seafront hotels, sinister empty mansions without a single light on; it was too early in the season for guests at the beach resort. Nick stumbled down a concrete ramp, and before he was ready for it, the hard ground gave way to sand. He pulled off his shoes and socks and carried them out toward the crash of waves. The sand hadn't been raked yet for summer, and jagged shells stabbed at his feet. He'd sobered up enough to realize how cold it was on the beach. On the horizon, a clean line of blue cut across the dark world.

Nick felt the urgent need to purge his body of Dulles Hawkes. If he could unzip his own skin, he would have done so; instead he began to strip, folding his clothes in a neat pile, which he left on the sand. Naked, he walked into the sea, the first waves sharp as paper cuts on his ankles. But the memory of Dulles on his body pushed him forward, and Nick held his breath as he hopped into the water and let the sea swallow him to his waist. Before caution could send him back to shore, he ducked his head under and swam out. A series of small fires erupted along his nerve endings, but he would need only another minute or two in the freezing surf to rinse his body of the contamination. He felt sick and half-dead, but he did not feel guilty. He would have felt guilty about Dulles if it had come down to money. But when he thought of the hour and twenty-three minutes he'd spent in the hotel room and the promise of more in the days to come, Nick didn't feel much beyond numb.

Still, a voice in his head told him to keep swimming out. That voice was as familiar to him as his childhood bed. It had been there, a bright, silvery menace in a corner of his brain, from as early as the age of twelve. *Keep swimming, go on, toward the line on the horizon.* It spoke to him of easy exits. But Nick disobeyed. He turned around and swam back to shore.

In the morning Nick took the vaporetto back to San Marco. It was a brutal ride with a drumming headache and no sunglasses. Sand flaked off his arms and legs whenever he moved them. He'd slept for too few hours, hunched under the shelter of a boardwalk concession stand.

Nick's sobriety returned in time for a new fear to grip him. It came in the form of the newspapers that several Lido commuters read as they crossed the lagoon. Nick tried to study the Italian headlines over their shoulders, waiting for them to turn the pages before searching the next collection of black block letters and pixilated photographs. Had any of the papers reported the death of a British tourist at a hotel by the train station? When the chinless executive in front of him read too slowly, Nick switched seats. But the mother nursing her infant wasn't much faster. Nick was desperate to find out whether Dulles's death had been ruled an accident or whether it was being investigated as a homicide. Surely the Hotel Grazia Salvifica was too stingy to have surveillance equipment on every floor. Surely, and yet he couldn't be sure at all.

He took out his phone. At some point in the night, the screen had cracked. But as he began to type into the web browser, he realized the mistake he was making. If Dulles's death hadn't yet been made public, the random assortment of nouns would read like a confession: DULLES HAWKES VENICE TOURIST FALL ELEVATOR MURDER HOTEL ACCIDENT GRAZIA SALVIFICA PUSH. In the event that the police ever checked his phone history, it would not be wise to predict killings on search engines.

Nick disembarked at San Marco and bought two papers at the nearest kiosk. He flipped through them as he headed toward Dorsoduro. From what he could glean, there was no news on Dulles. At another kiosk mere footsteps from the Accademia Bridge, he bought another paper, with the same result. Certainly even an accidental death of a foreigner would merit a write-up.

Nick loped into Campo San Barnaba mentally drained and physically exhausted, and yet he was still too jittery to surrender to Daniela's guest bedroom. He needed reassurance of some kind. Another mistake he wouldn't make would be to return to the scene of the crime, lingering outside the Grazia Salvifica for clues. Nick never wanted to go back to that street again. If he visited Venice in fifty years, he'd refuse to walk that section of the Strada Nuova.

He considered phoning Richard West or, better still, Eva. They might have already heard about Dulles. But both had been present when Dulles made plans to meet Nick at San Rocco, and he didn't want to stir up that memory in their heads. There was another person, more indirect, whom he could try. He searched his phone for Battista's number and dialed.

"*Pronto!*" said the familiar hostile voice.

"Ciao, Battista, it's Nick. *Come stai?*"

"*Bene*, Nick. How are you? Are you still in Venezia?"

"Yeah," he answered. Battista had been the nearest approximation to a friend that Nick had spoken to since the incident. Even still, hearing his voice shouldn't provoke the tears that flooded his eyes. "I'm still here!" he said emphatically. "How is everything?"

"So busy," Battista groaned. "*Pazzo!* More busy than when I saw you last."

"Yes! Ha! You're *really* busy!" Nick couldn't access his usual smooth conversational prowess. "Is all good with everyone? Any news?" He winced. Why had he asked such a clumsy question?

"Only Il Dormitorio, the *palazzino* next door. The guy who inherited it, he is selling it. I work on this with Mr. West too."

"Oh, wow!" Nick enthused. This was good news, and Nick needed good news right now. "Richard is considering buying it? It's a great investment."

"Yes, we will take it!" Battista said boastfully. "The guy is an *imbroglione, un delinquente*, how do you say it in English?" Nick could guess the meaning; he'd heard the same characterization of Clay a hundred times. "He wants five million euros! There is no way to pay that much. But we are smarter. We screw him over on the deal." Battista uttered the American term *screw him over* like a child practicing a dirty word. The second time was more convincing: "He is in a hurry to sell, so we screw him over completely!"

"That's great!" Nick replied. It was great. Let Richard seize the chance to offer Clay a trifle of his asking amount—four million, or three, or two. If it were up to Nick, he'd accept one. They could take whatever they got and be out of Venice in a matter of days.

Nowhere in Italy was far away enough from the elevator shaft on Rio Terà San Leonardo. They could fly to Indonesia or Australia or Cameroon. "How soon do you think he'll make an offer?" Nick asked. "He should snap it up before others learn it's for sale! Try to convince him, Battista. Make him buy it quickly!"

"I will try," Battista promised. "Mr. West promised me a bonus if I get all of the arrangements ready in time. That is why I cannot meet for a drink today. I am sorry."

"Yes, let's get a drink sometime. That's why I was calling. Ciao."

Nick stopped in a caffè and ordered an espresso. He tried to appear normal, lounging at the bar counter like just another expat enjoying a late-morning coffee. But when the espresso arrived, his stomach revolted. Did late editions of local newspapers still exist? Should he wait to check the kiosks again in an hour? His foot tapping furiously, he decided to text Eva a simple "Hi" to gauge the reaction it garnered. For the next twenty minutes Nick stared into the cracked screen at his own Hi, willing a response. No reply came. He placed two coins on the bar and left.

He'd pushed a man to his death. As he walked down Fondamenta Gherardini, that fact pounced on him as if it were a revelation. He'd have to carry that millisecond shove around with him for the rest of his life. From now on, he'd always be a murderer, even if it had been in self-defense.

He worried he'd lost his sanity somewhere in the past twenty-four hours. His reflection in the window of a mask shop confirmed it. Patches of sand caked his neck and ears. His curly wet hair had dried in the shape of a cresting tidal wave. He'd been walking around with the stench of the sea on him all morning. What was wrong with him? Why hadn't he gone back to his guest room right away?

He picked up his pace, ducked down the tunnel, and opened the metal gate onto the concrete garden. He shook the gate to make sure it had locked behind him, and hid his face from the neighbor smoking on his upstairs balcony. Nick was relieved to find the apartment empty. He shut the guest-room door, pulled down the window shade, and sat on the corner of the bed. Here in the soothing darkness, he felt safe. He was still sitting in the same position some hours later when his phone pinged with an incoming message. It was Clay, with good news from Paris.

CHAPTER 18

Was there a term for forgeries that looked *too* authentic?

Clay spread the forms out on the kitchen counter. Antonin had certainly come through for him. The three forged documents—a private agreement backdated to 1997, signed by Cecilia van der Haar, transferring ownership of the Venice property; a New York State notarized contract conceding power of attorney over the property to her brother and his subsequent heirs; and an Italian apostille festooned with more badges and stamps than a general's chest—looked more legitimate than the authentic scruffy, ink-blotted documents provided by Freddy's lawyer. Clay wasn't worried. Antonin had promised these papers would convince even the most diligent Italian notary, and it had only taken him a day of phone calls at the Ritz to conjure them. "I'm sorry I couldn't get them for you sooner," Antonin had said in all seriousness when the courier dropped the package at the hotel. "We are still a bit of the old world—slow on Sundays."

Clay caught the night train back to Venice. It had been barely an hour after his return when he received a text from West. Could I bring my wife and niece over this afternoon? West's impatience thrilled him. He decided to encourage it by writing back that today wasn't good because the realtor wanted to show Il Dormitorio to an interested buyer. This fake threat worked. West responded immediately with a message of polite panic. You already have it on the market?? PLEASE, Clay, let us have a look today. West sent a follow-up message thirty seconds later promising that he had an exceedingly generous offer in mind—plus it would spare Clay shelling out for lawyers and the agent's commission. Let's keep Palazzo Contarini among family, West implored. After all, up until the van der Haars, the house always belonged to one family. And I like to think it still does today. Maybe West didn't realize how much the van der Haar family despised one another. Or maybe he did.

I'll hold the agent off until tomorrow, Clay wrote back. How's 4pm?

The four heavy knocks behind the bookcase told Clay the time. He'd spent the day trying to get the house in order—which meant not so much cleaning as throwing out. He tossed several boxes of Freddy's inane flea-market finds, books encased in a blanket of mold, nearly a hundred broken picture frames, and half a dozen mouse bodies stuck to strips of glue. "Coming," he called, hurrying to unlatch the walnut door in Freddy's bedroom.

The sunlight pierced the gloom. Although Clay had cleared a path to the outer rooms, West entered with timid steps. The action seemed designed to communicate respect for a dead man whose bedroom walls he was anxious to tear down.

"I hope we aren't interrupting."

"Why would you be? We said four o'clock, right?" Clay refused to play along with the phony show of concern. But such small wins against West might not reflect positively on the final sale price. Clay stretched out his arm to mimic neighborly welcome.

The others followed, one at a time through the doorway, as if slipping through the crack in a border wall. Battista came first, uttering a frigid "Ciao" without making eye contact. His phone was already extended, ready to document every frayed wire and cracked tile. Clay wondered if Battista knew that he had also served as West's assistant. He considered whispering West's suit size to see if it worked like a secret code among inferiors. But it was evident that the young Italian had already been turned against him. Halfway into the bedroom, Battista muttered in rapid Italian, "You're asking Mr. West to pay way too much for this place." It seemed a test of Clay's fluency more than anything else. Clay fired back in Italian, "I guess that depends on how much he wants it."

Eva and Karine came next, the latter wearing a pair of beetle-black sunglasses. "It's embarrassing it's taken us so long to meet," she said kindly. There was nothing on the surface to loathe about Karine or Eva; it might be impossible to warm to any prospective buyer who trudges through your house, inspecting every wall stain and broken cabinet hinge as if it testifies against your personal character. But for Clay they nonetheless failed as deserving inheritors of Freddy's domain. Neither would understand the ugly romance of Il Dormitorio. No doubt the first thing they'd do would be to strip it of any lingering character, confusing hygiene with enhancement. Clay had grown up wary of people like the Wests; they were always desperate to save public parks by kicking out the people who actually needed them. Today, however, he did his best to make them feel at home.

Eva rushed through the bedroom to reach the common area. Clay heard her moans before he could follow her into the kitchen. She was orbiting the counter, staring up at the Blue Madonna.

"*Ohhhh*, it's magnificent. And it's a total wreck!" Both of these remarks were uttered with ecstatic delight. "My god, it needs so much work to bring it back to life. It's basically going to chip off in the next ten minutes!" Her small hands bunched into fists. Her skin was so pale Clay could see the blood running underneath it, like water under a frozen lake. Nick had said how much he liked Eva, but Clay didn't get the appeal. "What year was the fresco done?" she asked.

Clay cleared his throat. "Sixteen ninety-eight. It was painted for—"

"More than three centuries old!" Eva rhapsodized. "Before America was even invented. And if we don't restore it soon, gone forever. It feels like our duty, doesn't it?"

Karine snorted loudly. She was standing apart in the corner of the kitchen, her arms crossed and her sunglasses still on, despite the lack of sunlight on this side of the palazzo. She seemed to be reminding everyone that it was not Eva who needed to be convinced of the property's selling points. Eva ignored her, seeking out her uncle, who was currently running his hand down a piece of drywall.

"Uncle Richard, it's a masterpiece! It's exactly what you've been looking for! Can't you see how badly it needs to be *resuscitated*?"

For the first time, Clay experienced a touch of empathy for Richard West. His eyes kept scuttling between his niece and his wife as he tried to shape his mouth into an indeterminate line that would appease them both.

Clay suspected that Eva had probably colluded with Battista, because he filled the silence by gazing up at the murky blue fresco and piping out, "It is very beautiful, yes."

"Isn't it!" Eva agreed.

West strolled to the counter and stood next to his niece. He listened as Eva waved her fingers skyward and muttered to him about chemical compounds and plaster purifiers. It took a nudge from Battista to bring West's eyes down to the legal documents laid out on the countertop.

"Sorry," Clay said, stepping forward. "I put those out for the agent. It's the documents needed for the sale."

"Ah, perfect!" West said. He gave a cautious glance in his wife's direction. "If it's okay with you, could Battista take a few quick pictures of them?"

"Oh . . ." Clay demurred, although that had been the very point of leaving them out.

"It would move the process along, should we find ourselves settling on a price." Battista was already clicking away on his phone.

"Are there any other frescoes?" Eva asked greedily. Clay explained there were a few of lesser importance behind the drywall, along with some traditional stucco moldings.

"Pull down those walls!" Eva cried like a conqueror. "What a waste to keep them covered like this!" Clay wasn't at all charmed by West's niece, but he did appreciate her presence. She was practically selling the house for him.

Eva wanted to explore the other floors, and West walked over to his wife to coax her into joining them. "Come on, dear. You have to give it a chance." He threaded his fingers into hers and kissed her knuckles. It was impossible to gauge Karine's reaction through the buffer zone of her sunglasses, but as they mounted the steps Clay heard her whisper a clipped warning about their finances. "We can afford it," West whispered back. "When the new investments kick in, we'll be up again, higher than we were before." Battista jogged after them, and Clay was left alone in the kitchen to put away the documents now that they'd served their purpose. After ten minutes touring the house, Karine reappeared alone. She had removed her sunglasses and was squeezing them in her hand.

"Thank you for your hospitality," she said. Even without the sunglasses, Clay still couldn't read a verdict on her face. "It is a lovely house. And I'll admit it would add some needed space to our situation. God knows I need it when Dick gets on his conservation kicks."

He wondered if he'd misjudged West's wife. He liked the way she spoke to him—plainly, without artifice, as if she lacked hidden motives. She paused by the door to Freddy's bedroom. "It's a shame you're selling," she said.

"It wasn't an easy choice. But as much as I love Venice, it's, well—"

"—not a place for the young," she answered with a nod. "Or maybe it is. Maybe that's precisely why Dick likes it here so much. It's an adult playground, isn't it?" She glanced tiredly upward, not at the Ricci fresco but at a brown water stain on the ceiling. "You know, the clinic where I worked in Leipzig was devoted to cognitive neuroscience. My particular research was on the nature of the distracted mind, how the brain shifts in consciousness between immediate focus and wandering thoughts. The drift, the lag, the daydream," she said. "I had a lot of big ideas about what the brain was doing back then." She smiled, as if thanking Clay for indulging her. "It seems sometimes, in coming here, I've traded in for the daydream full time. Try as I might, I can't seem to shake myself into a lucid thought. It's all just drift and beauty." Karine abruptly slipped on her sunglasses. "I'm sure you'll receive a fair offer from Dick. Good luck with everything." Before she left, she gave him a pained smile, one that Clay felt sure she'd wear for the rest of her marriage.

He heard Eva and West descending the steps. "Did he have any relatives?" Eva was asking. "A boyfriend or a partner? Because it sounds like a great lawsuit."

"I'm sure there'll be a lawsuit!" West cried. "I'm guessing the last time that elevator was inspected was sometime right after World War Two, give or take a few months. It's typical Venetian negligence. They pass a zillion codes jamming everything up in bureaucratic traffic, but no one will actually show up to do the work. Honestly, the one good thing about that development in Mestre is that it's being overseen by foreign investors, which means it stands a chance of being built properly."

They rounded the corner into the kitchen, their arms interlocked. If Clay squinted, they would have looked like newlyweds shopping for their first home. "Nothing good should be said about that tourist development in Mestre," Eva chirped.

"Well, anyway," West conceded, changing the subject. "We can't blame the hotel entirely. I'm sure Dulles had about ten bottles of vodka in his system when he stepped into that elevator shaft. Accidents happen. You can't pad humans in Bubble Wrap!"

Clay froze upon hearing the name Dulles. It rang with a familiarity he couldn't pinpoint.

"He downed an entire bottle of vodka at what, noon?" Eva said. "I'm surprised he made it back to the hotel in order to fall down that shaft. It's a shame he did. There are so many canals that would have taken him."

"Dulles," Clay repeated aloud, trying to trigger his own memory.

West glanced over at him. "He was an acquaintance. Actually, you might have known him through Freddy. Dulles Hawkes, the antiquarian? They once did business together."

"He died two days ago right here in Venice," Eva added eagerly, as if boasting of her proximity to a tragedy. "He was visiting us, having a drink in our living room the day before he died!"

"Dulles was here?" Clay asked. "In Venice? In your living room?"

West flinched. His eyes nervously roamed the kitchen as if he'd blundered into a trap. He must have noticed the anxiety on Clay's face, because he reached his hands out beseechingly.

"I know what you're thinking, Clay," he said coolly. "But I

promise I did not summon Dulles here to do an appraisal of Freddy's silver. I hope we trust each other that much. I didn't hire anyone to do an assessment before I made you that offer. I had no certified knowledge of their value. That was our deal, and I wouldn't cheat you on it." Like a cunning little boy, West made sure that none of his sentences could technically be called out as a lie.

"We trust each other, don't we?" West went on. "We need a level of trust in order to move forward. Otherwise, it's probably wise to forget the proposal I had in mind for this house." He spun his wedding ring around on his finger while carefully gauging Clay's reaction. "Listen, Dulles happened to be in Venice on his way to Rome. He came by for a drink. He did have a peek at the van der Haar pieces, but that was after I bought them. Naturally, he raved about them." West made an attempt at an honest smile.

But it wasn't West's duplicity that had frightened Clay. When he heard Dulles's name, his mind flashed to Nick—specifically to the little problem over silver that Nick said needed taking care of. He had called it a glitch. Could Dulles Hawkes have been that glitch? Clay tried to imagine Nick as a murderer, getting rid of the drunk antiquarian in order to ensure his silence. But Nick wasn't capable of murder, and the harder Clay tried to picture his boyfriend in a series of homicidal poses, the more preposterous the enterprise became. Murder was too lonely a place for Nick. There was no way he'd resort to murdering someone over money.

"You said Dulles died in an accident?" Clay asked just to be sure.

Eva nodded. "The elevator at his hotel was out of order, and he fell from the fifth floor to the lobby. That's what the newspaper said."

"God, how awful," Clay moaned in relief.

Battista entered the kitchen, making a full panorama sweep of the common area with his phone. West clapped his hands at his young companions. "You two head back. I'd like to talk to Clay alone." Eva was already beaming in triumph as she and Battista made their way into the bedroom. West joined Clay at the counter.

"Thanks for letting us have a look," West said, his eyes on Clay, warm with possibilities. It reminded Clay of the moment they had met on the rooftop of the Peggy Guggenheim, after Clay had saved him from falling over the ledge.

"Of course."

"And for putting us ahead of tomorrow's buyers. Did they see pictures of the place or—"

"No, I didn't send any pictures yet," Clay replied. "The realtor just described it to them. French retirees, I think they were, looking for a place to fix up."

West spun his wedding ring again. "I've given the matter a lot of thought. To tell you the truth, we don't really need more space. But additional square footage isn't the reason for my interest. I feel I owe something to the legacy of the palazzo to bring it all under one roof again. I'm afraid of someone coming in and turning it into another rental for weekend travelers. That's not what these grand homes deserve."

Clay nodded. He would let West feel that he was doing something noble for Venice.

"Plus," West added, pointing to the fresco, "I know it isn't your fault and I don't want to speak ill of Freddy, but he should have done the work to preserve that Sebastiano Ricci. You have a responsibility to prevent treasures from turning to dust."

Clay nodded through this indictment too. He would nod through almost anything until he heard a figure tossed out.

"Now, I know you have these French retirees lined up," West said, "but I've asked a few real-estate friends for their advice. They told me, in its current condition, Il Dormitorio couldn't be worth much more than three and a half million on the current market. Your agent was flattering you by quoting a price of upper five." He laughed at the sheer absurdity of it. "Come on. No one's going to pay that much on top of all of the work needed in here in order to make it habitable. You could get a place so much larger for that amount. It's just not feasible. I think you'll find my proposal quite generous." He licked his lips and arched his pale eyebrows. "I'm offering four million euros even."

"Oh, I don't know," Clay balked. "Maybe I should wait a month or two and do a few open houses. See what interest there is."

"I thought you wanted to be out of Venice before summer?" West countered. "Look, I'll do one better. We can wrap up the sale as quickly as you'd like."

"It would have to be really quick and painless, because, honestly, the realtor swore to me that I could get at least—"

"I'll pay for the inspections and I'll even handle the legal fees. If it all goes through, that's four million euros in your bank account within the week. That's *four million* with no agents or outside intermediaries taking a cut. We'll do it the old Venetian way, fast and private. What do you say? You're not going to find a better deal out there. I promise you that."

Clay should keep haggling and hold out for more. He'd been too quick in accepting the lowball offer for the silver, and West was no doubt trying to fleece him again with a far lower bid than the house was worth. But he was tired of conning, tired of the lies and the tricks, and he didn't want to wait around for more glitches to appear that would threaten to take them down. Four million euros was an obscene amount of money. It was enough to start a brand-new life.

"Okay," he said. "All right."

West thrust out his hand, and they shook on it. "Excellent! I'll book an appointment with a notary." It felt like an ending, which is what Clay might have wanted out of it most.

He walked West into Freddy's bedroom. "I know this place holds a lot of memories for you," West said once he had crossed through the doorway, his eyes staring down at his own patch of terrazzo. Clay could already imagine that expensive flooring spreading like water through Il Dormitorio. "Whatever our differences, you're putting this house in safe hands. I'll take good care of it."

Clay shut the door and returned to the kitchen. He sat on the counter and stared up at the fresco. After Eva finished her restoration, the swimming Mary might survive another three hundred years. In that time she'd witness the rise and fall of many other families and sea tides. In three hundred years, all their names would be equally meaningless. Van der Haar, West, Guillory—just people who'd been here once.

Clay texted Nick, We'll be gone soon.

The next day was crowded with visitors. West sent two engineers over in the morning to inspect Il Dormitorio for repairs. A plumber arrived at noon, along with a city energy inspector who West had bribed for a last-minute appointment. As promised, West was doing his best to fast-track the sale. Eva dropped in unannounced at one thirty to take photographs of the fresco. Clay stayed out of everyone's way, busy notifying the interns of their impending eviction and dealing with the last of Freddy's possessions.

Most of Il Dormitorio's short-term renters took their expulsion in stride. Only one, a sandy-haired Ivy League brat from Connecticut, proved intractable, stomping his feet and claiming tenants' rights. It took an hour of compassionate sighing, a few veiled threats, and two hundred euros before he agreed to pack his suitcase.

By three thirty, Clay was trying to decide what to do with a set of Georgian chairs upholstered in beige needlepoint—really the only valuable furniture left in the *palazzino*—when his phone rang. It was Daniela. In lieu of hello, Clay answered with, "I swear he'll be out of your hair soon. Did he at least take you out to dinner?"

There was a long silence before Daniela responded. "Hi, doll. It's not that. But he *is* the reason I'm calling. He hasn't come out of his room in two days. I've knocked several times, and he always says he's sleeping." She paused. "I think you should come over."

Clay hurried out of the house and headed south. As he crossed the Grand Canal, he heard a faint chanting in the distance, like cicadas chattering on a forest's edge. These were human voices. Clay realized he'd been so engrossed in selling the house that he'd ignored the city around him. In retrospect, he recalled seeing banners suspended over bridges and white sheets hugging balconies that must have announced the details of today's demonstration. He saw them now. A rally was being held this afternoon for Venetian *residenti* at Piazzale Roma, the symbolic entry point to the city where the buses and cars dumped visitors from the mainland. The specific target of the protest was the massive development in Mestre, along with the project's phantom foreign investors. But for most of the Venetians gathering that afternoon under the hot spring sun, the real scourge was tourism itself. What would Venice be like without any Venetians living in it? There were only fifty-three thousand of these rare humans left, and that number was shrinking by a thousand each year. They were a people facing redline extinction, wiped out by foreign invaders who marched through their streets with cameras, shooting anything that didn't move. Their neighbors and children were sent into exile so their bedrooms could be Airbnb'ed for prime weekend rates. The love of the city had killed its people. Quite simply, Venice had been visited to death.

Clay passed dozens of protesters who must have just left Piazzale Roma. They carried homemade signs proclaiming VIVIAMO VENEZIA. NON SIAMO COMPARSE! ("We live in Venice. We are not extras!") or VENEZIA NON È UN PARCO DIVERTIMENTI ("Venice is not an amusement park") or MI NON VADO VIA MI RESTO ("I do not go away, I stay"). Others had simply adopted the iconic maroon-and-gold Venetian flag with the words RESIDENTE RESISTENTE stamped across it. Clay nodded in solidarity at the demonstrators. He wished he could swing by Piazzale Roma to raise his fist in support. But he was too concerned about Nick for any detours. He had texted him several times that morning, and he'd received ambiguous one-word answers in return: Great to Clay's news that the house inspections were under way; Anywhere to Clay's adventurous question as to the first place they should travel. Now those one-word answers seemed ominous. Clay purposely hadn't texted any mention of Dulles Hawkes to Nick, hoping the antiques dealer would remain forgotten at the bottom of an elevator shaft for the rest of their lives. But now his stomach was turning over, converting vague, unverified fears into very real pain.

The reverb of bullhorns pierced the air. The chanting grew louder as Clay cut a path near the Piazzale. He dashed down a tiny canal where the coppery water held the twitching reflection of the sky. Clay heard the Venetian chant clearly now.

Mi no vado via! Mi no vado via!

Mi no vado via! Mi no vado via!

I do not go away. I am not leaving.

He mouthed along to the words—although he *was* going away,

he *was* leaving. Maybe forever, and that was his real final goodbye to Freddy.

He turned down a sharp passage, in the opposite direction of Piazzale Roma. The cheering dissolved into a faint roar like television static in another room.

When Clay reached Daniela's apartment, a handsome older Chinese man with an oil slick of hair opened the gate. It was not ideal circumstances for meeting Benny, who was wearing a burgundy suit of lightweight velvet and a pair of dirty garden gloves. He'd been potting rosebushes in the strip of dirt that bordered the concrete, and he tugged off the gloves to shake Clay's hand. Daniela wandered outside in a loose silk dress, a shade of orange that clashed exquisitely with Benny's suit and her own red glasses. Daniela stared skeptically at the bushes, aware of their unlikely chances. Clay gave her a kiss on each cheek, careful not to smear her makeup.

"Is he any better?" he asked.

"I don't know what happened. He seemed so happy up until a few days ago and then? I went to the protest earlier today—god, it felt good to scream with my city—and when I got back he refused to open the door."

"I'll check on him."

"Take your time. Benny and I are having dinner with his family on Giudecca." She stared apprehensively at her boyfriend. "It's not a great night to meet your kids. The police are worried the demonstrators might get violent. And so they should get violent! But we could stay in and—"

Benny shook his head. "They're waiting for us, Dani."

Daniela pressed her mouth against Clay's ear. "God help me. Meeting a family at my age? I feel like some horrible mistake has been made."

"They'll love you," Clay assured her before doing his best rendition of Freddy. "Break their hearts, doll."

Clay entered the apartment and knocked on the guest-room door. He knocked two more times before turning the knob. The shades were drawn tight over the windows, and the covered skylight bore only the scant outline of a fading afternoon. The room smelled of sour boyhood. Clay placed his hand on the leg lump of comforter at the foot of the bed. The body underneath it barely moved. He walked over to the side. There was only the faintest rustle of sheets.

"It's you," the voice said. Nick must be looking up at him, but in the darkness Clay couldn't make out his eyes.

"Are you okay?"

"No, I'm not."

"Why don't you tell me about it?"

"I can't."

It was right then that Clay knew what had happened. He pulled off his shoes and climbed into bed next to Nick. Slipping under the covers, he slid his arm under Nick's back until his hand grasped his far shoulder. Then he collected all of Nick against his chest. He felt the pulse of Nick's breath and the shiver of his eyelashes on his neck. Clay wrapped his arm around this body. He wanted Nick to feel forgiven. He wanted him to know he was forgiven before he ever felt a sense of blame.

"You can tell me when you're ready," Clay whispered. "Until then, we'll stay just like this."

CHAPTER 19

Where do you go after Venice?

It was a question consuming Clay as he marched, documents in hand, toward his appointment at the notary. It had been a hard week for the city—angry protests continued to flare each afternoon and a car had been set on fire two nights ago on the bridge connecting Venice to the mainland. The week had been equally rough for Clay and Nick. Just convincing Nick to get out of bed those first few mornings felt tantamount to forcing a new religion on a person. Slowly, though, Nick had come back to life, a little more skittish and sheepish than before, but every day less inclined to disappear into the snuffed darkness of Daniela's guest room. Clay knew it was essential to put some distance between Nick and the scene of the crime. Leaving Venice as soon as possible was key, and Clay worked diligently on the last-minute preparations for the sale of Il Dormitorio. To hurry the process along, he sent West a bluffing text: Maybe it's best we wait until fall. I have to be back in NYC next week, and we've been rushing when it might be smarter to pause and consider our options. West asked him to hold on and within two hours he'd set their meeting at the notary for Monday at 10:00 a.m. "Think about the first place you want to go," Clay told Nick in an effort to keep him focused on the future. "Picture our next destination. It can be anywhere—seriously *anywhere* on the planet."

Strangely, when it came to choosing, neither of them could make up their mind. No place, near or far, seemed right. Bogotá. Cairo. Kuala Lumpur. Each exotic city was tossed out at random and dismissed with a shrug of doubt. Clay suspected that the stumbling block was money—for once, not too little but too much. The idea of living on an endless supply of cash proved as alien to both of them as visiting the moon—or, rather, like grafting the moon's sulfurous atmosphere onto Bogotá or Cairo or Kuala Lumpur. As different as their upbringings had been, they had both been raised incurably middle-class. As kids, Clay and Nick could each envision earning money or stealing money or even performing degrading acts for money. But possessing a surplus of it took on the absurd logic of a dream.

Clay finally made the decision for them. Last night, he'd texted Nick that their first destination right after the closing would be a train to Milan. And from Milan? Well, they'd figure it out once they got there. He thought it best not to upset Nick by mentioning that one of their chief search parameters might be "countries with no extradition treaty with Italy." After all, they'd be traveling with the extra baggage of fraud and murder.

Passing the train station, Clay took the white-stone Scalzi Bridge over the Grand Canal. The turquoise water rippled under its load of rush-hour traffic. At a kiosk on the other side of the bridge, Venetians snapped up the morning paper. They muttered in disgust over the latest turn in the Mestre imbroglio. Apparently the week of protests had induced an insider to come forward with a front-page-worthy reveal about the tourist development. As long as the headline didn't read YOUNG WHITE MALE WANTED IN SUSPICIOUS DEATH OF DRUNKEN BRIT, Clay took any news as encouraging.

He hurried through the spaghetti alleys of Santa Croce, hunting for the street that held the notary. Under Italian law, it was the buyer who chose the specific notary to oversee the closing, a stipulation not unlike letting the player cut the card deck after the dealer shuffled to ensure no collusion. But today's seller of Il Dormitorio had found another way to beat the system. Clay was armed with a folder of his forged documents mixed in with the legitimate ones. He also carried his passport, his bank details, and the original van der Haar deed from 1894 (a little relic designed to entertain West during the proceeding and keep his attention off Clay's trembling hands). He was as ready as he'd ever be to deceive his way through twenty minutes of formalities. At the end of those twenty minutes, four million euros would flow into his bank account. Yes, he was frightened. Terrified from throat to knee. But he could cheat a man he hated for twenty minutes in order to be free for the rest of his life.

His stomach seemed less convinced. Clay stopped at a corner to take a few settling breaths. He popped a chalky pink tablet into his mouth—his fourth that morning. *You can break down all you want after this meeting is over,* he told his stomach, a driver appealing to a sputtering engine to make it to the next highway off-ramp. *Get through this hour, and I promise you the best internist in Milan.* He pulled out his phone to check the time: 9:50. He had ten minutes to locate the notary.

He hurried down a passage that contained two bars and three mask shops but no notary. He careened left and fought past a barrage of deliverymen with their loaded metal trolleys blocking the path. The passage led to a Baroque church that Clay had walked by hundreds of times, and yet he couldn't mentally connect this landmark to his notion of where the notary was. He spun around, rebattled the deliverymen, and ended up on a tiny stone-carved bridge. The stomach tablets weren't working. He had five minutes until he was meant to be sitting across from Richard West to sign over the deed. Clay darted down a skinny alley that dead-ended in a canal. He was starting to panic, his folder of documents slick with palm sweat. He reversed and took a sharp right, only to arrive at the same Baroque church, where a group of Ukrainian tourists was now photo-stalking a flock of pigeons. The clock tower read one minute after ten. Clay picked up his pace, choosing movement over precision. Visions of West and the notary shaking their heads at his tardiness—*This kid can't be trusted, we'd better triple-check all of his paperwork*—flashed through his mind. It would be exactly like Venice to tangle him up one last time.

The city was no place for a sane person. Thus Clay took a nonsensical turn left, the very opposite direction from the way his brain told him to go. At five minutes after ten, he arrived at the notary's front door. A brass plaque over the buzzer announced CONSIGLIO NAZIONALE DEL NOTARIATO and notified visitors that the office was on the second floor. Clay pressed the buzzer and heard the drone of admittance.

As he stepped inside, the first tendrils of air-conditioning slipped across his skin. He saw the stairs in front of him just as he heard a voice yelling "Stop!" from behind him. Clay turned around in the entrance; the door smacked against his shoulder. A sprinting, olive-skinned man with curly black hair came to a braking halt in front of the building. He had a newspaper curled in his fist and was panting so hard he doubled over. Only when the man looked up did Clay recognize Battista.

"Crook!" Battista roared in English. "Cheater!"

It was Clay's worst-case scenario, the one he hadn't even allowed himself to entertain. He slipped his folder of phony documents behind his back. He considered barreling past Battista and hurling them into the nearest canal.

"All this time, he lied to me." Battista lifted to his full height and jabbed his own chest. "Mr. West made me work against my own city," he cried. "He made me betray myself!"

Clay had no idea what Battista was talking about, but it seemed unrelated to the documents in his hand. He felt a wave of dizziness pass through him. So close to disaster, he stood there somehow miraculously unscathed. Clay had been keeping the front door open with his shoulder, but the drone sounded again from the upstairs office.

"I'm sorry," he said to West's assistant. "I can't talk now. I have an appointment. I have to go up." He offered a sympathetic frown, as if to communicate that he knew better than anyone how manipulative Richard West could be.

"You don't understand!" Battista shouted, his voice breaking into a whine. He stepped closer and switched to his native tongue. "He made a fool of me, and why? For money. All this time, all these meetings where I bring blueprints and documents and bank checks, so stupid I was, fetching and retrieving like a dog, thinking we were working on conservation projects. That's what West *told me* we were doing, I swear that's what I thought!" The young man was on the verge of tears. He unrolled his newspaper and pointed at a photograph on the front page of a tan older man with rivulets of long gray hair covering his bald spot. A brown cigarette was clenched in the man's teeth. The headline outed him as the head contractor of the Mestre development, the local man performing the evil bidding of the anonymous foreign investors. The newspaper had sensationally dubbed him THE JUDAS OF VENICE.

"I have met this man many times," Battista whispered, as if

fearful that others on the street might overhear. "At hotels, at restaurants. I've passed envelopes and plans between him and Mr. West for months now." He shook his head. "Don't you see? West is one of the foreign investors in that development. Jesus, I'm so stupid! He's happy to restore an altar painting and get credit for saving Venice. But he can't resist making money, no matter what it destroys."

The buzzer droned again. Battista began to babble about his family—What if they found out that he worked for one of the developers? They'd disown him. He had lived in Venice his whole life. Where was he meant to go? Clay heard a commotion of voices on the floor above.

"I'm so sorry, Battista," Clay said somberly. "Richard West is a terrible person. I was his assistant once, and he screwed me over. I'll never forgive him for it. But, if you'll excuse me, I have to go upstairs now and sell him a house." It was a shame Clay couldn't explain to the unhinged young man the retribution hidden in that act.

As Clay turned to go up, Battista lunged toward him and grabbed his arm.

"No, you don't understand!" he said, his eyes bright with tears. "Don't you see? He's tricked you too. Don't go up there. It's a trap."

Prosecco at 10:00 a.m. did not strike Nick as the shrewdest way to kick off his last day in Venice. But Eva was in a celebratory mood, plus she wanted to say goodbye in person. Come on, swing by for a toast on your way out of town, she texted. I have exciting news!

Nick steered his heavy suitcase through the streets of Venice with his carry-on bag strapped on his shoulder. Even with his luggage he felt, for the first time in so many days, free, and light, and maybe, yes, even hopeful. The sun was warm on his skin, and the smell of brackish water teemed with amoebic life. Clay had saved him—that much Nick knew—and he would spend every day thanking him for that gift. Nick didn't mind the heft of his suitcase, or the shoulder strap digging into his collarbone, or the sticky heat of the late-spring morning, because it all pressed him firmly onto the planet and he wanted to stay here—with Clay—for as long as he could. Yellow signs pointed toward the *ferrovia*. Once Nick reached the train station, he'd buy two tickets to Milan and wait, mind empty, heart open, for Clay on the platform.

He wore his gift from Daniela, the Prince of Wales jacket. The tailor had done a nice job mending the sleeve; the rip was nearly invisible. Ahead, Nick spotted a postcard stand, and he stopped at it for a minute, realizing he'd forgotten to send his sister one. Now, on the last day, it felt too late. He'd write Margaret a postcard from wherever they ended up. Surely that destination would be *almost* as stunning as Venice.

It wasn't even ten o'clock yet when he reached the station—Clay wouldn't be free from the notary for at least another half hour—and Palazzo Contarini wasn't too far out of the way. Nick decided to push his suitcase in Eva's direction. Why not drop in to hear the news that she'd finally gotten her hands on the Blue Madonna fresco? He could wish her all the best. He'd likely never see her again.

In Cannaregio, Nick allowed himself a glance down the alley toward Il Dormitorio—for once, there was no chance of an accidental run-in with his boyfriend. Clay was signing his name to four million euros at this very moment. Nick entered the lush palazzo garden and stashed his suitcase and bag behind the flowering cypress. As he walked to the gate, he improvised a joke to tell Eva through the intercom: "Is this the Thank-God-Nick's-Finally-Leaving Party?" When he pressed the buzzer, though, a different voice erupted through the speaker. "Who is it?" Richard West asked.

Nick was thrown off guard. Shouldn't West be sitting across from Clay at the notary right now? He checked his phone to make sure of the time. It was only a few minutes after ten. The appointment should have just been starting.

"It's Nick," he said cheerfully. The gate clicked open, and Nick climbed the dark staircase. At the top, he found the door ajar. As he tried to push it open, however, the door hit against some unseen obstruction. Nick squeezed through the opening to discover the remains of a demo job. West's wall of chicken-wire bookshelves had been partially dismantled. The walnut door leading to the van der Haar *palazzino* now stood exposed. For Nick, this renovation was, at least, a positive sign, and it helped calm his anxiety. West clearly felt so confident about obtaining Il Dormitorio, he'd already started ripping down the physical barrier.

The man himself stood across the room at the bar. A shaft of sunlight cut blindingly across the floor, separating them. West wore his usual white linen shirt and pants. He was smiling in welcome.

Nick avoided the initial question that was blaring, loud as a siren, through his head: *What are you doing home right now?* Instead he sneaked it into a friendlier remark: "Look who I get a chance to say goodbye to! I thought it would only be Eva here this morning."

West hooked his hands on his hips and took Nick in with interest. His bare foot toyed with the brass brain doorstop on the floor. "So you're off to Milan for good today, are you?"

The mention of Milan spooked Nick. How did West know the city they had chosen for their escape this afternoon? Paranoia shot through him, running through every vein. Yet there was nothing cunning about West's smile. It radiated with genuine affection, and in relief Nick recalled his own excuse about the silver client in Milan.

"Yes, finally!" Nick answered with a laugh. "It's back to work, I'm afraid. I wish I could stay all summer. I really hope I can live like you do one day."

West clucked at the compliment. Nick noticed that he had extremely dexterous feet. He was able to grasp the brain with his sole and rotate it around on the terrazzo.

"Eva ran to the liquor store," West said. "She invited you over for prosecco before checking if we had any in the house. I tried to get ahold of Battista this morning to fetch some, but his phone doesn't seem to be on." West rolled his eyes at the unreliability of assistants. "Eva should be back in a few minutes. In the meantime, can I make you"—he scanned the contents of his bar—"a gin?"

"Oh, I can wait," Nick said amiably. "Is it just us?" He was hoping to tease out the reason that West was at home right now instead of at the notary.

"Yes, it's just us. I hope that's all right with you!" West poured out a pinch of gin for himself and drowned it in sparkling water. "Karine's out for the day. The dust from the bookshelves does a number on her allergies. It's best if it's just the three of us anyway. I've never seen Eva so excited. It makes me incredibly happy." He stirred his drink with his pinkie finger and sucked the tip for taste.

"Why is she so excited?" Nick asked. He couldn't decide if he was supposed to infer the reason or not. He was exhausted by the labyrinth of deceits. Leaving Venice would mean letting go of the lies. He glanced at the piles of books and disassembled wood. "Does it have to do with your recent renovation?"

"You could say that!" West replied giddily. He set his drink on the bar and wrapped his arms around his ribs, hugging himself.

Nick felt the vicarious warmth of that hug. West's win was also their win. Everyone was coming out ahead. Everyone had reason to celebrate this morning.

A *motoscafo* roared down the canal out the window. Nick waited for the engine to fade. "Does this mean Eva isn't returning to France in order to find a conservation job?"

"You don't know the half of it!" West cried. "You really should be thanked, because the silver deal laid the groundwork for reeling in the main prize. It established a level of trust . . . Well, not that I ever trusted that punk next door. Let me tell you, I was never fooled. I have a nose for scam artists." West tapped his right nostril. "You develop an instinct for them in business. But it's all worked out so nicely."

Nick smiled warmly through each insult of Clay. Let him hate the punk next door. What difference did it make now?

West let go of himself to wave at the wall behind Nick. "I never liked those shelves. But soon the wall behind it will go too. Eventually we can open up the whole house and return it to its original floor plan. I'm talking about exactly as it existed when it was built in 1473. I'm respecting the hell out of this palazzo's history, thank you very much! Far more so than the van der Haars ever did with their crappy partitioning job just to keep a toe in this town." West had finally collected all he could from the gilded American family. Now that he was free from his obsession, the van der Haars had deflated into the flawed human beings they had always been.

Nick stepped into the shaft of light, his hand shielding his eyes. "Are you saying you bought the house next door from the guy who inherited it?"

West nodded with enthusiasm. Then he modified that nod by tipping his head from side to side in an amusing "sort of" nod-shake. A giggle escaped his lips.

"You aren't going to believe what's happening right this minute!" West inched his sleeve back to check his wristwatch. "What's already happened, actually, as of fifteen minutes ago!"

"What is it?" Nick asked coyly. "What's going on?" He inched toward West to escape the sun.

"Well, it's safe to tell you. That kid, that *hustler* next door, is at the notary office right now, signing over the title to Il Dormitorio."

"Amazing! You're getting the whole house! Well done!"

"But, you see, I've known all along the kind of person he is. Did I ever tell you that he once worked for me as my assistant? This is the kind of person you don't trust as a rule. Which, of course, is why I asked you to examine the silver before I ever agreed to buy it. So when this kid comes back offering to sell me Il Dormitorio, I'm not some lamb quaking in an open field. I know to be careful around this Brooklyn gold digger." *Bronx*, Nick almost corrected.

West inhaled sharply. "I could smell it, you know what I mean? Like you must be able to do with fake antiques. I could smell the lies on him."

Sweat was prickling the back of Nick's neck. More than anything, he wanted to shut the curtains on the migraine of daylight seeping into the room. In the shade he could calm down and think rationally. "What did you do?" he asked, unable to contain the accusation in his voice.

"You're going to love it!" West promised. He pointed his thumb behind him at the bar. "Are you sure I can't fix you a gin?"

"I'm sure," Nick snapped. He tried to smile, but the muscles in his face were agonizingly tight. "What happened? What's going on?"

West didn't seem to catch the slip of Nick's mask. He was too high on his own triumph. "It's incredible! The kid bragged about owning the whole house. Like we were both equal under the same roof. He and I, *the same*, can you believe that?" West sputtered his lips at the absurdity of it. "Of course, that wasn't the case. He only got his hands on the half he cheated out of poor Freddy."

The image of Clay sitting in a notary office swam around in Nick's head as if it had fallen loose from a story that no longer made any sense to him. "If you figured out that Clay didn't own Il Dormitorio, why is he at the notary right now?" Nick couldn't stop shifting his weight from one leg to the other, as if neither limb wanted to bear the responsibility of holding him up.

West turned to retrieve his drink from the bar. "Battista deserves the credit for tracking her down. It wasn't easy. She's been living in Uruguay for the past twenty years, in a speck of a beach town called José Ignacio. It's just her and a dozen horses living in borderline poverty. The poor thing's half-senile. It's such a sad way to end up. I mean, she's *a van der Haar*! It goes to show: you have to keep replenishing your money supply, or there won't be any. I hope you've learned that lesson, Nick."

Nick shook his head, not because he was immune to lessons, but because the facts themselves weren't jelling in his head. "Who did Battista track down in Uruguay?" His voice quavered. "You can't mean Freddy's sister?"

West snorted in laughter. "Yes, Cecilia van der Haar! We tried to convince her to come to Venice to testify that she never signed away her half of the house, but she's too weak to travel. It's just as well. That woman is a nightmare, as nasty as the last century made them. But she was very grateful that we reached out to her. Understandably, she wasn't pleased that the same scam artist who worked over her brother was now trying to sell the family house from under her. Battista arranged for a local lawyer to take her affidavit and send it to us." West shook his head incredulously. "Can you believe it? I swear, *only* in Venice. It's always been a thieves' paradise." West took a swig of his drink. "But the good news is that Cecilia has agreed to sell me Il Dormitorio when it's all over. She's only too happy for the money. And my lawyer assures me no Italian judge is going to let Clay keep his share once he's convicted of real-estate fraud." West shrugged. "I think Cecilia understands who she's giving the property to and the amount of care I'll—"

"What will happen to him?" Nick asked urgently.

"To Clay?" West clinked his wrists together to signal handcuffs. "The *polizia* are at the notary with my lawyer. Once he hands over his documents, they'll arrest him. It's a ridiculously light sentence for fraud in Italy—three or four years. But at least he'll get some punishment for trying to screw me over." West scuttled toward Nick to clap him tenderly on the shoulder. The daylight proved too intense for him, though, and after a brief squeeze, he retreated to the shade by the bar. "I know I sound awful gloating about someone going to jail. I'm as sad about the situation as anyone. But that kid next door has always been a thorn in my side. He turned on me when I tried to help him once. Then he turned Freddy against me. Now I can finally say to his face, 'See, I was right about you.'" West stared dreamily toward the walnut door. "I'm always right about people. It's an instinct. Still, I can't believe that fucker had the gall to try to rob me blind."

Nick stumbled forward, making his way toward the satisfied smile on the other side of the sunlight. His fingers were strangling warm spring air. A flare of hate tore through him, a sick heat that made him feel claustrophobic in his own body. He'd felt it in the hotel room of the Grazia Salvifica, and he felt it now as he reached the pocket of shade where West was standing.

"Call it off," Nick said through his clenched teeth. "Right now. The whole thing. Call it off."

"Excuse me?" West was still smiling, but the expression had lost its wattage. His eyes creased. "Call what off?"

"The notary. The setup. Call it off!" Nick dug into his pocket and pulled out his phone. He tapped at its cracked screen with inept fingers.

"What are you doing?" West groused.

"I'm phoning Clay. I'm warning him."

"How do you have his number?" West took an instinctive step back. His eyes fled to the miniature skyline of glass bottles on his makeshift bar. "It's too late to warn him," West barked. "It's already happened. The meeting was at ten."

The phone slipped to the floor. Nick's fingers found West's shirt collar, and he dragged the heavy, older man up to his eye level. "You have to undo it! You'll say it's all a misunderstanding! You'll say you put him up to it!"

West's shock had finally solidified into rage. "Get off of me!" he yelled as he drove his arms between them and freed his collar from Nick's grip.

Shirt buttons pinged and scattered on the floor. Nick tried to follow the sound of a solitary button as it rolled across the terrazzo, but the image of Clay being led away in handcuffs refused to dissolve. A foot away, West was straightening his shirt collar, his face purple with anger. Nick tightened his right fist. He had never punched anyone before. But he had pushed a man down an elevator shaft. There was no end to what his hands could accomplish. He lurched forward, reeled his arm back, and struck West as hard as he could in the face.

The man crumpled so softly that it didn't seem connected to an act of violence. Nick's knuckles throbbed with pain, and the ache crawled up the bones of his wrist. He gripped his hand as he stared down at West on the floor. Specks of blood were blooming on his white linen shirt. West abruptly rotated onto his knees and began scrambling toward the bar. There must be a weapon stashed there, and if West got his hands on it, he'd surely use it.

Nick grabbed him by the belt loops and dragged him backward across the terrazzo. The older man tried to maneuver a flailing side-kick, but the motion capsized him and he tumbled onto his back. Straddling his stomach, Nick saw blood leaking from West's nostrils. His face had fallen into the shaft of sunlight, and Nick had the surreal impression of holding his head underwater in a stream, drowning him to death in the brightness.

A series of coughs sent West's skull tapping against the marble. He moaned, and for a second Nick felt a jolt of sympathy. But he remembered that this man had just thrown his boyfriend in prison, and his anger returned, doubling, as if seeping out of every crack inside of him. West gazed up, and their eyes met.

"*Aiuto!*" West shouted feebly. "Please, *aiuto!*"

"You fuck!" Nick screamed. "You conceited, greedy fuck! Who's going to help you now? *Who?* There's no one there!" West had taken everything from him, including the one person who could have stopped him from going further.

West licked the blood from his lips. "If you don't get off me, I'm going to kill you," he whispered matter-of-factly.

The sureness of that threat frightened Nick, more so because it was uttered by a man pinned to the ground who should be pleading for his life. "Yeah? Will you?" Nick said, trying to sound tough. "You're the one who should be scared."

West's hand shot up, his palm slamming into Nick's chin. Nick's vision went green and starry. But he managed to deliver another punch to West's nose that instantly dislodged his hand.

West looked like he'd been knocked out cold. His right cheek lay flush against the floor, and his eyes stared dazedly off to the side. But a faint, straining groan in the back of his throat betrayed him. Nick followed West's outstretched arm to his fingers, which were fastening around the brass doorstop. Just as West lifted it, Nick slammed his arm down. The doorstop skidded across the flecked marble, deep into the sunlight. Nick's knees hammered the floor as he scrambled for the bright metal orb. But West was a drowning swimmer trying to take him under too, clawing at his ribs and chest. Nick jammed a knee into West's neck, allowing him enough time to grasp the doorstop. He took the dense weight in his hand and climbed on top of West.

West was thrashing, arms flailing, lips swilling with spit. *"Aiuto!"* he cried again. "For god's sake, help me!" One of his thumbs nearly gouged Nick's eye. Nick had no choice. Neither of them did. He lifted the doorstop over his head with both hands. West's hips bucked, his feet kicked, his hand reached for Nick's throat. Nick's strength was flagging, but he brought the heavy brain crashing down.

The weight only nicked the side of West's head, the floor taking most of the impact. Blood flowed from a gash above the older man's ear, matting his white hair. The struggling had stopped. West was breathing evenly, looking up at Nick almost dumbly while sucking on his teeth. He was no longer screaming for help.

Nick grabbed the doorstop and rose on his knees, arching the weight high above his head for a second time. Killing West would free him—of what, he couldn't say exactly, but he wanted to be free of whatever it was. Murder offered itself to him like a shaded place to sleep. But in that instant Nick understood that if he killed again, he'd never find his way back. He'd be stuck in that shade, because there was nobody left to guide him out.

He rolled off West's body and set the doorstop gently on the floor. He pictured his bags stashed in the garden and the train station a ten-minute walk away and places without border checks or police. He got to his feet near the walnut door to Il Dormitorio. Just beyond that door were Clay's bags, packed and waiting.

Nick left the way he came. He didn't glance back at the man lying in the sunlight, staring up at the ceiling in the position of the dead.

There were fewer boats to the island in October.

Clay choreographed his train trip—Venice to Rome—and air flight—Rome to Lampedusa—with balletic precision to arrive just before the ferry departed. It was a long journey accompanied mostly by silence-hating toddlers and elderly off-season tourists. Still, Clay felt excited, albeit nervous. It had been five months. As the plane neared the island of Lampedusa, Clay studied the map in the back of the airline magazine. If Italy were a boot and Sicily a ball, Lampedusa was a fly buzzing on the playing field, which made the island of Linosa, what? A flake of skin? A bead of sweat? Some yet undiscovered microorganism that would either decimate or save the planet? Linosa dotted the Mediterranean Sea so far to the south that it seemed to want to belong to Tunisia. No Northern Italian that Clay asked had ever set foot on it. Clay gave Nick credit: he'd managed to find the most isolated spot, as far from Venice as possible while still technically remaining within the country's border.

Clay remembered the initial disturbing emails, sent via Daniela's address and never directly to Clay: If there is any indication they're on to me, I'll take the opposite route of the refugees, I'll smuggle myself into North Africa and disappear there.

Clay remembered the later life–affirming emails: Linosa is paradise! Black volcanic-rock beaches, prickly-pear cactuses, no banks, not even a single ATM! And I met this great guy Franco who's teaching me how to ride the only horse on the island. (Clay could admit to hoping that Franco was a cantankerous octogenarian with a soft spot for troubled Americans rather than a cute twenty-year-old islander.)

The more recent emails were terse and written, to Clay's amazement, in semi–decent Italian: It's safe now. I can't wait any longer. When are you coming?

"Go!" Daniela begged him. "If for nothing else, so that I can stop playing emissary between you two. Your Nicky really turned out to be the worst houseguest I've ever had. You know, he never did take me out for that thank-you dinner."

Was it safe now? Clay wasn't sure. On that vicious morning last May, Eva had returned to Palazzo Contarini from the liquor store to discover her uncle lying bloody and unconscious on the living-room floor. Richard West had been water-ambulanced to the emergency room at Ospedale SS. Giovanni e Paolo. In the three subsequent days that West remained stable but unconscious in the ICU, the Venetian police went to work investigating a violent assault that lacked a single eyewitness. Naturally, initial suspicion fell on Clay, and if it hadn't been for Battista supplying him with an alibi—as well as a dozen Venetians who saw him running around Santa Croce at the time of the attack—he probably would have taken the rap. Clay was too neat a package *not* to have done it. "I'm sure it's that neighbor!" Eva told the police. "They hated each other. My uncle didn't have another enemy in the world!"

Clay's interview with the detectives wasn't without its land mines. He denied possession of forged real-estate documents, and since he hadn't submitted any papers to the notary, he'd committed no actual crime. His story didn't sit well with the detectives, who were hungry for an arrest, but they were forced to let him go. They gave him a warning that his younger self would have swooned to receive from the local authorities—*Please don't leave the city in the foreseeable future. We will likely want to see you again.*

Eventually, Eva floated a second theory, outrageous even to her own grief-addled mind: "There was a young man, Nicholas Brink, who was supposed to stop by before he left town. At least, I invited him over. He never said whether he'd come or not. But it doesn't make sense. He was a friend. There'd be no reason for him to do something like that . . ." The detectives got as far as confirming that a man matching Nick's description had taken the 11:50 train to Milan. Before they could track his movements any farther, the suspect pool widened dramatically.

SAVE VENICE FROM THOSE WHO WANT TO SAVE VENICE. The newspaper headlines were merciless. Battista decided to step forward and publicly denounce his boss as one of the anonymous foreign investors of the Mestre development. The list of local suspects with a possible grudge against the victim ballooned to roughly fifty-three thousand. The detectives speculated that one of the protesters might have caught wind of the information before the media had, and decided to take matters into their own hands. The police still promised that an arrest was imminent, but Clay sensed that they'd soured on their taste for fast justice. The detectives, after all, were also born-and-raised Venetians. "We cannot rule out a random burglary," one of them told Eva within earshot of Il Dormitorio's windows. "A crime of convenience. Are you sure you shut the gate when you went to buy your prosecco that morning?" On day three, the hospital called with news. Richard West had woken up in the ICU.

West didn't speak. He couldn't. Or wouldn't. He was capable only of nodding or shaking his head before withdrawing into a blank, uneasy silence. MRI scans revealed no discernible neurological damage, although admittedly Giovanni e Paolo was a hospital with limited resources. It might simply be a matter of time before the trauma subsided and his speech returned. Clay watched from a garret window as Karine, Eva, and a hired male nurse brought West home on a *motoscafo*, carrying him in through the palazzo's canal-front doors, whose chain had to be clipped because the key couldn't be located. Clay wondered whether shame was the real reason for West's sudden muteness. If he didn't speak, he wouldn't have to account to old friends and new adversaries for his duplicitous involvement in the Mestre development. In any case, it was no warm homecoming. On the second night, a brick was thrown through the palazzo's piano nobile window. Trash was strewn in the garden. Vandals spray-painted TRAITOR and MAIALE CAPITAL-ISTA on the brick walls surrounding the house. Still, the detectives routinely visited West to see if his condition had improved enough to identify his attacker. Clay expected that sooner or later the aggressive, need-to-win West would conquer the meek and humiliated one, and Nick's involvement would come to light. But maybe West was more broken than Clay knew.

In the first week of June, Eva returned to Toulouse. At the end of the month, Karine decided to move her husband to the clinic in Leipzig, which offered far more advanced facilities for neurological disorders. There were no goodbye dinner parties, no last-minute visitors, no midnight disco music blaring through the walls. The

Wests closed the house and unceremoniously left by *motoscafo* one evening without any indication as to when they'd return. In her hurry, Karine neglected to board up the connecting door to Il Dormitorio. The day after the Wests departed, Clay opened the walnut door and saw the ghostly white-sheeted furniture. As he moved through the rooms, it occurred to him that for the first time in more than a century, all of Palazzo Contarini was home to a single inhabitant.

Clay stayed in Venice for the summer, still part owner of a toothpick of a palazzo. He heard nothing—not even an indirect word—from Freddy's sister in Uruguay. The Celsius spiked, and the days were swampy with heat and tourist fat and the nights were cramped and windless, the air as heavy as old paint. Clay loved it. He'd forgotten how dazzling Venice looked with heat-stroke and how each dark church was a cold gift of refuge from the sun. He spent most of his evenings with Daniela, but twice a week he'd meet up with Battista for a drink. They'd become close— the handsome Italian unemployed but determined not to leave for the mainland—and in their awkward pauses Clay felt a lingering possibility. What kept him from pursuing it was Nick, waiting in Linosa, waiting for West to come to his senses and name him, wait- ing to become a wanted felon, waiting for the police to match the fingerprints on the doorstep, waiting for the coast to clear. Three months went by and there was no accusation from Leipzig. Then four. In the end, Nick was waiting for Clay.

"I don't feel ready," he admitted to Daniela. "I don't know. I'm worried things have changed too much between us. I haven't seen him in four months. And, really, it's been longer than that, since we only met in secret the whole time we were in Venice. Hell, we were meeting in secret from the very beginning in New York."

"Welcome to how it's been for our kind for centuries!" Daniela exclaimed. "It doesn't make your relationship any less valid. Some might argue it makes it *more* valid."

He knew he should listen to her. But he was apprehensive all the same about the prospect of facing Nick.

"Anyway, I can't go yet," he reasoned. "What if the police track me? What if it's a trap and I lead them right to Nick? It might look suspicious if I left. They specifically asked me to stay in town."

Daniela conjured her best imitation of Freddy. "Now why on earth, doll, would you *ever* want to do what the police told you to?"

In Lampedusa, he took a taxi from the airport to the dock. He was driven through a town comprised entirely of two-story cement blocks, the metal grates pulled over whatever summer diversions they held. Not a soul in sight but for one boy on a corner, squatting down with scabbed knees, his head bent between his legs, his shoulders and neck covered in sand and dirt. He looked like he had been there for weeks. It was an eerie, inhospitable island.

"We don't get many like you," the taxi driver told him. At least, that's what Clay thought he said, his Sicilian dialect so difficult to untangle. Clay only half wondered what the driver meant by that remark. He watched the Mediterranean Sea fill his view out the window.

The ferry to Linosa—a blue island skipper that cut a razor path through the waves—took exactly an hour. The cabin's few occupants were elderly women and middle-aged men carting groceries, supplies, and caged animals back to the island. Clay tried to identify the animal inside the crate by his seat, but it was just a set of small, black, unblinking eyes in a cube of darkness.

When Clay had emailed Nick (via Daniela) the date and time of his arrival, Nick responded with a photo of himself on the horse he'd been learning to ride—a shaggy, brown-spotted mare, more bones than muscle, which suited Nick, whose face was hidden under the brim of a straw hat. Nick's message, all in English, was sprinkled in exclamation points—I'll meet you at the dock! Although you'd find me in five minutes wherever I was on the island! I'm "l'americano" here. That's more than just my nickname! Seriously, for the Linosians, I am America. They've known so few of us, everything I do and say has come to represent the character of our people! How scary is that? So, you're probably wondering about the horse. Well, I've taken quite a shine to riding. And I've been thinking, Freddy's sister is all alone in Uruguay with her horses. And she still owns half the palazzo. Who better to leave it to than the young, horse-loving American who wandered into town and kept her company in her final years? Something to consider on your trip down . . .

Clay honestly couldn't tell whether Nick was joking or not. No, they hadn't run off with four million euros. But they still had a couple hundred thousand from the silver, and that should see them through for a few years. For Clay, it was enough.

The island swelled on the horizon, high desert hills braiding together like a coiled diamondback. The water grew calm as it flattened into shallow turquoise. The ferry nudged the cement jetty. A paved road led up a hillside toward a huddle of single-story buildings, each painted a different bright fluorescent hue, as if to shout to those far out at sea, *We're here!*

Clay spotted him right away. He was the only tall man at the end of the jetty. His hair was curlier and blonder than Clay had ever seen it, a yellow bonfire, and he wore jeans and a black T-shirt with the sleeves rolled up to his shoulder blades. A deep tan blurred his features. But as Clay approached, he could see that Nick's face had grown thinner, the boy in him gone. His eyes were the same, though, and that was all the assurance Clay needed. They didn't run to each other. They didn't take each other up in their arms. They didn't kiss. The world was still too dangerous. But they were at home on the sea, and they would find their way.

ACKNOWLEDGMENTS

I n the summer of 1999, I lived in Venice for an internship at the Peggy Guggenheim Collection. My months there had a substantial impact on the writing of this book. I want to thank the Peggy Guggenheim—and its godsend of an internship program— for opening Venice up to me at such a young age. That said, I couldn't have captured this complicated, multilayered city without the help of key Venetian friends and experts. Chief among them is Toto Bergamo Rossi, who not only offered countless guided tours and a spare bedroom when needed but generously fielded a zillion disparate questions on the nature of palazzos, restoration materials, and Italian slang to give this story a firm foundation. Thank you also to Shaul Bassi, Simone Francescato, Pietro Rusconi, and Olympia Scarry for their own insights on Venice. A very special thanks to James Ivory for essential introductions.

Although I spent as much time as possible doing research in Venice, much of this novel was written in Paris. That would never have been feasible without the residency I graciously received from Maison de la Poésie. Thank you to Olivier Chaudenson, Caroline

Boidé Brénaud, and the entire staff, as well as to Centre International d'Accueil et d'Échanges des Récollets and the welcoming spirit of Chrystel Dozias and Aurélie Philippe. I could have stayed in that monastery in the 10th arrondissement for the rest of my days. Thank you to Tiffany Gassouk for being the woman who figures everything out, and to Alexander Hertling and Monroe Hertling for the Parisian dinner breaks.

The novel dips its feet in several specialized fields, and I am grateful for those patient professionals who shared their knowledge with me. On the subject of antique silver, thank you to Tim Martin, Jill Waddell, Ian Irving, Betsy Pochoda, and Tom Delavan. On legal matters, thank you to Meyer Fedida, Gianluca Russo, and Elana Bronson. On the study of neuroscience, thank you to my Récollets neighbor Daniel Margulies. A big thank-you to Daniela Guglielmino for correcting my Italian as much as one could.

No writing gets done without the guidance of my friend, adviser, sounding board, and support supplier Bill Clegg. Thanks to him and to everyone at the Clegg Agency—Marion Duvert, Simon Toop, and David Kambhu among them—for making it all happen. This novel was a labor of love, and my deepest appreciation goes to my editor, Jennifer Barth, for shouldering a good deal of this labor's weight and for seeing all of my good intentions and then forcing me to make them work on the page; her constant, unerring advice improved this story in countless ways. Thank you to Jonathan Burnham, who gets it and yet understands how it could work even better. Thank you to Sarah Ried for her tireless help. Thank you to the whole team at Harper.

This novel is, in many ways, a tribute to the wild, radical, street-smart souls who became the patriarchs and matriarchs of my adopted family over the years. I am particularly indebted to the late, great artist David Armstrong whose spirit hovered over me as

I wrote this novel; I pilfered his brownstone on Jefferson Avenue, his predilection for the endearment "doll," and his extraordinary photography archive as direct inspirations. Thank you to those friends who helped me down this road: George Miscamble, James Haslam, Lisa Love, Wade Guyton, Thomas Alexander, Joseph Logan, Zadie Smith, the folks at *Interview Magazine*, Leo Bersani, Patrik Ervell, T. Cole Rachel, T.J. Wilcox, Ana and Danko Steiner, and always the Cincinnati brood.

Insights,
Interviews
& More . . .

About the author

2 An Interview with
Christopher Bollen

About the book

11 Christopher Bollen on Writing
A Beautiful Crime

Read on

19 Have You Read . . . ? More by
Christopher Bollen

An Interview with Christopher Bollen

Christopher Bollen Is Pretty Sure He's Not a Sociopathic Murderer

By Mitchell Nugent

Originally published in Interview *magazine on February 4, 2020.*

IN THE WEE HOURS OF MARCH 18, 1990, two con men masquerading as Boston police officers burglarized the Isabella Stewart Gardner Museum, stealing a seismic haul of art by the likes of Rembrandt and Vermeer from the Venetian-style mansion. Three decades later, the robbery remains a mystery, and the art—which the FBI values at more than $500 million—remains unrecovered.

My mother's great uncle, Myles J. Connor Jr. was one of the first suspected of masterminding the theft. Connor, who was incarcerated at the time, was a notorious art thief in the New England area, but denied any real connection to the crime. Nevertheless, his early involvement inspired an urban myth within my family that caused cousins to scour dusty attics and relatives to ransack garden sheds in hopes of finding the Gardner treasures. Connor's ties also influenced my early obsession with crime novels, particularly those of Patricia Highsmith.

Reading *A Beautiful Crime*, I was immediately reminded of the Gardner heist. In the novel, the fourth written by *Interview*'s editor-at-large Christopher Bollen, two men also take advantage of a Venetian mansion—this time an actual palazzo in Venice—and leverage its ancient artifacts and history for profit. Unlike the Gardner heist, there's a gay love tryst, a murder, and an Airbnb crisis that's sinking a city underwater. In an age when con artists like Anna Delvey and Billy McFarland are becoming swindling sensations, I spoke with Bollen about his new novel, the glamour of the grifter narrative, and America's fascination with con culture.

MITCHELL NUGENT: *In 2016, Edmund White dedicated his novel* **Our Young Man** *to you. And this year, you dedicated* **A Beautiful Crime** *to White. How did you two meet?*

CHRISTOPHER BOLLEN: We met in the early 2000s through a mutual friend who was visiting from Seattle. I had always wanted to meet Ed for a number of reasons. One, because he's from Cincinnati and so am I. It's just amazing to have met someone who knows Cincinnati and wrote about it as well as he has, and in a number of his personal essays. All of his books are so seminal to me in terms of what you could do in literature—and also naughty in what you aren't supposed to do in literature. But he did it so effectively and so brazenly. He's been such a wonderful person ▶

to talk to about everything. It's such a treat to hear his amazing stories of life on earth. I did not expect or ask or have any idea that he would dedicate that book to me, but it was kind, and I felt so honored. And so, when the time came to write the dedication for *A Beautiful Crime*, I thought about what the book meant to me. To me, one of the assets I was going for in the book is the passing on of the gay identity and what it meant in the past to what it means for us now as a younger generation of men who are sort of dealing with this legacy. But the legacy and the rules have changed so much. And so I was just thinking of someone who I really admired who blazed the trail for me. White just seemed the right choice for it.

NUGENT: *You've cited* **A Beautiful Crime** *as your most personal novel yet. I've known you for some time, and I spotted Easter eggs throughout the book, from the Peggy Guggenheim internship to settings on the Upper West Side and an Ohioan as a central character. I'm not insinuating that you're a murderer too, but I wondered what other aspects of the novel are biographical.*

BOLLEN: Sometimes I'm relieved that it doesn't look like I'm going to have children because I don't know how I would tell them that I am not a sociopath or a killer. [*Laughs.*] Personal interest always becomes a huge part of writing books for me. Whatever I've become obsessed with, or have experienced, ends up being woven into the book. As you've said I was an intern at the Peggy Guggenheim Collection in 1999. That was a huge deal in my life then because I fell in love with Venice. It was the first time I lived outside of the country, and it was in the back of my mind the whole time—the early experiences I had there and how I got to know the city. But then there were parts of the book that were completely new to me. I knew absolutely zilch about colonial silver until I decided to, sort of out of thin air, include it as an element.

NUGENT: *That was going to be one of my questions for you—how you came upon the silver industry, and whether you were familiar with antiquities beforehand?*

BOLLEN: Not even a little bit. I must say that before I did the research for this, I couldn't have told you the difference between silver plate and real silver. To be honest, I needed an object. I wanted it to be something decorative. It was kind of touching upon the idea of what gay men have famously or notoriously been known to be good at, which is this Sontag idea of being aristocrats of tastes and how gay men have often dominated these worlds of decorative art. There's this sort of knowledge that's passed on between old and young men of what these values are. These are all dying art forms because I think, in a way, there's a loss of masterful understanding of them that was often passed almost like apprenticeships between gay men. So silver is kind of a luck in a way. It wasn't something I knew much about, but it seemed to check all the boxes of that. And there's this sort of ethical question to it in the book, obviously. As these sort of rarefied art forms disappear or become less and less important culturally, this next generation is sort of selling off the scraps of them for their own lifestyle. ▶

An Interview with Christopher Bollen *(continued)*

NUGENT: *Is there a particular anecdote from your Peggy Guggenheim internship that warms your heart?*

BOLLEN: Is there? I loved being an intern at the Peggy Guggenheim Collection. And it's just like [the character] Clay as an intern. I even loved doing all the guard duties. It's a very laborious job of standing still, but I really enjoyed it. You get to just stare at art and people all day long. And the funny thing is, I spoke very little Italian. I think I kind of lied on my application about being fluent.

NUGENT: *As one does!*

BOLLEN: I didn't really speak any Italian. But you learn how to say enough that it makes it seem like you speak Italian. So, like "*non toccare*," which is "do not touch." You could say that constantly and people would think that you were totally fluent. Then we'd have to give tours about Peggy. We did that once a week where we weren't supposed to talk about her sex life. But of course, when the director [of the Collection] wasn't looking, we would. [*Laughs.*] I have so many stories from that period. It was only three or four months, but it felt like five years. Every day was such an adventure.

NUGENT: *The novel suggests that a queer ecosystem doesn't really exist in Venice. Other Italian cities like Milan and Rome have substantial queer scenes and subcultures. Why do you think Venice differs?*

BOLLEN: That is such a good question. I had come to Venice in 1999 from New York. I was used to an international city with a very active gay nightlife. And Venice, for some bizarre reason, does not have that at all. There are no gay bars. Of course, things have opened up a lot there and it's been twenty years, but there still aren't any that I'm aware of. It shocks me because it's such an aesthetic city and such an international city. But it doesn't seem to have a very strong gay community, in that you can't easily find it. And it was a problem for me when I went there because you kind of just feel like you had returned to a very heterosexual environment. It probably has a lot to do with the way Italian culture treats someone's sexuality, and the shrinking community in Venice itself, and how given over it is to commercial tourism.

NUGENT: *I imagined Venice to be quite a glamorous place to go cruising, with its Grand Canal and deserted alleyways. I wanted to know what cruising was like before the advent of Grindr, but you kind of answered that question.*

BOLLEN: It's funny because Ed [White] always said that he cruised at the downtown fountain in Cincinnati, but I did not know of that as a cruising spot when I was a teenager in Cincinnati. And some people did say that late at night people would cruise in Venice down by Harry's Bar and just off San Marco. But I never knew that at all. There was a little sliver of the Lido that was a gay beach. It was called *Alberoni* and you could go there, but it took forever. You'd have to take a *vaporetto* out to Lido and then a forty-five-minute bus ride. And then you never knew what it was going to be like. So it was quite a commitment if you really wanted to go. ▶

NUGENT: *Did you live in a rundown palazzo, like Clay did in the novel, during your internship?*

BOLLEN: No, I lived in [the character] Daniela's apartment. I had made a friend there whose brother had owned or rented this apartment but never used it, so I took it over. It was absolutely amazing. Some people did live in rundown palazzos. But I found this apartment: it was on the ground floor. It had its own garden. It was shabby, but it was also, to my mind, so charming. And it was off Campo Santa Margherita, which was near the little bars that I liked to go to at night and not far from the Guggenheim.

NUGENT: *Now that I know the history of Daniela's apartment, did a particular place in Venice inspire the van der Haar palazzo?*

BOLLEN: No, not any one in particular. But there are so many of these creaky old spinstery palazzos there. And they're all so beautiful. So, it was sort of an amalgam of a few that I'd been in, and I picked the Cannaregio neighborhood [to set the palazzo in] because I thought it was a little more interesting and off the beaten path than anything on the Grand Canal.

NUGENT: *In your epilogue, you shared an anecdote about rummaging through late photographer David Armstrong's photographs. Did he inspire the character of Freddy van der Haar?*

BOLLEN: Yes, absolutely. David was not from an old-money Dutch family and wasn't as old as Freddy when he died, but David had such an amazing personality and was so hilarious and eccentric, and would always say the right wrong thing or the wrong right thing. I wanted that kind of character. David was just such a wild Bohemian. And that to me really represented the kind of creature that New York used to foster that you don't really find anymore. David even had a famous brownstone on Jefferson Avenue in Brooklyn [like the character Freddy van der Haar] where he would shoot a lot. And so I kind of took parts of David as I needed and put them into Freddy. There was a lot more Freddy, actually, in the original when I wrote the first draft. I was doing Freddy too much because I guess I love David so much, but I kind of pulled back a little bit. David was really, I think, sort of an overlooked photographer. And it seems to me that so much of the photography that's sort of in vogue right now is really based on his work.

NUGENT: A Beautiful Crime *is being compared to Patricia Highsmith's* The Talented Mr. Ripley *series, which is probably the best compliment I can imagine. What do you make of the comparisons?*

BOLLEN: I'm completely divided because I love Patricia Highsmith so much. I love how she can manage to juggle both the beauty of lies and the desires of lies with their evil underside as well. And all of the paranoia and murder and ugliness and nastiness that comes with it too. I think it captures so much about the American personality, or the urban American personality. I do think that there is a humongous difference between [*A Beautiful Crime* characters] Nick and Clay and Tom Ripley. Tom Ripley is a sociopath without a doubt. And I don't think that Nick or Clay is a sociopath at all. I think it's a very different ▶

motivation that brings about their own crimes than it is for Tom. So, for me, there's a difference in the motivation in the heart of the main character.

NUGENT: *Highsmith was often criticized for making Tom Ripley so empathetic and lovable, yet at the same time so wickedly evil. Nick and Clay aren't as extreme in their acts or as villainous as Ripley, but I was wondering why you think readers are so drawn to these kinds of crooked yet charming characters?*

BOLLEN: I think we're all kind of faced with the grifter, the charlatan, the fraud, the con artist. And I think it's obviously because the president is such a clear American figure. For a long time, we really admired that figure in the way that we admire the outlaw in America. It's really darkened because now the con artist is winning.

NUGENT: The Talented Mr. Trump!

BOLLEN: Exactly. I think, before, you kind of took joy in a criminal winning. There's a lot of hypocrisy in America of the bad and the good. And then you see the other side, so it's sort of the explicit version of what people are like. But now it's only too clear and real who's leading the country, so I think there's a little bit of a fright in that representation. It's such a New York characteristic, too, to fake it 'til you make it. You can win on competence and charm. Maybe we all think that we're kind of doing that. I feel like a lot of lies involve tap dancing when you're really not sure what you're doing. ∾

Christopher Bollen on Writing *A Beautiful Crime*

Venice Is Brilliant Inspiration for Any Writer—and Also Hell

Originally published by the Daily Beast *at www.thedailybeast.com on January 28, 2020.*

BEFORE THE HISTORIC FLOOD OF 1966, people rarely spoke about Venice sinking. That flood, triggered by a storm surge across Italy whipping up wind and water, increased high tide to over six feet and left nearly the entire city under water.

The 1966 calamity still holds the ominous record; it peaked at seventy-six inches; two inches higher than the tragic flooding that struck Venice in November 2019. Beyond the immediate devastation, the flood radically changed the city's identity forever. No longer was it merely the ultimate romantic fantasy capital. It now came with extremely modern psychological baggage—the ultimate ▶

romantic fantasy capital on the verge of extinction, the spectacular beauty on the way to the morgue.

That's the Venice we know today; the drowning museum swarmed by tourists who offer more harm than help. No wonder so many writers have been drawn to *La Serenissima* and have used it as a backdrop for their stories. The problems of the world are baked into its atmosphere, as complicated and unresolvable as its famous labyrinthine streets.

I stayed in Venice many times and for many seasons to research it as a locale for my new novel, *A Beautiful Crime*. I did not want to contest or correct the historical record or even imagine I could capture it in the round, to use an art term. I just wanted to get my slice of it right. Ultimately, I think the Venice depicted in the book is one in a state of crisis, caught in the jaws of a mighty shark: the old romance of it is disappearing and people are scrambling to hang on to whatever magic is left.

Leave it to Thomas Mann to get the city right. In a sense, he predicted the Venice of our age, or at least diagnosed our schizophrenic need to smother it with our love and attention even at the risk of death. *Death in Venice* was published in 1912, based off the author's own vacation on the Lido the year before, where he spotted a handsome Polish boy in the dining room of the Grand Hotel des Bains.

Through the course of the novella, the middle-aged, aristocratic, inspiration-starved Gustav von Aschenbach becomes increasingly fixated on the beautiful nymph-like Tadzio, to the point that he ignores warnings of the fatal cholera epidemic sweeping through the brackish canals in order to keep in close proximity to the young man.

As far as allegories go, Mann's is remarkably on point. Seduced beyond reason, Aschenbach can't get himself to leave Venice. His obsessive hunger to worship at the feet of beauty becomes its own kind of death wish.

The same could be said for the leviathan of mass tourism today, which is only too aware of the havoc it wreaks on the fragile ecosystem of Venice but can't square its destructive tendencies with its unchecked need to experience the city's treasures firsthand. (The local government routinely proposes ventures like charging an admission fee to the city, but here's an out-of-the-box idea: a small tax on every Instagram post, a surcharge added whenever the city's location is tagged by a non-resident account.)

The irony of Venice is that it is being destroyed by our love for it. If it were less essential to the world, it might have a chance at survival.

I share my fellow travelers' dilemma because I too have trouble keeping away. There are cities that writers love, and cities that love writers. Venice is certainly the former—admirers include Shakespeare, Byron, Henry James, and Patricia Highsmith.

But Venice doesn't open itself easily as a city for expat writers to set down roots, let alone a thriving literary scene. That might be due to the rigor of daily living conditions (its thorny, mazelike geography, the scarcity and expense of accommodations, the insurmountable swell of tourists).

Ezra Pound landed in Venice post–mental breakdown in the 1960s and stayed until his death; Joseph Brodsky would visit every winter on break from teaching in the United States, but made sure never to come in the ferocious, crowd-horded ▶

summers. (Both greats are buried on Venice's cemetery island of San Michele.)

Writers, like the rest of us, tend to come to Venice for short durations, and the nature, breadth, and visual poetry of the city tend to give the visit a feeling of a lone pilgrimage, a voyage outside of time.

No wonder so many depictions of Venice in modern English literature revolve around vacations. The Westerner ferreting out trouble on a Venetian holiday is a well-worn plotline that goes back to mannered fin-de-siècle mainstays like Wilkie Collins's *The Haunted Hotel* (1878) and James's *The Wings of a Dove* (1902).

It reaches its horror-suspense apogee in slim twentieth-century novels like Highsmith's *Those Who Walk Away* (1967), Daphne du Maurier's *Don't Look Now* (1971), and Ian McEwan's *The Comfort of Strangers* (1981). In each case, the city's confusing, misleading terrain mirrors the mindset of the visiting protagonists; thrust out of their comfort zones by a world that refutes rational order, the characters fall prey to seductive monsters and bouts of madness.

Twentieth-century literature often treats Venice as a loophole to European Enlightenment, a vexing, carnivalesque locale in sharp resistance to the hyper-organized urban grid or sanitized suburban sprawl. So far, in the twenty-first century, writers have tended to fixate not on its potential for Aschenbach strokes of insanity but rather the opposite: its tempting Tadzio-like display of pure capitalistic spectacle.

No novel epitomizes this slick picture of Venice better than Geoff Dyer's *Jeff in Venice, Death in Varanasi* (2005), in which an embittered British journalist runs emotionally aground in a ridiculous, moneyed, hysterically farcical insider art world of the Venice Biennale.

Dyer's Venice is one inhabited by name-dropping contemporary boulevardiers on the hunt for the latest shiny surface, a watery jet-set playground where "Venice had woken up and put on this guise of being a real place even though everyone knew it existed only for tourists."

Instead of an exotic refuge from the drudge of daily life, Venice works as an asylum for those most at home surrounded by pretty, empty reflections. No loophole, Venice has become the ultimate exemplifier of materialism without end.

Whatever your take on the city, it's damningly hard to capture it on the page. As any writer knows, the delight of writing about Venice with its sherbet-colored palazzos refracted in the waters of the Grand Canal is also its biggest obstacle.

Venice—because of its prismatic landscape of light and water—has always been a painter's paradise. The eighteenth-century Venetian painter Canaletto made an industry out of creating the ultimate postcard views of the city to sell to the English aristocrats on the Grand Tour; incidentally, prostitution was discreetly encouraged on the Grand Tour to ward off homosexuality among the young men around so much decadent art and beauty, and thus, Venice had some of the best brothels in Europe.

The city has been slightly less accommodating for filmmakers. In an interview I did last year with the Italian horror director Dario Argento, he stated that because of a slew of financial and practical considerations—namely navigating the bridges and canals with crew and gear and actors—he was never able to shoot a movie in Venice. ▶

Christopher Bollen on Writing *A Beautiful Crime (continued)*

For writers, the difficulty lies less with the oddity of the geography than it does with overfamiliarity. How do you describe a city that's already been over-described for centuries with so many gaudy adjectives? How do you make a place that holds a permanent lease in the public imagination new?

James noted this problem directly in his book of travel essays, *Italian Hours* (1909): "Venice has been painted and described many thousands of times, and of all the cities of the world is the easiest to visit without going there. Open the first book and you will find a rhapsody about it; step into the first picture-dealer's and you will find three or four high-coloured 'views' of it. There is notoriously nothing more to be said on the subject."

In other words, even if you haven't personally taken a gondola down the Grand Canal, because of its ubiquity in popular culture, you have. If a master like James felt defeated by the landscape, how will the rest of us fare with a city that hasn't changed much aesthetically since his time?

Equally frustratingly, Venice refuses to sit quietly on the page and let its main characters get on with the plot. It has such a loud, unwieldy presence that it constantly threatens to overshadow all the other details. It isn't merely the fact that a character never gets into a car to move between locations. It's that no simple stroll down the street is safe from the sudden appearance of a throng of German tourists all wearing feathered carnival masks.

To simply pretend the Venice of conspicuous consumption and budget tourism doesn't exist is tantamount to portraying New York City's Greenwich Village in the year 2020 without a single NYU student haunting the periphery. It's a fiction of a fiction. No, Venice is like Tabasco sauce: it takes over, it becomes the flavor of the meal. You don't write a book set in Venice. You write about Venice with characters set inside of it.

Mann's classic might deservedly remain the ultimate Venice novel, with all the rest of us toiling in its long, elegant shadow. Still, my favorite piece of Venice fiction is an under-appreciated short story by du Maurier that serves as a bawdy send-up of *Death in Venice*.

Written in the late 1950s, "Ganymede" centers on a middle-aged British classics scholar who arrives in Venice on a bachelor's vacation. It isn't long before this exacting visitor becomes smitten with a handsome young waiter working at one of the outdoor restaurants on Piazza San Marco.

Our pompous protagonist feigns devotion to this Tadzio double on overwrought Mann-like aesthetic grounds; it's clear, though, that pure lust is leading him to the same table on the square each night. In du Maurier's far less noble Venice, everyone is on the make. While the horny, self-deluded narrator attempts to get his hands on the boy, the boy's extended family is out to get their hands on this man's wallet—using young Ganymede as exquisite bait. Laughably, everyone's fantasies are exploitable and potentially fulfillable in this tourist town.

"Ganymede" doesn't end with a dying Aschenbach watching Tadzio frolic in the waves. Instead, du Maurier concocts a ludicrous waterskiing accident in the lagoon after the narrator is suckered into footing an exorbitant lunch bill. The magic of Venice is precisely that, in art and in life, both endings are equally likely.

It's easy to disrespect Venice. It's easy, as we watch the world burn, to write off Venice as a soulless, unsavable Disney World. Venice breeds as many cynics as it does enthusiasts—I have yet to meet a person who is wholly indifferent to it. ▶

About the book

I had the good fortune to live in Venice for several months in 1999 when, out of college, I worked as an intern at the Peggy Guggenheim Collection. Yes, there was plenty of Geoff Dyer–esque outrageous, rampant, billionaire spectacle culture on display (arguably, most of it on loan from cities like New York, London, and Los Angeles).

But there is a real city beyond—or braided into—the illusory one, a city that takes more digging to find than a few peeks out of a hotel window and a walk over the Rialto Bridge en route to an art party. It's a city that's learned to survive by camouflage; it's there because you don't see it. It's a city of some fifty thousand residents, the population shrinking by approximately one thousand each year.

For most of us, Venice has always been sinking. And yet, I predict we'll all be dumbfounded and more than a little regretful when it actually does. ◠

Have You Read . . . ?
More by Christopher
Bollen

THE DESTROYERS

ARRIVING ON THE GREEK ISLAND OF
Patmos broke and humiliated, Ian
Bledsoe is fleeing the emotional and
financial fallout from his father's
death. His childhood friend Charlie—
rich, exuberant, and basking in the
success of his new venture on the
island—could be his last hope. When
Charlie suddenly vanishes, Ian finds
himself caught up in deception after
deception. An enthralling odyssey and
a gripping, expansive drama, *The
Destroyers* is a vivid and suspenseful
story of identity and fate, fathers and
sons, and self-invention and self-
deception, from a writer at the very
height of his powers.

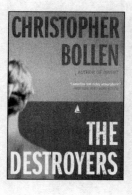

ORIENT

Orient is an isolated town on the
north fork of Long Island, its future as a
historic village newly threatened by ▶

the arrival of wealthy transplants from Manhattan—many of them artists. One late summer morning, the body of a local caretaker is found in the open water; the same day, a monstrous animal corpse is found on the beach, presumed a casualty from a nearby research lab. With rumors flying, eyes turn to Mills Chevern—a tumbleweed orphan newly arrived in town from the west with no ties and a hazy history. As the deaths continue and fear in town escalates, Mills is enlisted by Beth, an Orient native in retreat from Manhattan, to help her uncover the truth. With the clock ticking, Mills and Beth struggle to find answers, faced with a killer they may not be able to outsmart.

Discover great authors, exclusive offers, and more at hc.com.